New York Times bestsel ... as had over thirty novels published and has thrilled legions of fans with her seductive Dark Carpathian tales. She has received numerous honours throughout her career, including being a nominee for the Romance Writers of America RITA and receiving a Career Achievement Award from *Romantic Times*, and has been published in multiple languages.

Visit Christine Feehan online:

www.christinefeehan.com
www.facebook.com/christinefeehanauthor
@AuthorCFeehan

Praise for Christine Feehan:

'The erotic, gripping series that has defined an entire genre . . . I love everything [Christine Feehan] does'
J. R. Ward

'The queen of paranormal romance'
USA Today

'Gritty, brutal and wonderfully magical . . .
Unexpected and mesmerizing perfection'
Library Journal

'Once again, Christine Feehan brings a sizzling story of seduction and sorcery to her readers' Examiner.com

'Book after book, Feehan gives readers emotionally rich and powerful stories that are hard to forget!'
RT Book Reviews

'The amazingly prolific author's ability to create captivating
a ... d'

By Christine Feehan

SHADOW FLIGHT

CHRISTINE FEEHAN

piatkus

PIATKUS

First published in the US in 2020 by Jove
An imprint of Penguin Random House LLC
First published in Great Britain in 2020 by Piatkus

1 3 5 7 9 10 8 6 4 2

A CIP catalogue record for this book is available from the British Library.

ISBN: 978-0-349-42671-6

Printed and bound in Great Britain by Clays Ltd, Elcograf S.p.A.

Papers used by Piatkus are from well-managed forests
and other responsible sources.

For Julie and Sam.
With love.

FOR MY READERS

Be sure to go to christinefeehan.com/members/ to sign up for my private book announcement list and download the free ebook of *Dark Desserts*. Join my community and get firsthand news, enter the book discussions, ask your questions and chat with me. Please feel free to email me at Christine@christinefeehan.com. I would love to hear from you.

ACKNOWLEDGMENTS

As in any book, there are so many people to thank: Brian, for pushing me to get it done even when I was doing back-to-back traveling; Domini, for always editing, no matter how many times I ask her to go over the same book before we send it for additional editing. This one was tough!

CHAPTER ONE

Nicoletta Gomez sat in her very luxurious leather seat, trying not to look as if she were staring at or even noticing Taviano Ferraro. She'd asked him for this and, as always, when she'd asked anything of the Ferraro family, they had given her whatever she wanted. This was the first time she'd asked for something so ridiculous that she was embarrassed, but it hadn't mattered. The family hadn't flinched or hesitated. She sat in their private jet with three of her friends headed to Los Angeles to see a Kain Diakos concert because it was Pia Basso's birthday and that was her greatest wish.

Nicoletta was ashamed she'd asked. She didn't much like the way the three girls were acting in front of Taviano. They flirted relentlessly with him, and were constantly ordering his staff around. She sat silently staring out the window, wishing she'd never made the decision. As much as she loved Kain's music and thought it sounded so fun, asking a favor of the Ferraros wasn't worth it, not after all they'd done for her. Everything felt like a nightmare almost from the first, when she'd told Pia the Ferraros had acquired tickets for them and would fly them to Los Angeles and secure a hotel suite for the night.

Within hours, Pia, her sister Bianca, and their closest friend Clariss Naples were on Nicoletta about asking the Ferraros for an expense account to go shopping for clothes. Nicoletta was horrified. The girls came from affluent families, and she was not going to ask the Ferraros for money for them to purchase new outfits for their trip, not when they were already providing a jet, a suite at a luxury hotel and the tickets to a concert. She found it a little shocking that they would even consider it reasonable for her to ask.

They whined at her, reminding her that it was Pia's birthday, and then when she absolutely refused, wanted her to ask her foster parents, Lucia and Amo Fausti, to open their boutique, Lucia's Treasures, to allow the three to choose free clothing. That horrified her even more. She considered canceling the entire birthday event right then, but Clariss must have read her expression because she immediately burst out laughing and said it was all a joke and of course they were kidding. Nicoletta had been relieved, but now, thinking it over, she wasn't quite so certain.

The truth was, she didn't know or understand people. She'd spent the last few years avoiding getting close to anyone. She had too many secrets and was terrified of anyone finding out anything about her past. Now, she was beginning to have more confidence in herself thanks to her foster parents, counseling and, she had to admit, the Ferraro family.

Giggles broke out and she glanced up to see Pia almost fall into Taviano's lap. He caught her gallantly, his strong hands around her waist, steadying her, but there was no expression on his face. She knew that look from vast experience. Taviano wasn't happy. He never showed it. Never. But he had a temper and she didn't want to be on the wrong side of it, as she had been more than once.

She knew her friends thought he was absolutely the hottest man they'd ever seen, and she didn't blame them because—well—he was. He was tall with broad shoulders and, like his other brothers, totally ripped. Muscles everywhere, and, saying that, they looked amazing in the suits they wore. He had very dark hair, always just a little messy, which she loved, just the way she did the dark bluish shadow that seemed to be permanently on his strong jaw. She couldn't imagine him looking like a boy. He always looked like a man. He had the bluest eyes. A dark blue surrounded by very long black lashes.

Those lashes suddenly lifted, and she found herself staring into all that blue. Her heart nearly stopped and then began pounding. He did that to her. Always. She'd been a terrified teenager when he and his brother Stefano had saved her life and brought her to her foster parents, Lucia and Amo, the two most wonderful people on the entire planet. Just thinking about them made her want to cry.

Her foster parents knew all about her, everything that had happened to her, and they loved her through her nightmares and loved her through her insanity of parties and rebellion and trying to outrun herself. Taviano and his family had put up with her, watching over her, seeing to her education, even sending her to Europe and making certain she had the best counseling.

The moment Taviano released Pia, he shifted out of his seat and around her, ignoring the woman batting her eyelashes at him, and came straight to Nicoletta. When he did that, looking so directly at her, she immediately felt shy. She'd acted so crazy sometimes around him when she was younger, said things, and there had been that one terrible night . . .

She wanted to groan in shame, and it took all she had not to turn red with embarrassment remembering how drunk she'd been and how she'd thrown herself at him. It had been a really, really horrible night. They'd been very careful with each other over the next couple of years, and she always felt awkward around him. For the most part,

Taviano had avoided her, but he'd watched over her, just like the other Ferraros had done.

"What's wrong, *piccola*? You look upset. Your friends are having fun but you're over here staring out a window."

There was no reprimand in his voice. She realized there rarely was anymore. She looked for disapproval of herself often in others and was especially sensitive around Taviano. His sister, Emmanuelle, had pointed that out to her. She had given that a lot of thought and realized it was true. She looked down on herself and any little nuance others used was interpreted as disapproval.

"I feel bad that I got you into this, Taviano. I know you pulled the short straw coming with us. I didn't think that one of the family would be coming with the jet." She hadn't. She knew they'd send bodyguards, cousins of the Ferraros, but it hadn't occurred to her that a family member would deem it necessary to travel along.

He reached out to tuck a strand of hair behind her ear. The pads of his fingers were gentle as they moved along her cheek in a whisper and then over her ear. Her heart accelerated into a frenzy and her sex clenched. She was fairly certain if he kept it up her panties might melt off, but she didn't dare move or even breathe deeply.

"I came because I wanted to come, not because I drew a short straw. When you go somewhere, Nicoletta, a member of the family goes, or we send a cousin, someone trusted. We don't let strangers watch over a treasure, and you are that to us. To me. Have your fun with your friends. You never ask for anything for yourself. It is always for Lucia and Amo or someone else. Even this was for . . ." He glanced over his shoulder and gestured. "Enjoy your time with your friends while you can," he reiterated.

She forced herself to draw in air even though she knew it was a mistake. Taviano always had a distinctive masculine scent about him. She would be able to find him in the dark. The scent wasn't strong, and she didn't think it was a cologne; it was his skin, a faint spicy trail she wanted to follow that made her feel safe every time she got near him. Intellectually, she was certain she felt that way because he was the one who had come at her darkest hour, and when she inhaled and drew air—and him—into her lungs, she felt that sense of well-being.

"Thank you, Taviano. You're always so generous. You and your family." She nodded toward Pia and Bianca, who were dancing to one of Kain's most popular songs. Clariss was downing a strawberry-filled flute of champagne. "They're having a fabulous time, drinking your best champagne."

"That's what it's for. I see you're not drinking."

This time she couldn't control the blush. It started somewhere low and crept steadily up her neck to her face. She avoided his eyes. "I stopped drinking some time ago."

There was a small silence. "Nicoletta."

"Mmmm?" It was the best she could do. She fiddled with her phone, pretending she was occupied with a text message.

"Look at me."

It was a command, nothing less, and she was used to obeying a Ferraro command. No one disobeyed them. It just didn't happen. She had to steel herself to meet his gaze. It took courage, but she managed to raise her lashes and meet all that dark blue. It was like looking at a turbulent night sky. Every time she did it, he robbed her of her ability to breathe.

Nicoletta was hopelessly in love with him and there was nothing she could do about it so she didn't even try anymore to fight it. She had made up her mind a couple of years earlier just what she was going to do with her life—she was going to be like Emmanuelle and Mariko Ferraro. They were quiet about it, but they were warriors, exuding confidence, commanding respect, and she was slowly coming to find that belief in herself thanks to them.

The one thing the Ferraros had drilled into her over and over, wanted her to believe and given her as a gift, was that she could rise above everything that had been done to her—everything that had been taken from her. She could be a phoenix, rising like that firebird from the ashes of who she had been. She was determined that no one would ever be able to hurt her like that again, destroy her or anyone she loved. She would be a strong, confident woman and ensure that her daughters would be as well. If she had sons, she was determined they would be like the men in the Ferraro family, because she didn't know better men.

"That night was not your fault. It was mine," Taviano said, his voice very firm, but his tone was low, gentle, just the way he almost always spoke to her now, ever since that horrible night when she'd acted such a fool. "We are careful in our family not to drink to excess. You are aware of that. You're one of the few we allow close to us. Only one of us can do so at a time; that night was my night, and I indulged too much. I should never have gone after you when you were partying, and I was angry. I knew better. My brothers should have stopped me. You have to let it go."

She shook her head, her gaze flicking past him to her friends, who fortunately weren't paying much attention to their conversation. "I'm ashamed of the way I treated you after all you did for me. I really am, Taviano. I think I wanted to run away from myself." She knew that was what she'd been doing. She'd loathed herself, and she didn't think she was worth anything. In some weird way she was punishing herself for the things her step-uncles had done to her—things she had been helpless to stop. "Every time I saw you, you were a reminder . . ."

"You don't have to explain. I'm well aware." Taviano brushed his fingers down her cheek very gently.

She caught her breath. There was something about the way he touched her that got to her every time. He put goose bumps on her skin. Sent a rush of heat through her veins. Fire always danced low and wicked at that touch. It had been that way almost since the first time she'd opened her eyes and stared into his. She'd been so young and so old. So terrified of living, and humiliated that he knew what had happened to her over the last few years. She could barely stand looking at him or his brothers. At any of his family. They knew.

Yet because of them, because of his family, because of Taviano, she had learned to have confidence in herself. To believe she was worth something. Her recovery was due to the Ferraros and their endless patience with her, and of course the counseling they paid for. But also, she was certain, it was due to Lucia and Amo Fausti, the family the Ferraros had chosen for her. Her foster parents had loved her through the worst of her striking out at everyone—mostly striking out at herself.

"Just have fun, *tesoro*. We're going to worry about us and our relationship another day, but this day is for you and your friends."

Her heart jumped and then clenched hard. It took discipline not to rub her chest. She was acutely aware of his declaration but had no idea what he meant. Their relationship? He rarely spoke to her, in fact he usually avoided being alone with her, not that she blamed him. The family relationship? She hoped they weren't thinking of cutting ties with her. She'd toed the line, done more than what they'd expected of her.

She glanced at the three girls. Pia was glaring at her. It was her birthday and she wanted the attention, especially Taviano's. He was wealthy and gorgeous and reputed to be dangerous. The combination was heady. Nicoletta was embarrassed that her three friends were throwing themselves at him, but she couldn't throw proverbial stones—she'd done it, too. She'd been younger and drunk and feeling worthless, but she'd done it. The results had been disastrous, and she would never forget that lesson. Never. Not for as long as she lived.

The blush was back, and immediately Taviano reacted as if he knew exactly what she was thinking, and he probably did. She could swear he read minds—at least he seemed to read hers.

"You have to let it go, Nicoletta. We were both very drunk that night."

"I was very drunk. You at least didn't lose your mind completely." She whispered it to him, afraid the others might hear, even though they were a good distance away and the music was loud.

His eyes, already so blue, darkened with something that looked so close to desire her stomach dropped and her sex clenched. His breath was suddenly warm on her neck, her ear, sending a shiver of need down her spine. She couldn't look at him. She didn't dare. Not when every cell in her body was alive with need and awareness and he was so experienced he could read a woman like an open book.

"You might think of it that way. I look back on that night often and wish I'd had a little bit more to drink." His voice, as always, was low. Velvet soft. He murmured the declaration into her ear and the words burned into her mind, etched there like some beautiful calligraphy that was written in stone.

Her gaze jumped to his and she couldn't look away. He could seduce her so easily, and yet she'd offered herself to him and he had rejected her completely. She knew women came easily to him. He was in every glossy magazine, photographed with models and actresses on his arm. He went to charity events and parties, and women were all over him. The paparazzi managed to capture his life almost daily.

The paparazzi hung around the Ferraro Hotel and the Ferraro territory as well as anywhere any of the Ferraro family might be in order to capture pictures of them, especially if they might be able to get them in compromising situations. Taviano was the last eligible bachelor, the last single Ferraro brother, and women flocked around him, hopeful that he would choose one of them as his bride. He didn't date. He didn't even hook up for a night, at least no photographs had proven that lately, so he seemed to be pursued all the more, as if he had a secret life and the world was determined to uncover what it was.

"What does that mean?" She managed to choke out the question. Because what did it mean? She had been totally humiliated that night. She'd thrown herself at him and he had rejected her.

There had been kissing. So hot. He'd devoured her. She hadn't known anyone could kiss like that. She'd thought she knew what kissing was. She'd thought she could control sex, but she'd suddenly realized she knew nothing at all about it. Taviano had kissed her like she was someone special. Someone who meant something to him. He had held her with care. His mouth had been gentle, but firm. He had taken control, leading her, not the other way around. Then things had just spiraled out of control.

She had shed clothes. She remembered that, offering him everything. Wanting him with every breath she took. She needed him to erase everything that had gone before. His mouth had done that, so hot, so strong, she hadn't known her body could feel that way just with his mouth on her breast. His fingers on her nipple, his hair brushing over her skin. The way the bristles on his jaw rubbed along the curves of her breasts. She'd had the marks of that stubble, his teeth and fingers, for a night and a day, and she wanted them forever.

"It means I can still taste you. I go to bed with your taste on my tongue and wake up with it there. I ache thinking about you. It means you aren't safe forever, so you'd best have your fun with your friends while you can, because you aren't a child anymore."

It was a declaration. A challenge. Maybe even a throwing down of a gauntlet. Nicoletta drew back in her seat, uncertain how to react. It was the last thing she expected him to say. He meant it, too. Taviano didn't say things he didn't mean. His blue eyes glittered at her until she held her breath, afraid of moving.

She sat for a long time trying to figure out what she was going to do. If Taviano really persisted in attempting to seduce her, he wouldn't have to try too hard. She knew that. How could she ever forget what it felt like with his mouth on her? Traveling down her body? His tongue on her skin?

His lips worshiping her? Then moving up between her thighs so slowly she wanted to scream. Nothing had ever prepared her for such a thing. She had no idea sex could make her body feel so good.

Then he had abruptly stopped. He'd pulled away, cursing. She'd chased after him, hands on his trousers, feeling his thick arousal, tugging on his zipper, desperate and determined to get at him. His hands had caught at her wrists and stopped her, pulling her off him. The moment he'd let go of her, she'd been back, knowing he was aroused, knowing he couldn't hide that he wanted her. She'd known what she could do, that he wouldn't be able to stop once she had her mouth on him, but he'd been furious with her, once again stopping her, giving her a little shake.

They'd exchanged words. Her taunting, trying to tempt him, using her body shamelessly, pointing out that he wanted her, trying to get to him with how good she could make him feel with her mouth, with her body. He had tried to stop her. Looking back, she was utterly humiliated remembering just how often, just how he had tried to dress her himself, the different ways he'd tried to defuse the situation between them.

She'd been so hurt and angry and drunk that she'd continued to escalate it. She could barely make herself face the things she'd said and done that night until he'd suddenly dragged her naked body right over his lap and delivered a spanking onto her bare bottom. It should have reduced her to a child. It should have humiliated her beyond reason. The last thing it should have been was erotic, and it had made her want to weep with need.

Taviano caught her chin in his hand. "You have to stop. If you don't, you're going to give me no choice but to shock your friends. I promised myself I'd wait until you turned twenty-one, and that's in a few more weeks. I already know that's too damned far away."

She wasn't about to ask him what that meant, either. She simply nodded to indicate she'd do her best to forget that horrible night ever happened, but she knew she never would. She thought of it every single day. It had been the catalyst for her to change her life. To want to make something of herself. She had given up drinking and trying to hurt herself for things in her past she hadn't been able to control. She decided to control herself and take responsibility for herself at least.

She wanted to protect Lucia and Amo and make certain they were never harmed. She knew she could never have Taviano Ferraro, but she could take advantage of the hand the Ferraro family held out to her and the education they were offering. She was intelligent and learned quickly, and she pushed herself from that day forward. All of the Ferraros helped her. Taviano was around, because the family was very close. She avoided him as best she could, and he seemed to avoid her, which was helpful when she didn't know how to act around him.

She searched for a safe topic. "How is Cristo?"

Taviano laughed softly. "I'm not going to let you be a coward forever, Nicoletta, but any time we can talk about my nephew, I'm all for it. And Crispino is doing quite well, as you should know, since you watch him for Francesca every chance you get."

"I love all that curly hair he has. It's so beautiful," Nicoletta said. She did. Francesca told her that the moment Stefano saw his son born with thick black curls all over his head, he immediately named him Crispino. His uncles and Emmanuelle, his aunt, adored him, and all of them spoiled him, but Nicoletta was determined she was going to be the favorite. He was the sweetest boy ever.

"It's good that you spend so much time with him," Taviano said.

"Francesca needed a lot of help after he was born," Nicoletta said, "and I was there with Mariko and Emmanuelle, working on self-defense. It was natural to help her with the baby. There's no way not to fall in love with him. He's just so adorable. I'm there nearly every day."

It was a silly thing to say. Taviano would have that information. She might work at Lucia's Treasures for her foster parents and also at the flower shop occasionally, but she never missed a lesson in self-defense. She took her training very seriously and studied with one of the women or one of Taviano's brothers. They weren't easy on her, either. She went home with bruises, and every muscle in her body aching, but she didn't care. She wanted to be as good as they were—which seemed unattainable, but that didn't deter her from trying. Everyone had to start somewhere.

She recognized she was fast. Very fast. She had good hand-eye coordination. She could hit hard and accurately, the same with kicking. She picked up the techniques they taught her quickly and was always thirsty for more. She didn't want praise—she wanted critiques that would make her better. She never wanted to be a victim again. Never. She was determined to learn to turn her mind and body into the best weapons possible to defend herself and others if needed.

"He's already got Stefano wrapped around his little finger," Taviano pointed out. "That little boy is going to rule us all."

Nicoletta laughed. She couldn't help herself. Taviano sounded so rueful and he looked so handsome, with his dark hair spilling across his forehead and his blue eyes mournful, as if all of them loving his nephew so much they could never speak harshly to him was a bad thing. Not a single Ferraro raised their voice to Crispino. The child was told "no" when he was too adventurous and might have gotten into something that could harm him, but the "no" was never delivered in a harsh manner, and he was removed gently if he refused to obey.

Nicoletta followed the lead of the Ferraro family when she watched the boy, treating him exactly the same and sometimes dancing him to sleep or cuddling him longer than necessary just because she needed it more than he did. Often Lucia and Amo would come over just to hold the boy as well. They loved watching him grow.

"I was astonished at how quickly he grew in weeks and

months, from rolling over to crawling and sitting and then standing. Sometimes I think I was less prepared than Francesca and Stefano," Nicoletta admitted to Taviano. "He would cuddle with me at night, and I just felt this amazing closeness with him. He made my heart feel so—" She broke off, feeling silly again.

When she lifted her lashes, Taviano was looking at her with that focused stare that always made her stomach do a slow rolling pitch that ended up with a million butterflies taking wing and fluttering, so that she wanted to press her hand there and give it away that he was wreaking havoc on her body with just a look. He was dangerous to women and in particular, to her.

"What?" she demanded.

"I like that Crispino makes you feel that way. You dance with him."

"How did you know?" she demanded. She did, all the time. "You're never there when I dance with him."

"*Piccola*, Stefano has security cameras everywhere, you know that. He has apps on his phone so that at any given moment he can see his boy and know that he's safe. We make certain you're safe at all times. You have always known this. We've never hidden that from you."

His voice was gentle. That velvet moving over her skin. She didn't know if he spoke to everyone like that or just her. Maybe she was the only one who actually got that sensation when he talked in that low voice, but it was so real it was physical.

"I just forget," she admitted. "I'm glad Stefano watches out for Cristo that way." She'd shortened the baby's name right away, and Lucia and even Francesca called him Cristo, but the men in the family rarely shortened his name.

"He likes you to dance with him, but Stefano said the other night when he was fussy, he was forced to do some dancing to put him to sleep." Taviano sounded pleased with that. In fact, he smirked a little. "All of us are hoping Francesca managed to get a video of that."

"You know she did." Nicoletta couldn't help laughing. "Stefano's going to give me another lecture. He's always telling me that Cristo needs to be able to soothe himself to sleep and I shouldn't dance or cuddle him to sleep."

Taviano's smile faded. "Don't let him fool you. He still rocks that boy to sleep sometimes if he wakes up more than once in the middle of the night. He did all of us when we woke up. Is he giving you lectures? Harsh ones? Because Stefano can sound harsh even when he doesn't mean it that way. If he does, Nicoletta, I'll have a word with him."

That sounded ominous. More than ominous. By his tone, he was upset with Stefano just at the thought of him lecturing her, which was ridiculous, since Taviano did it all the time. Well . . . until that night. Since then, he'd kept his distance. He had a temper, and she didn't want him at odds with Stefano, especially over her. Not with the Ferraros always being so good to her and to the Faustis. She knew they made her foster parents' lives so much easier, and she appreciated everything they did for them because she loved Lucia and Amo so much.

"Stefano has been wonderful to me, Taviano. He doesn't really mind me dancing around with Cristo, he just likes to sound all tough when he tells me that he has to do it because of me. He loves getting up with his son in the middle of the night. Francesca says any alone time he gets with that boy is his favorite time because he's always so busy."

"I believe it. He took care of all of us when we were little. Our parents weren't much on babies or toddlers," Taviano disclosed. "It was always Stefano who changed diapers and fed us bottles or comforted us in the middle of the night. God forbid a Ferraro child dare have a nightmare, or not know how to use a toilet at birth."

Nicoletta put her hand on his without thinking about what she was doing. She never thought in terms that Taviano might need comfort, that he might have come from an imperfect situation, because he seemed so omnipotent. He was always so completely uncaring about what others thought of him. He didn't seem to need anyone at all. The moment she touched him, she realized what she'd done and started to pull her hand away. He covered her hand with his, pressing down, holding hers trapped between his.

"You've met Eloisa. She's as cold as ice."

Taviano, like the rest of his brothers and his sister, rarely called his mother by any other title than Eloisa, her given name. They referred to her in public as "mother," but Nicoletta had been around them in private too long not to catch on to the fact that to the siblings, she was always Eloisa.

"I thought she was just that way to me."

"No, she's that way to everyone, her sons included. She's worse to Emmanuelle and even more so to her daughters-in-law. She saves her venom for you because you mean something to all of us and she knows it."

She wasn't touching that one, either. There were just too many things Taviano was alluding to, and she couldn't keep up with him, or even have hope. He'd totally shot her down once, and that had been enough to shatter her heart. She wasn't going there again. She couldn't and keep her hard-won confidence. She had been around him and his family for three years. In that time, no matter how big a fool she'd made of herself, or how much she'd hated herself for what had happened to her, the Ferraros had been patient with her.

Taviano had never told anyone of her conduct that night. He could have. He could have told her foster parents. He could have told his family. He had never changed his patient ways with her. Or his caring. He had been careful not to be alone with her, and truthfully, that hurt, but she understood and even was grateful. She had made changes, studying the way she should have. Listening to the counselor and trying to implement what was said. Putting her trust in Lucia and talking things over with her when she found herself particularly upset and having nightmares. Opening herself to loving again. And that meant herself as well.

She had to find her own strengths and weaknesses. The Ferraros had offered to train her in self-defense, and she'd taken them up on that offer. That meant getting close to their family, and she wasn't sorry about that. They took her in and acted as if she were a part of them. They didn't hold back at all—other than Eloisa, who treated her with the utmost disdain, but she was never at Francesca and Stefano's penthouse, which was where Nicoletta went for training. She only ran into Eloisa when the woman came to visit Lucia.

Nicoletta was in love with Taviano. It wasn't just about sex. It wasn't just about him saving her life. There was a difference in the way the Ferraros were in private with their family and the way they appeared in public. She was always treated like family. Always. She saw the real Taviano and she loved everything about him. How gentle and kind he was. How he could get that flash of temper that could erupt and burn hot and go away just as fast, so that he was laughing. The way he held his nephew so gently, whispering to him, laughing, pushing a stroller down the street, and later, holding his little hand.

Taviano sat on the floor and played instruments with Crispino or raced little cars, sometimes rolled balls across the floor. It didn't matter what kind of toys his nephew wanted to play with, he was ready, and he had infinite patience. She loved that about him. All of his brothers and Emmanuelle appeared to be the same, but she could never quite take her eyes off Taviano when he was with Crispino.

Nicoletta also loved his relationship with Emmanuelle. The two often laughed together. All the brothers were protective of their sister. She envied Emmanuelle that at first, but then realized they seemed equally as protective of her. Then she became aware of a deep sadness in Emmanuelle, and she found herself growing protective of Taviano's sister for no reason she really understood other than she seemed very sad at times.

Emmanuelle traveled quite often, staying in New York with her cousins, and sometimes going to Italy to stay with relatives there, but after a few months, she would return and bury her face in little Crispino's neck and proclaim he was the love of her life and she could never leave him again.

"Why is Eloisa so cutting to Emmanuelle, Taviano? She visits Lucia often, and sometimes Emmanuelle comes with her, and when she does, Eloisa says really snarky things to put her down in front of Lucia. I mean, she says them about me, but I expect that."

Taviano frowned. "What do you mean, she says them about you? I specifically asked Lucia to report to me if Eloisa was upsetting you with her visits."

"She isn't upsetting me. I was asking you about Emmanuelle."

"I was asking you about what Eloisa says to or about you," Taviano said, his voice turning hard. "Answer me, Nicoletta."

She rolled her eyes. "Oh, for heaven's sake, Taviano. You know very well the kind of sneering voice she uses and the cutting remarks she makes."

He stood up, towering over her. His face became stone, eyes glittering down at her, two twin gems that looked suddenly frightening. "Answer me, Nicoletta," he reiterated.

She didn't hesitate, heart kicking into overdrive. "I'm beneath Lucia, and Eloisa has no idea why Lucia and Amo would take me in. I'm old enough now for them to kick me out, and they've done their good deed and don't have to continue to flog themselves mercilessly for sins they never committed in the first place. I'm going to turn on them and rob them blind. I'm going to stab them in their sleep. I've already brought trouble on the Ferraro family, look what happened to Vittorio right outside their home because I was crawling out the window trying to have a rendezvous with some boy. I'm a slut and whore and I sleep around, she has that on good word, and she's only trying to spare Lucia heartache. Naturally that isn't all said on the same visit; she spreads it around. Lucia, of course, stands up to her, but there it is."

His face darkened as she spoke, and she could tell he was

having trouble holding the infamous Ferraro temper in check. "You should have told me. Lucia should have told me."

"It doesn't bother me. Eloisa is never going to like me. A lot of her friends don't like me." She gestured toward Pia and Bianca. "Their mother pretends to like me, but she doesn't. Pia and Bianca are probably my friends because I'm a stepping-stone to you. Their mother is hoping you'll marry one of them."

"Are you fucking kidding me, Nicoletta? Why would you arrange to take them on this trip if you know that?"

She gave him a half smile. "I'm a little slow on the uptake. I didn't get that until I watched them with you just now. I could be wrong. I hope that I am. I think Clariss is a genuine friend, but at this point, I'm still not sure I'm that good a judge of character. Lucia is still helping me with that. She's amazing in that department."

"Don't do that again, keep something from me, like Eloisa talking shit about you."

"She talks shit about Emmanuelle, Taviano. I would think you'd be more concerned about that."

"She's done that since the day Emmanuelle was born, *tesoro*. My sister has never been good enough for our mother, and she never will be. Francesca will never be good enough. I don't suppose any female ever will be in Eloisa's eyes." He shrugged his shoulders. "You don't see her at Stefano's home for a reason. If she keeps talking shit about you, you won't see her at Lucia's, either."

"She's Lucia's friend, Taviano," Nicoletta said, trying to be gentle. She could feel his fury. He was really angry with his mother.

"I don't much give a damn. Go have fun with your friends. I'm going to talk to Lucia and find out how long this bullshit has been going on."

"Please don't upset Lucia."

"I would never upset Lucia," Taviano said, his voice softening. "I mean it, *piccola*, go have fun. You have this one more night and then we're talking." Abruptly he was gone, walking down the aisle toward the front of the plane where Demetrio and Drago, his second cousins, were sitting looking very relaxed, but again, Nicoletta knew better. They might be related to Taviano, young and good-looking, but they were trained bodyguards and they were very good at their job. Her friends weren't any more of a distraction to them than she was.

Nicoletta stared after Taviano, unsure what to think. She pulled out her cell phone, wanting to call Lucia for reassurance. She'd come to rely on her. Lucia was an older woman, steady, sweet and unfailingly strong. She'd had tragedy in her life. First the loss of her young daughter to cancer and then the loss of her remaining son after he came home from serving in the military and was shot by a random murderer outside a theater.

Nicoletta had come to Lucia and Amo, seventeen and wild with grief at the loss of her parents and striking out with anger at the terrible things done to her by her three step-uncles for the past three years while she'd been in their custody. Her foster parents seemed to understand her and had the patience needed to let her grieve and strike out. They connected to her on every level, and it was impossible to love them any more than she did.

"Aren't you going to join us?" Pia asked, her voice petulant. "I thought this was supposed to be a party."

Nicoletta looked up with a small smile. "You look like you're partying to me. For your twenty-first birthday, on a private jet, drinking the best champagne, going to the concert of your choice, I'd say you're partying."

"What was all that?"

Nicoletta shook her head. "All what?"

"You and Taviano? You looked as if you two were having a private conversation."

She shrugged. "Just family stuff. Nothing huge. We were talking about Francesca and Stefano mainly."

"Family stuff? You're *family* now?" Now there was a bite to her voice.

Pia was definitely jealous. She'd had enough to drink to show it. Nicoletta stood up with another smile. "Yep. I'm family. If I wasn't, we wouldn't be on the jet, headed to the Kain Diakos concert, now, would we? Let's get some dancing in before we get there." She caught Pia by the arm and hurried back to the other two girls.

Immediately they were laughing and dancing. Clariss had more strawberries than champagne, but she still pronounced it the best she'd ever tasted. Nicoletta indulged in eating quite a few strawberries, found whipped cream and added that to them just for fun. Bianca drank two more flutes filled with strawberries and champagne, but Pia was mostly just drinking. That worried Nicoletta. They weren't even at the concert yet.

"Slow it down, girl. If you drink too much, they won't let us in."

"Who cares," Pia said. "We can just stay on board and spend the night here. Why did we need the hotel when there's a bed? Or you three can go to the hotel and I'll stay here with Mr. Hotness. He's been looking at my boobs all evening."

Nicoletta tried not to smile. Taviano was looking down at his phone, and even though he was wearing that stone expression the Ferraros tended to wear in public, she knew he was not happy. He certainly wasn't staring at Pia.

"You wish, Pia," Clariss said. "We're going to the concert, so switch to something else. You're not ruining this for us. Besides, you love Kain. I thought you were going to have his babies."

Pia brightened. "I am. I *so* am."

She threw her arms around Nicoletta and hugged her hard, staggering a little so they both nearly went down. Nicoletta had to balance for both of them.

"I'm sorry. I love you, my friend. I was *so* jealous for a minute because I had this idea that Mr. Hotness was going to marry me and carry me off to a place where my mother couldn't yell at me anymore and destroy everything I try to do. That was a dream that will never happen though. Instead, I'll have Kain's babies."

Bianca shook her head. "Mom will never stop trying to marry us to the richest men she can find. She's not happy with Dad, but she still wants that life for us. I'm absolutely crazy about Enzo Gallo, not that he would ever look at me. If he did ask me out, Mom would be so ugly to him that he'd only do it once, but honestly, I'd be willing to sever ties with my family just for a chance with him. Not you, Pia, just her. I'm so tired of never being able to talk to a man who interests me."

"I had no idea," Nicoletta said. "You live on your own. You both work."

"It was the only way to get out from under her, but we're not out from under her. Every time we get a job, she goes to our boss and sabotages it for us," Pia confessed a little drunkenly. "Then we're behind on rent, and it sucks always looking for jobs because it looks like we keep hopping from one place to the next."

Clariss sank into one of the seats, reaching for a strawberry, dipping it into the whipped cream. "That's awful. You should have told us. I would have helped. You could have moved into my apartment. It's small, but we could make it work."

"I could have talked to Stefano," Nicoletta said. "He would have found jobs that she couldn't sabotage." She nudged Bianca with her hip. "And I do know Enzo Gallo. He's the Ferraros' cousin. He works as a bodyguard. I can casually introduce you if you haven't actually met him. In fact, I can arrange a few times to run into him when he's not working. I kind of know where they're going to be sometimes."

Bianca shook her head but then changed her mind. "You'd do that?"

"I want to know if Stefano could really find us jobs Mom can't screw up for us, Bianca," Pia said. She slurred her words a bit, but she was looking very sober as she looked directly at Nicoletta.

"I honestly believe he would," Nicoletta said. "Stefano can do anything. If you and Bianca really want to work, then of course he'll find you a good job."

"One where we make enough money where we can be independent? I don't mean tons, just enough to pay rent and eat," Pia persisted. "Not pity money. We'll work for it."

Nicoletta nodded. "I'm certain he would, but he'll only do that kind of favor once. You can't screw up," she cautioned. "Stefano isn't the kind of man you cross."

Pia nodded. "I get that." She stuffed a strawberry into her mouth. "That's an even better birthday present than the Kain concert. And I love him. I'm going to have his babies."

"No, you're not," Bianca protested. "I'm not going to get stuck providing for us while you get all the sex and stay home with the kids, you hussy."

They all laughed and began dancing again. Nicoletta decided maybe she was better at picking friends than she'd thought.

CHAPTER TWO

The air was electric as only Kain Diakos and his band could make it. Nicoletta felt vibrations in the air, surrounding them, everywhere. The music pounded through her veins, set her blood on fire, so that she threw her head back and raised her hands in the air, her feet stomping out the beat while her body swayed. Like everyone around her, she had to be up on her feet. Dancing. Singing. Eyes glued to the stage and the magic happening.

The stage would be dark one moment and then light would burst across it, colors dripping down in all shades, and Kain would move through those various hues with his sensual body, delivering his lyrics in his beyond-sexy voice. If Nicoletta hadn't been so far gone on Taviano, she would have been pledging the heavens that, like Pia, she would be having Kain's children. He was awesome. His songs were beautiful. Lyrical. His body was ripped. Hot.

His mother was Ethiopian, his father Greek, and he got the best of both worlds when it came to his looks. His eyes were dark chocolate, his hair black and very curly, wild enough for some of the curls to drip down his forehead when he moved on the stage, which only added to his sexy appearance. He produced his own music, wrote his own songs and burst onto the music scene so fast, no one saw his star streaking to fame until he was already there.

His following began online, his concerts were sold out nearly the first hour the tickets went on sale and he was winning every award possible. Nicoletta knew he was only going to get bigger and bigger in the music industry. She liked that he was up-and-coming but still hands-on with the stage productions so that his vision of music and stage went together. It added to the feel of the music and the way it was presented, so that when you were actually there, the notes vibrated through your body as the lights dazzled your eyes and put you into the song with him.

She loved his voice. She loved the lyrics. She loved the actual rhythms and the guitar riffs, the drums, the way everything came together with the lights, and the energy of the crowd. Pia, Bianca and Clariss were gyrating and waving their arms, jumping up and down and dancing with the others.

Nicoletta found herself pulling more and more energy off the crowd, the stage, the singer and the incredible music. It fed her soul. Her body sang, feeling renewed and strong. She loved going to concerts. Lucia had been the first one to take her to a concert, and the moment the singer had come out onstage and all those things had come together—crowd, music and singer—something in her had reacted to that energy, and she felt a difference almost immediately. It was healing to her. Spiritual almost. She'd told Lucia, and Lucia had acted on it. Wonderful Lucia. Giving her everything and anything she needed.

She'd been to many concerts and then she'd discovered Kain's music. He'd just been starting out online, but she played his songs over and over and danced in her room to them. When she couldn't sleep and the nightmares were too close, she listened to them, sang the lyrics and let them carry the worst of her past away.

His concerts were incredible, lifting her, elevating her to another place. Unlike the other women in the crowd, who came for the sexy man and his voice—most of whom were young and well dressed, many of them actresses, models or even singers themselves, well-known celebrities who followed Kain now—she came for the entire package, including the energy of the crowd. It swallowed her past. Ate it up. Gave her back her life.

Pia bumped her with her hip. "Isn't he amazing?" She shouted it.

"He is." Nicoletta had to agree.

"I'm in love!" Clariss yelled.

"Me, too," Bianca said. "You can have his babies, Pia. I'll work and support you."

Pia blew her sister kisses as the band swung into the next song. They were in the front. Naturally, Taviano had gotten them the best seats possible and they could dance right up to the stage where the bodyguards allowed them close. The lights played over them and cameras panned, throwing images up on the huge screens behind and on each side of the band. That way even in the far back, everyone could see Kain and the incredible sexy movements of his body as he made his way across the stage with his blend of hip-hop and R&B.

His music was at times elegant and dark, but always hypnotic. The atmosphere he created with his songs and voice was mesmerizing. When he added in his stage presence and lighting, the moody colors and pounding beats, he enthralled an entire audience from the moment he stepped on stage.

Nicoletta turned her face up toward him, arms reaching, basking in his magic, needing his dark, twisted lyrics that always spoke of the worst of times somehow finding their way to becoming right. The steps were long, the road rocky and painful, the losses heavy, but the agony was worth it in the end. She knew that road. She'd traveled it. She was coming out the other side.

She always felt as if Kain had journeyed similar paths, or how could he write songs so filled with the truth of exactly what it was like to suffer the worst that humans could do to one another and then give hope? He gave hope to millions of listeners through his lyrics. When she closed her eyes and just let his voice and the sounds of his band bathe her skin, flow into her veins, taking her further and further from those few short years when she lived in New York with her three step-uncles . . .

"Nicoletta?"

She blinked, trying to make the voice Pia's or Bianca's. It was too deep. A man's voice. One with an accent. One far too familiar. She turned her head and found herself staring into a pair of speculative dark brown eyes. The man was close to forty. She recognized him immediately and her heart dropped—nearly stopped beating. Armando Lupez. He was Benito Valdez's right hand.

Benito Valdez was the head of the bloodiest gang, the Demons, with headquarters in New York. Unfortunately, Benito, just out of prison, had fixated on her and demanded her step-uncles turn her over to him. Right before that had happened, she had been rescued by the Ferraros and just disappeared. No one knew where she was or what had happened to her. She'd been living in Chicago and just assumed that over the intervening years, she'd been forgotten.

All around them darkness embraced the crowd, and lights pounded on and off, the colors once again spreading like a magical web. The pulse of the music should have made those colors bright and harmonic, but instead, they felt sinister and threatening. She glanced past Armando to see two more men she marked as gang members, flanking him. She didn't recognize them, but that didn't matter; she knew the Demons had chapters in other cities.

Armando smiled, a slow, evil smile. He had his phone out and showed her a text. "Saw you up on the screen looking so fine and sent Benito a pic. You just get better with age. He said to bring you on home. He has special plans for you."

Nicoletta didn't wait. She kicked him hard, smashing her boot into his groin and pulling out her phone as she did so. She didn't wait to see Armando fall. She shoved at Pia and Bianca to get them moving. "Come on, Clariss, we have to go now. Run. Get to the other side of the aisle."

They were slow, not understanding, but she grabbed at Clariss's arm and dragged her as she ran toward the other side of the venue, thankful they were in the very front. There was a crowd they had to thread through, but most were standing. As she ran, she texted Taviano with one hand. De-mons here. Spotted me. Chasing me now. Tell me what to do.

Get to west exit. I'll be there. There was no hesitation. None. He answered her as if he'd been waiting for an emergency.

She sent the thumbs-up emoji.

Could Taviano get there that fast? He hadn't come to the concert. He was waiting on the plane. She had to believe him. She risked a quick glance to see the exit sign shining in green on the west wall. The distance seemed insurmountable, especially since Pia, Bianca and Clariss insisted on turning back as Kain and the band swung into one of his biggest hits.

"Nicoletta," Pia wailed, "what are you doing?"

"Run," Nicoletta said, pushing her again, pouring urgency into her voice.

She glanced over her shoulder. The two men who had been behind Armando were shoving women out of their way and coming after them. A few women screamed, but with the screaming of adoration for Kain up on the stage, it was impossible for security to tell that anything was wrong.

"I'm in heels," Bianca complained. "What's wrong?"

"Those men are after us and they'll kill us," Nicoletta hissed. "Before they do, they'll rape and torture you. They're members of the Demons gang. Now run."

"Is this a joke?" Pia asked.

Bianca slipped off her heels but paused to look back at the two men coming toward them. One of them shoved a woman so hard using the flat of his hand between her shoulder blades that she went flying over the back of a seat. Bianca gasped and sprinted around Clariss to take the lead. She had no idea where she was going.

"The exit! The west exit!" Nicoletta shouted, trying to be heard above the music and the screaming of the crowd.

"Which way is west?" Pia asked, following her sister.

They were running straight down the aisle now, trying to avoid those standing and dancing. Weaving their way through the tight crowd was difficult and slowed them down. Pia, Bianca and Clariss were hesitant to push their way through. When Nicoletta glanced over her shoulder, the two men were closer. She could see their features now. One man was definitely younger, closer to Taviano's age, and the other was around Armando's age. Both looked scary and determined. She knew that if Benito asked for something and he didn't get it, he was a very vindictive and dangerous man. If he got it, he always returned favors. They would want favors from the leader of their gang.

Abruptly, the three women in front of her stopped moving. The crowd was thick and refused to part to let them through. Bianca looked back at the two men, saw they were close and ran into one of the rows of seated people, pushing through, trying to get to the other side. She murmured, "Excuse me, excuse me," over and over. Pia hesitated and then followed her sister.

"Bianca, Pia, no! Come back this way!" Nicoletta shouted. Neither even looked back. She doubted they heard her over the loud screams and the pounding beat of the music.

She made a grab for Clariss, who chose a different aisle to do the same thing, making her way toward the middle, where the three women hoped to run back toward the entrance doors.

Nicoletta had to make a choice: follow them, or make

her way to the exit and get to Taviano. She inserted her shoulder between two women who seemed to be glued together and pushed between them, ignoring their angry outburst at her. She felt someone grab at her arm, but she pulled it through, keeping the two women between her and the men following her as she tried to get between several more women bunched together. They were jumping up and down, clutching one another and having fun, just as she'd been doing up front.

These women were much more aggressive, not wanting to move and angry that she would try to invade their space. She tried several different ways around them, and none would relent and give ground. She glanced back, and not only had the two men gotten past the first two women, but Armando was with them and he had a gun out. One of the women spotted the gun and his evil smile.

"What the hell? What do you think you're doing with that? He after you, honey?" She waved behind her, stepping forward a few inches to give Nicoletta enough room to slip by her. Just like that, she'd gone from angry to protective. She was probably at a Kain concert because his music spoke to her—a survivor of some horrendous event as well.

Nicoletta could see the west exit sign. There were only a few people between her and where she needed to go. She didn't see how it was possible for Taviano to reach the venue before she could reach that exit. The temptation to do as her friends had done and go toward the middle was huge, but she believed in the Ferraros. If Taviano said he'd be there, somehow, he would.

She threaded her way through the next group, this time two men and three women. She heard the gun go off and more screams. Her heart thudded, and she prayed Armando hadn't shot the woman who had stood up for her. She didn't look back. She pushed harder, shoving her way past the men and nearly knocking down one of the women. Just as she reached the shadow the light was throwing across the floor, Armando grabbed her by her hair, yanking her head back, and she immediately reached back to stab at his eyes with her thumbs, but he turned his head to the side.

"You little bitch. You're going to pay for that," he snarled.

She raked the heel of her boot down his shin and, at the same time, slapped both hands over his to force the hand holding her hair flat on her scalp. She dropped low and spun around and then stood up fast, hoping to break his wrist. He howled and let go of her hair. She tried kicking him in the groin but he jerked his body to the side.

"Behind me," Taviano ordered, coming out of nowhere.

She didn't hesitate. She leapt to get behind his body. As she did so, two guns fired almost simultaneously. Something hot buzzed past her head and hit the wall behind her. Gasping, she caught at the back of Taviano's shirt as he staggered back.

"Are you crazy? Benito will kill you if you touch that girl," Armando snapped. "Get her friends. Get the other bitches. She'll come with us, won't you, Nicoletta? When we cut them into pieces, she'll beg to come with us."

Taviano smashed his fist into Armando's face and dropped him like a stone. Before either of the other two men could turn their guns on him again, Nicoletta stepped in front of him.

"Go ahead and shoot me. Benito will skin you alive and you know it. And then he'll kill your families."

Taviano's arm snaked around her waist and he dragged her back toward the glaring light of the exit sign.

The men left Armando struggling to stand and took off after Pia, Bianca and Clariss. Nicoletta caught at Taviano and started toward the door. He stopped her.

"Not that way, *piccolo*. You're my woman. You're about to find out what it is to be a Ferraro. Step into the shadow and keep your body behind mine."

She'd never liked the feeling of being in the shadows, and yet she'd always been drawn to them. They'd always made her feel as if her body were being torn apart, but she knew she could hide in them; she'd done so on several occasions, just not always successfully. "You've been shot, Taviano. You need help. We have to get you to one of the medical facilities."

"We'll get there. I want you to do exactly what I say."

He turned to face her. When he did, she could see the blood splashed on his jacket. He wore that same immaculate, classy, very expensive charcoal pin-striped suit that his entire family wore. The tie was a darker charcoal and the shirt was lighter charcoal. The men and even Emmanuelle always looked so distinctive, but she had to admit, when they got close to the shadows, they seemed to fade into them.

He cupped her chin with his palm. "You have to trust me like you've never trusted me before. I'm going to ask you to do things that are going to frighten you, and you're going to have to do them without question. Can you do that for me? We don't have time for anything else." He was whispering, his voice incredibly low, but she heard every word.

She didn't hesitate. All she did was look at the blood on his jacket and into his eyes. The music had faded. Everything around her faded but Taviano and the blood.

"Take off everything you're wearing. Everything including your underwear, Nicoletta. Your earrings are fine. Lucia gave them to you. I had them made for you and asked her to give them to you. My cousin made them. You'll wear my shirt." He was stripping off his jacket and, one-handed, removing his shirt as he spoke. He was fast, too.

She didn't look at him and she knew he didn't look away. It was her boots that gave her the most trouble, but she got them off and the shirt on in record time. She knew about hiding in the shadows naked. She'd done so. With her clothing on, she'd been found every single time.

"When we go farther into the shadows, you don't let go of me, you understand? No matter how it feels, no matter what, you don't let go. Keep your eyes closed tight. You're going to feel sick and disoriented."

She was already feeling sick and disoriented. Her body felt like it was in pieces, as if when she'd removed her clothes, the material had been the only thing holding her together. Now, with just his shirt, nothing would hold her skin on, and she was being pulled apart piece by piece. The feeling sickened her. It helped when she closed her eyes, but she was terrified she was going to vomit all over Taviano.

"I've got you, *tesoro*," he whispered.

His mouth moved so close to her ear, she felt his lips brush her earlobe. He wrapped his arm around her and locked her to his side. She immediately put both of her arms around his waist as far as she could and held on as tightly as she could, pressing her head into his side. She had no idea what they were going to do, but somewhere in her mind, there was a vague recollection of being in a similar situation and feeling this exact sensation.

Then she was moving so fast it felt like she was on a speedway, the fastest bullet train or park ride. Faster even than that. Her stomach dropped and rolled and was somehow left behind, or she would have spilled the contents down his rib cage. She knew her arms were around his waist, but her flesh was literally peeling off the bone in tiny pieces and flying away. She couldn't look because she knew she would see only a skeleton holding on to Taviano.

She wanted to scream, or at least call his name, but she couldn't. She couldn't make a sound. Not even open her mouth. She refused to open her eyes, and he'd said not to. If she did, she feared her eyes would be sucked out of her face, just like her flesh had been torn off. If she lived through this, if she was intact when he stopped, she was never, never doing this again.

Just as abruptly as they seemed to speed, they came to a halt. Taviano held her steady for another moment, and then his hands went to her shoulders. She wrenched away from him, stumbling, her stomach heaving. She threw up over and over, emptying the contents into the corner of the small, dark room. She was grateful it was dark and ashamed she couldn't handle however they'd gotten there. She didn't even want to know how they had.

When she turned back, he handed her a wet wipe and a bottle of water. He had already slipped off the jacket and she could see his upper body, the rock-hard abs and his thick chest that always took her breath away. Now, all she could really see were the shocking streaks of blood splattered across it, coming from his left arm.

"Taviano." She whispered his name, horrified that she was vomiting while he was bleeding. She wasn't that kind of woman. She could fix horrible gashes. The sensation of her body being torn apart must have been happening to him as well, and with a wound like the one he had, the traveling could only have made it worse.

He towered over her, looking down at her face, his eyes gentle. "Are you all right?"

"Yes. No. I honestly don't know. Are you? What was that? How did we get here?" She waved her hand at him. "Don't tell me."

She looked around, half expecting to find that they were exactly where they had just been, because if they weren't, how had they traveled somewhere else? And why would she think that was what they had done? And she did think that. They were at a first aid station. No one was in it. She hurried over to the shelves, looking to pull out a first aid kit. She opened the one she thought would have the items they would need.

This wasn't her first time traveling in the shadows. She'd done this before alone in her room, by accident. And she half remembered another time with Stefano and Taviano. She didn't want to think about it. She didn't have time to process it yet.

Taviano came close to stand beside her. Just his scent drove her crazy. Masculine. So distinctive, sexy, even when it was mixed with the coppery scent of blood.

"I have to clean this wound and we have to get back to the airport immediately."

He was all business, pulling out the items that he needed from the first aid kit. Whoever had shot at them missed her by quite a margin and had taken just a chunk of his skin from his arm. It looked like it hurt. He rummaged through the box, looking at the various threads to sew up his wounds with.

"What are you looking for?"

"Silk, it has to be silk, otherwise we'll need to take thread from my shirt."

In the end, that was what he did. She frowned, watching him. He was fast at it, too, as if he'd done it a million times. She took the needle from him after he'd cleaned up the blood and dosed the wound with antibiotics.

"They went after my friends, Taviano. They're going to hurt them. I think Pia and Bianca may have gotten away, but Clariss was way behind the other two. I just left them. I ran straight to you." She felt ashamed for leaving her friends, so much so that she concentrated on staring down at the stitches, keeping them tiny and even.

"*Piccola*, look at me."

His voice was so gentle, it turned her heart over. He waited until her gaze met his. "You did exactly what I asked you to do. If they'd gotten their hands on all of you, they would have killed your friends in front of you."

"Can you find them?"

"My first priority has to be you."

She was watching him closely, and his blue eyes darkened and shifted for just the smallest moment, but it was enough. "You know where they're going, don't you?"

"Nicoletta."

"You do, Taviano. You know. I don't have a lot of friends. Pia and Bianca told me things tonight that made me very aware they are my friends. I'm not about to let them down. Clariss has always stood in my corner. Always. I know what those men will do to them, and so do you. Even if they weren't my friends, I couldn't leave them behind. I'm asking you to help me save them. I can't live with myself or with you if we just go off and leave them and be safe back in Chicago."

"You aren't going to be safe in Chicago, Nicoletta. Neither are Lucia or Amo. I've already texted the family to get them to a safe place. The moment Benito Valdez finds out from his people here where you've been living, he's going to be headed straight to Chicago, and he's going to bring an army with him. Your friends have cell phones and IDs on them. It isn't going to be difficult to get any information out of them about you that Benito wants."

She hadn't thought of that. She caught at Taviano's arm, suddenly torn between trying to locate her friends and rushing back to help protect Lucia and Amo. "I never thought that they'd be in danger. What are we going to do?"

"One step at a time. Stefano and the others have that under control. We have to control the situation here. We need to get you back to the plane. Everyone there is on alert because, again, the girls will give up that location as well."

She lifted her chin as sudden awareness dawned on her. "The hotel. They'll go to the hotel. Especially if Pia and Bianca went to the hotel. That's where they'll go, isn't it, Taviano?"

He sighed and slid his arm into the sleeve of his jacket. "Yes."

"Then that's where I'm going. And I'm going to kill Armando Lupez. You have no idea the terrible things he's done. He deserves to die, Taviano. They rape girls so easily, young girls, destroying them even when they know the girls will take their own lives. They think women have no rights. They use us and then throw us away. They beat us and force us to do whatever they want and laugh while they do it. They force the girls to service their friends or other men for money and get them hooked on drugs so they can use them on the streets. They make them mules for carrying the drugs. These are bad men." She made every effort to keep her voice under control, and it took effort when she wanted to scream at him to listen to her, to understand and believe her.

He put his arms around her and pulled her close. It was only when she put her head on his chest that she realized tears were running down her face. She didn't cry. She never cried. She'd stopped doing that when she'd barely been fifteen, but once she started, she couldn't seem to stop, and she didn't have time to fall apart, not if she was going to save her friends. She needed to persuade Taviano that he had to help her because she couldn't do it without him. If he thought she was too emotional, knowing him, he would take her straight to the plane and take her somewhere out of the country.

She lifted her head to look at him. "You said I never ask you for anything for myself."

"Don't, baby. Don't ask this of me."

"I have to."

"Then I'll get you to the plane, have Franco, our pilot, fly you the hell out of here somewhere safe and I'll go back for your friends."

"Not without me. I'm asking you, Taviano. This is what I'm asking. Give me this. I can do this with you. I know you and your brothers, even Emmanuelle, can do this. Let me. Teach me."

He swore in Italian and pressed his forehead to hers. "*Tesoro*, this does not bode well for me for our future. If I agree to this, if we go to find your friends, Nicoletta, you have to do everything I say when I say it, just like before. That's important. There's no room for error. This is life or death. Do you understand me? You could die if you don't. I could."

She could tell by his voice he meant exactly what he said. With anyone else she might have dismissed the orders as melodramatic or a man wanting to control her or the situation, even with what was happening, but the Ferraros weren't the type of men to cross. They said something, and you knew they meant it and spoke the truth.

She nodded. In any case, this was Taviano. For whatever reason, she would follow him to the ends of the earth.

"We don't seek revenge because someone hurts us. We seek justice. We mete out justice. You have to learn to push emotion from your mind. It won't be easy, but you have to do it. Can you?"

She wasn't certain she could actually do that. Could anyone when it was so personal? She had seen Armando Lupez rape young girls. Very young girls. He had beaten them and given them to others in his gang. He had trafficked them and used them up. She despised him with every breath she took. How did one keep from being emotional? She couldn't lie to Taviano. She wouldn't.

"I'll try, Taviano, but the things I saw . . . The things Benito Valdez and my step-uncles did to me and I saw Armando doing to others, I just can't forget what that was like. I can't. I'm not going to tell you that I can. I want him dead. I never want him to be able to do those things to another girl. He has to be stopped."

"Ordinarily, a complete investigation is done, and it is proven that he is guilty. Investigations are always carried out by two separate teams, and they are very thorough so that there are no possible mistakes. We never take a chance that an innocent person is ever accidentally taken."

She pulled back. "Do you think I'm lying to you about Armando? I *saw* him. He did those things in front of me. They were lessons for us. To keep us in line."

"No, *piccola*, I don't think you're lying, I'm explaining how the system works. You need to know. You're getting a crash course."

He sounded very patient, and she was ashamed that she'd jumped down his throat. He was giving her what she'd asked for, and she wasn't even really listening to him. She realized he was really giving her something huge, a crash course in the family business. Secrets no one knew. No one else would ever know. They had always treated her like family, and Taviano was putting his faith in her.

Nicoletta took a deep breath and swallowed her screaming demons. The ones that visited her in the middle of the night and whispered to her when any man came too close. She forced herself to look at Taviano, the one man she did trust. The one she believed in. He was a Ferraro, and he had saved her when no one else had even noticed she was being eaten by the wolves.

"I'm sorry, Taviano, I'm listening. I'm a little freaked out, but I'll catch up."

"I know you will. We just don't have any time. You want to do this, we have to move now, if we're going to beat them to the hotel. They'll be getting the information out of Clariss fast and moving on it. All they need is the keycard, and she'll tell them everything they want to know immediately. Hopefully, they'll bring her with them. If they do, and Pia and Bianca got away and are there already, we're good. If not, we're going to have to find her. That might be more problematic."

Nicoletta didn't want to think how they would be getting information out of Clariss. "You mean we're going to be traveling the way we did to come here again, don't you?" She couldn't think about what was happening to her friends. She had no control over that. The thought of once more being torn apart by the shadows was appalling, but she'd asked Taviano to take her with him. If that was how he was traveling, then she was sucking it up and going with him.

"Nicoletta, I know it's terrifying to travel this way, and it's painful, but it's fast and we have the advantage. We can never be traced by law enforcement. We can disappear instantly if we need to. You always have to hold on to me. Keep your eyes closed like you did and don't let go. Hold tight. I can't lose you. If you let go, there is no way for me to recover you. My younger brother died traveling this way. It's dangerous."

"I understand. I'm not about to let go of you." She wasn't, either. She was going to hold on so tightly she would leave her fingerprints etched permanently into his skin.

"When we get there, no matter what's happening, you do exactly what I say. I don't care whether they point a gun to one of your friends' heads, you do what I say. I can move from shadow to shadow fast. They don't know that. You have to trust me in every situation to get us out of it."

"I can do that, Taviano."

Nicoletta had seen what the Ferraros could do. She'd been a terrified teenager, threatening to take her own life because her step-uncles were going to turn her over to Benito Valdez, and she wasn't going to let them. She'd rather have been dead. Stefano and Taviano Ferraro had appeared out of nowhere and snapped the necks of her step-uncles as if they were twigs, taken the gun from her and saved her from the worst fate possible. They'd done it in seconds.

Taviano tipped her head back and, to her astonishment, brushed his lips across hers. Her stomach did a slow roll even as she was acutely aware her breath wasn't minty fresh anymore. He locked his arm around her waist and stepped backward, pulling her with him deeper into the shadow.

"Hold on, *tesoro*."

Instinctively, she wrapped her arms around him and pressed her face tightly into his side, closing her eyes, inhaling his scent, taking him in deep, needing to immerse herself in him, her heart pounding in dread of that wrenching of every bone in her body. Her skin tore off in pieces, flying from her. She felt herself coming apart and she clutched him harder, desperate to crawl inside him. This time it was much worse, most likely because she knew what to expect.

There was a sound like the buzzing of a million bees rushing through her head. Her body was thrown sideways. She was almost jerked from Taviano's tight grip, but he held on when she would have lost him, and that scared her more than anything could have. It felt as if they were twisted and then spat in a different direction. The buzzing was gone, and the sound was more like the roar of a freight train bearing down on them. It was terrifying. She squeezed her eyes closed even tighter and pressed her face into his ribs, renewing her grip on him.

The next wrenching moment came, tossing them in what

almost felt like the opposite direction. Again, her arms slipped, and she was flung back away from him, but he kept that iron bar locked around her back, holding her to him, so that she wasn't lost. Her lashes fluttered but no light came in, just shadows passing so fast it was insane, impossible, making her dizzy and sick. None of this could be real, and yet it was all too real, a horrible nightmare she couldn't get out of.

Nicoletta had molded herself into being a survivor. Into being strong. She could curl up into the fetal position and hide, or she could pull herself together and accept what was happening. She forced her body to relax into Taviano's. When she stopped being so rigid, so tense, she felt the subtle movements of his body. If they were actually molecules moving through the shadows that fast, they were doing so together and, like riding behind on a motorcycle, she would be able to follow his lead rather than get flung around every bend and corner.

She realized after a time that Taviano wasn't being thrown around just anywhere—he was choosing a route. He knew exactly where he was going. She tried to relax, although it wasn't easy. The noise was horrendous. The feeling of being constantly torn apart, the wind blowing *through* her body, the sensation of her bones missing, was sickening. Sometimes she couldn't feel Taviano. She just kept her eyes closed and moved with him, relying on their strange connection, that weird bond that she'd felt but tried to deny from the very moment she'd opened her eyes on the plane and looked into his after they'd first rescued her.

She would never forget that moment. Those dark blue eyes and the way, for the first time, she'd felt safe, when she should have been terrified in such an unfamiliar situation with total strangers. She'd been without her own clothes. Fear had come eventually, but strangely not when he was with her.

She hadn't wanted to feel anything for Taviano because every time she was close to him, the physical attraction was so strong she could barely contain herself. She froze around any other male. She didn't want to be in the same room with them. But she wanted to rip Taviano's clothes off and get as wild and crazy as possible. That only made her feel dirty. She loathed herself. She'd gone off the deep end and acted out, finding the worst kids to run with, drinking and sneaking out her window at night, not studying, refusing to go to counseling. Hurting herself. She was meanest to Taviano because she was so attracted to him, not just physically—which didn't make any sense, since she couldn't stand the thought of a man putting his hands on her—but emotionally. Until that night when she'd gotten so drunk and thrown herself at him.

There were so many jerking turns, she should have had whiplash by now. She was so lost in the darkness with those horrible sounds, like trains and bullets and sometimes bees. She tried to match the noise to the speeds they traveled, recognizing that each sound was specific to a speed, anything to get her mind off the disorienting, sickening feeling of no longer having flesh or muscle. Sometimes the sensation of blood splattering over her face was all too real, and then it would feel as if she didn't have a face and the bones of her skeleton were flying apart as well.

Abruptly, like before, they came to a skidding halt, one that sent her body jolting forward but felt as if she wasn't all there. *She* was there, her mind, but the rest of her hadn't had time to catch up. Her actual flesh-and-blood body was still back there in the shadows, caught somewhere, held prisoner. She didn't open her eyes but clung to Taviano while her stomach churned madly and her head pounded so severely she thought her eyes and ears might bleed.

Bile rose and she tasted it in her mouth. She turned her head, trying to pull away from Taviano, but she knew she could never stand if he let her go. Her legs felt like noodles, no bones, and if she opened her eyes and saw light, she'd not only vomit but her head would most likely explode.

"Nicoletta?"

She became aware of Taviano rubbing his hands up and down her arms to warm her. She was shaking she was so cold. Freezing. Shivering.

"Can you open your eyes yet?"

She shook her head, tentatively testing to see if she could bring one hand up to cover her mouth, trying to convey to him that she was going to be sick. When she did, he immediately turned her away from his body and shuffled her forward a couple of steps. She bent toward the perfect carpet and gagged, over and over. Once she started, she couldn't seem to stop, or at least it felt that way. They weren't at a first aid station where he could find her wet wipes and a bottle of water. She was destined to be gross no matter what. She was really showing him what she was made of.

Nicoletta made every effort to force her body under control. It wasn't easy, and she was terrified of opening her eyes. She knew, the moment she did, her head was going to shatter into a million pieces. Still, she lifted her lashes slowly, with great reluctance. They were standing well back in the shadows in the hallway of the luxury hotel just outside the suite where they were staying.

Colors exploded behind her eyes, and her head throbbed and burned. Her vision was blurry, and strange geometric patterns faded in and out in graying patterns in front of her. Her throat felt raw. She cleared it several times. "Is anyone in there?"

"I'll check. I don't want you to move. Stay right here and don't make a sound. Even if Armando comes and has your friends with him, he won't be able to see you if you don't move," Taviano cautioned.

She wasn't about to move. She couldn't, but she wasn't going to tell him that. She nodded, trying not to sway. Trying not to let him see she was going to fall on her face any second. She'd asked for this, and she was putting them both in danger. She wasn't going to be the weak link by being utterly helpless.

She had experienced the shadows and what they could

do to one's body when she was fifteen and alone. It had been accidental, but it had happened, and she'd chosen to try over and over to re-create that experience in order to escape her uncles, even for a little while. She would choose the pain and fear in order to help her friends and stand with Taviano every time.

She hadn't told a single member of the Ferraro family about that experience—or any of the others that had happened to her—because the idea of it had been so bizarre. She already thought she looked like a crazy person to them. She wouldn't have blamed them if they wrote her off the way Eloisa, Taviano's mother, had. Nicoletta was familiar with the strange pull of the shadows on her body, and for her friends and especially for Taviano, she would definitely endure it.

CHAPTER THREE

Taviano knew he was out of his fucking mind for letting Nicoletta look at him with her big dark eyes and wrap him around her little finger the way she'd been doing for nearly three years. He was risking everything bringing her with him on a hunt like this one. Why? What in God's name was wrong with him? He knew the answer. He'd better have that answer when Stefano demanded it of him, because he was going to be stripped of his right to be a rider for breaking every sacred rule they had.

What he was doing went against his family's code. He was risking being banned from riding, something that would kill him. He couldn't imagine existing if he couldn't use his talent, but he couldn't deny Nicoletta, not when he knew what she'd been through. Not when he knew what these men had done to her. Not when he loved her with every breath he took. He wasn't a man given to love many people. That kind of emotion was reserved for his family.

His shadow had tangled with a young girl's three years earlier and sealed his fate. He had known even then that he belonged to her. She hadn't known it. She'd been wild with grief at the loss of her parents and the sexual, physical and emotional abuse heaped on her by three men who had been virtual strangers to her and then by a brute of a man, Benito Valdez.

He remembered the rage welling up in him that had never quite receded. He had wanted to wipe out the other members of the gang, but Stefano had been the voice of reason. The Ferraros weren't about that. They brought justice. The gang knew nothing about the Ferraros. They'd never heard of them. They had no way of knowing what happened to Nicoletta or even if she was alive.

Taviano didn't want to leave her vulnerable, there in the hallway with only a shadow to protect her. Anything could go wrong. She was fragile. Anyone could see that. She was pale beneath her beautiful olive skin, swaying on her feet, one hand clamped over her mouth to prevent another round of vomiting, and she kept closing her eyes against the dim light.

Traveling through the shadows was hard on an experienced rider, let alone one who had never done it before. She had no business moving through the shadows without being trained. It was far more dangerous than he had explained to her, and it had certainly taken a toll on her. The only reason he believed she could safely travel through with him was because she'd done it before, and every member of his family had noticed the way her body reacted whenever a shadow fell across her.

Typically, one capable of riding, if untrained as they grew older, became almost immune to the pull of the shadows until eventually it was impossible to actually use what had been the ability. That hadn't happened with Nicoletta. If anything, the gift had seemed to grow, not lessen.

Cursing, knowing he was absolutely wrong for allowing her to be with him, riding the shadows and chasing after the men who gave her such nightmares, he leaned forward and brushed a kiss on her forehead. "Don't move," he reiterated. He couldn't be in two places at one time, so he had to hurry.

Taviano chose a slender shadow, one of the feeler tubes that was slick and fast, felt like lightning and could rip one's body apart into millions of pieces. He would have never taken Nicoletta with him into one of those tubes. Even experienced riders were sick after using them to travel in, but they were fast. This one delivered him beneath the door and right into the suite.

He'd gotten one of the best the hotel had to offer for the four girls without being too outrageous. He wanted Nicoletta to have fun with her friends. The suite was thirty-three hundred square feet of luxury and was located exclusively on the hotel's top floor. Drago and Demetrio had told him that made it easier to provide security for Nicoletta, not that he'd been worried at that point. There hadn't been any reason to think that she was in any danger.

There was a full kitchen, a library and a wet bar, as well as two bedrooms and two and a half bathrooms. The luxurious living area gave the suite a very upscale homey ambiance, and the wraparound balcony offered exceptional views of the city.

The room had the faint scent of mixed fragrances. He'd been there earlier, as the four women had gotten ready for the concert, all of them excited and laughing. Nicoletta rarely laughed. She didn't talk as much as the three others, and when she did, her voice was always pitched very soft, but he always listened for every word. For all her wild-child ways, she brought a sense of peace to him when he'd never felt that before. He hoped he brought the same to her.

He moved from shadow to shadow, going through the suite, making certain Armando Lupez or any of the members of the local chapter of the Demons hadn't gotten there before him. Pia and Bianca Basso sat on the bed in one bedroom, suitcases out and packed, cell phones in hand, texting but talking to each other even as their fingers and thumbs were busy sending out messages, presumably to Nicoletta and Clariss.

"What happened, Bianca?" Pia asked. "What exactly did

Nicoletta say to you? Did you see Clariss? I didn't see anything. I just ran because you did, and Nicoletta kept saying to run. I didn't even see Clariss."

Bianca looked like she'd been crying. She nodded. "These men had guns and they were chasing after us. I didn't know them. They seemed to know Nicoletta. She was really afraid of them. One of them grabbed Clariss. I saw them pull her backward by her hair. I don't know what to do. I can't get Nicoletta on her phone. We can't just leave her. Or Clariss. If we call the cops, I don't even know what we'd say. If we call Mom, she'll freak out, and we can't call Stefano because we don't have his number."

Taviano rode the shadow back to the front door of the suite, opened it, left it propped open and hastily went to Nicoletta. She'd gotten sick again, but she was steady as she took his hand and entered the suite, hastily calling out to her friends.

Pia and Bianca came running, charging out of the bedroom, nearly knocking Nicoletta down as they hugged her. Taviano stood behind her, his arms around her, holding her so she wouldn't be taken to the floor. The two sisters blurted out so many questions at once there was no way to sort them out and Nicoletta didn't even try. Taviano took charge.

"We're going to have visitors soon and they aren't going to be pleasant. You'll have to save the questions and explanations for later. Nicoletta, you need to wash up and change so you can go with Pia and Bianca to a safe house with my cousins. I've put in a call to them . . ."

He had cousins, riders who would help if he needed it, and who would also make certain Pia and Bianca were safe—and, most importantly, that Nicoletta was.

She shook her head. "Absolutely not. Don't bother arguing with me, Taviano. I'm washing up, but I'm going with you to find Clariss. Get this done, keep Pia and Bianca safe, and we'll find Clariss. If she's with them, we'll go home together."

He shook his head. "Absolutely not."

"We'll talk about this later."

Taviano wanted to strangle her. She was more stubborn than he'd ever thought possible, but he should have. She would have never managed to survive all she'd gone through if she hadn't been able to dig down and find that will and do whatever needed to be done. He didn't have the time to argue, and she knew it.

"Use Pia's or Bianca's cell if anything goes wrong to inform Stefano immediately. He'll call our cousins. They know the situation and are on their way to us. They'll identify themselves to you, Nicoletta. They'll use the family name and Stefano's name. If that doesn't happen, you don't leave that room. Are we clear?"

"Very."

"Then go."

Nicoletta indicated the bedroom with her chin, and her friends obeyed. He thought that was telling as well. Nicoletta was younger and much more fragile-looking. She was curvier, yes, but beneath that darker skin, she was pale and sick-looking, clearly not recovered from her ride in the shadows. But she was completely confident, and Pia and Bianca went with her immediately, without hesitation.

Taviano heard the furniture being moved in front of the door. That was his woman, not taking any chances. She had the good sense to know another barrier might be needed just in case. Taviano could get in, but no one from the Demons could enter, at least not quickly.

He moved through the living area, dimming the lights, making certain to cast shadows where he wanted them. He hoped they would bring Clariss. If they did, he could leave Pia, Bianca and Clariss with his cousins and go straight home to be ready when Benito Valdez came with his army to take Nicoletta. Benito had four brothers, and once he was dead, they would have to contend with them, but his family could hunt them. They would have no reason to associate Nicoletta with the Ferraros. They might still try to find her, but the Ferraros would be actively looking for them.

It was only a few minutes later when the keycard was slipped into the lock and the door was shoved open fast. Two men stepped inside, weapons drawn, Armando Lupez behind them, his nose crooked and very swollen, both eyes already looking bruised. He was also armed. Their gazes thoroughly swept what appeared to be an empty room and then they lowered their weapons and grinned at one another, carefully closing the door.

"Little bitches haven't come home yet," Armando said. "Rocko, check the other rooms just to be sure. Jorge, stay with me in case they come in."

"Maybe they went running to the plane?" Rocko suggested as he started toward the library.

"Not without their clothes and jewelry." Armando snickered. "These are rich little bitches, don't go anywhere without their things."

Taviano chose a shadow that would slide in right behind Rocko. He entered the library before Rocko because the tube was fast, but it gave him that moment to collect himself before the man crept in, his gun once more in his fist, sweeping the room, coming in deeper in order to make certain no one was hiding behind any of the chairs. Taviano emerged from the shadows behind him, caught his head in his hands and, using the signature move of all shadow riders, broke the man's neck.

"Justice is served," he murmured softly and lowered the body to the floor.

Dispensing justice in a hotel room rented to the Ferraros was strictly forbidden. They were always protected. They always had alibis. Stefano was going to lose his mind over this one, and frankly, Taviano wasn't certain how this was all going to be explained. Hopefully his cousins in Los Angeles had cleaners in their family as good as those of the Ferraros in Chicago. Pia and Bianca couldn't see any of the bodies and couldn't know the men had actually come there to find them. They had to think the gang members had never found them. He counted on Nicoletta to provide some sort of distraction.

He stepped into the shadow and took it back into the living room and rode it straight behind Armando Lupez. He was second-in-command to Benito Valdez, and no matter which chapter he was visiting, he would be in charge. No one was going to want to tell Benito that Armando was dead. That would throw everyone into total chaos. Jorge would run straight back to wherever they had taken Clariss, giving Taviano the opportunity to follow.

"Rocko, what's taking so long?" Jorge demanded, turning toward the library. He took several steps in that direction when there was no sound. Both men had seen Rocko enter, and he hadn't come back out.

Armando exchanged a long look with Jorge, and both once more drew their weapons and started toward the library, coming up on either side of the door. The Demons risked a look through the open door, but the room appeared to be empty. Armando indicated for Jorge to enter first. Jorge nodded and stepped inside, immediately going to his right to give Armando a clear shot if anyone should leap out at him. He began to make his way slowly around the furniture in the room. Suddenly he stopped, his eyes on the body on the floor.

Taviano rode the shadow directly behind Armando. He waited a moment, right in the mouth of the tube, breathing deeply, collecting his body, letting the pain in his arm dissolve along with the sickness from traveling such a gut-wrenching, fast shadow, before stepping right behind Benito's right-hand lieutenant, catching his neck in both hands and delivering the signature kill.

Riders began training as toddlers. It wasn't as easy as it looked in movies to break a neck, and that particular move was introduced even when they were young, just two, in games and in the strict training regimes they underwent.

They practiced endlessly all their lives, and even now, they continued to train.

Taviano broke Armando Lupez's neck fast and professionally and lowered him to the floor gently. "Justice is served." He slipped back into the shadows. He needed to be able to follow Jorge when he ran, and he was going to run.

He rode a shadow into the bedroom. Pia and Bianca were in the bathroom. Nicoletta was sitting in front of the bathroom door, looking very determined.

"They're sitting in the bathtub with the doors closed around them."

"Clever girl. I knew you would think of something."

"It suddenly occurred to me if you had to—" She broke off and looked back at the door to the bathroom, shrugging. "It was just smarter to make certain no one saw or heard anything."

"You have to go with the cousins, *tesoro* . . ."

She shook her head. "Don't protest. Just listen. Clariss has been with them too long. I know what they're probably doing to her. I've been through it. She'll need me. A woman with her. I can't let her be raped, possibly tortured, and not be there for her. I *have* to go, Taviano. Please understand."

He closed his eyes briefly. Unfortunately, he could understand. It was the one argument she had that made sense. The only argument she could give him that he couldn't say no to. "We're going to have to move fast. My cousins should be on their way up now. They'll take Pia and Bianca to a safe house."

"They're worried about their mother. She may be super controlling, but they love her, and they know she loves them," Nicoletta said.

"She's safe. Stefano has her safe. We'll make certain they know that. I told the boys to bring you some clothes. I love you in my shirt, but I don't like other men seeing you like that when I know you aren't wearing panties."

She blushed. "I'd hoped you'd forgotten."

"I'm not likely to forget something like that." He moved

the chairs that were in front of the door and headed out of the bedroom. "Let me make certain Jorge made his run for it. I'll let the cousins in so we can hurry after Clariss. They'll clean things up and then get Pia and Bianca out of here."

It wasn't as easy as he made it sound, and when his brother found out what he'd done, there was going to be hell to pay at the very least and his career to lose if Stefano deemed him that careless—and he was afraid that might happen. He couldn't think about that now. He had a purpose, and that was to get her friends to safety while protecting his woman.

He rode a shadow into the living room and found the suite empty. He wasn't surprised. Jorge had no reason to stick around. Two men had their necks broken, and there was no sign of anyone in the suite. There had been no sound. Just like what had taken place nearly three years earlier, when Nicoletta's three step-uncles had been found with their necks broken. No one had been seen going into the house or coming out, yet her step-uncles were dead, and Nicoletta was missing. Jorge had made a run for it.

Unexpectedly three men appeared in the room with him. Like Taviano, they were tall and muscular, wearing pinstriped suits that fit perfectly on their very athletic frames. They had dark hair and eyes and strong jaws, and looked both attractive and dangerous.

Taviano greeted them fondly. "Maximino. Remigio. Marzio. Thanks for coming."

"The others let your boy slip through. Severino is following him at the moment." Severino was the eldest of the six Ferraro brothers in Los Angeles. Like Taviano, they had only one sister, Velia. She was the youngest, and they adored her and were protective, although, as a rider, she was just as fierce as they were.

"He'll switch off with Tore."

Taviano frowned. "You couldn't ride the shadows here, because you had to take Pia and Bianca out of here for me.

That already puts you in jeopardy. You don't exactly have alibis when they discover the dead bodies of our enemies in this hotel. It isn't like we can remove them safely."

"Leave that to us," Maximino said. "We'll take care of things. Velia sent your woman clothes." He handed Taviano a small bundle. "She said to say she wished she could meet your Nicoletta, and she was looking forward to joining you later this week to do just that."

Taviano nodded, grateful he had the kind of family who would put themselves at risk without hesitation when called. "Have your brothers pull back though. I can get Jorge and his friends to give us their location without compromising your family. We've been careful to make certain our family is never where the cops can point their finger at us. This is where you live. If they spot your cars on the street cameras following a gang member and then you're associated in any way with anything that comes back to this hotel room, it could get nasty. Pull your brothers back and trust that I can handle that side of things."

Maximino nodded. "I'm on it."

Taviano couldn't do more than grip his cousin's hand, walk into the bedroom and hand the clothes to Nicoletta before returning to the living room to find Maximino and Marzio had already removed Armando's and Rocko's bodies from the suite, as if they'd never been. Where they'd taken them and how, he had no idea. He'd only been gone a few moments.

"Cameras?"

"Taken care of," Remigio assured.

Taviano nodded to Nicoletta as soon as she was dressed. "Have Pia and Bianca join us, *tesoro*, we have to leave quickly."

Nicoletta knocked on the door loudly and the two sisters emerged, looking a little frightened. They hugged Nicoletta hard. Taviano took their hands gently and immediately introduced them to his cousins. The three Ferraro brothers were at their most charming and helped the women close their suitcases and talked them into allowing the brothers to put them up at the luxurious Ferraro estate, right on the beach.

When they expressed worry about their mother, the cousins assured them that their mother was going to be flown there in Stefano's private jet, so no worries, and they would have separate apartments from their mother right on the beach for their stay. Since they'd missed out on the concert and Kain was a personal friend, they would do their best to see if he would come for a weekend and swim and relax with the girls. Pia and Bianca were so thrilled they almost forgot that Nicoletta was staying behind with Taviano and that Clariss was still missing. Taviano assured them that Clariss was going to be fine and he was taking care of it.

"Last chance, *piccola*," he whispered, as his cousins took Pia and Bianca down the elevator, both women laughing and talking, excited and hoping there really wasn't trouble after all. They had been drinking, and they hadn't seen that much to make them think that anyone was really after them. There had been gang members with guns, but maybe it had all been a mistake, the gang after them because they were wealthy or something. Clariss may have gotten lost or she could still be at the concert and just wasn't answering her phone, as the cousins implied.

"I have to help Clariss, you know that, Taviano. In any case, I wanted to be with you the entire time, but I realized to protect you, I needed to keep Pia and Bianca occupied. What happened? What did you do?"

"I served justice on two of them." Taviano took her hand and led her to the door. "Once we step into the shadow again, Nicoletta, the same rules apply. You have to hold on no matter how dicey it gets. This is your third time in under two hours. That's unprecedented for an inexperienced rider."

"I wouldn't ask to go with you if it wasn't for Clariss. I wouldn't, Taviano. I know what it's like to be raped like that. I don't want her alone . . . I'm sorry I'm putting you in this position."

He swept his hand down the back of her head, trying to console her, to console both of them. He wouldn't have allowed her to go for any other reason.

"Listen to me, Nicoletta, this is important. Your body is getting torn up. You're already experiencing side effects. All of us did in the beginning. Nosebleeds. Body aches. Your legs won't want to work. You have to tell me, you can't get brave and think it won't matter. It will. That's not courage. Not telling me will only jeopardize both of us. I have to know where your body is and how it's holding up at all times. I can counter some things by the shadows I choose to use."

"It makes a difference?"

He nodded. "Everything makes a difference. When we have time, I'll explain things to you, but for now, you're just going to have to trust in everything I say to you."

"You've gotten me this far. It does seem like something out of a science fiction novel, but sometimes, that very first time, when I was being taken out of the apartment, from there to the airport, when I woke up in the jet, I remember some of it."

Taviano stared down into her upturned face. That beloved face. He could hardly remember anymore when he'd come to love her. Maybe from that very first moment when their shadows had connected and he'd felt that jolt of absolute awareness of her go through his body. Or when his chest hurt so damn bad when she spoke, like a key turning in a lock, opening a passageway he'd kept closed and barricaded, even protected by barbed wire, but somehow with just the soft musical notes of her voice she'd found her way in. It could have been when she'd awoken screaming and fighting on the plane, a little warrior woman, ready to battle a hundred men if necessary, her eyes looking into his, terrified but determined.

He'd drown in all that beauty. In all that feminine warrior-woman fight. He loved that. He loved that she would have taken him on in a heartbeat. She'd softened. Relaxed. Not for the others—for him. Looking right at him. Recognizing him the way he did her. He framed her face with both hands. She'd given him this—that trust—even back then, when he hadn't yet earned it. There had been those times she fought herself and fought him. Not because she didn't believe in him but because she wouldn't believe in herself.

"Before we go back into the shadows, Nicoletta, you have to know, I know I was born for the sole purpose of being that man who will stand in front of you. When you're there in that dark place, where it feels like a thousand demons are tearing you apart, know I'm there with you. Always, *tesoro*, because you are my treasure and my only. You'll always be that for me. You'll never be alone there, even if it feels that way. In your mind, reach for me and you'll find me."

He took her mouth. Those lips. That mouth. She tasted fresh and clean. She was his everything, and she tasted that way, as if she had been created especially for him. Sin and innocence blending together, an incomparable rush. He kissed her gently, wanting her to feel loved. Knowing she would need that in the cold of the shadows, something light to hold on to when the demons came to tear her apart.

He wanted to be gentle for her, knowing what she'd suffered. Knowing what had been done to her. He'd sat through her nightmares hundreds of times, listening in the dark to her screams, feeling the tears on his own face when she couldn't cry. She didn't know he was there with her at first, in the beginning. He knew she would have been embarrassed. As it was, she was humiliated that he knew what had been done to her. Then later, when she did know because he couldn't bear it any longer, she had used him as a punching bag, and he'd let her. Often, he'd held her, rocked her, let her learn to cry all over again on those long, sleepless nights.

He tried to keep his kisses under control, but they ignited

together, two matchsticks, creating an explosion. Flames began to lick at his skin, dance in his veins, smolder in his gut and rise higher and higher, spreading from his groin until his entire body seemed to burst into a wild inferno. It was crazy and it was exhilarating. Only Nicoletta could do that to him. He was always in control. He'd thought it had been the alcohol before. He knew now it wasn't so. She slid her arms around his neck and kissed him back, her mouth moving against his, her body melting into his as if she'd caught fire, too, and they shared the same skin, the same never-ending passion.

He lifted his head, reluctantly breaking them apart, breathing deeply, forcing air into his lungs when he wanted everything Nicoletta, including that fragrance that was all her. "You ready for this? Because we're going to get Clariss back. I'll need you to make certain that whatever happens there, Clariss doesn't see me do anything to harm anyone. That's more important than anything else, Nicoletta."

He tucked her wild hair behind her ear and tracked her cheekbones with the pads of his fingers. He loved her soft skin and the way she had such perfect bone structure—at least to him, it was perfection. He admitted to himself that he was very enthralled with everything about her.

"I wouldn't mind doing a few of them in myself," she said, sticking her chin in the air. "Seriously, Taviano, you're very protective, but you don't understand . . ."

"Your number one goal is always to protect the family. Our reputation must be protected at all times. Our cousins just put themselves on the line for you, me and your friends. We always establish alibis so there is no question that we are innocent if someone points a finger at us. Clariss has been taken by this gang. We don't know why. We followed and attempted to get her back. If some of them turned on each other when we freed her, we know nothing about that. Do you understand, Nicoletta, because if you don't, I'll get the cousins back here to take you with them and I'll do this alone."

He poured absolute conviction into his voice. There was no backup when it came to protecting the family, and she had to realize it. No matter how much he loved her and wanted to give her the world, he wouldn't budge on that. It was a rule the family followed—every branch of the family followed. Every member had to be protected. He was willing to risk his career for her but not his family's safety.

Nicoletta nodded, looking him in the eyes. "I understand. I didn't think about that, Taviano. I just despise them so much. I need to understand how all this works. I don't really know what you're talking about, but I'm trying. I'll do whatever needs to be done. I'm just so scared for Clariss."

Taviano was well aware Nicoletta didn't know much about the family business. How could she? She might be considered family, but she wasn't privy to what they did or how their business was carried out. His brothers and sister knew that Taviano planned to claim her, to marry her and bring her in, but until that happened, she couldn't know, and in some cases, a partner might never know everything.

"We'll talk about this more when we have time," Taviano promised. "Are you ready for this? You can't let go. It's going to be very intense. You have to hold on even tighter than before. You were doing great, learning to use your body by following mine."

"I can do it."

He could see the reluctance but also hear the determination. His woman was a fighter. He took out the burner phone he'd gotten from his cousin, the one he'd programmed Clariss's number into. He knew if he called Clariss's number, one of the Demons would answer, and that was the point.

He punched in the number, and after several rings, Clariss's voice, very shaky, responded. Nicoletta started to answer, but Taviano shook his head, scowling at her.

"Clariss. Drago here." He hoped she would remember the bodyguard's name and realize no member of the gang would know who he was. "Where are you, babe? I'll come pick you up. Nicoletta said you were separated at the concert."

There was the sound of a scuffle, a muffled scream, and then a man took over. "You want this bitch?"

Taviano counted to ten before responding. "Who is this?"

"Does it matter?" the voice barked curtly.

"You have my girl, it matters," Taviano snapped. "What the hell is she doing with you?"

"Where's Nicoletta?"

"Why would I care? You got my girl. You don't want to mess with me."

There was a snort on the other end of the line and Clariss screamed, clearly in pain. Nicoletta stepped toward Taviano and the phone, one hand over her mouth to keep from crying out herself.

"*You* don't want to mess with *me*," the man snarled. "I'm Iker, vice president of the Demons, and you're so screwed. You want this bitch of yours back in one piece, you'd better find Nicoletta and bring her to the warehouse on South Street. You have an hour to get here." He added the exact address.

"I don't know this city. How the hell do I do that? And Nicoletta's off somewhere partying. I have to find her first."

"The longer you give me with your bitch, the more fun I have with her," Iker threatened, laughing, and he ended the call.

Nicoletta caught at Taviano's arm, and when he winced, her eyes widened, remembering his injury. "I'm sorry. I can't imagine what it must be like to go into the shadows with a bullet wound. I know what they're doing to Clariss right now. They're horrible people. We have to get there fast. I don't care what you have to do, or how dangerous it is to travel that way, just please get us there, Taviano."

"You don't know what's going on there, Nicoletta. They don't know what's really happening with us. She's all they have left to bargain with to get you back. They can't torture her, or even pass her around, or they take a chance at losing her. They already have to tell Valdez that they lost you and his right-hand man. They don't have Pia or Bianca.

They don't have the bodies of their own men and they don't know if those men are dead or alive. They aren't going to take too many chances with Clariss just to satisfy some idiotic urge. They have other women if it comes to that."

Nicoletta took several deep breaths, trying to get herself under control. "All right. Are we going right now?"

"I'm just going to ditch the phone, and then we're gone." He broke it apart and scattered it throughout the various garbage containers, in the bedrooms, bathrooms and hallway, knowing the maids would clean up.

Stepping into the mouth of the widest, slowest shadow tube, he pulled Nicoletta into his arms and waited until she wrapped herself tightly around him. He felt the tremors running through her, but knew if he suggested again that she stay, she wouldn't. He dropped his chin onto her head.

"Press your body as tight as you can into mine. Feel every movement."

"Sometimes it feels as if we have no skin or bones," she admitted reluctantly.

"I know, *piccola*, the sensation is a horrible one, but just keep pressing tightly to me, and no matter how strange we feel, try to follow every movement of my body with yours, even if it feels as if we aren't even there. Keep your eyes closed and breathe me in. You'll recognize my smell, right, Nicoletta? You'll always know my scent, the way I do yours."

He waited for her to nod for him. She took another deep breath, her gaze clinging to his, that trust there in spite of her fear. *Dio*, he loved her all the more for that trust. He knew he wanted to earn it more every single day. He wanted to deserve it.

She'd been through the fires of hell when she'd been so young, and yet she'd come out the other side, and here she was, standing with him on unfamiliar ground, doing something most people would run screaming from, looking him in the eye and giving consent when she knew it was going to hurt like hell. More, she was doing this for her friend, to be there for Clariss when she knew what could possibly be happening to her. That moved him all the more.

He bent his head to hers and brushed his lips very, very gently over hers. "I knew the moment I saw your courage on that plane, Nicoletta. I knew you, what was inside you, and I knew I had to learn to be man enough to deserve to call you mine. I swear I'll get us through this."

He tightened his hold on her and waited until she pressed her face tightly into his rib cage and he felt the flutter of her long lashes as she closed her eyes. Her arms locked, and he stepped deeper into the tube. At once it took them, pulling them apart, tearing at their bodies to send them hurtling through like an underground subway system. He had to remain alert to exchange one shadow for another, making his way through the city to their destination.

Every rider had to have the ability to map out any city and keep those coordinates in their heads at all times. They couldn't get turned around or lost. They moved so fast even in the slowest shadows that it would be impossible to make guesses; they had to know exactly where they were going ahead of time.

He made several leaps from one shadow to the next, trying to avoid the smaller feeder tubes that would have gotten him to the warehouse Iker had instructed him to go to, but those were so fast and so hard on the body that he didn't want to chance taking Nicoletta into one again. As it was, they would still have to ride one more time to the airport, back to the plane. Four trips in one evening. He couldn't imagine what that was going to do to her. He should have never allowed this, but she was right—if Clariss had been gang-raped, she would need a woman and a friend.

The city flew by, lights and cars and colors flashing, along with various sounds blasting and rumbling through his head. He kept his arms tight around his woman, making certain that when he stepped from one shadow to the next, or had to make sharp turns, he did so as carefully as he could so that there was no chance of her slipping away from him. Those first fast turns in the feeder tubes had terrified him. He'd almost lost his grip on her, and he knew once he did, it would have taken a miracle to find her. She would have gone one way and him another.

The warehouse was coming up fast and he slowed their progress, letting their bodies catch up. Even so, they'd traveled a great distance and the sensation was sickening, even to him. He was a very experienced rider. He'd been in and out of the shadows from an early age. His mother had demanded all of them start moving in the shadows when they were as young as five. Stefano went with them, but they were able to condition their bodies to the continual pull of the shadows on them as they sped through. In the beginning, they stepped in and then stepped out. Nicoletta had been thrown in and expected to acclimate.

He took them inside the warehouse. From the outside it seemed smaller than it actually was. Inside, it appeared cavernous. His family owned several warehouses in industrial parts of Chicago. All had legitimate trades in them. If they were raided or the cops came around at any time and looked at any of the businesses the Ferraros actually owned themselves, the bookkeeping was impeccable and aboveboard. Nothing was ever out of place.

If there was a hint of criminal activity in any of the companies renting space from them, they terminated the lease immediately if an investigation proved the illegal endeavor was in fact taking place. The results were handed over to the cops. The Ferraros didn't allow anyone to commit crimes on their properties, yet Taviano knew how easy it was to hide that kind of activity if one wanted to get away with it. His family, more than once, had to interrogate a prisoner in one of their warehouses and then make that prisoner disappear without a trace. There could be no hint of that man ever being on their property, or them being connected to him in any way.

Taviano half expected the warehouse to be set up as a legitimate business. The Demons had been around for a long time, and Benito Valdez was considered a savvy leader. He'd gone to prison, but the cops hadn't gotten him on any of the charges they'd wanted to take him down on, like murder—which they knew he'd committed—or trafficking, or drugs, or gun running; they'd gotten him on tax evasion. He'd served a short sentence, and while he was in, he'd continued to run his gang and continued to grow his chapters.

Under Valdez's leadership, the Demons had quickly risen to become one of the most feared gangs, taking territory from other gangs, swallowing smaller gangs and taking over their enterprises: drugs, prostitutes, trafficking and anything else they had. It was join with them or die. They didn't give much quarter. Valdez kept his chapters in line by sending his trusted lieutenants when he deemed it necessary. They had no compunction about putting a bullet in the head of any president of a chapter that wasn't in compliance with Valdez's dictates. He was ruthless with the members of his organization, yet just as generous with his favors.

The warehouse was anything but a legitimate business, and Taviano could see that Iker had his own side operation separate from his local president, Tonio Valdez, Benito's brother. He must have been really upset when Tonio had been appointed the president in Los Angeles and had taken over his position.

Armando Lupez hadn't come to Los Angeles on vacation. Benito Valdez must have sent him there to bring Iker into line. That told Taviano a couple of things immediately. Iker had an ego, and he didn't like either of the Valdez brothers telling him what to do, especially Benito when he was in New York. Armando wouldn't have come alone. He would have one or two others with him as well. But why had he been slumming at a concert, then?

Jorge was most likely one of Iker's men. He'd run straight back to the warehouse. That meant somewhere among the men with Iker, there were a couple, at least, from New York. They would be the ones with the real authority, although Iker wouldn't necessarily hold to that.

Iker was a thug, and prior to Tonio Valdez taking over, Iker had run his chapter that way. There was no finesse at all. He most likely had men still very loyal to him. Benito might be into raping women and doing whatever he wanted as far as showing he was all powerful to his men, but he kept his shit tight when it came to his business. Iker wanted the neighborhood and the local cops to fear him. The warehouse was a place of obvious torture. The tools were there. There were bloodstains on the concrete floor. Meat hooks hung from the ceiling. This was a deliberate show to any who might oppose Iker and his men. It was a legitimate cop's dream. There had to be enough evidence to convict Iker and his men of any number of crimes.

Clariss was seated in a leather chair off to one side of the room, very close to what appeared to be an office. She was hunched into herself, knees drawn up, her hair over her face and her hands covering her chin and mouth as if trying to keep from making any noise. She wasn't tied up, and he couldn't see any blood on her. She didn't look as if she had been sexually assaulted, although it was coming. Armando had most likely made it very clear that she was needed to get Nicoletta back, and whoever he'd left behind with Iker was most likely the one threatening her. That didn't mean they hadn't knocked her around to intimidate her. Men like Iker and Armando believed women were nothing and that they had every right to do whatever they wanted to them.

This situation was a potential powder keg. Iker paced back and forth, swearing under his breath. Every now and then he glared at a man in a red shirt who stood off to the side, just to the right of Clariss. The man leaned against the wall, looking casual, but he was anything but. Taviano could see he was armed to the teeth, and his hand was never far from his gun. Taviano was certain the man in the red shirt was from New York. Iker was far from happy that he was there.

"Just relax, Iker," another man said. "I think it might be a good idea to call in your president, Tonio. Let him know what's going on here. You're the VP, and I get that you can handle this, but Armando's dead and things have gone sideways."

Iker spun around and glared. "Don't fucking tell me what to do, Santiago," he snapped. "You, Armando and Carlos come in from New York and try to tell me how to run my town. Tonio was the one to play the big man and send Armando to the concert. He got him killed, not me. It's bullshit for you to come here thinking any of you know LA better than I do. You don't know the first thing about what goes on here. And now some little bitch has Valdez hot, and we all have to jump because he needs to scratch an itch, that's just bullshit, too."

Santiago exchanged a long look with Carlos, the man in the red shirt. Yeah, Taviano was right, they'd come there to bring Iker in line. He wasn't going to get in line. He was angry that Benito's brother, Tonio, had come in from New York and taken over the chapter a couple of years earlier.

Iker broke off to swear at them, a long string of expletives, but neither reacted, although Taviano suspected both wanted to take out their guns and empty them into the man. There were six other men in the warehouse including Jorge. Those men had to be Iker's. Taviano didn't blame the two Demons from New York for not carrying out their orders right that moment. They would have been gunned down in a bloodbath had they killed the LA vice president.

Taviano had a lot to work with though. He couldn't have Clariss know he had been at the warehouse—or that Nicoletta had. She had to be rescued, but not by them. Iker had to die and so did the other members of the Los Angeles chapter of the Demons, but again, not where she knew who killed them.

He assessed the situation in a matter of a minute, and in

that minute, his body was catching up. Nicoletta's was finally doing the same. He had chosen a shadow far from the others in the warehouse, and they were in the mouth of it, where the others couldn't see or hear—and it was a good thing, because Nicoletta went to her knees, and this time she was vomiting a mixture of bile and blood. Not much blood, thankfully, but there was some pink mixed in.

CHAPTER FOUR

No matter how sick she was, Nicoletta still seemed aware they were in danger. Taviano could tell she was making every effort to muffle the sounds of first the horrendous vomiting, then the dry heaves, followed by gagging. She tried to lift her head a couple of times, but clearly, pain crashed through her skull and neck, and she grabbed both sides of her face and held on.

"You have to breathe, Nicoletta. Take in air. You don't yet know how to breathe in the shadows properly." He should have thought of that. So many things to teach her. He was so wrong for allowing this. Now they were in the situation and he couldn't get them out of it. They couldn't be seen anywhere near the warehouse. No car could be brought near it. Was their safety worth risking her life?

"I'm sorry, *piccola*, I shouldn't have taken you with me. You aren't trained. Your body isn't conditioned for this kind of travel yet." He swept back her hair and did his best to try to massage her neck and shoulders to ease the cramping.

"Not you, Taviano," she denied, her voice stuttering a little. "Not your fault."

He didn't want her to talk. It was obviously too much of an effort. He sank onto the floor and pulled her onto his lap, away from the corner where she'd gotten sick. They were in the darkest part of the room, but where Iker had deliberately placed overhead lights that could swing and cast macabre shadows that would add to the sinister atmosphere and strike fear into enemies.

Those shadows were everywhere, allowing Taviano full access to almost anywhere in the warehouse. He needed to start a gun battle and allow the Demon members from the two chapters to take one another out. In order to do that, Clariss had to be protected. His mind worked to solve that piece of the puzzle even as he rocked Nicoletta gently back and forth, breathing deeply, willing her to follow the rhythm he was setting for her.

She kept her head down and her fingers pressed to her face. With her hair falling around her, he couldn't see her expression.

"Are you bleeding?"

She hesitated as if she might attempt to deceive him, but then remembered his warning. "A little. My nose. I think my left ear. My head feels like it was in a vise. Is that normal?"

"It happens. Usually at first, or when we're in a fast tube, like a feeder tube. Your body isn't conditioned to this type of travel. I shouldn't have allowed it without bringing you into it slowly and letting you get used to it. I was being selfish, Nicoletta."

"That's not true." She started to shake her head and stopped immediately. "You wanted me on the plane. I pretty much begged to stay with you. Don't make this your fault. This was our decision. I wanted to be with Clariss if she needed me. Did you see her? Is she all right? Did they hurt her?"

"It doesn't look as if they raped her."

"Thank God."

"I need to know if you're all right, Nicoletta."

"It's a headache. I've had them before."

"Like this?"

"Ummhmm." She didn't nod, but he had the impression of her nodding. "I was hiding in my room when Diego, my step-uncle, came to get me. Cruz, Alejo and Diego would sometimes come together, and other times one would come alone, but it was always horrible when they did."

He stroked soothing caresses down the thick, luxurious length of her hair, all the while watching the tension building between the two factions in the warehouse. "How old were you?"

"It was when I first went to live with my step-uncles in New York. I was only fifteen. My parents had just died in a car accident, and I was sent to live with those terrible men in a completely different environment. I didn't know them. I'd never met them. I went from a loving home to a nightmare situation. I didn't understand what happened, why I was suddenly just handed over to these strangers. I didn't realize they were my father's brothers."

He knew she was so shaken up by the fact that the Demons had Clariss in their hands and she had narrowly escaped the same fate Nicoletta had suffered that she told him the truth. He kept rocking her, soothing her, all the while watching the building tensions, waiting for his moment.

"Your mother married their brother and he adopted you when you were four, but they never lived near his three brothers. He'd gotten away from the gang and made a life for himself," Taviano supplied.

"I didn't know that. I only knew that I'd lost my parents, and suddenly I was with these three men who ripped apart my body every chance they got."

Taviano closed his eyes briefly, grateful for the dark of the shadows. He'd heard her screams, shared the nightmares, but knew he would never come close to knowing what it had been like for a fifteen-year-old innocent girl to go from a loving home to three grown men brutally using her whenever and however they felt like it.

"That time, when Diego came, I had been in the shower, and I was naked. I found a shadow and just stayed there, shaking, my hand over my mouth, frozen. His brothers came in to help look for me. They thought I'd gone out a window. They ended up searching the house. My head felt like it was splitting in two when the light finally moved, and the shadow was gone. I couldn't move. I just lay on the floor, curled up in a ball. My nose was bleeding then, too."

"What happened?"

"They took turns raping me. And beating me. They were really angry when I didn't tell them where I'd been."

Taviano forced down the bile rising in him. He couldn't protect her from what had happened to her in her past. She'd risen like a phoenix, more powerful than ever, an amazing woman, a fighter, one willing to learn that every defense was an offense. Learn that her brain was her greatest weapon. Learn the Ferraro family business. Follow his lead even when she wasn't certain where they were going because she trusted him that much and she had observed all along that the Ferraros were far more than what they appeared to the outside world, and she wanted to be a part of that.

She had come to terms with her past. He knew those terrible years of repeated rape and beatings had shaped her and would rise up at times to strike at her unexpectedly, just as the things that had happened to him in his past could do the same, but they had both emerged victorious, stronger, both fighters.

Although Benito Valdez still lived, the three step-uncles who had violated her were dead, killed by Stefano and Taviano, left on the floor of their apartment for Valdez and his lieutenants to find. Stefano and Taviano had taken Nicoletta with them into the shadows, but she had been unconscious—at least they thought she'd been. He was coming to find out she hadn't been quite as unknowing as they believed.

Nicoletta was extremely strong, and Taviano was proud of being her partner. He brushed a kiss on top of her head, still rocking her. Still breathing for her.

"Can you still see her? Clariss?"

That told him she still wasn't opening her eyes, that the light would hurt her. He was going to have to move soon. The tension in the warehouse was stretching to a breaking point and he wanted it to go his way. He glanced at the clock on the wall across from him. Drago and Demetrio would be there any moment to retrieve Clariss and take her to join Pia and Bianca if she was uninjured. If she was hurt, she would be taken to a private doctor. Her parents would be flown in to join her and they would be placed in a safe house until the danger was over. The bodyguards knew better than to show themselves inside the warehouse or interfere in any way until he gave them the sign to go in and get Clariss.

"Yes, she's fine at the moment. I'm going to have to leave you right here, *piccola*. Will you be all right? You can't move. Everyone is armed. Stay close to the wall and low to the floor. Also, stay quiet."

"I'm good. I know the rules. Tell me what you're going to do."

"I'm going to get them to shoot each other without shooting Clariss, or us. That way, we're not in any way involved in this mess."

She tried to look up at him but moaned softly and covered her face with her hands. "I am going to have so many questions for you when I can see again and we're alone in a place where we're not in danger."

He kissed the top of her head again and gently put her against the wall. "Stay put. You're right at the mouth of the shadow." He wanted her there so there would be less stress on her body and hopefully the headache would ease fast. If it didn't, in spite of the danger of discovery, she would be going back with Clariss in the car to the cousins, and then Drago and Demetrio could escort her to the plane.

"I'm not moving," she reiterated.

Taviano didn't wait. He caught a small feeder tube that took him straight across the room to Carlos, the New Yorker in the red shirt. He was closest to Clariss and seemed the most protective of her. In a pinch, Taviano would bet Carlos would dive for her and take her to the floor to keep her from getting shot. If he didn't, Taviano would have to do it and hope she never saw who actually tackled her.

Iker and Santiago exchanged a few more heated words, Iker essentially telling Santiago that he could do anything he wanted with "the bitch" and he wasn't waiting around for her boyfriend to show up. He had things to do. Santiago sent him a smile that all but said that he was a dumbass hothead and was going to die the moment they had him alone.

Taviano stepped into a shadow that slid up behind Iker. The vice president of the local chapter had a bad habit of caressing his weapon as if it were a woman. He would take it out of his waistband and wrap his fist around the grip so he could stroke the barrel with his finger. Taviano knew it was a ploy so that when he really wanted to shoot someone, they had already been lulled into a false sense of security.

This time when Iker performed his little "habit," Taviano guided the VP's arm toward the wall between Carlos and Clariss so the gun lined up perfectly, his touch so light, it was impossible to feel. The moment both people were in the clear, Taviano allowed only his hand to momentarily emerge from the shadow, squeezed the trigger with his gloved finger, then he was gone, sliding back into the tube. Immediately, he caught the feeder so that it brought him straight back to Clariss.

Carlos reacted just as expected, gun drawn and firing steadily at the enemy as he knocked Clariss from the chair and covered her body with his own. The New York Demon had chosen his targets already and he took down three almost before he hit the floor. Iker turned and shot at Santiago as he threw himself down and rolled toward his men, shouting at them to kill the New Yorkers. He had no idea what had happened or what had caused his gun to fire, but Santiago was relentlessly shooting at him.

Carlos turned the desk over for protection and dragged Clariss behind it. She didn't struggle against him but didn't help at all, reacting more like a rag doll, which alarmed Taviano. She seemed almost in a comatose state to him. Carlos gave her a harsh warning, ordering her to lie on the floor behind the overturned desk and not move. The moment he scrambled to the corner, peering around it, seeking targets, she lifted her head and took a quick look from one end of the room to the other, trying to find an exit. Clariss was an intelligent woman, pretending to be cowed when she wasn't. Taviano allowed himself a sigh of relief.

Carlos took aim at one of the LA Demons and squeezed off a single shot. As he did, Taviano rode the shadow that came in to the right of him. It was a tricky angle, especially as the shadow narrowed, and he didn't want to be seen by Clariss if she happened to turn her head and look toward Carlos. Taviano slid feetfirst, catching Carlos in the rib cage and hip, sending him sliding into the open, exposing him to his enemies. Iker rose up on his knees and poured bullet after bullet into Carlos's red shirt. Simultaneously, Carlos shot Iker, creating a zipper up the middle of his body from groin to throat. Iker fell backward onto the concrete and Carlos simply lay still.

Santiago and the remaining three Los Angeles Demons continued to fire at one another. There was no doubt that Santiago was the better shooter. Taviano began to make his way toward Santiago. He was very close to where he had left Nicoletta, although he had his back to her and was about ten feet to one side of her, but it was too close for Taviano's comfort. He was grateful that Clariss had kept it together and hadn't screamed, but she was definitely thinking about trying to head for an exit. She just had to keep her head down until the shooting stopped.

The three remaining LA Demons split up to come at

Santiago from different directions. None of them paid attention to Clariss. She crawled toward the nearest exit. It was the door to the office, which would be the front entrance. Taviano had told Demetrio and Drago to wait outside the warehouse. He knew they had to have heard the shots and would be anxious. The moment that door cracked open they would be there, guns drawn.

Santiago fired and the three local Demons returned shots in a deadly barrage. Clariss pushed the door open and Taviano saw his bodyguards catch at her and drag her out, slamming the door closed behind her. Their orders were to put her in the car and get her out of there. Now he had no choice: he would have to take Nicoletta through the shadows in order to get her back to the plane unless he found a way to call them back. Silently, he swore in several languages.

He wanted to allow Santiago to kill all but one of the locals before they shot and hopefully killed the New York Demon. The gun battle was fierce, the three locals trying to maneuver Santiago into crossfire. He shot one of them in the leg, taking him down to the concrete floor, rolling to get a better aim as he fired continuously in an attempt to kill the gang member. The local tried to make a run for it but with his injury, couldn't get up. Santiago's barrage of bullets ended his life.

As Santiago rolled back to get under cover, the local to his left shot him in the leg and head. Taviano saw both bullets score. Santiago flopped over and then lay still, the gun still in his hand.

Taviano slid out of the shadows just behind Santiago. He had to use Santiago's gun to kill the last two remaining locals. He didn't want any evidence leading to any of the Ferraros being at the warehouse. Clariss would tell the police that Demetrio and Drago had come to get her, that she'd crawled away by herself and they'd gotten there just as she exited. It was the truth as she knew it.

He took the gun from Santiago's open palm, his eyes on

his target, the local who had killed the New Yorker. The man was close and moving closer, sure that Santiago was dead but cautious all the same. Taviano had lost sight of Jorge. The last he'd seen of him, the man had been slinking toward an exit, still firing toward Santiago but, as earlier in the suite, looking toward self-preservation first. The Los Angeles Demon was approaching, in direct line now. Taviano rose up and shot him, almost point-blank. He made each bullet count, firing two in the throat and one between the eyes.

At the first sound of gunfire, Nicoletta forced herself out of the huddled ball she'd been in. Everything hurt. Every single inch of her body. Even her toes. But she'd asked for this. Even demanded it. On some level she'd even known, because she'd been experiencing it on minor levels on her own. She hadn't known one could move from one place to another, but she had moved in her bedroom when she lived with the step-uncles. She had just thought she was going crazy.

She'd tried multiple times after that to re-create that experience, but she hadn't been effective in completely hiding or moving from one place to another. Now she realized she'd been naked then, in the shower when she'd heard them coming for her. She hadn't wanted to face her step-uncles naked, so she rarely took her clothes off, and her showers were super-brief. Now she realized her clothes had been the problem all along.

She pressed her fingers to her mouth. They were trembling. Her lips were trembling. She forced them to stop. She had learned to take control of herself. She had Emmanuelle and Mariko Ferraro to thank for that. They worked with her when they trained her on self-defense. They talked to her constantly about not just training her body but training her mind as well. What defense actually was. What power was. What it embodied. What control was. What that embodied. She saw those traits in both women, and more, she *felt* both power and control when they walked into a room. They embodied both traits, and she wanted that kind of confidence and to command and earn that same respect.

Nicoletta ignored the fact that her head wanted to explode and her body felt as though it was in pieces. She knew it wasn't. Her skin covered her bones. She had only to open her eyes and look, and she would see for herself. It was only in her mind, a trick. The mind was powerful. Vittorio Ferraro lectured her on that subject as he trained her on speed and how to throw a proper punch and kick with maximum power so that when she struck, she was focusing that strike on a tiny area, but the penetration was so deep that it could shatter bones or destroy organs inside the body.

Focus, little sister. The punch doesn't stop at the surface. You want to penetrate, go out the other side. You kick through *the obstacle, whatever it is.*

How many times had he said that to her in his patient, soft, commanding voice? Vittorio never raised his voice. Never was exasperated or impatient. He pushed her hard, but he worked just as hard, giving her his time generously and repeating lessons when she asked him to go over a technique she wanted to improve.

Her lashes fluttered, protesting, a kind of terror seizing her at the idea of allowing light in, but she was determined to overcome fear. She was with Taviano for a reason. She didn't want to be deadweight that he dragged around. She wanted to be a partner, useful to him. If that was going to happen, she had to open her eyes, and she had to do it now. She was going to use every lesson the Ferraros had taught her to get back on her feet and get over the effects of the shadow riding. If they could do it, so could she.

She opened her eyes very slowly, all the while hearing the sound of guns going off. She was afraid for Taviano and Clariss. That fear for them, more than anything else, helped her to overcome her own terror of her head exploding. Pain burst through her skull as the light pierced her eyes, but when she blinked rapidly, she realized that the shadows dulled the brightness to a dimmer gray, helping to mitigate the effect.

It suddenly occurred to her that every lesson in the Ferraro training dojo ended with sitting on the mats, legs tucked up, breathing deeply, meditating. The breathing was always the same, slow and even, and they corrected her breathing almost more than they corrected her fighting techniques. Taviano had used that same breathing to slow hers to match his. She used it now and kept breathing, just the way she'd been taught, and found she could recover faster.

The numbness in her body, the feeling of paralysis, lessened, as did the images in her mind that she wasn't all there. She looked down, half expecting her skin to be gone, but there it was, covering her arms and legs. Her body was intact and that helped push away more of the sensation that she was no longer in human form. Breathing deeply, she pressed her hand against the wall of the warehouse, her first physical sensation. The contact with something solid really grounded her.

The gunshots continued, louder now, as she recovered, the sound ringing in her ears. She turned, back to the wall, heels digging into the concrete, and forced herself into a standing position, pushing up hard, using her unsteady legs and her hands on the wall. It felt good to find muscles, wobbly or not. She willed steel into her body. She was an asset, not a complication.

She was Taviano's partner. She was born to be his partner. That had been her secret mantra for the last couple of years, when she'd been working so hard to overcome her hatred and loathing of what her step-uncles and Benito Valdez had done to her. She was not going to allow those men to take away what her parents had so lovingly provided for her for so many years. What Lucia and Amo had done for her these last few years. Or the opportunities the Ferraro family had given her—the training and education, the counseling and compassion.

She trained with the Ferraros and then went to work, all the while going over their instructions in her head, every movement, every single thing they said to her. She didn't forget anything. That was another gift she had. She remembered everything. Sometimes it could be a curse, but in this case, it was a major help. The smallest detail was etched into her brain. She practiced in her mind when she couldn't practice with her body.

At home, she gave Lucia and Amo her undivided attention, and then, the moment they retired for the night, she was in the garage, where she'd set up a gym, and she was training again, working on the speed bag, the heavy bag, and kicking and punching and practicing rolls and falls. She knew the Ferraros had trained from the time they were very young. She had a lot of time to make up, but she was determined to do it.

When she wasn't working out physically, she was hitting the books. The Ferraros were intelligent. That was apparent in their conversations. They spoke several languages. They could converse easily on just about any subject. She immediately set out to catch up on her education, at first in order to be able to converse with them, but then because her mind became thirsty for knowledge. There were apps on her phone, and she went to bed every night speaking other languages and woke in the morning practicing them.

Leaning against the wall for support, Nicoletta forced her chin up and made herself look out of the shadows and really focus on the room and every individual. Clariss was on the floor, crawling toward the exit. No one seemed to be aware of her. There were bodies on the floor and a great deal of blood. She knew she should be bothered by that, and there was a part of her that was upset that she wasn't. Living with her step-uncles had changed something in her.

She searched the room for the one person who mattered most to her. Taviano. He moved from shadow to shadow, and even she couldn't see him until he emerged behind a fallen shooter and took the gun from his hand. He rose up as a man approached, the weapon extended. Taviano shot him at least three times, point-blank.

Her heart in her throat, Nicoletta caught sight of Jorge, the one other person she recognized from the concert. He had been with Armando, chasing after her. Clearly, he had begun to make his way toward the exit of the warehouse, near where she was, just as he'd done at the hotel, but he turned back when he saw Taviano.

She had no choice. Her body *had* to work. Nicoletta launched herself out of the shadow, rolling in a tight somersault, to come up under Jorge's gun arm. She slammed her head under his chin, driving upward using her entire body, her heels and knees, nearly lifting him off his feet. At the same time, she used her fingers to force his hand open, hitting his pressure points so his fingers spasmed and the gun fell to the floor. She kicked it away and followed Jorge as he fell away from her, driving her stiff fingers into the dent at the base of his throat, imagining them coming out the other side of his neck.

She pulled back as he went down to his knees, coughing. She kicked him hard in the solar plexus and then spun around when she felt hands on her waist.

"*Piccola*, it's just me. Slip back into the shadows." Taviano stood in front of Jorge with Santiago's gun. "We can't have evidence that we were here, although you saved my life. Let me finish this."

He spoke gently, as if she might shatter—or condemn him because he was going to pull the trigger on Jorge, the man who would have killed him. She could pull the trigger. Would that make Taviano think less of her? Because she wasn't that compassionate woman, her heart soft and concerned with how to help the poor boys who lived such a bad life that they joined gangs and decided raping girls and selling them was a great pastime and way to make money. She was never going to be that woman. *Never.* She wasn't going to pretend to be, either.

She did just what he said, walking back, skirting around

two dead men to get to the corner where the dark shadow lay like a stripe leading out of the warehouse. Once she was at the mouth of the shadow, she watched as Taviano made his way back to where Santiago was. He lined up the shot so it looked as though the New Yorker had actually fired the gun that had killed Jorge. She locked that information in her mind. It was another detail that couldn't be forgotten. That was how the Ferraros kept away from police attention. They made certain that everything added up for forensics. Taviano replaced the gun carefully in Santiago's open palm exactly as it had been when he removed it and then he rode the shadow back to Nicoletta.

He looked around the warehouse. "Do you see any cameras? I interrupted all transmissions, but I could have missed something."

She should have thought about that. Stefano had told her more than once that she always had to pay attention to cameras on the street. When she walked down a street, he wanted her to practice noticing how many businesses had them. Which ones were real and which were fake. Could she concentrate on them and stop them from recording? She'd never tried something like that, and she'd thought he was crazy until Ricco had demonstrated.

Secretly, she'd begun trying to stop a small recording device she had. She'd managed to interrupt it a grand total of three times for all of two seconds. She'd been proud of herself until Stefano had sternly told her to keep it up, that she needed to be able to knock out cameras for long blocks of time if need be. She didn't understand how being able to have that kind of control would come in handy until this moment. Now she wished she'd spent more time on practicing and less time on sleeping. It just seemed that she often fell into bed exhausted after long training sessions.

"Would they have cameras attached to the beams up in the ceiling for any reason?" she ventured. "It seems kind of silly, but when I took a quick look around, they seemed to have an abundance of cameras. I thought it was a bit narcis-

sistic. If Iker was narcissistic, he might have cameras showing every angle of his performances, because although I
didn't see him most of the time, he sounded like he was
performing to an audience."

Taviano looked so pleased with her it was all she could
do not to grin. She looked down at her hands, happy to see
that her fingers were intact.

"Give me a minute to check, *tesoro*. I'll be right back."

Nicoletta watched him move easily from the mouth of
the long wide shadow to the smaller feeder tube, and then
he was gone from her sight. She knew *tesoro* was *treasure*,
and it was an endearment the way it was used, but the family always had endearments for her. Vittorio, Ricco, Giovanni
and Stefano almost always referred to her as "little sister,"
mostly in Italian. Sometimes it was "little one." They had
accepted her as family, and it had taken a long while for her
to realize that. Now she knew.

Taviano, thankfully, had never treated her like a sibling.
He rarely trained her. He seemed uncomfortable putting his
hands on her, and she couldn't blame him after the disaster
of that night when she'd been so terribly drunk and flung
herself at him. She kept from groaning, still embarrassed at
her behavior that night. Taviano might be able to excuse it,
but she wasn't quite there yet. She might never get there.
She'd come a long way and her confidence level was rising
every minute, but not around him. Maybe it never would.

Taviano slid back into the shadow beside her. She was
astonished how silent he was when it had been surprisingly
loud traveling through the shadow.

"You were right, Nicoletta. There were actually two more
cameras. I took a minute to make certain the feed wasn't going to a remote site and then I removed the insides and turned
them off, with the wires not hooked up, as if they hadn't finished installing them completely."

"You think the cops will buy that?"

He shrugged. "It doesn't matter what they do. Clariss is
our tie to the warehouse. Drago and Demetrio have taken

her to the cops, and she'll give her statement. After that, she'll be taken to the cousins and reunited with Pia and Bianca. They'll be well looked after."

While he explained, he carefully cleaned up all evidence of her getting sick. His cousins had done so at the hotel. He had to make certain it was done at the warehouse.

"The cops will launch an investigation once they see the slaughter at the warehouse, but what are they going to find? My cousins weren't near the warehouse, and neither were we. Pia and Bianca will tell the cops that you're with me. And you are. We're going to fly off in the jet together."

"I'm sorry I got sick." She nodded toward his hand and the wipes he'd found to use.

"Wait one minute." He found a Dumpster some distance away and tossed the wipes in the thing, certain the cops wouldn't dig that far, and then returned to her.

"Can you handle one more time in the shadows with me?"

Nicoletta's stomach did that weird pitch and roll it often did when she was around him. She could handle one more time going anywhere with him. She managed to lift her lashes just enough to sneak a quick peek at him, and his dark blue eyes were so focused on her she nearly choked. He could burn a hole right through her looking at her like that. She nodded because she really couldn't speak.

Taviano took her hand. "You're going to have to look at me, *piccola*. I need to know you can do this. We're going to have to make a short stop in Vegas and then head home."

"Vegas?" That made no sense.

"I'll tell you when we're safe on board. We've got to get out of here, but I have to know you really can do this."

"There seem to be quite a lot of things you're going to tell me once we're on that plane," she said, attempting humor when her entire body rebelled at the idea of going with him once more on the long journey to the airport through the shadows.

His arms tightened around her. "I've got you. I'm in your head, Nicoletta. In your mind. If it becomes too difficult, and you can't feel me anywhere else, look for me there. Feel me there. The shadows can fool our physical bodies, and can twist our perceptions, but our brains remain intact. You can find me there, and I can find you. If you search for me, our connection will grow stronger. Our shadows are already twisting together. They've been doing so every time we've been close for the past three years. You had to have felt it."

She'd felt the connection between them growing when they were close, but she'd thought it was only on her side. She'd tried to stop it. She'd done everything she could to stop it. She'd used alcohol, tried to hurt herself, been rude and cutting to him. He was so attractive. Physically, he was just about everything a woman could ask for in a man. Sometimes it was all she could do to keep from staring at him, but he was so much more to her than his gorgeous looks.

"You ready?"

There was no way for her to be ready, but they had to get this done, so she nodded. She had a lot to think about. Taviano had given her an unexpected gift, just the way all the Ferraros always gave so generously to her. Why? Why had Stefano and Taviano singled her out and brought her home with them? What had brought them to New York and to her step-uncles that night?

Taviano gripped her hard and stepped into the long, thick shadow. Instantly she felt the pull on her body. It was strong, tearing at her skin and muscles. She closed her eyes and pushed her face into his rib cage, breathing in his scent. Taking him into her lungs while she could. Everything about him always made her feel safe.

Taviano was right about their connection. She had put a gun to her head when her three step-uncles had come for her, telling her that Benito Valdez had demanded they hand her over to him. They said it was an honor that he wanted her to be his woman. She knew better. He'd demanded that her uncles share her on more than one occasion, and he'd deliberately hurt her, laughing when he did so. He was a brutal, uncaring man.

She had eyes. She saw how the president of the Demons treated women. He ran a human-trafficking ring. He could say what he wanted, but she wasn't having his babies and then being trafficked while he kept the children and took the next girl who caught his eye.

It had been Taviano who had taken the gun from her hand. He had come out of nowhere, out of the shadows, killing her step-uncles and removing the gun so gently. She would always remember the way his voice had reassured her. She'd been out of her mind with fear of Valdez, determined to end her life. Wanting an end to the beatings and rapes. She'd fought every day since her parents' funeral, when she'd been handed over to them, and she couldn't fight anymore.

Taviano's touch had been so gentle, his voice like a soft warmth over her skin, a stream of reassurance that enveloped her in a cocoon that separated her from the rest of the world. Then he had her in his arms and his brother was asking her if she wanted to live. Looking at him, at Taviano, she knew she did when she had been so certain before that she didn't.

The wind whipped at her body, flogging the skin from her, flaying at her muscles to expose her bones. She squeezed her eyes closed tighter and pressed her face firmly into Taviano's side, breathing the way she'd been taught every single night at the end of her training. The ending to her nightly sessions hadn't been to wind things down or meditate like she thought; there was a much deeper purpose, one that helped immensely when in the shadow tube. The more she used the breathing, the better she stayed in control. That allowed her not to panic and lessened the terrible impact of the shadows tearing at her body.

She tried to breathe him in again, to stay connected physically, but there in the shadow tunnel, their skin and bones were gone and there was nothing left of either of them. She shuddered, trying not to be afraid. She'd done this now enough times to know she could get through it and still live. Still be alive. Still be intact and whole. Still be Nicoletta with Taviano. Whatever that meant. Could she be in his life, close to him, when he spent so much of his life partying with other women?

Seeing him with other women had been so painful to a young teenage girl who had viewed herself as unclean. She'd loathed that she was the way she was and he was so perfect. The women hanging on his arm had been so beautiful and elegant. She had looked at every picture, unable to stop herself, poring over the magazines at night in her room, and then ripping the photographs up so she wouldn't fixate on them. That had started her destructive behavior. The drinking. The cutting. The sneaking out at night. She'd been so unfair to Lucia and Amo.

The Ferraro family always had someone watching over her. Much to her consternation and shock, it was usually a family member. That didn't make any sense. They were playboys. They had money. They had no reason to care about an orphan who didn't care about herself, yet they were always there, picking her up, taking her home, making certain she had whatever she needed available to her.

Taviano had always been close, and she'd felt that connection between them growing, just as he had pointed out, no matter how much she'd wanted to deny it or wanted to sever it. When she'd flung herself at him and he'd rejected her, she had made up her mind to change her life for herself. Her mother had been strong. He'd reminded her of that. He'd reminded her of a lot of things that night.

She'd been ashamed of herself. Not because she'd been gang-raped, not because she'd been helpless to stop it, but because she'd been so self-destructive, refusing to reach out and accept the help so many people offered her. Her parents, whom she'd dearly loved, would have been so upset with her. She had vowed to be the person they'd raised. Independent and strong. A fighter. She'd been that once and she would be again.

Whatever was between Taviano and her she would have

to accept as well. She couldn't sever that tie. The connection was so strong that at times she swore she felt him moving in her mind. She loved him that much, but it didn't matter. She wasn't going to have a one-sided relationship.

She practically worshiped Taviano. He cared for her the way all the Ferraros did. He alone was physically attracted to her—she was very aware of that fact. She also knew that wouldn't last once he'd had her. He seemed to go from woman to woman. She knew that all the Ferraros had reputations, although they didn't seem to cheat on their wives. She watched them closely. Taviano was the lone holdout, the last of the wild Ferraro playboys, and speculation was rampant that he was looking for a bride, with several articles written on the possibilities of his choice of wives. She knew, because she'd read every one. Not once had lowly little Nicoletta been among those suggested for him.

CHAPTER FIVE

Taviano carried Nicoletta down the aisle of the plane to the bedroom. He cursed with every step as he hurried to get her to the bed where he could examine her for injuries. "Get us into the air, Franco," he called out. They needed to get the hell out of Los Angeles. "Drago, the first aid kit, the large one," he added, his voice clipped.

He set Nicoletta down on the comforter and she instantly turned on her side, trying to curl into the fetal position away from him. He put a hand to her belly to stop her. "I'll need washcloths and towels and warm water." He took the large case from Drago and put it on the bed beside Nicoletta.

"*Piccola*, stay still. Let me see how much damage there is. How bad is the headache?" Thankfully the lights were dim, and the shields were down on the windows in the bedroom. She had her eyes closed and her hands over her face, but between her fingers he could see trickles of blood sliding down her face. "You're going to have to move your hands."

"I can't."

He wanted to smile at her protest, that soft little voice that came at him out of the dark. Very gently he laid his hand over hers. She didn't try to stop him when he enclosed her smaller fingers and pried them loose, uncovering her face. Even so, it was difficult to see her pale face in the dim lighting of the plane.

The jet gave a shudder as it began to move on the runway. Franco spoke, telling them to prepare for takeoff. Demetrio Palagonia leaned in from the other side of the bed to hand Taviano a warm washcloth.

Taviano took it with a brief smile of thanks. This was supposed to be an easy, casual run to a concert, not a dangerous mission that put them all in jeopardy. They'd handled it, but Stefano wasn't going to be happy. Taviano had left his phone on the plane. He couldn't take it into the shadows, and he wasn't going to see what his brother had to say to him yet.

By now, his LA cousins would have told him that Pia, Bianca and Clariss were safe and staying with them until given the word that they could go home. When Stefano asked why there was no mention of Nicoletta, he would be told that their sister had provided clothes for her to ride the shadows, so no worries on that score, and Stefano would lose his ever-loving mind. Taviano couldn't blame him, but he didn't want to hear about it, not yet.

The plane was in the air and Taviano breathed a sigh of relief as he wiped away the blood. Thankfully the twin trickles came from Nicoletta's nose, not her eyes and ears. He had mostly been afraid of a brain bleed. She'd seemed to handle the last ride better than all the others put together. He wasn't certain why, when this ride should have been the worst, but her body had moved with his, as if they'd been born to ride together.

He cracked an ice pack, wrapped it in a cloth and applied it to her forehead after sweeping back her hair. "Drago, there's an eye mask in the drawer right beside the bed. Would you mind getting that out for me?"

"No problem."

Drago pulled it out and helped lift Nicoletta's head so Taviano could slip the mask over her head to cover her eyes.

"You're good, *il mio tesoro*. Just relax. We're in the air. Your friends are fine. You've got a small nosebleed but that's all. Not as bad as before, and you weren't even sick."

"Don't say the word *sick*," she cautioned.

"I'll be more careful," he promised, exchanging a relieved grin with his cousins and nodding when they indicated they would leave him alone with her.

He waited until both left the room before he removed his shoes and slipped up onto the bed with her. He was damned tired, and it was going to be a very long night. He had some explaining to do.

"I can't believe how fast you learned, Nicoletta." There was pride in his voice. "The entire family has noted how quick you pick up technique and retain it, but riding the shadows is something we learn from the time we're toddlers. We start with simple games and progress from there, but you were just thrown in at the deep end and acted like a pro."

"I threw up over and over, Taviano. That's hardly being a professional," Nicoletta protested, a note of sarcasm creeping in, telling him she didn't like praise she didn't feel she deserved.

"You don't understand. Some riders train for years and still can't take being in the shadows. They end up not being able to do the work because it's too difficult. You're going to be twenty-one in a few weeks, Nicoletta, and you were able to ride four times in the same day without training. That's unheard-of. No one, to my knowledge, or the knowledge of our family, has done such a thing. If I lose my fucking career over this, I want you to know I'm so damned proud of you, and it was my choice to do it."

He meant it, too. It had been his choice to bring her with him. It had been a risk, but he'd *needed* to bring her. He would have to answer to Stefano, maybe even go before the counsel. If it went that far, if Stefano insisted he be brought before the counsel, then he would be banned from riding, but he knew he would have done it all over again, because Nicoletta needed him to give her what she asked for. He might be able to make himself explain it to Stefano, but never to the counsel, so he hoped it didn't go that far.

There was a small silence. Nicoletta put her hand to her head and slowly drew the ice pack from her forehead and then removed the eye mask. He could just make out her eyelashes fluttering as she turned her head to look at him. Ignoring the light, restraining hand on her belly, she sat up.

He saw what that movement cost her. There was a momentary flash of pain on her face. Her body hadn't recovered from the brutal travel in the shadows. It wouldn't for a long while. Still, she turned on the bed, pulling her legs up under her as she faced him completely.

"What do you mean, lose your career?"

He winced. He still hadn't recovered from riding the shadows, especially with a wound. He should have guarded his words more carefully.

"I promised you I would explain things to you, didn't I?"

Her eyes searched his face and then she nodded.

"You may as well get comfortable. I'll get you something to drink. Something icy cold. I know from experience your throat is feeling parched." It was true, but there was a part of him that was stalling, and he knew it.

"Yes, I need something cold to drink, Taviano, but before anything else, you need to explain what you meant. Why would you lose your career because you helped my friends?"

"Not because I helped your friends, Nicoletta." He got up and made his way to the small bar there in the bedroom. It was fully equipped, just like the one in the other room. He got her a cold water. Like him, Nicoletta didn't drink alcohol anymore. "Because I allowed you to see what we do."

"I already suspected what you did. I had done it myself,"

she pointed out, taking the bottle from him. "Well, I hid, sort of. But I still suspected you did something in the shadows."

"That's beside the point. You didn't have a clue how to ride them. There are rules that all riders follow, and for good reason. Those rules are in place to protect all riders. All of the families, not just ours. If you were to tell what you know to an outsider, you could ruin everyone."

"Why would I do that?"

He shrugged. "Any number of reasons. Money comes to mind. People do all sorts of things when they're angry or hurt or drinking, or just because they can. You and I both know things can take a very ugly turn very fast."

She was silent, regarding him over the top of the bottle of water, her gaze thoughtful. "How do we keep you from getting into trouble, Taviano? I asked you to help my friends. You tell me what to do and I'll do it."

"Marry me." He said it abruptly. Too abruptly. He knew the moment the words had left his mouth that he'd mangled the moment. He sounded harsh and implacable, much like Stefano when he was decreeing that the world had to do as he dictated.

She looked shocked. Even a little horrified. She blinked rapidly, and for a moment he thought her lashes looked wet, as if there might have been tears on them, but she turned her head away, shaking it and then putting the water bottle to her mouth.

He made every effort to soften the impact of what he was saying. "We're heading to Vegas. If you're willing, we can get married there. Me taking you into the shadows and explaining the family business to you will be more acceptable if you're actually married to me. Stefano will be pissed as hell, but there's a chance he'll let me stay a rider."

Dio. He'd always been good at talking his way out of anything. What was wrong with him that he couldn't get the right words out for her? She was stiff, her shoulders set, her face angled away from him so her luxurious, thick, long black hair flowed down around her shoulders, hiding her expression from him.

"I see. How long will you have to keep up the pretense?"

"What pretense?"

"That we're married." Her voice was strictly neutral.

"What the hell does that mean? We're going to Vegas. You just said you'd do whatever it takes to help me out. Marriage is marriage, Nicoletta. You don't get married and then what? Get unmarried? Divorced? Once we're married, we're fucking married. There's no pretense. I don't lie to Stefano or to the family."

"Lovely. Well, that just sounds lovely, then."

He really had blown it big-time. He took a deep breath and shut down the infamous Ferraro temper. He was angry with himself, not with her. "Look, Nicoletta, I know you deserve the works, a big church wedding, and we can have that. We can make that happen when this is all over, one with everyone there. I want that for both of us, but I'm going to be honest about what's happening here."

She turned her head then and her dark eyes met his. He was older than her by several years, but right then she looked at him with too-old eyes. "Do be honest, Taviano. I would appreciate it."

He reached for her hand and threaded his fingers through hers. "When I first encountered you, a little over three years ago, our shadows touched. Maybe you didn't feel it the way I did, but I knew then that we were connected." He'd already told her that much. He tightened his hold when she tried to pull away. "Over the years, our shadows continued to entwine, and now they're so tangled together, if you look at them, Nicoletta, you won't be able to tell where one starts and the other lets off. They're one and the same."

She shook her head, but she stopped pulling away from him.

"When a rider marries and his partner accepts and comes into his or her world, she accepts the rules that govern that world. Their shadows twist together like ours have and make an unbreakable bond. It's unusual for the shadows to do what ours have prior to a union, but everything about you has been unusual."

She moistened her lips, frowning a little. "I don't exactly understand. If you saw that our shadows were already tangling together, then you had to be worried that you would have to be my partner even back then. Now I can understand why you were always so angry with me. It makes so much more sense."

"It wasn't like that."

She shook her head again and looked away from him.

He swore under his breath. "I was never angry with you, Nicoletta, only at what I couldn't fix. Men want to fix things."

"Just keep explaining."

He wished he still drank alcohol. "Once married, there's no divorce, no parting without severe consequences to both parties."

Her eyes were back on his face. Unblinking. Watching him carefully. Taking in everything he said. She looked very sober. No expression. He couldn't read her, and that was extremely unusual. As a rule, Taviano could read Nicoletta like an open book.

"Please explain 'severe consequences.'"

He ran the pad of his thumb over the back of her hand. Stroking little caresses. He needed them more than she did. He needed to reestablish the connection he'd come to rely on. It had grown strong between them, but just that fast, she'd pulled away from him. He was used to her near adoration. She wasn't adept at hiding it, although she tried.

He had waited to claim her until he felt she was old enough. She'd been through far too much, and sexually, he knew he was demanding. He'd spoken to counselors about what to expect, and every one of them had said to go slow, to let her set the pace. That meant not to claim her until she was older, to give her time. Waiting had been difficult, especially when she'd had another man declaring he was in the running.

Taviano wasn't certain if Nicoletta even knew Dario Bosco had made his own claim on her. Taviano had shut that down hard, telling him and his family that Nicoletta was engaged to him. That had been two years earlier and no one had said one word to her, which was a good thing. She would have ripped his head off.

"Taviano, are you going to answer me?"

"Yes, I'm just trying to figure out the best way to tell you. I keep blurting shit out and saying it all wrong. I'm not doing this well, Nicoletta."

"I'm getting the gist of what you're telling me."

She might be understanding the premise, but she wasn't understanding him and the way he felt. "If shadows are merged so they become one and the two riders decide to part ways, the one who is the actual rider forfeits his or her ability to be able to ride. He can't go into the shadows as he once did. It's like living a half life. That would happen to me if we decided to end our marriage."

"And me?"

"You would forget that you ever knew me. If we had children, you would forget you had them. If others pointed them out to you, you would have no feeling toward them. In some ways that is a protection for you, but it is also a kind of hell. I would always remember you."

She stared at him for nearly a minute in total silence. Then her long, thick lashes fluttered, calling attention to the tips and the way they curved up at the ends. "This is insane. You just said our shadows are already merged together. It doesn't matter if we're married or not. It happened almost immediately."

He nodded. That was the truth. It happened the moment he was in the same room with her, that first time in New York when Stefano was there to bring justice to her three step-uncles. He'd felt the jolt of that first connection. It had hit hard, and when he'd looked at the shadow, his hand already curled through hers, he had seen that first knot forming.

The second time had happened on the plane when he'd gone to the bedroom in case she'd woken up and was frightened. The light, as dim as it had been, cast their shadows on the wall. He remembered looking up in a kind of horror to see the two shadows weaving together, as if someone were using knitting needles to intricately tie them together.

He should have talked to Stefano about it, but he'd looked down at her face, that angelic face with the lashes lying like two thick crescents on her bruised skin, and he'd known he was born to be hers. She might have still been a child, but someday she would need more than she did right at that moment, and he would have the time to shape himself into the man she would not only need but hopefully want.

"So almost from the beginning, you knew that you would have to be with me, or you would lose your ability to ride the shadows." She gave a delicate little shudder, as if she couldn't imagine why anyone would want to ride the shadows.

He nodded. "I knew. Each time we came in contact, our shadows merged, and the weave grew tighter. I felt it. I knew you did as well."

"Why didn't you stay away from me, if you knew it was happening? You came night after night, Taviano."

"Our lives are different from others. We look as if we have freedom, but we don't. If we can't find the person we choose on our own to marry, the one we love, by a certain age, then a marriage is arranged, because it is necessary for a rider to produce children."

She stared at him as if he'd grown two heads. "No one can force you to marry someone."

"It's done out of duty. We are born into a family that carries a heavy responsibility. Those of us who accept that responsibility will allow an arranged marriage if we can't find a partner in the time allotted."

"But my shadow snared yours, and you just let it. I suppose that's kind of like an arranged marriage, isn't it?" There was a touch of sarcasm, or maybe tears, in her voice.

He shrugged. "The point I'm making here, Nicoletta, is we're here now, in this place. I took you into the shadows, which was strictly forbidden. I gave you a glimpse of the life we lead. I can bring you all the way in or leave you behind right now. You have to choose."

She took a long pull from the water bottle and then pressed it against her throat. "Don't be an ass, Taviano. I already told you I would do whatever it took to help out. I asked you for help with my friends. I insisted on going with you. All along you kept giving me an out. I kept going with you and asking for more. Every choice was mine. If we have to marry, you need to know you aren't getting any bargain."

She hesitated, moving the bottle from her throat to her forehead, pressing it there and then taking a breath to continue. "In spite of the fact that I threw myself at you when I was drunk, I haven't been with a man since I was a teen and I was gang-raped repeatedly by my step-uncles. The only other man I've been with was Benito Valdez, and that was rape every single time. I fought and lost the battle. I don't even know if I can have sex, let alone enjoy it. I don't know if I can have children, if that's what you're looking for. I don't know a lot of things that would be helpful when one is thinking about marriage."

Taviano noted she avoided looking at him, when before she'd been so direct. "*Tesoro*, there is no need to worry. We'll cross that bridge when we come to it."

"It's a pretty big bridge. You cheat on me and we're done. I'm not the kind of girl who puts up with that kind of thing. You knew what was happening and I didn't. You could have stopped it, but you didn't, so no matter what, those are the consequences."

"I want you to be very clear on that, Nicoletta. I couldn't have stopped it. Shadows are a force of nature. They connect. They twist together. I knew it was happening, and yes, I could have made an effort to stay away." He hadn't because he'd been so drawn to her. He had wanted—even needed—a closer connection with her.

"Just tell me about what it is you do. What the family does. How it all works and why you're so secretive."

He might as well. He'd already gone this far, and she had promised to marry him. If she didn't, he had no choice. He would have to break it off with her, and that would destroy both of them. She would forget everything he told her.

"I'm sure, in the years you've lived with Lucia and Amo, you've heard the rumors about the Ferraro family."

"Of course. That you're members of a crime family. That you're mafia. That you have a territory, and the Saldi family is the greatest enemy. Naturally I've heard the gossip."

"What else?"

She sighed and pressed the bottle to her forehead again. He knew immediately that the headache still persisted. "Some say that if a family has a problem, one can request a visit with Eloisa, and she will listen to that problem and make it go away."

He nodded slowly. "That is what they say. So, if in New York, a social worker goes to my cousin's grandparents, former riders, and requests a visit with them, they grant it of course. An afternoon tea. Perhaps coffee. Here, in Chicago, the social worker might meet with Eloisa for the same thing, a simple tea, just a nice friendly visit. In Los Angeles, you met a couple of my cousins. Their grandparents also would meet with that same social worker upon a request and also sit down to a nice cup of tea or coffee for a pleasant visit."

Nicoletta frowned at him. "There are riders in New York, Chicago and Los Angeles?"

He nodded. "Also in other countries, although we are very few and getting fewer."

"Children?" she guessed. "It's probably difficult to find each other and have children."

He wasn't going there yet. "In our world, these former shadow riders are now known as 'greeters.' All riders are born with the capability of hearing lies. Some, obviously, are better at it than others. We develop the gift as we grow. I'm certain you have the ability."

Taviano waited for her to nod. Her gaze was on his face, and that steady stare was a little disconcerting. He'd wanted her to understand his world, but her comprehension level and learning speed was astounding. She was picking up what he was saying far too quickly, jumping ahead, without further explanation. He wasn't going to be able to hold anything back. If he did, she would guess accurately anyway.

"In the first part of the visit, the greeters simply talk with the visitors, establishing their patterns of speech and breathing. Then they ask them why they've come. The visitor lays out their problem. We'll use the social worker for our example." He kept his gaze steady on her face. "She has a young girl that she's worried about. She can't get her out of the terrible abusive situation she's in. Her parents died in a car accident and the teen was placed with her only relatives, but they are members of an infamous gang."

Nicoletta stirred then, her rigid shoulders jerking, her head pulling back. She slid off the bed and went to the bar, pulling out another cold bottle of water from the mini fridge. Leaning against the long, low-slung dresser that ran along the curved wall of the aircraft, she nodded at him to continue.

"They threatened her family when she tried to have the teen removed, but she knows they've raped her, and she's seen multiple bruises on her. She's afraid of the gang, but she can't leave this girl in that situation. She doesn't know what to do. She has some money saved up for her retirement, and she's willing to give all of it as a fee if the family can do something to get this teen out of the situation and bring some justice for her."

Nicoletta had broken out in a sweat. She pressed the water bottle to her face, stepping to one side so no light, even as dim as it was, could touch her.

"Are you all right?"

"Did she really do that?" Nicoletta whispered it. There were tears in her voice.

"Yes."

"I didn't know."

"You weren't supposed to know. Anyone knowing could get her and her family killed. The Demons are vicious. There could be no signs pointing back to her."

"I thought I had been completely abandoned. She came to see me and they pushed her around. I had two workers before her. They both raced away. She looked at me, and there was something in her eyes, and then she left, and I never heard from her again. They laughed and said no one would ever come for me."

"They were wrong, weren't they?" Taviano said softly.

He ached with the need to go to her. She looked so alone. He'd seen her like that countless times in the last few years. Standing straight. Looking just like she did now, upright, refusing to be broken when she was so torn up inside. He knew what those men had done to her, and she hated that he knew.

Still, he was going to be her husband. He wasn't going to do what he'd been forced to do for the last three years. He slipped from the bed and went to her, choosing to ignore that she froze like a little rabbit when he got close.

"The social worker laid out the problem, and my cousin's grandparents in New York listened very carefully, tuned for lies. Tuned for truth. They say nothing, only listen. It's always possible an enemy has slipped in. Or someone from law enforcement. It happens often. Our family is often tested. When the visitor is finished speaking, they murmur great sympathies but promise nothing. They say how sorry they are. They ask a few questions for clarity. They might ask them to write down names. They never offer to help. The visitor goes away wondering if they wasted their time."

Taviano slipped his arm around Nicoletta's waist and urged her toward the two round chairs near the entryway of the room. The chairs were very comfortable, and he wanted her to rest while she could. Her body needed it whether she recognized it or not.

"There is always an investigation. There are two sets of

investigators. The first team finds out everything they can about the client. The second team investigates the actual crime. Both have to be human lie detectors and they have the capability to influence others to want to talk to them. They investigate quietly and very carefully in order not to tip off the cops or anyone else who might be interested in the same crime or people."

Nicoletta allowed him to urge her toward the chairs. She sank into one with a small sigh and immediately put her feet up on the built-in ottoman, leaning her head back and closing her eyes. "I have to say, I could live in this plane, Taviano. Is it yours? If it is, it's a seriously good reason for a girl to want to marry you."

"Kissing me is a seriously good reason for a girl to want to marry me."

She opened her eyes and scowled at him. "Now's not a good time for that. Keep talking. Vegas can't be that far from LA by plane."

He pretended to sigh, but at least she was back to being more like herself. "Investigators have to be family members and they have to have specific psychic gifts. Once the investigation is complete, greeters, investigators and shadow riders all have to agree before the job is taken. To do that, the rider has to know every fact about both parties. Where they lived, who lived with them. Their routine. Their friends. Everything. That's vital. First, we can't make a mistake, and second, we don't want the rider in jeopardy if at all possible."

"Essentially, a rider is an assassin." She turned her head and looked at him coolly, beneath the fan of her dark, thick lashes, daring him to tell her the truth.

His heart jumped in his chest. He'd laid it out for her, using her own case as his example, and she was still judging them harshly. He might have expected that from someone else, but not from her. He didn't view himself as an assassin, but he supposed the outside world would see him that way. He didn't make a kill personal. He meted out justice to those who slipped through the system. Sometimes the task was something as simple as getting back money that was taken from an elderly person in a scam. It didn't have to be a broken neck.

"Often we're called on to mete out that kind of justice, yes," he admitted.

She turned her head again, staring through the open bedroom door into what would be the wide formal dining room. When the family was aboard, that was the part of the plane most used. They sat around the large table and interacted, mostly laughing together and enjoying one another's company.

"Why were you in New York instead of the ones who live there? You said you have cousins who live there."

"Once an investigation is complete, the riders come in from a different city. They fly in essentially looking to party. The paparazzi hound them, taking tons of pictures. Cousins who live in that city greet them and they party the night away with well-known actresses or singers, anyone who would also be pursued by the paparazzi. The idea is to get into as many magazines and newspapers as possible. It's all about alibis."

"While you're all visible, someone they never saw is in the shadows doing the deed."

"Exactly."

She turned her head then and his heart nearly stopped when she sent him a little half smile. "Nice gig. You really thought up a foolproof plan. No wonder you all like to be in the spotlight so much. I should have figured that out all by myself. I'm a little disappointed in myself that I didn't."

Relief was overwhelming. She wasn't as opposed to what they did as he'd first feared. She continued to look steadily at him. "That's why you didn't go after Benito and Armando then. They weren't on the list. No one had sanctioned them, so to speak."

Something in her voice put his warning system on alert. His woman might just be a little bloodthirsty. He'd just explained the system to her and the need to make certain it was never personal. He knew that wasn't always possible, but they still had to try. He was going to have to watch her.

"I will admit, I read the reports and they were very detailed. I knew what he had done to you and I wanted him dead. It felt very personal to me even then. Stefano refused. It wasn't sanctioned, and we weren't on the Demons' radar. They would have no idea what happened to you. You would be safer if you simply vanished. I wanted you safe."

"I wanted them all dead."

He was silent. If he had to admit it aloud, he had to agree.

"Tell me more. I interrupted you, and I'm sorry. I didn't mean to. I find this entire business extremely fascinating. I can imagine Stefano doing it, but not Francesca."

"Francesca was never trained as a rider. She was born capable, but never trained, and she doesn't ride the shadows. Stefano would lose his mind if she tried. She's the heart of our family and always will be. Ricco's wife, Mariko, is a trained rider, and she's fast and excellent at it. Sasha, Giovanni's wife, isn't, but she could have been. Again, she will never be a rider; however, she's a force of nature and a powerhouse. Grace, no way will she ever be a shadow rider, and Vittorio would lose his mind, just like Stefano would if Francesca wanted to be one."

Taviano could feel Nicoletta's eyes on him, but he deliberately didn't look at her. Instead, he stared up at the ceiling of the plane. He made her ask.

"What about you, Taviano?"

"What about me, Nicoletta?"

"What do you expect from your wife? Do you expect me to be the heart of the family like Francesca? Or a force of nature like Sasha? Or like Grace, sweet and accommodating of everything you want? Or like Mariko, a rider?"

Taviano thought it over, taking his time, wanting to answer her honestly. "I would like you to be the heart of our family like Francesca, and you're already a force of nature like Sasha. I would love that you'd be sweet and accommodating, even thoughtful of my needs and wants, the way

Grace is with Vittorio. As for a rider like Mariko, no, I don't want that. She takes her own rotation, just as we all do. I would be opposed to that. If I had my preference, I would want us to work together, like we did. Of course, you need far more training, both in the shadows and out, but I think we'd make a good team. That would be my preference. So, it isn't an expectation, Nicoletta. It's a preference."

"I don't know that I have the self-discipline needed to keep my personal feelings out of the work," she admitted with marked reluctance. "How do you do that?"

"Practice. Work. Everyone has good traits and character flaws, Nicoletta. Some of the flaws can be both good and bad. The problem is, people don't want to acknowledge they have them, or they simply use them as an excuse. They'll say they're stubborn, as if that excuses their behavior. It doesn't. If they know they're stubborn, they have to work doubly hard not to be. I have a terrible temper, as you well know. I work on it all the time. Sometimes I'm successful, other times I'm not. I'm not proud of it. I despise the fact that I'm not disciplined enough to overcome letting that damn thing rule me. I don't like hurting people I care about. I know I've hurt you with things I've said in anger. We just keep at it."

She nodded. "You think I can get to a place where I won't throw up when I'm with you in the shadows?"

"You didn't on the ride back to the plane."

She gave him a faint smile. "I'm pretty certain there was nothing left to come up."

He held out his hand to her. "You're going to do fine, although I'm going to warn you, even after we're married, Stefano may be so pissed at me that he'll strip me of my right to be a rider anyway. This might not fix everything."

"Why Stefano?" She took his hand. It was slow, but she did it.

"He's the head of the Chicago family. His word is law. Eloisa used to have a say, but not anymore. I'll abide by whatever Stefano says. He'll be fair. Angry with me, but fair. I put you at risk. Just so you know, the family didn't take any money from the social worker, Nicoletta."

"Someday I'd like to go back and thank her in person. Maybe it would be nice for her to know that she made a difference in someone's life. Lucia and Amo have been wonderful to me. I couldn't ask for better foster parents. I wish they could be in Vegas with us. They aren't going to be happy, even though I can explain that it's really kind of a bogus wedding."

His eyebrow shot up. "Bogus wedding? What the hell is a bogus wedding?"

"Not real. You know, like one of those Elvis wedding things. Isn't that what we're doing? Sort of doing this fast and fake so Stefano will be happy, and then doing it again when Lucia and Amo and the others are around?"

He wanted to say yes. He wanted to give her that big church wedding—and he would. But there wasn't going to be anything bogus about this wedding. "This wedding won't be fake, *piccola*. We're getting legally married. We'll file the papers, and then go home and let Francesca and Grace plan our big event. Grace is all into that. You can give all the input you want. You tell them what you want, and it's yours. Go all fairy tale if you want. Hell, I'll dress up as Prince Charming in those silly striped white tights for you, but this isn't going to be an Elvis-slash-bogus wedding."

"You're so lying right now. You would never in a million years dress up as Prince Charming in white or striped tights."

"Okay, I am lying about that," he conceded. "It's not good when my fiancée can hear lies." He pushed out of the chair and went to the bedside stand to open the drawer where he'd placed the small jewelry box. All along he'd thought to ask her to marry him. Of course, he'd been planning to ask her officially. He'd all but told her that this was the end of her freedom, so she needed to enjoy it while she could.

His cousin Damian Ferraro, from New York, was a very talented jeweler who made very special jewelry designed to be able to go into the shadows. He was famous for designing the perfect ring for an unseen, unknown lady. Taviano hoped he had created magic for Nicoletta. Like his brothers, he hadn't looked to see what Damian had made for his woman. He'd been a little afraid to see.

He brought the small jeweler's box out just to make it official. Because Nicoletta didn't have many things good in her life, he went down in front of her on one knee and opened the box with his thumb, shifting it so she could see inside.

"I'm asking you officially to be my wife, Nicoletta. I want you to marry me and spend your life with me. I promise I'll spend the rest of my life doing my best to make you happy." It was a lame proposal because looking at her robbed him of speech, which didn't seem possible.

He wanted to give her the world. Take away every bad memory she had and replace it with something good. She thought she was in little pieces, scattered on the ground. He'd heard her say that once when she'd torn up a photograph of herself Lucia had taken. She'd been crying and she'd called herself trash. She'd burned the image and placed the ashes of the picture in the trash can "where she belonged." He'd hated that. Now he couldn't even give her a proper proposal because she left him without words. But she liked the ring. He saw that on her face. It was a flawless dark indigo blue diamond. Like his eyes. The stone had a lush elegance to it. He could have passed it off as a sapphire with its fiery sheen, but the cushion-cut diamond, set in a platinum band, was too rare and beautiful to be compared with anything on the market. She would be unable to wear the engagement ring in the shadows, but the wedding band was made of a special alloy she would always keep on her finger.

"Taviano." She barely breathed his name.

"Say yes."

"I can't wear that."

He took it out of the box and pushed it onto her finger. It slid on easily, just the way he knew it would. Damian had a way of knowing, without ever meeting the woman who would wear the ring. The stone looked perfect against her skin. She looked down at her hand and then up at his face.

"You need to say yes, *tesoro*," he coaxed.

"I said yes, but I'll say it again. Yes, but—"

He leaned in and brushed a kiss across her lips to stop whatever she was about to say. *Yes* was just fine with him. He knew she was afraid she wasn't going to be good enough. He knew she would be. He had his own secrets. His own past. He was no saint. She'd have to live with that.

He took her hand and pressed a kiss over the ring. "Franco just said we're going to be landing. Let's do this, and then we'll face Stefano." He hesitated. "One more thing. The wedding band stays on your finger. This comes off before we take to the shadows, so in an emergency, if you're wearing it, you'll have to get rid of it."

She shook her head. "Taviano. No."

"We'll have plenty of time to think of plans just in case, but you have to keep that in the back of your mind."

She pressed her other hand over the ring. "Maybe the ring is magic, and it will protect us. It feels as if it could be."

"Let's hope so."

CHAPTER SIX

What the hell were you thinking, Taviano?" Stefano snapped, glaring at his youngest brother. "You could have killed her. Instead of sitting on the couch with you right now, you could be carrying her out of a tube in your arms dead."

It was easy enough to see that the head of the Ferraro family was furious. Nicoletta curled closer into Taviano, uncertain whether she was doing so in order to protect him or have him protect her. She had seen Stefano angry, but never like this. His rage radiated throughout the room—not just the room, it filled the entire penthouse apartment. She was afraid even that gigantic space couldn't possibly contain the fierce emotion and it would leak downstairs and affect the people staying in the Ferraro Hotel.

Taviano glanced down at her the moment she moved into his rib cage, and his arm dropped from the back of the couch to her shoulders. The heat from his body seeped into the cold of hers. He had a way of always calming her when she wanted to run. He didn't seem that affected by his brother's wrath, not the way she was. She wanted to find one of the shadows and try to hide herself, even knowing the toll it would take on her. That made her feel like a coward, but she didn't like raised voices—especially men's raised voices.

"He's not angry with you, *piccola*," Taviano explained, his voice gentle. He dipped his head so his lips were close to her ear. "Our brother Ettore didn't make it out of the shadows. It was Stefano who found him. He has every right to be angry with me. The risk was very real."

"But I'd done it before." Nicoletta lifted her head, forcing herself to meet the fury in Stefano's eyes.

It was difficult to be surrounded by all of the Ferraro brothers at once. Even though the room was very spacious and extremely luxurious, warm with Francesca's homey touches, having all of Taviano's brothers around her took discipline not to panic. She knew being in close proximity with too many men was still a trigger for her. She'd discussed it often with the counselor, and how she could best handle that and hopefully overcome it.

"When I was a child, I sort of played in the shadows, not riding them, or really hiding in them, but I was really drawn to them and would jump in and out of them, always feeling that weird pull on my body. That wasn't the same, but I think maybe in a way it prepared my body for the feeling of being in the tube."

She had played often, and even as she got older, she couldn't stop herself from jumping in and out of the shadows, like a child playing hopscotch. She'd felt silly, but it had been a compulsion.

"Then, after my parents died and I was given to my stepuncles, when I was taking a shower and I heard one of them coming for me, I inadvertently found myself hidden from him. He called to the others and they hunted for me, but they couldn't see me."

She *detested* talking aloud to the entire group of Ferraros about what had happened to her. It was too personal.

At the same time, she would do anything to make things right for Taviano.

"I didn't realize that I could move in them, but I did it accidentally. Once that happened, I tried to do it deliberately."

She detested that Taviano was being yelled at because of her. He didn't show hurt or anger, nor did he try to defend himself, even when he knew his career was on the line. She wanted to defend him. At the same time, she could barely breathe.

She wanted to go home, get to Lucia and Amo. Emmanuelle was there, and Mariko sat quietly with her hands folded neatly the way she did, looking graceful and poised. Two women. That helped, but Nicoletta really wanted to be away from there. Away from all of them—even Taviano. Especially Taviano. She was beginning to sweat, although she felt cold and clammy.

There was silence after her statement. Stefano's dark blue eyes seemed to pierce right through her skull into her mind, into her soul, where he could see things she didn't want him to find. Taviano's arm tightened around her, and she realized she was shaking. She hadn't lost it in the shadows. She hadn't lost it when there was gunfire. She couldn't make a fool of herself and lose it with his family.

She'd been to this penthouse hundreds of times. She'd played with Stefano's son. She'd worked out in his training hall with his brothers—all the men in this room that she was now so nervous with. What was wrong with her that she was so close to a full-blown panic attack? She knew them. She liked them all. They'd been good to her. Protected her.

She wiped at the sweat on her face and tried to take a breath, but her lungs felt raw and burning. Her vision blurred. There were too many men surrounding her. Too many of them.

Stefano leaned toward her, his dark eyes steady on her face. "What do you mean you've done it before? You actually went into the shadows deliberately, Nicoletta? You knew you could hide there? Not be seen?"

She nodded. Desperately drew in air, taking a deep, quick breath. The pressure in her chest increased, her heart pounding to the point that she was afraid it might burst. She pressed her hand hard against her breast and forced herself to answer. "Yes. When I was a teen, they came for me when I was showering, and I was terrified. The things they did to me . . ."

Now she couldn't breathe. She could barely see. Her vision had tunneled until everything was going black with the exception of Stefano, who was straight in front of her. "Taviano." She whispered his name, her fingers twisting in his shirt, gripping him tightly as she had in the shadows, terrified she would make a fool of herself, panicking in front of his family.

Instantly he was crouched in front of her, his forehead pressed against hers. "Just breathe with me, Nicoletta. It's just you and me. Breathe. *Tutti qui sono famiglia.*"

She found herself looking into his eyes. Taviano. She loved him. She detested him. He wrapped her around his little finger. She adored him. He made her feel safe. She breathed with him because she would do anything for him, and he was asking her to breathe with him. She knew enough Italian to know he was saying everyone there was her family. She also realized he'd said it deliberately in Italian because he wanted her to distinguish between his family and the ones claiming to be her family who had been so abusive toward her.

Once she was able to breathe again, she slipped her arms around his neck and held him for a moment, gathering her strength before facing Stefano and his brothers. They were intimidating men when they were on their own, but together, they were a force. Taviano slipped back onto the couch beside her as if nothing had happened, his arm once again sliding around her shoulders.

Nicoletta lifted her chin. "I still have panic attacks when

I'm in close confines with several men. I'm sorry, it just happens out of the blue and I can't seem to control it. It doesn't always happen, and I've worked on it, but my counselor says that it might continue to happen for the rest of my life. I'll keep trying to get on top of it, but who knows if I'll be able to."

"It was probably Stefano and his God-awful temper," Vittorio said.

Nicoletta sent him a small smile, not quite daring to look at Stefano to see how he took that little dig. She couldn't control the color rising in her face. She was embarrassed that she had to admit she had panic attacks when the Ferraros seemed to be so perfect and confident. Apparently Taviano was going to be the one stuck with the "flawed" wife. Eloisa was going to have a field day with that one.

"Francesca is always on me about my temper," Stefano admitted. "I don't want anything to happen to you, Nicoletta. Going into the shadows is dangerous. If you aren't trained properly, it can take a toll on your body. More importantly, you can get lost there."

She nodded. "I was well aware of that. The one time I did move accidentally, I was hiding from my step-uncles and I found myself from one side of the room to another place, and I didn't know how I got there. It was very disorienting. They were angry with me when they found me, and the consequences were very brutal, but I was so sick and feeling so lost, as if I wasn't all there, that the things they were doing to me didn't really register until afterward. In a way, the consequences were a blessing. I wasn't as afraid as maybe I should have been."

There was silence after her declaration, and she felt the rising tension in the room, that sudden flare of anger tamped down in Taviano and reflected in his brothers. She glanced up at his face for a sign of what she was supposed to say to ease the tension in the room. She was at a loss with all of them.

Taviano's fingers found the nape of her neck and began

a slow massage. She sat very still, not knowing exactly what to do. No one had ever touched her like that, and the feel of his fingers on her bare skin, pushing into her muscles and nerve endings, sent a heat wave through her. It was a kind of slow seduction of the senses. It was frightening and exhilarating at the same time.

"Relax, *Tesoro*. Stefano might choose to eat me, but you will go unscathed in all of this," Taviano whispered into her ear, amusement in his voice.

The touch of his warm breath added to the feeling of seduction, and that little undertone of amusement created an intimacy between them. She imagined that was what it was like between two people who really were in love. His lips actually brushed against the lobe of her ear, feeling cool and firm, sending a roller coaster crashing through her stomach.

"Were you aware that we were shadow riders?" Stefano asked, his voice pitched very low. Again, his gaze was fixed on her face. He looked suspiciously very hawklike.

If Taviano's strong fingers hadn't chosen that moment to settle around her neck possessively, and there was no other word she could think of to describe the feeling, she might have run from the room. Stefano was expecting the truth. She was well aware that every one of the Ferraros was like her, they could hear lies.

"Yes, at least suspected," she admitted. "I watched all of you and the way the shadows swallowed you up. The time the truck tried to run Ricco or me down, one of us, and he pushed me out of the way, he was so fast, too fast. I watched him quite a bit after that. I was fast like he was when I did things. I have a memory that few others have. I can hear lies. I have these strange gifts, and all of a sudden there were others that seemed to have them. Of course I paid attention. I saw whenever you disappeared into the shadows. And I remembered you taking me through one of the shadows to the plane when you were getting me away from my step-uncles."

"And yet you said nothing," Stefano said.

She ducked her head. "I loathed myself. And you. And Taviano. You knew what they'd done to me." She whispered it, feeling the grasping hands on her body. The way they forced themselves on her, the pain of the intrusion. The laughter as they brutally used her again and again, switching places so casually.

Taviano stroked his fingers gently on her face. "*Piccola*, who is your man? Your *compagno*? Your *marito*? Look at me. See only me." Very, very gently, he framed her face with both hands and turned her toward him. "Open your eyes, Nicoletta, and see me."

She lifted her long lashes because she was used to doing what Taviano asked of her. He was the one man in the world she trusted when she wouldn't trust any other. There he was with those dark blue eyes of his, looking at her as if she were the only woman in the world. She had no idea how he could do that—focus so completely on her—but he always did. She couldn't help but smile at him. She couldn't help the way her heart reacted with that instant joy. She *adored* Taviano. No matter how often she told herself she was going to get her heart broken if she didn't protect herself, she couldn't stop the overwhelming emotion he produced in her. It just spilled over, like some volcano welling up out of nowhere.

"This is going to be your life with me, you know that, don't you?" She cupped the side of his face, hating that he had been forced to marry her. That he had known three years earlier and had been helpless to do anything about it. She had always wondered why he had been so angry. He'd been abrupt with her, those dark blue eyes so moody, his handsome face never quite facing her when all the other Ferraros did. Their shadows had twisted together, and he'd been caught in a trap, just as surely as men had been caught in years gone by when girls had purposely gotten pregnant. She hated that for him.

He leaned into her, covering those scant inches between them, and brushed a kiss across her lips, trailed more kisses down her cheek to her shoulder. Light. Gentle. Barely there. She felt his mouth like a hot promise. He might as well have pressed a fiery brand straight through skin and muscle and etched his name into her bones forever.

"*Dio*, Taviano," Stefano snapped. "I'm supposed to be passing sentence here. You're tying my hands."

Taviano sank back against the leather couch, taking Nicoletta with him. She couldn't help noticing the others smirking a little as they exchanged looks with one another. She didn't quite understand what that all meant, but she knew those looks were at Stefano's expense. He was both sibling and parent to his brothers and sister, and it wasn't always the most enviable position to be in. Right now, she felt a little sorry for him.

"Nicoletta is *famiglia*." Stefano pinned his youngest brother with a stern eye.

Immediately Nicoletta felt the difference in the room. All humor was gone. Whatever Stefano was about to say, he meant business; all of them were listening, and every single one of them, Taviano included, would abide by what he said. She slipped her hand into Taviano's and tightened her fingers around his, willing to show him support as best she could.

"She's loved by all of us. You claimed her three years ago, so yes, you have that first right to her, but she is *famiglia*. We do not fuck around with *famiglia*. We don't take chances with *famiglia*. Never with our women. I will admit, there were extenuating circumstances I was unaware of. The fact that Nicoletta had already been in the shadows and was experimenting on her own—which, by the way, is extremely dangerous and is now *forbidden* to you, Nicoletta."

Stefano turned the full impact of his deadly dark stare on her. "I hope you understand what I am saying to you. As head of this family and as the leader of the shadow riders of Chicago, you are forbidden to experiment on your own. You will be trained properly if Taviano and I agree that you can safely maneuver inside the shadows. But you will never try to do so alone. Is that understood?"

There was no way in hell she was going to defy Stefano Ferraro. She nodded. "I understand, Stefano. Absolutely." She might not like that Taviano and Stefano had a say in what she could or couldn't do, but she'd hear them out before she entered into an argument about whether or not she could go into the shadows again. She believed in Taviano, and he'd already told her his idea for his wife was to work *with* him.

Stefano turned his attention back to his youngest brother, and Nicoletta held her breath. Unknowingly, Taviano tightened his fingers around hers, nearly crushing her hand. She didn't protest, realizing how difficult this was for him. He would accept whatever Stefano decreed, but being a rider was who and what Taviano was. If that was taken from him . . .

"I'm very aware your shadow had already tangled with Nicoletta's. Everything about Nicoletta is unprecedented. Everything. Still, the rules we have are in place to protect the family. Telling her what we are and what we do and how we do it could have placed all of us in jeopardy."

Ricco shook his head. "That's not entirely true, Stefano. I've given this a lot of thought. Their shadows were already so merged by Nicoletta's second year here, they might as well have been married. Taviano couldn't have survived as a rider if she had left. We all talked about that. We knew if she married someone else, we would have had to dissolve them first. We'd lose Taviano as a rider at that time, there was no getting around it. No matter what, he was going to have to share information with her. If she agreed to marriage, she would know, and if she didn't, she wouldn't remember."

Nicoletta avoided Taviano's gaze. She couldn't look at any of them. It felt more than ever as if she'd trapped Taviano into marriage. Maybe it wasn't her fault, but it was still the end result—he had to marry her. He didn't marry her because he loved her, or even because he was so physically attracted to her, he couldn't do without her. He had to marry her in order to continue his career as a shadow rider.

Her stomach lurched and she pressed a hand deep. Her life was a mess. She wanted to go home to Lucia and Amo. There was unconditional love there. She felt it every time she walked through their door. She mattered to them just because she was theirs. They were like that. It wasn't because her shadow was different or that it happened to tangle with Taviano's; they just loved her.

She realized she had started to rock herself, another bad habit she had developed that she'd been working on breaking. In the course of less than an hour in the company of the Ferraro family, she'd had panic attacks twice and was now rocking herself.

"Not all partners know what we do," Stefano denied. "They don't always want to know everything."

"Nicoletta, obviously, is not one of those partners," Vittorio said. "She already realized we were capable of disappearing into the shadows. Taviano had to get to her fast when she alerted him to the danger. He took her out of harm's way, just as any of us would have done. She asked him to help get her friends free from the Demon gang members."

"All of which, until that point, seems reasonable enough. At that point, no matter what she wanted, or said, he should have taken her back to the plane or had the cousins take her ass to the safe house and sit on her until he cleaned up the mess."

Stefano made his opinion absolutely clear. There was no doubt in Nicoletta's mind that he would have done exactly that. He wouldn't have cared what she thought or felt. He would have taken her somewhere safe and forced her compliance. To him, there was no other reasonable course of action.

She flicked a quick glance at Taviano's brothers. In spite of the fact that Ricco, Giovanni and Vittorio had stood up for him, it was clear from their expressions that they agreed with Stefano. Her heart sank. When she was younger, she'd often thought of Taviano as a dictator, a man who insisted on things his way, but as she had grown up, she'd realized he was looking out for her. Now, she could see he was different from his brothers in some ways. Many ways. This was one of them, and it was going to hurt him.

Stefano's dark eyes were back on his youngest brother's face. "Why? You broke the rules of the *famiglia*, of the riders, and you must have had a compelling reason or you would never have risked everything to do so. I know you, Taviano. You love what you do. You're good at it, and you know we need you. We need every single rider we have. Our numbers are decreasing, not increasing. Tell me your reason."

There was a long silence. For the first time, Nicoletta sensed Taviano hesitate. He actually felt uncomfortable. She was very tuned to him and knew it was because they were so connected. He could read her every mood, just as she could read his, and she was the reason he was unwilling to tell his brother why he had risked everything to take her into the shadows because she'd asked him to.

She wanted to know. More than anything, Nicoletta wanted to know, but this was Taviano, and what he did was life. She took a deep breath. "I can go into the other room and give you privacy."

It hurt to make the offer, but she would do anything for him. Even this. And this hurt. They were supposed to be partners. She had sacrificed, going knowingly into a loveless marriage, when she was already so in love, which made it so much worse.

Taviano put his finger under her chin and tipped her face up to his, studying her expression. It hurt to let him see that she was trying not to show she was unhappy. One long finger slid over her cheek.

"If you can be so courageous, Nicoletta, so can I. This will be difficult for both of us. This has to do with you. If you want to, stay, but, *tesoro*, it won't be easy to hear."

She nodded because she could see it was difficult for

him. She had no idea what that meant, but at least it put them in it together. He settled back against the leather, his arm once more circling her shoulder, his fingers urging her to sit back as well. It took a moment for her to realize he was waiting for her to settle close to him before he started, so she fit herself next to him, her thigh touching his. For no reason at all, her heart began to pound. Anxiety was already setting in for both of them.

"We had the reports from the social worker as well as the investigators, which were much more thorough and detailed. I read those reports far more often than I should have. It made me crazy. When it was my watch, I would sit in Nicoletta's bedroom while she slept. She had terrible nightmares."

Taviano scrubbed his hand down his face, as if that would stop the memories from coming. Nicoletta could feel the waves of anger pouring off of him. She didn't look at the others. She'd lived through those nightmares. She didn't need to see reports. She knew firsthand what was in them.

"I'd watch her fight, hear her pleas. No one should have to suffer what she did. No one. She was mine to protect. I wasn't there for her. I couldn't do anything to help her. I watched her try to self-destruct and I knew why. I even understood. I felt so damned helpless. I still do. Who does that to a beautiful young woman? What possesses anyone to do that kind of thing to someone else?"

Nicoletta could feel Taviano shaking. There was genuine distress there. Not just anger. Real distress. She knew he was close to tears. That would kill her, if he broke down. He was so strong. So invincible. She was rising up, a powerful woman in spite of what had happened, in spite of the brutality done to her. She was becoming someone confident, someone she had been destined to be all along. Maybe different, but still strong and compassionate, a woman able to function and live her life, choose her own way. She had chosen Taviano.

She turned her head up to his and nuzzled his neck just

to show solidarity. She didn't know what else to do. She didn't want to make things worse emotionally for him, but she wanted to find some way of showing him she stood with him. She had learned to distance herself when any discussion of her step-uncles was taking place. For the most part, she had become good at that.

Nightmares persisted. She had plenty of triggers she still worked on. She didn't like discussing the details of what had happened to her, but if her counselor insisted when the nightmares got too bad, she did. This was about Taviano. She could do anything for him, and she would. He made her feel safe, and she would find a way to make him feel just as safe.

"The nightmares were so bad at times that I found myself going to the house when it wasn't my time to watch over her. I would soothe her. Sit on the side of her bed and talk to her, sometimes wake her." He cupped the side of her face, turning her head toward his. "Do you remember?"

He asked her so softly, so intimately, she didn't think anyone else could hear. Of course she could remember. She felt the tears burn behind her eyes. She knew tears burned behind his because they both had shed them. Holding each other. She'd fought him at first, and then she'd let him share those terrible times. She hadn't wanted to. She didn't want anyone to know, least of all Taviano. Beautiful, perfect, handsome Taviano.

Three men forcing themselves on her at the same time. She had told him everything, sobbing, sometimes even hitting him, punching, her body wrapped up in damp sheets, thrashing wildly, a mess. Taviano had been there night after night, and during the day she'd be so humiliated she'd snipe at him and be ugly, yet he'd come back to get her through the torment of reliving the ugliness that had been her unrelenting night.

He told his family about those nights, holding her while he did so, rocking her like he had every night. What it was like for her. For him. How it felt for her to have to know the family was aware of what had happened to her. What it was like for him to have to know he couldn't undo one single moment of her torment.

Through it all, she felt his rage, and it felt so personal, not just for her but for him as well. As if when their shadows twisted together, everything that happened had been shared, or he felt it, because he was shaking just as much as she was. There were beads of sweat on his forehead. One trickled down the side of his face she knew he was unaware of.

Taviano looked at Stefano. "She never asked for anything for herself. Not one single thing. I knew the consequences. I was willing to pay them, Stefano. Those men were the ones who wanted to take her back to what her step-uncles had done to her. They had her friends and might already be raping them. She couldn't have that in her mind. I knew that. I knew what was going on in her head. How could she not be thinking of what they'd done to her and what might be happening to her friends? When she insisted on being with me, I wanted to give that to her. I *needed* to give her that."

"More than you needed to protect her?" Stefano asked.

Nicoletta gasped. She nearly came off the couch, both hands curling into tight fists. "He *did* protect me. All the time. He didn't let me do anything at all. I wanted to do more than watch, believe me, but he refused to allow it. I sat in the shadow while he took all the risks."

Stefano pinned her with his dark eyes, clearly bent on intimidating her, which might have worked if she wasn't so angry with him for continually implying Taviano wasn't looking after her.

Taviano hid a small grin, but his eyes were laughing. "*Piccola*, he's just doing his job. I put Nicoletta's protection above all else. I was concerned with her traveling in the shadows so much. It was unprecedented for someone un-trained to go that many times, and the first couple of times were hard on her body, but she learned fast. She has an ex-tremely fast learning curve. She got better and better at it."

Stefano sat back in his chair, shaking his head. "Everything about you, Nicoletta, is unprecedented. You make this very difficult."

Nicoletta glanced around the room. It was the first time she'd forced herself to look up in a while. Taviano's family were all exchanging those small smiles again. Relief spread through her. She knew immediately they wouldn't be doing that if it wasn't going to be all right.

"Nicoletta is going to be trained, Taviano," Stefano announced. "Thoroughly trained. She won't be on rotation with you as your partner until I okay it. I don't care if she stands in front of you and cries her heart out." He paused and turned to her. "We're stepping up your training. If you thought it was tough before, think again."

She had thought it was tough before. She nodded. "I understand."

"Before anything else, you have to ask Grace and Francesca to plan your wedding immediately. Lucia, Amo and Francesca are going to be so upset that they weren't there. They deserve to see both of you walk down that aisle, and they're going to get that."

It was a decree, nothing less. If that was the price Taviano had to pay in order to remain a rider, it was clear he was willing to pay it. He gripped her hand, his finger sliding over the twin rings on her hand, the beautiful indigo diamond and the plain alloy band with the inscription in Italian: *Amore Eterno.*

Nicoletta wasn't certain how she could get through another wedding, especially with Lucia and Amo watching, not dressed in a gown she knew Lucia would want her to wear, with Taviano waiting at the end of the altar. She briefly closed her eyes and willed herself not to cry. She was too emotional.

"Are we finished? Is everything all right? I thought I could go home and you all could plan the war or whatever. I want to spend time with Lucia and Amo."

There was a small silence. She hadn't meant for anyone

else to hear her, but it was evident they had. Taviano brought her left hand up to his mouth and he kissed her wedding rings. "Lucia and Amo have been taken to a safe house, *tesoro*, just in case Valdez gets someone into our territory without our knowledge. It's highly unlikely, but it could happen. We want them safe. Grace and Francesca will consult with Lucia to make certain to incorporate whatever she prefers into the wedding details along with whatever you want."

"I want to talk to Lucia." Nicoletta found herself glaring at Stefano, as if he were personally keeping Lucia and Amo from her. She felt that streak of stubbornness that had always benefited her when she needed it most rising swiftly. It was what had kept her alive in the worst of circumstances. She refused to give in. Refused to give up.

Taviano handed her his cell phone. "She's programmed in. She wants to talk to you as well. She's close by, so we can visit with her when we know exactly what we're up against." He looked up at Stefano. "Have any of the cousins reported in?"

Nicoletta took the cell phone, feeling silly. She didn't know why she'd reacted the way she had to Stefano, only that she didn't want another wedding. She really didn't. She couldn't say that, not to any of them. How could she explain it? That she loved Taviano, but he didn't love her the same way? That she was ashamed that he had to marry her, and she felt she was taking advantage of him? That she wasn't good enough for him? There it was in a nutshell. The real reason.

She didn't want to walk down that aisle, most likely in a church, wearing a pristine white wedding dress, feeling like she was covered in slime knowing the man waiting for her didn't really love her and never would. He would see her always as the woman who had trapped him with her shadow.

It would be hell for her after seeing the way Stefano adored Francesca, and Ricco, his beloved Mariko. Giovanni clearly loved Sasha, and Vittorio never took his eyes off of Grace when she was near him. Taviano would be the only one of the Ferraro brothers trapped in a loveless marriage. He'd told her that if they hadn't found the one person on their own they wanted to marry who could provide shadow rider children, a marriage would be arranged for them. Nicoletta knew, for Taviano, she was that woman. Eloisa and Stefano hadn't arranged the marriage, but their shadows had.

She tuned out the discussions of their cousins reporting on the Demons gang activities and looked down at the phone in her hand. Lucia's name was right there. Her thumb slid across it, and her heart jumped. Suddenly the need to hear her voice was overwhelming, and a lump rose in her throat. She didn't want to be in this room with these men and Emmanuelle. She wanted to be home with Lucia and Amo, where she didn't feel so inept and imperfect.

"Excuse me. I'll just go into the other room and make this call," she murmured and stood up.

The moment she rose, Taviano did as well. His brothers did, too. Her heart nearly stopped. She wasn't certain why they all stood up, and for a moment she thought they might be trying to prevent her from leaving.

Taviano gestured toward the door. "You know your way around the apartment. The sitting room is empty. You'll have complete privacy there, *piccola*."

She couldn't answer him. She just nodded and tried a smile, but she was all out of them. Her facial muscles refused to cooperate. It seemed as if, since they'd been in the chapel, Demetrio and Drago as their witnesses, she was all smiled out. She had barely spoken to Taviano once she'd actually signed the papers tying them together.

When the official had asked her if she took Taviano as her husband, she'd stopped, looked Taviano in the eyes and asked him if he really wanted to do this. He'd said yes. Very firmly. She'd agreed to marry him. Then again, before signing, she'd asked him. Taviano had been extremely resolved, certain they were doing the right thing, so she signed the papers, but not before reminding him he hadn't had her sign a prenup. She needed to tell Stefano to have their lawyer make one out immediately.

With shaking hands, she pushed open the door to the sitting room and took a deep breath of the clean, fresh air. Francesca had a way of making everything in the penthouse feel homey and welcoming. More, there was always a faint, elusive scent that was barely there, but it made its way through the house so it smelled of clean air after a rainstorm. She looked around at the warm room with the plush, inviting chairs. She'd been in here many times, entertaining Crispino. She'd played on the floor with him, on that thick rug that covered the warm wood floor. Nicoletta curled up in one of the chairs and wrapped a throw blanket around herself when she realized she was shivering.

She hadn't gone into the plane's bedroom after their wedding, suddenly too afraid to sleep in the same bed with Taviano. She'd never been afraid or nervous around him. Never. She'd slept in the same bed with him countless times, because it had never really occurred to her when she was a young teen that he was at all interested. He'd never acted it. He'd rocked her to sleep after a storm of tears or terrible nightmares.

Now, everything had changed. They were married. She didn't want to be alone with him. She was terrified he would want her physically and equally terrified that he wouldn't. She made no sense, none. She knew she was bordering on psychotic behavior, and she needed Lucia. She wished she had someone else she could trust to talk to, but even friends like Pia, Bianca and Clariss were not ones she would ever talk about her past—or about Taviano—with.

She drew her legs under her and made herself very small as she pressed Lucia's name and watched her lifeline video call the one person who she knew loved her unconditionally—who loved her generously. When Lucia's face came up on the screen, Nicoletta saw her through a haze of tears. She reached out to touch her face.

"You're so beautiful, Lucia. I can't tell you how much I

love you and Amo. I'm so sorry for all of this. I hate being away from you. I hate it so much."

"Nicoletta, baby, why are you crying? Tell me what's wrong. I can have Stefano bring me to you right now, or you to me. Are you hurt?"

Nicoletta could hear the true anxiety in Lucia's voice. It was never about herself, always about the other person. That was Lucia. She cared deeply about her friends and family. Nicoletta had learned so much from her in such a short time and wanted to be like her. She wanted so much more time with her.

"I'm not hurt. Taviano was with me. He took great care to make certain all of us were safe. Pia, Bianca and Clariss are with his cousins in LA. I think the Ferraros flew in their parents to make certain they were safe as well. I just don't like being away from you."

"Is Stefano bringing you here?"

Nicoletta cleared her throat. "There was a little complication, Lucia. I don't really understand it, but Taviano insisted that we needed to do it, and I went along with it. Now, I think I was just scared and maybe I don't know . . ." She trailed off, and a fresh batch of tears flooded her eyes and spilled over again. "I'm sorry. I don't know why I can't stop."

"I'm going to have Amo call Stefano, honey. He can send a car for me. If you're not in danger where you are, then it should be safe enough for me. Otherwise, he should have brought you here immediately." Lucia was very firm.

Nicoletta shook her head. "Don't do that." She dashed at the tears running down her face. "I married him. Taviano. We're married. I'm sorry, I wanted you there. We're planning a big wedding here. I mean, Grace and Francesca and you are supposed to plan it, but we're secretly married. That's the complication. The thing is, Lucia, he doesn't love me. I don't know why I said yes, when I knew he didn't love me. I shouldn't have. I love him. I always have, you know that. I shouldn't have said yes. I knew better. It wasn't right. I don't know what I'm going to do."

She was wailing. Crying like a baby. She *never* did that. She wanted to run. She ran all the time now, but this time she just wanted to run the streets up and down for hours until the chaos in her head subsided and the heartache went away.

"*Cuore mia*, take a deep breath. Taviano Ferraro does not do anything he does not want to do. It is impossible not to love you. You are still having a difficult time learning to love yourself, so you don't always believe others can love you. You have given Amo and me our lives back. Our hearts when they were torn out of us. You have become our heart. Stop crying, my little love. Just breathe. When was the last time you went to sleep?"

"I don't know," Nicoletta answered honestly. "I just want to come home to you. I want to feel safe."

"Don't you feel safe with Taviano? You always told me you felt safest when he was around."

"I'm just so confused right now, Lucia. I don't know what I'm doing. I don't know what's right or wrong. I feel like I put everyone I love in jeopardy, maybe the entire neighborhood. This gang has no hesitation in killing people. Men. Women. Children. They don't care. I don't know what to do."

"What you do is trust in those you've always trusted in, Nicoletta. Nothing has changed. Taviano is still the same man. I'm still your mother. Amo is still your father. The Ferraros have always claimed you as family, and they will be even more adamant than ever. This is *your* neighborhood. Even Eloisa, as mean as she can be, will stand with you because you belong here. Not one single thing has changed. You put your trust in that. You put your trust in the Ferraros. In Taviano. In me and in Amo. We won't ever let you down."

Nicoletta wanted to hold her and hug her so hard. She had come to Lucia only three years earlier a mess, a complete mess. Lucia had loved her through the worst of times. Nicoletta knew that no matter what, Lucia would stand with her. She did trust her advice—How could she not?—but Lucia couldn't understand about Taviano's reasons for marrying her, and that she couldn't reveal to her. As much as she loved Lucia, that was a Ferraro family secret, and she couldn't share—not even with the woman she called her mother.

"I'm fairly certain Benito Valdez, the president of the Demons, who is the one causing all the problems, hasn't made his move to come here yet, Lucia, and I can get Taviano to bring me out there. I can stay with you until things really start heating up, and then I'll come back and see what I can do to help."

"Do you think that's wise? Shouldn't you stay with your husband?"

"Don't call him that," she objected immediately just as Taviano slipped through the door.

His eyebrow shot up. He walked across the floor, not even making a whisper of a sound, took the phone out of her hand and grinned at Lucia. "She should stay with her husband." He winked at Lucia. "How's my second-favorite woman in the world?"

"I've been downgraded, I see."

"It is true, but only one small degree." He laid a hand over his heart. "You will always have a piece of my heart."

"I will concede," Lucia said, and blew kisses to him. "I love you, Nicoletta. I will see you soon. Take care of each other."

"Wait." Nicoletta nearly leapt off the chair. She got tangled up in the blanket as Lucia hit the disconnect button. "Damn it. Don't let her go. I have to talk to her." She knew she sounded desperate, but it was because she didn't want to be alone with Taviano. She couldn't be alone with him. "Can you just drive me to wherever she is? That would just be better. I can stay there."

"No, *tesoro*, you can't stay there. You're coming home with me. What kind of message does it send to the family if my new wife runs home to her mother the first night of our marriage?"

"Taviano."

"Nicoletta."

She sighed. "I'm really tired."

"Then let's go home."

"I have to remind Stefano to talk to the family lawyer about a prenup. You didn't have me sign one, Taviano. That could be a really big problem."

He caught her hand and hauled her out of the chair when she'd withdrawn back into it, almost like a turtle. Wrapping his arm around her waist, he pulled her tight against his side. "First, there is no divorce. I went over the terms and I was very clear on that, so there's no need for a prenup. Second, if you did leave me, you wouldn't remember you were ever married to me no matter how many people pointed it out to you."

"Great," she muttered. "Sounds great to me. You're going to be sorry. I'm good at spending money."

"You're lousy at spending money, Nicoletta. I know everything there is to know about you, and you don't spend anything. Every penny you earned working you turned over to Lucia—which, by the way, she put in the bank for you. You didn't even buy new clothes."

"Because Lucia insists on giving me clothes all the time."

They were at the elevator. Taviano waved to his brothers and Emmanuelle, and Nicoletta lifted her hand, acknowledging them. She wasn't certain just what to say or what had been accomplished in their meeting.

"She loves to give you things." They stepped inside and the doors closed, leaving them alone once again.

CHAPTER SEVEN

Taviano's home was a modern estate built in the hills overlooking the city. Like his brothers, he owned several homes, but he didn't bother to mention that to Nicoletta, knowing it would just freak her out more than she already was. He hadn't told her the ring on her finger, the one she continually turned back and forth and clearly loved, was worth a small fortune and then some, because she would have taken it off and never put it on again. Some things were just better left unsaid as far as he was concerned.

She'd been acting strange ever since Vegas. Clearly, she was afraid of being alone with him. He hadn't expected that. It had occurred to him, as it had to Stefano, that she might have problems when Stefano demanded a family meeting of the riders, with all the brothers in the close confines of one room. He thought he was completely tuned to her, ready after years of waiting for her to grow up, but now, he realized, even without the terrible trauma she'd endured, he didn't know everything there was to know about her.

Nicoletta slid out of the car the moment it pulled up to the house, not waiting for him or the bodyguards to get there first. He was going to have to talk to her about that, but since he was certain it was safe, he let it go. She had her head tipped back and was looking up, as did most people when first encountering the architecture. He had as well.

He had found the estate while looking for land; he had wanted acreage, not necessarily for an actual house. He had houses. He wanted land he could surround himself with, to give himself a little bit of a buffer from the rest of the world when he needed it, especially there in their chosen hometown. The family loved Chicago. They loved their neighborhood and the people in it, but sometimes, especially after they had to pore over the reports of a particularly ugly investigation and learn every aspect of those involved and then serve justice, retreating to somewhere peaceful was imperative.

He watched her face, needing to see if she loved his home the way he did. It would be her home, theirs—where they would raise their children. He had studied the layout carefully before purchasing the property, making certain, as Stefano had drilled into all of them, that if they did have families, they could protect their wives and children from any harm from every direction. He had done just that.

There had been a long-standing feud hundreds of years earlier in Sicily between the Ferraro family and the Saldi family. In the territory where both families resided, the Saldis were the unspoken leaders and the ruling crime family. In spite of the fact that they always had an uneasy truce, the Saldi family had asked the Ferraro family to merge with them, and the Ferraro family had refused.

The Saldis often aided the people in the territory against the crimes committed on them by the local government, but then the price could be bloody or steep and the Ferraros would aid them. The Saldis didn't like the interference. When the invitation to join forces was refused, the Saldis sent their soldiers to kill every man, woman and child in the Ferraro family. Only a few escaped, going "underground." They fled the country, disappearing into other countries around the world. Those who managed to escape were mainly shadow riders. They vowed such a thing would never happen to any family member again, and rules were put into place and they began to grow in numbers. As they did, the Ferraros grew even more vigilant.

He watched as Nicoletta stood in the drive, hands on her hips, looking up at the high-pitched roof that was much more than a roof. The entire covering of the house was really an art piece and a fortress at the same time. The architect had built the rooftop to be a lookout, a place he could go to see the city and the surrounding hillsides from every direction.

The owner could set his high-powered telescope up to study the stars, something one couldn't do in Chicago. He could land his helicopter right on the center of the roof when he needed to, yet the landing place was invisible from nearly every conceivable direction. That was what had given Taviano the idea to have the rooftop be more than the art piece the architect had designed it to be.

There were gables and cathedral ceilings, dormers and rounded turrets that rose into the sky like towers on each corner of the house, giving it the appearance of a castle. Those turrets effectively gave him places of cover when he might need them if he had to defend his home with a rifle. He had lights to shine around the yard to cast shadows in every direction, to give his family ways to disappear should they need it.

Nicoletta turned and looked at him and then back at the house. He walked up to her, standing close, but didn't make the mistake of touching her.

"You live here? You bought this place?"

"I thought it was beautiful. I was looking for somewhere peaceful and wanted land. I didn't expect the house. The roof alone intrigued me. Up there, at night, you can see the stars and they go on forever. You can't see them in the city because the lights are too bright. Out here, there aren't any lights. I bought up as much land as possible around me, just as Vittorio did. He actually was the one who gave me the idea. He can see the stars. I wanted to be able to do it as well. I've got an amazing telescope."

He loved the telescope he had and hoped Nicoletta would become as passionate about stargazing as he was. He often went onto the roof and just spent time studying the various constellations. He particularly liked to look for new galaxies. That was one of the things he thought would intrigue Nicoletta and maybe help bind her closer to him. For now, it was the house he was counting on—the house and the surrounding woods. He hoped they would have the same effect on her they had on him—bringing her peace.

He waited, not pushing her to go inside. Vines crept up trellises and reached toward the closest bushes so that it was impossible to tell where the actual start of the plants surrounding most of the house was. The plants crept back toward the woods and then into the trees so that flowers adorned the trunks as if they were in a jungle setting. The original owner had managed to create a space close to the house that simulated a rain forest. Taviano knew that that alone was worth the price the man had asked. Looking at Nicoletta's face, he knew he would have paid ten times the amount.

"This is so beautiful. Does that path continue all the way through?"

"Yes." He'd walked it dozens of times. At first he'd wanted to make certain he could escape if an enemy came for him, and then he'd discovered that the woods were alive with wildlife and birds. The sounds they made calling back and forth to one another soothed him almost as much as or maybe even more than the classical music he listened to when his mind was in complete chaos from rereading those vile reports on Nicoletta.

She turned her face up to his and for the first time since Vegas, there was a hint of real joy there. "It's so incredible,

Taviano. I can't believe this place really exists. I would love to show it to Lucia and Amo someday."

"I imagine they'll be here often, *tesoro*. In fact, there is a guesthouse. It is possible they might want to move closer when they get a little older. That way we can look after them. We won't put it to them that way, of course. We will find a way that shows them we really need them close to us. I've given it quite a lot of thought, and I think they'd like living here."

Her dark eyes drifted slowly over his face. It was impossible to tell what she was thinking, when before she'd always been such an open book to him. He let her look her fill. He wasn't going to apologize for worrying about Amo and Lucia. His entire family was concerned for them. Stefano and their oldest son, Cencio, had been friends and served together in the military. Stefano was close to Cencio's parents, and when their son had been murdered, he had taken them personally under the protection of the family. That hadn't been a hardship, since every single member loved them.

"I appreciate that you think about their welfare, Taviano," Nicoletta said. "I love them very much, and I can tell that time is wearing a bit on them. I've been a little worried myself. I've been trying to learn the business so I can take it over for them and run it. I don't know what they have in the way of retirement . . ."

"They have always been considered *famiglia*, but now, they are even more so, if that is possible. I think if we have them close to us, neither of us will worry."

He could see the relief on her face right before she turned away from him to look once more toward the woods and the narrow path leading into the darkened interior.

"They'll love it here, Taviano."

She took a deep breath and walked toward the front door. There was reluctance in every step, so that by the time she made it up onto the wraparound porch, with the columns and turrets at the corners, she was no longer looking up at the house but down at the artwork on the flooring the previous owner had built into the entryway.

"I think they'll love living here as well. We're just far enough away from the city that when we're on the roof we can see the stars. No one can do that. It's a miracle. Lucia and especially Amo will love going up and viewing the stars that way even if they can only see them through the telescope."

He reached past her and opened the heavy front door, crowding her just a little with his taller body so that she stepped into the cool foyer.

"Is it easy to access the roof? I noticed that Amo is having a difficult time lately climbing stairs. Even just the three back stairs from the alley entrance. He's far slower, although he always plays it off like it's no big deal. I try to carry the heavier boxes for him, but that just upsets him more, so I make sure the car is pulled up very close to the stairs and try to shove them up onto the platform so he doesn't have to actually carry them up the stairs themselves."

He wished he'd gotten her talking about her foster parents earlier. She never seemed to notice what was happening around her when she did that. The foyer had opened into the much more spacious front room. If he hadn't been sold on the acreage and rooftop, he would have immediately been sold on that room alone. The high ceiling was pure art form, with the carved galaxy chiseled so elegantly into the white-blue marble that one had to look several times to notice the entire universe mapped out overhead in all its splendor. The universe spread across the huge milky-blue ceiling, culminating at the top into what appeared to be a round circular "knot" but was really a door that opened onto the roof. His house was that great.

He kept his gaze on Nicoletta's face and his fingers threaded through hers, wanting to keep her moving. It was late and they were both tired. She could get the big tour the next day, but tonight he wanted to establish that they'd both be sleeping in the master bedroom. It wasn't going to be the easiest thing to do, not when she was so skittish, and he knew what she was the most worried about—with good reason.

"There's an elevator to the roof that Amo and Lucia can take," he assured her. "I'm glad you mentioned that he was beginning to have problems. I'll keep a closer eye on it and tell the others to watch out for him as well. He has a lot of pride."

For the first time, he saw a genuine smile reach her eyes. "All of you men do. I think there's something in the drinking water."

He flashed an answering grin. "I guess I can't argue with that."

"We're walking too fast, and you're not letting me look at anything."

"You can look tomorrow. It's late, and we both need sleep. If you don't, I do. My arm is hurting like a son of a bitch." It wouldn't hurt to remind her he'd been shot and was in no shape to jump her—although that wouldn't stop him for a second if she gave him the go-ahead, which wasn't likely.

The hallway was wide. He liked open space, and the house gave him that. The master bedroom was its own suite. He could just live there and be happy. The hallway ended at the wide double doors. Nicoletta stood staring at them without saying a single word. There were dim night-lights spilling shadows from sconces above their heads and decorating the halls with familiar tubes that called to him, but he kept his eyes on his reluctant little bride.

"Nicoletta." He said her name softly and just waited. Breathing in and out. Willing her to turn and face him. Willing her to breathe with him when he could feel the tension in her rising all over again.

She stood staring at the double doors and then looking down at the beautiful stonework in the floor before she finally turned around, her long lashes fluttering before she lifted them to look at him with her astonishing dark eyes.

"I'm still the same man I was when I first got on the plane with you. Nothing has changed since then. What are you afraid of?" He asked the question as gently as he knew how. She wasn't just afraid, she was terrified, and Nicoletta terrified could be anything—a runaway, or just plain lethal.

Those long lashes fluttered again, and along with them, his stomach muscles did the same. She didn't look away. She might be terrified, but she had courage and she stood her ground, just the way Emmanuelle would have done. His heart nearly broke for her. She was magnificent. Beautiful. Tragically so. It was all he could do not to sweep her into his arms and hold her to him. Her chin lifted a little defiantly.

"That's not true, Taviano. You tied yourself to me. You married me."

He wasn't certain what the big deal was. "We've always been tied together. You knew that. You've always known it. I sat on your bed every night for three years, *piccola*. I held you when you cried. I listened to the horror of what those bastards did to you, and I let you use me as a punching bag when you needed to. I rocked you when you couldn't sleep. We've been tied together for years, Nicoletta."

He waited a heartbeat. "Even after, even when we didn't talk because we both knew what was between us, we were tied together these last two years. You felt it. Don't tell me that you didn't."

Color swept into her face, but she didn't look away. "I detest that you know what those men did to me. I really do. I've come to a place of acceptance, I think, at least I'm getting there, but I still hate that you know all the details. It makes it difficult to look you in the eye, or to think about ever . . ." She trailed off, clearly embarrassed to bring up the real reason she was so upset with being alone with him now.

Sex. He'd never pushed his needs or desires on her. He wanted her with every breath he took, but he was careful not to ever make it a thing with her. His need of Nicoletta wasn't just sex, and it never would be. He could wait until it developed naturally with her, and he was confident it would. She might be afraid it wouldn't happen because she was so traumatized, but she was attracted to him, and she wanted him with the same urgency. She just got spooked when it came down to it. He was determined to be patient.

He'd talked to some of the best rape counselors in the world on what to do and how to handle the situation between his woman and him. The answer was always the same: *She* needed to handle it. She needed to set the pace. She needed to feel in control, and he had to let her. That was a hard one for him, when he needed to feel that same control, but he loved her that much to give it to her. Where and when that had begun, Taviano wasn't certain, but the emotion had grown until it was so strong, he knew his path was locked with hers.

"We'll have sex when you're ready for it, Nicoletta," he assured her. "There's no hurry. We're still back on step one. Let's get comfortable with each other and remember we're best friends—"

She shook her head. "You never give me anything of yourself, Taviano. Nothing. You know everything there is to know about me, the worst things one human can know about another human, but you don't ever give me back anything that would make me feel as if I was special to you, a part of you."

Everything in him stilled. Came to a complete halt. His heart even seemed to cease beating. He had always known this moment would come. There couldn't be the two of them without it, yet it could tear them apart as surely as it had torn apart his family. He couldn't look at her. There was no meeting her eyes any more than he could meet his own eyes in the mirror in the morning when he got up. He couldn't look at his mother when she walked into a room, and he had never looked at his father. Never. Now everything in his life came down to this one moment. This heartbeat of time.

If he gave her the truth of himself, shared his past with her as she had shared hers, would she give him the same acceptance or reject him the way his parents had rejected him? He couldn't lose her. He couldn't lose riding the shadows, it was all he had. He was a rider. That was who he was . . .

He ducked his head and stared at the toe of his immaculate shoes, breathing deeply, trying not to think that she could be in any way like his mother. Trying not to believe that his Nicoletta could in any way be like Eloisa or Phillip. Still, if he didn't choose to give himself to Nicoletta, share who he was, what he was, any part of the real truth behind the man who was Taviano Ferraro, then what he had with her would never be more than a sham. He didn't want that with her, and she was far too astute to believe any lie he came up with.

Cursing in his native language, Taviano reached past Nicoletta, fingers settling around the doors to push them open, his taller body forcing her smaller one to step inside the master bedroom. He was more aggressive with her than he'd ever been. He felt aggressive. Belligerent. Angry. Fearful. So many emotions. But then he'd been feeling them ever since Stefano had demanded to know why he'd allowed Nicoletta into the shadows with him.

"You want to know about me? Something no one else knows? Not Stefano? Not my brothers or Emme? Only my lovely mother, Eloisa? Or my now-dead, loving father? Do you want to know how she chose her husband and riding shadows over her son and his mental and physical well-being? Do you want to know what my father had to say about his own son?"

With every word his heart pounded and his chest hurt. Adrenaline poured into his body until he was shaking so hard he could barely control himself, when he was all about control. He suddenly couldn't breathe. He slammed the doors closed with the flats of his hands and strode past her through the bedroom, straight to the bar.

With trembling hands, he reached for the bottle of Scotch. Hell, he didn't need a glass. Nicoletta's hand got there first. She took the bottle from him and set it back on the bar.

"Don't tell me, Taviano. If it hurts that much, you don't need to share it. I understand what pain and humiliation are. I know what letting someone see the worst of your shame is. It isn't worth you drinking, not to me."

He caught both of her upper arms and dragged her close, looking down into her upturned face. She was fearless, looking back at him, her eyes wide. She met his gaze without flinching, no matter that he deliberately let her see the unrelenting fury that burned like a raging volcano, deep and wild, ready to explode.

She ignored the rage in him, the fact that everyone knew the famous temper the Ferraro brothers shared and that she was alone in a house far away from everyone else with him.

Nicoletta laid her palm gently against his rough jaw. "You can tell me something humorous about yourself. Something everyone but me knows, Taviano. It doesn't have to be a secret you don't want to share."

If she didn't have his heart already, he would have surrendered it right then and there. He pulled her in tight against him. "This is our home, Nicoletta. I want you to love it, so if you want to change anything about it, feel free to do so. I'll get your name on the accounts tomorrow morning. That way, if you want to go furniture shopping, or anything else, you can immediately."

He kept holding her, knowing he was going to tell her there in their bedroom, the place they would sleep together. He looked over her head toward the long row of glass that looked out toward the woods, where there was a riot of green even in the dark. The various shades shimmered in the faint lights created by the custom night-bulbs coming off the eaves from the roof. Each light was dim and cast multiple shadows depending on the angle. It had taken years for one of his very talented relations from one of the other branches of Ferraros to develop those bulbs.

"And you're going to be the only person I tell my secrets to. I'm not big on sharing." He whispered that truth into her ear, hoping she understood that the things he told her, he wanted kept between them.

Nicoletta stepped back and he reluctantly released his hold on her, feeling as if he were giving up his lifeline. She'd thought he'd been hers. All along, she'd been his. She tipped back her head and looked up at him. She understood. He saw more than understanding in her eyes. Compassion. That look that he'd seen so many times for others.

She'd never understood that he'd watched her closely. The Ferraros protected her because she was capable of producing rider children. That meant she was guarded carefully as the treasure she was. If she wasn't for him, or one of his cousins, they would have put out the word and other riders would have come to meet her, hoping they would connect with her. As it was, Taviano knew he had been the reason their shadows had tangled together so quickly.

He had taken his shifts protecting her like the other family members, but in watching her, he had paid particular attention to how she treated others. That was very important to him. Even when she first came as a foster teen, a wild, angry, hurt and humiliated young woman, she had been so careful with Lucia and Amo. She'd responded to them almost immediately and was never disrespectful to them. He watched her help them in the store and work hours to help take the load off of them. She pitched in to clean and even cook. She spent time with Lucia in her favorite tea garden and helped her pull weeds around her koi pond.

Nicoletta never failed to be polite to others, but more than that, she was genuinely good to children in the parks, stopping to help them if they needed it. He saw her tie shoes, push children on swings, brush away tears, sort out problems and help them with whatever was needed. Little boys and little girls flocked to her.

She read books to children and often watched them, giving young mothers or single fathers a much-needed break while she ate her lunch in the park. She developed a regular grocery program for the elderly in the community fairly quickly, checking with them before shopping for Lucia and Amo. One neighbor had turned into two and then four. At last count, there were sixteen elderly couples or single men and women living in the neighborhood she checked with before going to the grocery store. And she was always patient.

She often picked up dinners for various people at odd hours. Mostly it was single mothers, but sometimes, again, it was the elderly. She even cooked meals at their homes. She never talked about doing it for them. Not to anyone. Lucia hadn't known until one of her friends accidentally let it slip. She'd been sworn to silence.

The look on her face when Francesca had put Crispino into Nicoletta's arms for the first time had been enough for him. She'd looked as if she'd totally fallen in love with the little boy, so spellbound by him. He wanted her to look at their child like that. He wanted her for his wife and the mother of his children. He wanted the kind of compassion she showed for the neighborhood elderly and single parents to extend to those they knew, no matter their circumstances. He had looked for that trait in a wife his entire life, as long as he could remember, and she'd turned up in a ratty little apartment in the worst of circumstances, and now he was taking a chance on losing everything.

"The things you—or your family, for that matter—tell me, I would never share with anyone else. It isn't their business, but you in particular. You're my . . ." She trailed off and looked around the room, as if that might give her an answer as to who he might be to her.

"Husband," he supplied. In spite of the churning in his gut and the bile in his throat, he couldn't help the small amount of amusement rising. "I'm your husband." He took her hand and rubbed his thumb over her ring. "If nothing else, this should help you remember."

She pulled her hand away and glared at him. "I remember. There's nothing wrong with my memory. Where are you sleeping? Because I'm going to throw myself on the bed, and as soon as I do, I'm going to sleep."

She wouldn't be, he could almost guarantee that, although maybe that would be a good thing. If he stalled long enough, they'd both fall asleep and the moment would pass. She was giving him every out. If he took it, there would be no going back, and their relationship would never be what he wanted or what either of them needed.

"The master bath is through those doors."

The doors were glass, and once opened, revealed the enormous two-person double sink with a marble top and gold faucets. A deep Jacuzzi tub dominated the side of the room facing the woods, along with the wide double shower and the rows of various showerheads.

"Who lives like this, Taviano? There are so many dials and things, I couldn't possibly figure out how to use the shower," Nicoletta said.

"I'll show you." She made him want to laugh. The way she glared at him like it was all his fault that the man who constructed the house had built it as if with Taviano in mind. "But not tonight. You've had a shower. You can just brush your teeth and hop into bed. Your clothes are already in the drawers and closet. Emmanuelle and Lucia added more."

Before she could protest, he added one of the best reasons she couldn't protest. "As riders, we have to wear certain fabrics. All of your clothes are best constructed in those materials. You can't just get them off the street. My family makes them specifically for riders."

"Right, okay, that makes sense."

He heard the relief in her voice. He turned to the door to the left of the double sink. "This leads to my closet. The right door is yours." He didn't look at her face as he opened the door and walked into the enormous room that opened up even more as he walked inside. One could fit a small apartment in the closet. He didn't look back to see what she was doing. He was damned tired, and he needed to pull himself together. Too long in her company was wreaking havoc on his body, and now, the emotional overload was adding to his fatigue.

Coming out of the shadows always brought on a rush of sexual urgency. It was hot and it was powerful. Having Nicoletta right there only added to the immediate need he had fought off for hours. The pain in his arm had been pushed back, and now it came rushing to the forefront, just to add to the fact that tonight was officially going to be a bitch of a night.

He didn't like to sleep in clothes. He was a restless sleeper and he often got up and walked around the house in the dark and then went back to sleep. For Nicoletta's modesty he pulled on a pair of loose-fitting drawstring silk pants that were designed to slip into the shadows if need be. There was never a time that the attack on their family was forgotten, and the riders were provided with every type of clothing to get them into the shadows under any circumstances no matter where they were should they be attacked.

When he walked out of the closet to the double sink, Nicoletta was already back, brushing her teeth, her hair in a messy knot on top of her head, the way she often wore it before braiding it to go to bed. She wore a little pair of boy shorts and a short tank by one of the newer designers. It was sexy chic, and on Nicoletta, Taviano had to admit it worked. The material was thin and nearly transparent, an ombre effect that started light and ended in a darker color at the bottom, just at the end of the short little shirt.

He tried not to stare, but it was nearly impossible to keep his gaze from returning to her breasts as she bent toward the sink.

She rinsed her mouth out and glared at him, her gaze jumping to his chest and then remaining there, her lips forming that rounded O he liked to see, which gave him a few fantasies of his own. She waited until he finished brushing and rinsing before she turned her back on him and marched to the bed, flipping back the covers.

"Where are you sleeping, Taviano?"

"Right there in that bed beside you, Nicoletta. And don't get weird on me. We've slept together before. This is the master bedroom, and this is where we're both going to sleep." Decisively, he pulled back the covers on the opposite side of the room from her.

She paused in the act of getting into the bed. "It isn't the same and you know it. You weren't . . ." She trailed off again and pointed to his chest. "And I wasn't . . ." She made some ridiculous circle with her fingers that seemed to encompass her sexy little supposed-to-be-non-sexy lingerie.

He burst out laughing. "Use your words, *tesoro*. I usually can interpret, but this time, I'm failing."

Nicoletta sat back on the edge of the bed and laughed with him. "I think I'm so tired there aren't any words. You took off your shirt. It's kind of distracting."

"Since I'm your husband, I'll take that as a compliment. Slide into bed and stop being afraid. I told you, you're very safe with me. You've always been safe with me."

An expression slipped across her face and was gone before he could fully capture it, although he had a photographic memory and knew he would be able to pull it back up later and study it in detail. She'd looked almost sad instead of reassured.

"Just don't use the word *husband* anymore. Let's go to sleep and we'll call it good until tomorrow. Too much happened, and we can leave it all until we both get a good night's sleep."

He waited until she slid under the covers, and then he slipped under them as well. Thankfully, she'd turned to face the long bank of glass that showed the woods just outside, extending branches with leaves and vines twisting and waving in the slight breeze. He fit his body around hers, one arm around her waist, locking her close to him. She had curled up, drawing up her legs, making herself small the way she did. He was used to her doing that; she had for as long as he'd known her.

Taviano was much taller than Nicoletta was, and he pressed his hips tight against her bottom, expecting her to protest. She must have felt the tremor that ran through his body, because for once she didn't object to his very close proximity. She didn't turn, nor did she stiffen. She stayed very still. He kept his head above hers, staring out at the trees as they swayed slightly, dancing just that little.

"Young riders are traditionally sent out to other countries to train around the age of fourteen. There is a family in France, the Archambault family, you know Elie, and it's a big deal to get an invitation to train with them if you're under twenty. Stefano was invited numerous times but he had turned them down because he watched over us. When I was nine, he was invited again, and that time, he decided to go. My other brothers were all out of the country and Emmanuelle was with our aunt in New York. I was the only one left here, so Stefano thought it was okay to leave. I told him I would be fine. I knew how to cook for myself. Eloisa and Phillip were never around anyway, and I'd be all right."

Taviano paused for a moment, rubbing his chin on top of her head, the shadow along his jaw catching in her silky hair, tying them together just as their shadows did.

"This family in Italy that we knew said they would train me, and Eloisa and Phillip wanted me to go. That way all of us would be gone at the same time. Stefano didn't want me to be sent out so young, but they insisted. Stefano knew the family in Italy. He had trained there as well, so he agreed and he went to France. I spent three months in Italy with them and then I was supposed to come home, that was the deal Eloisa and Phillip had with Stefano, but apparently when the time was up, my parents didn't want me back, and Stefano wasn't home."

He couldn't help the rage building in him from transferring to the grip he had on her, and he had to make an effort to relax his hold. Adrenaline gave him the shakes, and he needed to jump up and pace almost as much as he needed to hold on to her, afraid she would desert him the moment she knew the truth.

"Eloisa and Phillip made some deal with another family of riders, two cousins, not very well known, the only two left from that particular family. They were older, two men in their forties. All the other families had students. No one investigated them. I was sent directly from the Italian family to them, and I know they weren't investigated because the family was reluctant to send me and asked Eloisa and Phillip twice if they were certain. They said no one ever used that family anymore."

Nicoletta started to turn her head, but he couldn't look at her, so he pushed his face into her shoulder, forcing her to stay still. She pushed her body back against his, almost as if she knew what he was going to say.

"I was with them for three months. It was the longest three months of my life." He rubbed his face against the back of her head, her hair once again tangling in the rough stubble along his jaw. "It wasn't as long as you were with those assholes that you were given to by the state, Nicoletta, but it seemed forever to me. I don't know how you did it. I had my tenth birthday while I was there, and it was a nightmare. I've hated birthday celebrations ever since."

Her hand slid over his, the one locked around her waist. She pressed her palm tightly over his and then her head bent toward her other hand, and her mouth came down over her palm, her teeth biting down as if to keep from screaming for both of them.

"I was afraid they would kill me before I could get back to my family. They threatened to kill me if I told anyone. I think they were going to arrange an accident, but then Eloisa showed up to take me back. Stefano had come home, and he was furious. I told Eloisa everything on the plane ride home."

Abruptly, he stopped speaking. He couldn't find his voice. He was that scared, hurt ten-year-old boy all over again, when he had closed that door and thought it would remain closed so many times over the years.

"What did she do? She must have been so angry." Nicoletta's voice was muffled. It sounded as if she was crying.

"She looked at me so coldly. I thought maybe she was frozen. Like ice. I kept thinking that. That she was ice inside, and I wished I was ice inside. I wanted her to put her arms around me, but I knew she wouldn't. She just stared at me. And then she told me we had to talk to Phillip first, before anyone else."

"Phillip? Your father?"

"Stefano is my brother. He might be older than me, but he's still my brother, and at that time, Eloisa was the head of the Ferraro family. What she said went. Phillip was a rider, but he didn't like it. He didn't train the way he should have, and he didn't ever go into the rotations to work as a shadow rider. Eloisa was the respected rider. She didn't say another word to me until we reached Chicago and Phillip met us at the house."

Again, Taviano had to pause. He tried not to think or feel like that ten-year-old boy. He'd seen the distaste in his father's eyes. The utter repugnance. "My father never looked at me after that day. He told Eloisa that if she made it public that his son had allowed two forty-year-old men to play with him for months, he wouldn't stick around. It was bad enough that he had to know about it and see the kid every day."

"What?" Nicoletta's outrage spilled over, not only in her voice but in her body as well. The rage that was in him poured off her. "That's insane. Your own father had that reaction? You were ten years old. How could you stop two forty-year-old men? That's crazy, Taviano. Utterly insane."

"He couldn't look at me. He wanted Eloisa to ship me back to Italy. He told her another family of riders would be happy to have me. He all but insisted. In the end, they compromised. She didn't want to lose her status as a rider, so there could be no divorce. That meant no counseling for me, and no one else, particularly Stefano, could know what happened, but I had to remain in the home. Phillip gave in and allowed me to stay so that Stefano wouldn't have any idea anything was wrong, but he still refused to have anything more to do with me."

"I can't believe your mother would be okay with that. That makes no sense. What about any other child sent to those terrible men?"

"Those men, who I'm not certain were really on the books as riders anymore, were found dead with their necks broken a few weeks later."

"That had to be Eloisa, right? At least she did that for you."

"I wanted to think Eloisa killed them to serve justice or to avenge me, but my guess is she did it to keep anyone from finding out the actual truth of what happened, especially Stefano. He might have killed her. He still might if he finds out."

He was making that a distinct warning. It wouldn't serve any purpose telling Stefano, nor would he want him—or the others—to know after all this time. He understood why Nicoletta had trouble looking at him when he knew so much about the details of her past and what her step-uncles and Benito Valdez had done to her. He hadn't filled in the details for her, but it had all been done to her, so she knew. He didn't want to have to face Stefano and the storm that would follow when his brother realized he hadn't been protected as a child. It would be difficult enough to face Nicoletta in the light of day.

CHAPTER EIGHT

Nicoletta squeezed her eyelids tight against the hot tears she couldn't stop on Taviano's behalf. She should have known. He held himself in such rigid control at all times. He wanted to be the one in control. He was watchful. Careful. Saw everything. Was aware of everything.

He had always been so good with her. So understanding. No matter how terrible she'd been to him. How many times she'd said mean, cutting things and tried to push him away. He understood, and he kept coming back. He knew. Another wave of love for him washed over her. He hadn't had anyone, when he should have had an enormous family to help him through. That was almost worse than what she'd been forced to deal with.

"Your parents, Taviano. What were they thinking? You should have had counseling and so much love and support, just what you all offered to me."

"My mother was thinking she didn't want to give up being a rider. If Phillip left her, that's what would have happened."

"She chose riding over her son? Never. Never in a million years, Taviano. Oh my God. I can't stop crying. You have to help me stop."

He shifted back and turned her into him. She found her face pressed against his bare skin, and she was breathing him in. That scent that was only his. Only Taviano.

His arms were around her, holding her tight, the way he'd held her so many nights after her nightmares had awakened her. No one had held him. No one. Not even when he was ten years old.

"Stefano would have held you, Taviano. He would never have rejected you."

"I know, *amore mio.*"

Her heart leapt at his use of the endearment and the quiet acceptance in his voice. God, why did the world have to be such a vile, ugly place? The Ferraros appeared to have everything. Taviano was a golden prince. Damn Eloisa and Phillip to hell for their selfish decisions.

"We're not doing that." Her declaration came out muffled and her lips tasted his skin. He tasted like love and temptation. "We're not *ever* doing that."

"What aren't we doing, *piccola?*"

His tone was gentle, in total opposition to her decisive, belligerent, ready-to-go-to-battle war cry. She didn't care. She meant every single word of her declaration.

"We're not sending our children off to foreign countries and strangers to train them no matter what the traditions are. If you insist, or Stefano does, then I'm going, too, and I'll be sitting right there to make certain no one touches one single hair on their heads."

He rubbed his thumb over her forehead and then pressed his lips there twice. Her heart jerked hard in her chest before settling down to a wild rhythm that threatened to pound through her veins in tune with her overwhelming connection to him.

"I'm with you one hundred percent, Nicoletta."

"How can you stand to look at her?"

"Eloisa?"

"She says the ugliest things to Emmanuelle and all the other women and yet you know what she did. If the others knew . . ."

"And they never will. She changed after that. I didn't see it at first, because I was a kid and I was so hurt. I withdrew and acted out. I hated myself. I didn't want to be around my brothers, especially Stefano. I was afraid he would see something was different, something was wrong with me. That I was 'dirty.'"

She couldn't help squirming uncomfortably. She understood exactly what he was talking about. It was no wonder he knew exactly what she had been doing in those first few years. He'd been so young, with no one to turn to. No one to guide him through. His own parents had effectively cut him off from all help.

"I realized, as I grew older, that Eloisa, although she'd been a shit mother to us when we were babies, had gotten better when we started training. She laughed more and did things with us. She'd begun to interact with us. She wasn't the greatest, but she seemed to be learning, especially with Emmanuelle. Eloisa reverted back to her cold ways after the incident. I think that's why Emme is so much more tolerant of her than the rest of us. She remembers that and is always trying to get it back." He nuzzled the top of her head. "Or maybe Emme's just more compassionate than the rest of us."

She wrapped her arms around his neck and pressed into him. "I don't know how we're going to do this, Taviano. You deserve so much more than you're going to get with me, but I swear I'll always have your back, no matter what comes at us."

"I'm well aware of that, Nicoletta."

He pressed another kiss onto the top of her head and then with his casual strength, turned her so that she once more faced away from him, settled her into her favorite sleeping position and then wrapped himself around her.

"I really hope your sister tells Eloisa we're married tonight so she can stay awake all night and lose her freakin' mind."

Taviano laughed softly. The warm air blew against the back of her head, sending little shivers of awareness down her spine. If she hadn't been so exhausted, so emotionally overwrought, she would have responded physically, but she closed her eyes and savored the idea of lying in bed with Taviano while his mother stewed somewhere, furious that he was with Nicoletta.

"I think we're going to spend a lot of time working on meditation."

She loved the genuine laughter in his voice. Just the fact that she could make him laugh after his disclosure made her happy. Taviano, like his brothers, was a gentleman. He was very used to getting his way. He could buy and sell small countries. He owned anything he wanted. In the time she'd been around the Ferraros, she'd come to realize, for all their wealth, the core of who they were came down to one thing—family.

When the doors were closed, they were very different from the men and women they showed to the public. They might appear to live glamorous lives. They raced cars and attended all types of charity functions. They were invited to every party. They jetted around the world, chasing the best snow, the best view of the northern lights, whatever it was they seemed to have gotten in their heads that day, or they visited cousins to party.

They always wore their signature suits, looking handsome, and Emmanuelle, stylish and beautiful. They were the Ferraros. Untouchable. They smiled, but those smiles were rare and certainly didn't reach their eyes, which made them appear all the more mysterious and dangerous. Rumors were abundant, mostly because they were beyond wealthy and their origins were Italy and Sicily, so they had to be in organized crime; others said they were self-made, but no one knew how their massive fortune had been acquired.

Nicoletta had seen them completely differently from the

personas they projected to the world. Behind closed doors they were a close, loving family. Aunts and uncles to little Crispino, they vied for his attention and spoiled him until Stefano objected and removed him from them and spoiled him by becoming a gym, allowing his son to climb all over him, making his brothers, sisters-in-law and wife laugh at him.

They genuinely laughed together. They preferred to spend their time together. They cooked meals; in fact, she'd learned that Taviano was an excellent cook. Francesca loved to cook, and the two of them were usually the ones to put together the meals so they didn't have to eat out, where others could intrude on their privacy.

When Vittorio had introduced Grace into the family, she had been accepted immediately. More than accepted, she had been embraced by the various family members, as had Sasha when Giovanni had married her. Lying there, with Taviano wrapped so closely around her, Nicoletta realized that his family had accepted her as well. She had been the one to hold back.

"I wish you'd had a choice," she murmured. She was so sleepy she knew he probably couldn't understand what she was saying. Her words sounded, even to her own ears, as if they were blending together.

His arm tightened for a moment around her waist. "There's always a choice, *piccola*."

"Not if you're a rider, it seems."

He used a remote with his free hand and brought down privacy screens to black out the windows so they could sleep in when the light came in the morning. "There's always a choice, Nicoletta. I'm not Eloisa. As much as I love being a rider, I had a choice from the beginning whether or not to allow my shadow to tangle with yours. I will admit, I didn't realize it would happen so fast, but I still made that decision. After that first knot formed, I could have stayed away, but I didn't. You were the one without a clear choice because you didn't know the consequences until I told them to you. I couldn't do that right away for obvious reasons."

"Taviano, why did you—"

"Go to sleep, *tesoro*. We'll be sorting through quite a few things in the morning. I'm tired and I need to lie down."

She had a hundred more questions for him. Mostly, she needed to know if he really thought that he could fall in love with her. *In* love was far different from loving. She had no doubts that Taviano loved her. She knew that he did. She felt it every time she was with him. She not only loved him; she was *in* love with him. He was always going to be her "only." The one. She wanted to be the same for him.

She knew the moment he finally fell asleep, his body relaxing fully against hers. He was warm. Not just warm, almost hot. His arm was a weight around her waist, but she found she liked having it there, when she'd always wanted to be able to run at the least sign of danger.

It was strange to be lying in bed knowing she was Nicoletta Ferraro, Taviano Ferraro's wife. She found that the idea gave her a little thrill, when before she'd been so upset that she'd let him talk her into it. Now that Taviano had shared his past with her, given her something no one else but his witch of a parent knew, she felt as if she belonged with him. She fit. Maybe not perfectly yet, but she could have his back.

She was tough. She had survival skills. Emmanuelle and the others were teaching her how to not only get better at defense and offense but also be better at handling people. She was learning the skills necessary to fit into the places the family went, their charity events, the clubs, the places she would never have considered going. Now that she was Taviano's wife, she would learn faster. Lucia would help her, and Francesca was an amazing tutor. Before, Nicoletta detested asking for help; now she had a perfect reason.

She had no idea how she was going to fit in to Taviano's world, but she was going to do her best, because someday she would have his children, and they weren't going to be ashamed of their mother. She drifted off to sleep, determined to find a way to make things work with Taviano, to make their relationship strong and very real.

* * *

Taviano woke to the angry vibration of his watch. It took only a moment of inhaling and becoming aware to know Nicoletta was in his arms. She hadn't moved. For once, she'd slept quietly, his larger body surrounding hers. He found himself smiling as he gently and very carefully pulled his arm from around her waist and rolled to the side of the bed. Raising one of the many privacy screens to allow some light to spill into the room, he saw it was a beautiful morning.

Three messages had come in while he slept. Typically, he awoke when he received a text, but he hadn't. Two were from Eloisa. One from Stefano.

I will not tolerate this, Taviano.

This had better not be true.

Stefano's message followed: Eloisa is in an uproar.

Taviano found himself grinning for no reason at all. He looked down at the woman lying motionless, curled up like a little kitten in the middle of his very large bed. There was his reason, right there. She had given him a reason to make his world right again.

Nicoletta turned her head and lifted her long lashes. He loved those lashes. The way they were so thick. The way they curled at the tips. "What?"

He caught up his phone and showed her the text messages. "Eloisa is on the warpath. She will not tolerate this. I suppose our marriage is the 'this' she is referring to."

Nicoletta sat up immediately, pushing at stray strands of thick, dark hair falling around her face. She didn't seem to notice the way the strap of the tank on the right side had fallen off her shoulder and most of the top curve of her right breast was exposed, a tempting allure that drew him like a magnet.

"Oh, no, so early in the morning, too."

He turned, put his knee on the bed and leaned into her, brushed a kiss on her lips and then bent his head to that curve there was no way to resist. He was gentle, his mouth moving over her breast, tongue tasting, teeth easing the material down until he uncovered her nipple. If she had moved away from him, he would have stopped. She didn't. If she had stiffened, he would have stopped. She didn't.

Her gaze met his, searched his. He let her see his desire. He wanted Nicoletta to know that no matter what, he found her attractive. More than attractive. He took his time lowering his head a second time, waiting for her to pull back. His mouth closed over her breast, drew it into the heat of his mouth. He was careful to be gentle, not let the wildness in his nature and his need of her get the upper hand, not even when hot blood rushed through his veins and hit his cock like a fireball.

He didn't use his hands. He didn't in any way act possessive, when he was all about possessive. He was born for this woman. His soul matched hers. Fit hers like a key. His body was made to pleasure hers. He knew it as surely as he knew he was a Ferraro. Still, he was careful, because Nicoletta had to know she was safe with him, especially when they came together in their bed, no matter how they came together.

He lifted his head, kissed the red mark he'd made and then brushed another kiss across her upturned lips. "Good morning, *tesoro*. You're irresistible with the light shining on you that way. And it really isn't all that early. It's close to noon. You take a shower while I see what I can find us for breakfast."

Nicoletta touched the mark on the curve of her breast with her fingers. "She's going to come here. Eloisa. She's probably already on her way."

"No doubt." He couldn't look away from the way her fingers held his mark to her, almost as if she were protecting it. Then she stroked a little caress across it. His heart reacted with a strange jerk.

"I'm a grown man, Nicoletta. She can't very well come here and order me back home or threaten to cut me out of the family fortune. First, I'm independently wealthy, and second, she can't cut me out of the trust. Stefano is in charge of the riders and he is head of the family. She has no control in my life and hasn't since I was ten."

He realized that was true. He had turned to Stefano for everything, cutting out his parents, and Eloisa and Phillip had allowed it. If Stefano had noticed that he shouldered more responsibility in the raising of Taviano, he never said so, but then he wouldn't.

"What do you want me to do when she gets here?"

"I'm not certain yet," he said honestly. He didn't know. "I believe Eloisa is ashamed of the choices she's made over the years. I've had a lot of time to think about things. She hasn't been able to look at any of her children since making her decision. She grew colder and pulled away from all of us. Maybe she loved Phillip, and all she had left to her was riding shadows, because Phillip didn't love her. He didn't love any of us. He was selfish and vain. All he seemed to care about was other women. He used shadows to have affairs, further twisting Eloisa into a bitter, lonely woman."

Nicoletta leaned her chin into the heel of her hand and stared up at him with her large dark-chocolate eyes. Last night she had wanted to hunt Eloisa down; this morning, there was a small hint of compassion in her eyes. His warrior woman could definitely be a rider. She would learn to balance the need for vengeance with the will for justice.

"The death of my youngest brother, Ettore, really separated her from everyone. He was born premature and very fragile, his lungs weak and his body unable to deal with the terrible toll the shadows took on the riders. Stefano warned our parents repeatedly that Ettore shouldn't be a rider, but imperfection was never tolerated in the Ferraro family. Phillip just didn't care enough to bother, but Eloisa was fierce about our reputation, and she believed that Ettore simply needed to work harder to bring his body to maximum physical perfection. Others had done it, and so could he. He died in the shadow tube, and Stefano has never forgiven her. More importantly, she has never forgiven herself."

"It's so sad. All of it. On the outside, so many people envy what the Ferraros have, yet no one really knows what other people go through, do they?"

Taviano shook his head. "I think Eloisa has always felt alone. My grandparents really loved each other. And they loved us. But they weren't quite so wonderful with their children as we'd all like to think. They were so wrapped up in each other they ignored them, leaving them to be raised by a series of nannies and then shipped off to families in other countries to be trained."

"The traditions Eloisa followed."

He nodded. "She didn't find a partner, so they arranged a loveless marriage for her. Sadly, she fell in love, but Phillip didn't. He courted her and pretended, but he didn't really care. For someone like Eloisa, that made it all the worse. I'm certain she felt a fool. I've often wondered if that's why she objects so strenuously to Francesca. She can see Stefano loves her so much, and it scares her for him. The same with Ricco and Giovanni and now Vittorio. She doesn't want them to suffer the way she did." He shrugged. "Who knows what goes through her mind. I've spent far too much time speculating on her behavior."

He held out his hand to Nicoletta, and she took it immediately. He wanted her showered and dressed before Eloisa arrived—and he knew she would be coming. She was like a storm, and he felt the brewing already stirring up the air. He pulled his new wife to her feet.

"I'm certain Eloisa interferes in our lives now to prove to herself she can't have a relationship with any of us. She was particularly horrible to Francesca, who truly, in all of our opinions, is the kindest woman on the planet. I think Eloisa is terrified of being accepted. Of actually having a relationship and loving someone and having them hurt her. She doesn't know how to relate to anyone anymore with the exception of Henry. He grew up in her family, and she spends all her time with him now, She's different with him.

He's not a rider—he works with the cars. A good man and very loyal to our family."

Nicoletta was silent for a moment, and then she met his eyes. "She's too ashamed, the way I was, so she's self-destructive and pushes everyone away from her. That's what you think, isn't it?"

"Not like you, *piccola*. I was thinking more like me. You aren't anything like she is."

Nicoletta shook her head but didn't react to his statement. "I'm going to take a shower. You go find us food. If she's really on the way, I hope you realize that no matter how much compassion you have for her, what she did was wrong. You're her son, and even now, you're trying to find excuses for her. I'm not going to get over it that easily, and she's going to be tearing into me. It might be a good idea for me to go for a walk after breakfast. That path in the woods looked really intriguing."

Was he making excuses for Eloisa? Had he been unconsciously trying to find reasons for his mother's behavior his entire life? It was possible. Children did that. Was he still doing it? "You aren't deserting me and leaving me to the wolves."

"At least you know Eloisa is a wolf, *mio marito*."

She flounced off toward the master bath. Within minutes he heard the shower come on and then a squeal and more water running and more squeals. Laughter followed. She definitely was adventurous. She hadn't come back to ask him to show her how to use the various dials. She also hadn't asked him for a map of the house. He liked that she at least identified him as her husband and that she hadn't pulled away when he'd kissed her good morning and spent time with his mouth on her breast.

Taviano dressed carefully, but in casual clothes. They would be meeting with Stefano again very soon. Stefano had already devised a plan to take down Valdez and his army of gang members. The Ferraros would prefer to take the fight to them, keep it out of their own territory if possible. They knew Valdez would send his men there, hoping to catch them unawares and get to Lucia and Amo so Nicoletta would come quietly with him.

Benito Valdez didn't really know Nicoletta. If she did come quietly with him, she would slit his throat the moment she got the chance. The man would never be able to go to sleep again. If the Demons did manage to get their hands on anyone Nicoletta loved or cared for, she knew the Ferraros would be coming through the shadows for them. She would just have to provide a distraction.

Taviano looked around his kitchen. He loved to cook. Now, having his woman in his home, the kitchen was suddenly completely different. He opened the crisper and found the vegetables he'd ordered delivered for their morning breakfast. He began quickly grilling them for omelets.

Nicoletta came into the kitchen looking beautiful in a light blue blouse tucked into a darker blue flowing skirt he was certain Lucia had chosen. A wide hand-painted leather belt cinched her small waist. The outfit was classic Lucia's Treasures and looked as if it could be worn on the streets of one of the smaller villages in Italy or in New York and fit easily into either place. That was the beauty of Lucia's fashions.

"Something smells delicious."

"Coffee's on." Taviano indicated the pot in the corner of his workstation. He was already working on his second cup.

"I love the way coffee smells first thing in the morning," she admitted. "And don't you love the sound of those birds?" She did a little spin and then poured the coffee into a cup before going to stand beside the open door. The screen was in place to keep insects out, but Taviano loved the sounds of the birds as well, especially when he was cooking.

"Sometimes I play music, but most of the time, I just listen to the birds and the frogs, although they only sound off if it's early or right after a rain." He indicated the smaller table inside the rounded alcove. He preferred that space to eat breakfast unless he was eating outside.

He turned his head toward the front of his house. "She's here."

"How can you tell? There wasn't a car."

"She used the shadows. Feel the difference in the energy, Nicoletta." He kept his voice low. "You can always feel an intruder. Our home has a specific energy. A particular set of notes to it. Call it a vibration. Once you get it, you'll know when one note is jarring or out of place. Our family never jars, not even Eloisa, but the notes play differently."

Nicoletta didn't argue or act like he was crazy. She didn't even lift an eyebrow at him. Instead, she nodded her head, frowning a little. Concentrating, as if listening, or trying to feel what he was explaining to her. She reached out and touched her fingertips to a shadow and then threaded her other fingers through his. At once, the jolt of their connection hit them both hard.

Taviano hadn't expected their combined energy to be so potent. He should have. Their power was growing, so the sexual component between them had to be as well. Sex, power, their minds merging; the connection was so strong, just their fingers threaded together nearly pulled them from their chairs into the thin tube she had placed the tips of her fingers into.

He used the strength of his body to hold them in place. "Breathe. Use the meditative breathing."

Nicoletta heard him, although he spoke in a mere whisper. She began immediately, matching her breath to his. He could feel his mother getting closer, the weight of her disapproval obvious with every step she took. Her dark censure sank into the flooring and spread through the house like doom, moving ahead of her.

"Feel her? She's close to us now. In the hall."

"Yes." Nicoletta breathed the word back to him. There was triumph in her mind. Excitement that she could feel the energy vibrating through the house, even though it was negative energy.

Nicoletta pulled her fingertips from the shadow and picked up her fork. She let go of Taviano's hand and casually pulled her legs up under her skirt as Eloisa walked into the room. Taviano had seen her do that so many times, tuck her legs onto a chair in tailor-fashion, making herself smaller. It had never bothered him until now, until this moment when his mother had entered their home and he wanted Nicoletta to realize that Eloisa was in Nicoletta's territory, not the other way around.

As always, his mother looked elegant. There was no other word for Eloisa. She might storm into a room like a wild tornado, but she commanded it and drew every eye. She was tall and beautiful, timeless in her beauty. Her hair was still thick and dark, streaked now with silver, but classy, as if she had been kissed by the sun. When she walked in and the morning sun hit her, she looked as if she might have wings. He knew that look was very deceiving.

"Good morning, Eloisa."

"Good morning, Mrs. Ferraro," Nicoletta added.

Taviano wished he was sitting next to his bride instead of opposite her. Her voice was soft and musical, but just that little bit hesitant, and he knew his mother would catch that, chew her up and spit her out. If he had been sitting close, he could have shielded his bride, put his arm around her, at least protect her a little with his larger body.

"I despise being called that," Eloisa hissed, glaring at Nicoletta.

"What would you prefer I call you, then?" Nicoletta asked.

Eloisa put her doubled fists on her hips and leveled her cold gaze at Taviano's wife. "I would prefer that you didn't speak to me at all."

Before Taviano could reprimand his mother, Nicoletta nodded. "I would prefer that as well, but in my home, which is here and, obviously, with Lucia and Amo, you can do your best not to be rude or don't bother coming around. Outside of either place, we'll agree I won't speak to you and you don't speak to me."

Taviano could barely keep the grin from his face. His woman was no shrinking violet. She might not want to be rude to Lucia's friend, his mother, but she wasn't going to take Eloisa's bullshit anymore, not after his revelations.

The color drained from Eloisa's face. "How dare you speak to me like that?"

"Why? Because of your age? What have you ever done to earn my respect? Not one single thing. You haven't shown any compassion toward me and what happened to me, but why would you when you couldn't show it to your own child? You don't have to like me, Eloisa. In fact, I don't care one way or the other if you do. But you aren't going to be rude to me in my own home. You aren't going to be rude to me in front of Lucia and Amo anymore because it makes them uncomfortable, and when you leave, Lucia cries. You're bitter and angry because you made very bad choices, and you refuse to stop making them, as if somehow that's going to justify what you did. Here's a news flash for you." Nicoletta leaned forward, staring her mother-in-law straight in the eye. "There is no justification."

Eloisa's face changed from icy hauteur to sheer hatred. She actually shrieked, her hand flashing out, fingers curved into a claw, long nails like hooks slashing at Nicoletta's eyes. The sound of Taviano's hand connecting with her wrist was loud as he slammed his mother's arm away from Nicoletta, who had turned just enough and shockingly fast so that the claw barely missed her face. He'd hit his mother's arm hard, so hard he was afraid he had bruised her at the very least, maybe even cracked a bone. He hadn't had time to soften the block, fear for Nicoletta uppermost in his mind. Eloisa looked as shocked as Taviano felt. He'd never seen his mother lose control. She could have blinded Nicoletta.

"I'm sorry," Eloisa whispered, cradling her arm. "Really, Taviano, I don't know what got into me."

"Let me look at your arm."

She shook her head and stepped back. "It's all right. It was a mistake coming here. None of you listen anyway.

You do what you want. What Stefano thinks is best. He always thinks he knows so much more than I do."

Nicoletta got up and went to the freezer without saying a word. Taviano pulled a chair out at the table and got his mother to sit. His woman handed him the ice pack as she sauntered back to her chair, not even pausing so that Eloisa didn't seem to notice. He wrapped the pack around his mother's arm.

"We listen to you, Eloisa. Even Stefano listens. We're loud and we argue, but we take what everyone says into consideration. It's a generation thing. We're noisy. In the end, we do what's right for the family."

"Do you? Are you certain of that?" Eloisa asked.

Taviano picked up his cell and texted Henry, the man who had taken care of their family the longest. He'd been in their lives as long as he could remember. He loved cars and kept theirs in perfect running order. He seemed to love Eloisa no matter how she acted. He would bring a car out to the estate to take Eloisa back. Taviano didn't want her riding the shadows with an injured arm.

He poured his mother a cup of coffee and added cream. She never took sugar in her coffee or tea, but always took cream. "Would you care for an omelet?"

He glanced at Nicoletta to see if she was eating. She hadn't been eating very much lately, and to him it was worrisome. Her nightmares tended to come in bouts, and he'd noticed patterns. She often stopped eating for days before the nightmares became severe. She was pushing the food around on her plate.

Eloisa shook her head. "No, I ate earlier. I had some reports to finish and send to your aunt and uncle. Taviano . . ." She hesitated. "I thought we put all that behind us. You're a grown man now."

Nicoletta sat up, her back ramrod straight. Taviano had to find a way to silence her. She was furious all over again. There was no way to "put it all behind them." His mother couldn't understand that. She never would. She didn't want to understand it. He saw no reason to have it out with her.

"Where are you going with this, Eloisa? Just come out and say it. You're not one to beat around the bush. If you have something to say, just tell us."

"If you bring this up now, even after all these years, you know your brother. He'll lose his mind. We already have enough to contend with, thanks to . . ." She trailed off and studiously looked out the window to the beautiful view of the woodlands and brush. "We just have enough going on right now without your brother getting crazy. I don't know why you felt it necessary to tell her anything at all . . ."

"You mean share my past with my wife?"

Eloisa flinched. "Really, Taviano? Your wife? Who is she really? Do you even know?"

"Yes, Eloisa. Like you, I did my homework. Stefano, you, the entire Ferraro family, from the lawyers to the Archambault family, no doubt, investigated her lineage." Taviano couldn't keep the sarcasm from creeping into his voice.

He took several deep breaths to try to keep his temper from flaring. He wanted his mother safe, and that meant keeping her there until Henry arrived with the car. "Seriously? You know damn well who her mother was. She was Leora Aita, from a very respected family that in the old days, long before they were stamped out by the Saldis, produced riders. A few of the Aitas escaped that massacre, but no one heard of their children producing riders after that tragedy. Leora married Asce Archambault, a cousin of the riders of France. He died when Nicoletta was two. I know you have this information, Eloisa."

Sometimes his mother exasperated him on so many levels. She made no sense at all. She had protested every one of his brother's wives, when all of them had come from good families and could produce riders for the Ferraro family. The only conclusion he could draw was that she objected to the fact that they were love matches rather than arranged marriages.

Eloisa had the reports on Nicoletta's birth mother and father. She knew as well as he did the family she came from.

The Archambault family—riders or not—were renowned in their world for the strength of their psychic talents.

Taviano glanced at Nicoletta's face. She had gone unnaturally still. Her dark eyes were on him, not his mother. Again, when normally Nicoletta was an open book, now she was impossible to read. He didn't like the fact that she was so withdrawn that when he shifted to connect their shadows, he didn't feel the jolt of awareness that always slammed so hard and deep into him. She'd taken herself somewhere else, and it was deliberate. She was protecting herself, and it wasn't from his mother—it was from him.

"Yes, I'm very much aware that Leora had the good sense to marry an Archambault. I'm certain they directed her toward a cousin because she wasn't a rider, but still, it was probably a good match. But when he died, she chose to marry far beneath her. That nasty family from New York. The Gomez family. They were all gangbangers."

Color swept into Nicoletta's face and her knuckles turned white where she gripped the edge of the table.

"Nicoletta was adopted by Desi Gomez and taken out of New York, far from his brothers and the gang he was born into. He stayed away from all of his relatives. He worked hard and built a good life for himself and his family. He was a good man, Eloisa. Everything said about him was good. Even the cops had good things to say about the man. It wasn't his fault that he was killed in a car accident."

"It was their fault that they didn't have anything prepared for their daughter just in case they died, so she wasn't sent to his brothers, now, wasn't it?" Eloisa demanded, her voice snide.

Nicoletta stood up. "I suppose so, just as it was your fault that you sent your ten-year-old son to two horrible men against the warnings of the family he was with because you were too lazy to take care of him on your own, and then you were so selfish you didn't get any help for him because you didn't want your precious life disturbed in any way."

She ignored Taviano, not even looking at him as she

slipped past and opened the kitchen door, controlled violence in her movements as she closed it.

"This isn't going to work, Taviano. She's going to say something in front of Stefano. You know she will." Eloisa cradled her injured arm to her and shook her head. "What a mess. I knew she would be impossible to deal with."

"You think you can cow everyone by being ugly to them, Eloisa. You push everyone away and then wonder why you don't see your grandson or have Emme around anymore. Nicoletta is my choice. She was my choice from the moment I saw her. I knew she was mine. You don't have to like it any more than you have to like any of your other daughters-in-law, but you won't talk about her parents like that in her home and upset her, not if you want to come here. You're banned from Stefano's and that's a tragedy, when Francesca would always welcome you. You're banned from Vittorio's because you're nasty to Grace."

Eloisa rolled her eyes. "Grace. She's a doormat for Vittorio and he spoils her rotten."

"She's not a doormat. If he spoils her, how can she be a doormat? That doesn't even make sense. She loves him, and it's their relationship. She likes pleasing him. He likes pleasing her. They work together. That's how it's done, Eloisa. People find other people that fit with them, the way Nicoletta fits with me." He glanced down at the text message. "Henry is here with the car. I'll be happy to walk you out."

"I don't think she fits quite as well as you think she does," Eloisa said, standing. She gave him a little smirk. "She wasn't in the least bit happy you and the family investigated her. She doesn't understand money, and she never will. Don't bother. I found my way in. I can find my way out."

CHAPTER NINE

Taviano wound his way along the narrow path through the thick trees and brush into the deeper interior. The woods had been planted years earlier and had a good heavy growth. The vines creeping up the trunks gave off a perfumed lilac scent. Birds called to one another and he could hear the wings fluttering as they moved from branch to branch overhead. Instead of the lightness he normally felt when he took this trail, there was a heaviness that weighed on him.

He took in several deep breaths not only to calm himself but to calm Nicoletta, knowing that the heaviness was coming from her. It was embedded into the path itself and he felt it with every step he took. He moved slowly, not wanting her to feel as if she were being chased. Nicoletta could be lethal. She was a runner. And she was hurt by the things his mother had said about her adopted father. Desi Gomez had raised her from the age of two until she was fifteen, and from everything Taviano had read in the reports, he'd been a good man and an even better father. Nicoletta loved him just as she loved her mother.

He reached for her, for the connection between them. It was strong whether she liked it or not. That connection was forged in something very powerful. The shadows were tangled and knotted and merged because of what they shared, the ultimate ugliness that had created two strong warriors.

"You loved your parents. I don't know that I can say that. I may have loved the idea of parents, but I can't say that I love mine. I want to. I want to say Phillip was worth something, but he wasn't."

He didn't raise his voice very loud. He didn't have to. He was close to her. "Not to any of his children, and he treated Eloisa so horribly that it may as well be called abuse. He didn't hit her, but it was emotional abuse. We all saw it. He knew her parents had drilled it into her that riding the shadows was her duty and that she had been born to do that and only that. It was her only worth. That gave him leave to do anything he wanted, and he took it. I detested him. All of us did. No, I can't say that I ever loved him."

Silence met his declaration, but she heard him. He knew by the sudden stirring in his mind. It felt feminine. She'd been crying, and that broke his heart. "I don't like that you choose to cry alone. When you cry, Nicoletta, I prefer that you do it with my arms around you."

Birds called back and forth, a loud noisy monologue that seemed to be over some kind of intruder the flock took exception to. The air would fill with small birds swooping and climbing high and then diving gracefully all together so they looked like one large shadowy machine chasing off a predator. He studied the images and knew she was doing the same thing.

"Are you comparing those birds chasing off the hawk to you chasing off my mother?"

There was the impression of a shrug. Their connection through their merged shadows was very strong and she wasn't blocking it anymore. He was grateful for that, although he could feel her hurt and anger. Even her disdain. "Maybe not just your mother. Maybe you and your entire family with the way you treat people, Taviano. You're so casual about your entitlements."

He kept walking. Quiet. Controlled. Padding along the path like the predator he was. She knew he was one. She knew his entire family had been born predators. They were raised to be very skilled at what they did, and they had grown into extremely lethal beings. She was right that there was a sense of entitlement to some of their ways. They always investigated anyone who came close to them. They didn't think anything about it or what effect it might have on the person being investigated should they find out. They'd never much cared one way or the other. The investigation was always thorough and a fact of life.

At times they offered a token resistance, but they always knew it was going to be done. When Nicoletta had been brought home to their family, there had been no question about doing an investigation, especially when they were asking Lucia and Amo to take her in. The Ferraro family was sponsoring her. They would mentor her, assume responsibility for her. Naturally, they would want to know everything they could about her.

Once the anomalies had begun to show up, the fact that her reflexes had grown faster, her movements in the shadows had increased, not decreased, so many things with Nicoletta that all of them noticed when training with her, they'd investigated even further, going so far as to make inquiries into the families in Europe, specifically the Archambault riders as to what psychic abilities their cousin had possessed.

"I suppose it seems that way, *tesoro*." He moved steadily, right behind her, just out of her sight. The birds had settled back into the trees now that the hawk had been driven away.

"It doesn't seem that way, Taviano, it is that way. All of you do whatever you want to do. You walk over other people. If you want something, you just take it. Or buy it. And you're so casual about it. Eloisa is so cutting, not just to me but to anyone she thinks is inferior to her. What makes her so much better? Her money? Money doesn't make anyone better."

"No, *piccola*, it doesn't." He hated the sadness in her voice. Everything she said was true from her perspective and yet it wasn't.

"Grace is so amazing. She really is. She's like Francesca. Truly nice, and yet Eloisa looks down on her like she's nothing, just the way she does Francesca."

"Tell me why we're having a discussion about Eloisa and her opinions on anyone." He was too close now. He inhaled and closed his eyes as he took her scent into his lungs. He didn't want to move up on her until she was ready to face him. "You shouldn't care about her opinions."

"I don't."

There was confusion in her voice, and he knew he needed to see her face. She'd stopped walking. "You do or you wouldn't be so upset. You're very upset."

He pushed aside the heavy heart-shaped leaves and fragrant clusters of flowers hanging from a basswood tree and she was sitting beneath it, knees drawn up, arms wrapped around them tightly, gently rocking back and forth. She didn't look up when he sank to the ground opposite her.

"Nicoletta. Tell me why you're so upset over the things Eloisa has to say about everyone."

She reached down and gathered up dirt in her hand, slowly letting it leak through her fingers to the ground. "You're all different. You have to be. You can't be like everyone else. I thought I could be like you, but it's really not possible. I'm never going to fit in. At first I wanted to blame it on the fact that I was raped."

She used the back of her hand to rub her forehead, as if she might have a headache. Taviano didn't interrupt her, although he wanted to. He wanted to reassure her that she belonged with him no matter where they were or who he was. He forced himself to remain silent and hear her out.

"I realized, when Eloisa was talking so disparagingly about my mother and father, that I remember the way my mother would take me through the neighborhood, and we'd go to the park or library and wave and say hello to everyone. She knew everyone by name. They knew her. She liked them. She laughed all the time. She didn't talk behind their backs. Not ever. She would have been so angry with me if I had done so. She gave me those lessons, Taviano, from the time I was little. People mattered to her, not money."

"You mean the way they do to Francesca and Stefano? Or Grace and Vittorio? You aren't as close with Giovanni and Sasha, but Sasha is just as down-to-earth as Francesca and Grace. Giovanni is the first man to look out for those less fortunate. Trust me, Sasha would box his ears if he ever got too pompous. Mariko doesn't have a mean bone in her body, and Ricco is very kind. We work hard, Nicoletta, and most of what the public sees is so we can have alibis for what we don't want them to see or know about our real business."

She nodded. "I understand that. On the other hand, it's so easy to just get on your private plane and go to any hotel and buy out an entire floor or the entire hotel if you want."

"So, what you're upset about is the fact that we have money."

"I'm upset because you married me, Taviano, for all the wrong reasons, and I let you. I just let you. That's why I'm upset."

He studied her averted face. He could feel distress pouring off of her in waves. "You couldn't care less about money. You didn't marry me for that."

"Don't pretend you don't know why I married you. This is humiliating enough. The good thing is, we didn't consummate the marriage. We can get it annulled."

"That's not going to happen." He was very firm about that. "There are perks to all that money, Nicoletta, and the lawyers I have access to. One of those is getting my way. You better believe there won't be an annulment or a divorce. I made that very clear. We need to stop going round and round on this issue and focus on moving forward."

"You're very frustrating, Taviano." She sent him a look from under her long lashes that made him want to lean across the small space between them and kiss her. "Do you see how entitled that makes you? You're just proving my point."

"Why? Because I'm honest about what I want? I told you from the beginning I wanted you. I knew it was you. I didn't make any bones about that. You ran, and I chased after you."

"You rejected me when I threw myself at you. It took a lot of courage to try to seduce you."

"We were both drunk, Nicoletta. That isn't courage, it's alcohol. The minute you freaked out, and you would have, what if I didn't have the control to stop? Where would we have been then? Do you have any idea what it cost me to turn you down? I've had a permanent erection for far too long. It was indecent because you were too young, and I was supposed to be looking out for you."

"You did look out for me. It's not your fault that I fell in love with you."

"Why the fuck do you have to say it like that?" Temper swirled in his gut in spite of his determination to go carefully with her.

She winced. He rarely swore at her, especially since that night two years earlier. "Like what? How do you want me to say it? It's the truth."

"Like loving me is the worst thing that anyone could possibly do. I'm sure that's how my mother feels. Hell, I drive Stefano up the wall all the time as well. Maybe he feels that way, too."

"Don't be an idiot, Taviano. All you have to do is look at Stefano when he talks about you or to you and see the love on his face. It's hard to miss. Your entire family looks at one another like that, but especially Stefano. And I don't say it like loving you is the worst thing that anyone could possibly do. It's difficult when it's not the same kind of love given back."

He stared at her, hoping that somehow clarity would come to his brain. He considered himself an intelligent man, but he got nothing just looking at her. "At this moment, Nicoletta, I really want to shake you. You aren't making any sense, when I've always considered you sensible. My family is going to be showing up soon, and I'd prefer not to be pulling out my hair when they arrive, so do a better job of explaining what the hell that means."

She heaved a sigh as if he wasn't quite bright. "I know you love me. How could I not? You've looked after me for the last three years. There's a difference between being in love with someone and loving someone. You can love children, Taviano, and siblings, and parents, but you aren't *in love* with them. Do you see the difference?"

"Why do you think I married you?" She exasperated the holy hell out of him sometimes.

She shrugged. "Obviously, the investigation turned up the fact that my lineage would produce the right babies you needed, and our shadows tangled together way early and you couldn't get out of it. You were kind of trapped into it."

"That's what you think?"

"Yes."

"First I'm entitled and privileged, and then I'm this poor sap who was trapped into a loveless marriage by my own shadow. You know what I think, Nicoletta? I think you're a little afraid to face the truth."

"I've never been afraid to face the truth, Taviano. I'd rather just know it and deal with it than skirt around it or wonder all the time."

"The truth is, I'm so in love with you—and have been for so long—I don't know how I would survive without you. If you decided you couldn't handle what we do, although shadow riding is who I am, I would find another way to live just to be with you. I knew some time ago, long before you knew, that I was born to be that man, the one to make your life the best it can be, and I intend to be that man."

Nicoletta stared at him, her mouth slightly open, her

eyes wide with shock. Clearly, it was the last thing she'd expected him to say.

He stood up and held out his hand to her. "The ants are going to eat you alive. Come on. We have to get back to the house. Stefano wants us to take the fight to the Demons instead of letting them get to us if at all possible. He's got plans so they're coming to the house. They gave us a little bit of time because they know we're on our honeymoon."

She put her hand in his and let him pull her to her feet. "Are you serious?"

"About my family coming here? The ants? The honeymoon? Which we'll take after the real wedding. We are having a real wedding no matter what," he added decisively. "I'm certain Grace has half of it already planned out with Francesca and Lucia by now, and it's not quite noon."

"Not any of that. Loving me."

"Oh. That. I'm very serious, Nicoletta, and you should have known. I've never let you out of my sight. I ran off every boy that ever wanted to ask you out on a date. Two years ago, I informed Dario Bosco we were engaged so he'd back the hell off."

She gasped. "No way. That's why he quit calling me."

"That, and I threatened to knock his head off if he went behind my back and tried to undermine me. Of course, the family helped by keeping you busy, and Lucia and Amo were wonderful and aided me as well. It was a great conspiracy."

"They knew?"

"I told them I was going to marry you. I was just waiting for you to get to be a decent age. I couldn't very well ask you to marry me when you were underage."

"I wasn't underage."

"Eighteen was underage to me."

"I felt like a million years old."

He put his arm around her shoulders. He knew exactly what she meant. Sometimes he felt the same way. He'd often looked at her when she'd been trying to fit in with the other schoolgirls and he'd known it would never happen. Her childhood had been ripped away, just as his had been.

"How could I not be in love with you, Nicoletta? And why would I ever allow my shadow to tangle with yours so fast? I'll admit it was a little shocking even to me, the way they bound together, merging so quickly, but I didn't do anything to stop them. I didn't want to. I knew immediately you were the one and I was going to have you." He sent her a quick grin. "Once Stefano and the others realized our shadows were so fully merged, they got behind us very quickly."

"You're kind of devious, aren't you?"

"You're just now beginning to notice that about me? Absolutely I am, make certain you remember that. And I'm bossy, but in a good way."

"Is there a good way to be bossy?"

"My way is," he assured.

They walked together, matching steps on the narrow pathway until his exasperation got the better of him. He stepped in front of her, effectively halting her, and framed her face with both hands, forcing her to look up at him. "Woman, I just declared I'm madly in love with you, and I get nothing. No reaction whatsoever from you."

A slow smile spread across her face until her dark eyes lit up. His stomach did a slow roll and his cock reacted with a hard jerk.

"I'm a slow processor."

"My ass you're a slow processor. You're deliberately trying to make me crazy."

"And succeeding. I really hate that you investigated me."

"My family did that. And now it's *our* family, technically."

Before she could argue with him, he bent his head and took her mouth. He loved that mouth of hers. The pouty lower lip that had always dared him to bite it. He didn't. He kissed the hell out of her. He started slow. Gentle. Coaxing. She opened her mouth and let him in, and they both caught fire.

Flames licked over his skin and heat rushed through his

veins. He shifted his hold on her, sliding one hand behind her head to hold her in place, his arm a bar around her, locking her body to his. She melted into him, going boneless, her smaller, softer body intensely feminine. He felt every curve, her breasts tight against his lower chest.

A single sound escaped her throat, a moan, sexy and low, one that reverberated through his body and went straight to his cock, carried on that wave of rising heat. The flames leapt higher. Warning bells went off in his head. *"Dio, Dio, amore mio*, we have to stop."* He whispered it against her lips.

"I know. I can't."

He couldn't, either, but he had to. She wasn't ready. She thought she was, but she wasn't. He wasn't risking losing her because he hadn't waited. He hadn't been careful enough. Kissing was okay. Stripping her naked in the forest and taking her like a man starved was not. He heard himself groan as he found her lower lip, that beautiful pouty lip he dreamt about, caught it between his teeth and bit down gently, somewhere between punishment and a sensual enticement.

Nicoletta gasped, and he licked at the sting and then kissed his way down her throat before holding her against him so tightly with both arms he couldn't tell if it was her heart pounding or his. He nuzzled the top of her head.

"Dio, bella, we're going to go up in flames if we keep this up."

"I was all for it."

Her voice was muffled against his chest, but he felt her breath with every word, warm and tempting, her lips like a sinful temptation against the thin material of his shirt. She wrapped her arms around his waist, nuzzling his chest.

"You're not helping me."

"I know. I'm sorry, and you're being so good, Taviano. I do appreciate it, too. Well, I do and I don't. When you kiss me, I think I could really have wild, amazing sex with you. I want to. I really do."

She lifted her head and looked up at him, her dark eyes

meeting his. She didn't try to hide the mixture of love and desire. She looked a perfect blend of sin and innocence. Lust and trepidation mixed together in one tempting package.

"We'll get there, but when it's right."

"How, Taviano? I'm so scared I'll never be able to get there. When you're kissing me, I can't think straight. I'm not afraid. I just want you. But when I stop to think about the rest of it . . ." She trailed off, shaking her head.

"Have a little faith, *piccola*. I have no doubt we're going to have amazing sex. Don't be in such a hurry."

Her hand slid down his chest to stroke over the material stretched so tightly over his aching cock. "I do have certain skills, Taviano. I'm really good. I made certain I was really good. I can at least take care of this for you, so you don't have to walk around hurting all the time."

The temptation to let her was strong. Her fingers felt like magic, and his cock didn't just ache. Frankly, it was painful. There was something in her voice—in her expression. And he'd been there himself. "Why did you make certain you were really good?"

He felt her instant withdrawal. Her body stiffened just that little bit and separated from his by an inch or so. Her mind, so closely connected to his, slipped away. Their shadows, always tangled, always merged, began to shift, as if they might try to uncurl those tight knots.

He caught her chin. "Nicoletta, we tell the truth to each other. That's how I know how to keep you safe and to guide us through any sexual missteps. There are bound to be many. I don't want problems we can avoid, so that means communication. You think I didn't have to learn what oral sex was?"

"Then you probably know that if you could get them to use your mouth, they often couldn't use other parts of your body, although in my case there were three of them, so sometimes that didn't work so well anyway," she said.

He caught the sheen of tears before she blinked them away. "Yeah, *piccola*, I learned that trick, but there were two of them, so it didn't always work for me, either. I think we'll wait until we're mutually satisfying each other, not using oral sex out of fear."

"Do you think that's why I was offering?"

"I think you're very frightened, Nicoletta, of not pleasing me. Of not being able to have sex the way you think I might want to have it."

She ducked her head. All around them the birds sang, calling out to one another, but she was no longer hearing the soothing symphony. She was screaming inside. He could hear it in his own mind. That was how close they were, even when she'd tried to separate them.

"You're very experienced, Taviano. I've seen the magazines. You've had so many partners. So many women. I've had those three monsters and Benito Valdez, who, quite frankly, was as big a monster as all three of the others combined, and I hated every second I was with them. I despised sex. Nothing about it was good. Nothing. Not one single thing."

He rubbed at her lips with the pad of his thumb. Her skin was so incredibly soft, but it was the woman and everything about her that melted the ice in him, that hard place inside him he had thought impossible to ever get past to find the real man.

"That wasn't sex, Nicoletta. That was rape. That was brutal animals trying to hurt you, to prove they had power over you. They didn't. They never could. What it wasn't, was sex. Sex between two people who love each other should be beautiful. It should be slow, staring into each other's eyes, so intimate you know you belong together for eternity. It should be fun. It should be slam-against-the-wall, can't wait to fuck. It should be anything you want it to be because you're so in love you need to give each other so much pleasure you can't stand it. But always, *always*, Nicoletta, whatever two people in love do, it's consensual."

He brushed a kiss on her soft, tempting lips because he couldn't stop himself. "If you get scared at any point and you want to slow down and take a breath, you say so and we slow down. You want to stop, you say so, then we stop. We try something new and it scares you, you say so and we stop and discuss whether you want to keep going or not. You don't like something, we stop. End of story. Anytime you say no, it's no. That's sex with the one you're in love with. That's sex with me. That's why it's so important to always communicate honestly with me about what you're feeling, and I promise I'll do the same."

She stared up at him for a few more moments and then she nodded, her impossibly long lashes fluttering in that way that always moved him.

"That's why I love you so much, Taviano. You manage to make me feel so important to you. No matter what. You make everything all right."

"Everything is all right as long as we're together. We're stronger together, Nicoletta. You always have to remember that. Eloisa might try to take us down. Others might. They don't matter. It's always going to be you and me."

She took a deep breath and nodded. "Let's go back to that beautiful home you managed to find, although I can't believe you really can see stars. No one can see stars anymore."

"We can." He poured confidence into his voice, allowing her to change the subject. They needed to switch to something much lighter. "We're very far out."

"The city is too lit up. I think you have to be in the middle of the lake in order to see them. I looked it up once. I asked Lucia and Amo about going to an observatory, and even there, it's not a really good shot at seeing them."

"It is here. The artist who built the house chose the location far enough away, across the lake and deliberately with seeing the stars in mind. He was an astronomer at heart, which is why most of the art pieces in the house or built into the ceilings and walls all have to do with the universe and galaxies."

They managed to walk side by side, with her tucked beneath his shoulder for most of the way, until they neared the house, and then he took the lead. She tucked her hand into his back pocket. She'd done that once or twice before, and Taviano liked it. Eloisa would lose her mind if she ever saw Nicoletta do something like that.

He knew that his relationship with Nicoletta would be very different from his brothers' relationships with their spouses. He might be dominant—the Ferraros were born that way, and being riders only brought out that trait more—but he needed a warrior woman, a partner. He had known he wanted a woman who would work beside him. He hadn't thought that until he met Nicoletta—until she opened her eyes on the plane heading back to Chicago and he looked into all that rage and confusion. That fight. Those eyes held the same emotions his held every time he looked in the mirror.

He opened the kitchen door and stepped back to allow her into the house first. The dishes were still on the table right where he'd left them when he'd gone after her. Eloisa was gone. Thankfully, Henry had taken her away in the car, so Taviano didn't have to worry about her riding the shadows with an injury. She no longer rode the shadows to bring justice to those who deserved it. She had taken the role of a greeter, but she still used the shadows to move around when she wanted to secretly get from one place to another fast.

Nicoletta immediately cleared the table and helped him clean the kitchen. "I would have thought you would have an entire staff working for you."

"They clean," he admitted. "But not my dishes. I'm one person. When I'm here, I like to be alone. I cook, and I do my own dishes. I have a couple of people who will come in after, and a regular cleaning crew while I'm gone, but otherwise, I just want to be left alone."

"I like that," Nicoletta said.

"Good." He shot her a grin. "Because when we're at the stage where you're comfortable having sex, I'm fucking you in every room, on every table, over every couch, on the rug in front of every fireplace and on the roof as well. We don't want to be stumbling over staff while we're doing that."

Color swept up her neck and into her face. She arched an eyebrow at him. "All those places? Really?"

"And the bed. We have a lot of beds to break in. There's a swing chair out on the porch as well. And a porch railing."

She burst out laughing, just as he'd hoped she would. "You have sex on the brain."

"I've come here a lot in the last three years, *tesoro*. I spent a lot of time fantasizing about the two of us." It took self-control not to drop his hand to his cock and show her just what went on when he was fantasizing. "Did you? About me?"

She nodded, the blush starting all over again. "Yes. All the time. Especially in the bathtub. Once, you almost caught me. You came into my bedroom just as I was finishing up."

"Finishing up?" he echoed. His heart accelerated. He remembered that night so vividly. He had come into her bedroom through the window. He'd heard the splashes of water in the tub. Moans. So soft. She sounded frustrated. Near tears. He'd stood just outside the door, one hand on the doorknob, knowing how inappropriate it would be, how wrong of him, but it was clear she was sexually frustrated and in need. He wanted to be the one to send her over the edge. To help her get where she needed to go. Instead, he'd done the right thing and backed off.

"I didn't know what I was doing. I still don't. I think I'm so afraid of feeling anything because it was all so wrong. Everything was so wrong."

He hated the defeat in her voice.

"Nothing is wrong now. Everything we do will be right," he promised. "We'll try a few things to see if you like them. Nothing scary."

She laughed unexpectedly. "It's all going to be scary."

"Isn't that half the fun? I'm not scary, so it's just what we try. You can relax and only worry about whether or not it's too good."

She snapped a dish towel at him. "How can something be too good?"

He grinned at her. "Ask me that question after the family leaves."

The smile faded from her face. "What?"

"You heard me. I've decided I'm going to start with just laying you down on the bed, spreading you out and devouring you. Eating you like candy. I bet you taste like honey and lavender. You always smell like that."

The blush was back. "Taviano." There was cautious excitement in her voice.

"Nicoletta." There was teasing firmness in his.

"I'm not going to be able to concentrate on whatever Stefano says, you know that, right? I'll be thinking about you trying to do that."

His eyebrows shot up as he handed her the last cup. "Trying? *Amore mio*, have a little faith. I have spent more than a few years thinking about how you're going to taste. I will savor every drop and make certain you enjoy every moment. There's not going to be any worries about that, but you may find it might be too much, in which case I'll give you a moment to catch your breath before I start again." He gave her another wicked grin, caught up the towel and hung it on the rack to dry in the sun and took her hand.

"You're really enjoying yourself, aren't you?"

He was. There was no question about it. She was in his home. Finally. Nicoletta. His Nicoletta. His ring was on her finger. The ring his cousin had made specifically for the right woman, and it fit perfectly, much like Cinderella with her glass slipper. She might have an army of gangbangers coming after her, but she had an entire family of riders swarming to protect her, and he would bet on them every time.

"Didn't you have second thoughts?"

"Of course I did," he admitted. "I'm a man. I was a bachelor. Women threw themselves at me. The thought of marriage, being with one woman for the rest of my life, was a very different prospect. That was fleeting, I'll admit. And only when I thought about an actual relationship. It isn't like I had a good example with the parents. But then I kept going to your room every evening and talking to you. Listening to you. Laughing with you or holding you when you were crying and knowing how strong you were to survive what you did."

She shook her head as she settled into the chair in front of the fireplace. "Both you and Stefano act as if I saved myself. I was going to kill myself. That was my only way out. They were going to hand me over to Benito, you know that. You came in when they were desperately trying to save themselves. They knew if they didn't give me to him, he would kill them. If I was dead, he would kill them. That's the kind of man Benito is. I wasn't brave right then. I was a coward. I couldn't face Benito and what I knew he had in store for me."

"I thought you were very brave. You saw us kill your step-uncles. You might not have known how we got there, or even how we killed them, but they were dead, and you knew we were the ones responsible. I took your weapon from you, and I asked you if you wanted to come with us. You said yes. That was brave, Nicoletta. You said yes and we'd just killed them."

"I looked at you and knew you were better men."

"When you woke up on the plane, you knew we'd stripped you naked. You were wearing my shirt. You didn't scream, and you didn't fight me. You just looked at me and then to the door, and you went back to sleep. That took courage."

"You drugged me."

"You remember being in the tunnel. You weren't that drugged."

She kicked off her shoes and drew her feet onto the chair, a small smile on her face. "That's true. I do vaguely remember. That's why the feeling of being in the shadows was somewhat familiar to me. It was looking into your eyes, Taviano. I just trusted you. I did. I can't tell you why, but I did."

He poured them both a chilled glass of water before sinking into the chair beside hers. The glasses were placed on the small figure eight table between the two wide-cushioned chairs. The detail in the little table was exquisite. It was another one of the artist's creations that he'd left behind with his house.

Taviano thought the figure eight table fit perfectly with the two laid-back seamless chairs he'd bought at a gallery. The material was painted in bold stripes and round circles; the colors, muted purples and blues, reminded him of the night skies. Because the chairs were wide and overstuffed, they were extremely comfortable. Eloisa thought his "Bohemian" style of house and décor was atrocious, and she wanted him to allow her interior designer to take over, but he liked his unorthodox home and every art piece in it.

"I love all the sculptures you have," she said, as if she could read his mind, and maybe she could. They certainly were bound together. "I always wanted to learn to make pottery."

Something to give her. He could do that. She never would ask. He flashed her a smile. "Lucky for you, we have a little studio just waiting for someone to be interested enough to make pottery in it."

"I tried learning out of a book. It doesn't work that way."

"I happen to know people. Real artists, the best at their craft. They'll show us."

"Us? You'd do it with me?" There was a note of excitement in her voice.

"I told you, I'm the kind of man who wants my wife for a partner. You do it, I'll try it at least. I haven't shown you the training hall yet, but we have a full-sized gym, a meditation room and a pool for training. We have a shooting range, too."

"I still want to keep studying, Taviano. I can't fall behind on languages. Fortunately, I learn fairly easily, but I don't like taking time off."

"We'll put together a schedule. I'd like it better if Lucia and Amo would move to the guesthouse now, but I don't think we'll talk them into it this soon," he said. That meant they would have to schedule in time for visits.

"They like being close to Lucia's Treasures," Nicoletta admitted. "I can't imagine them moving this soon, either."

Taviano wasn't giving up all hope. Lucia and Amo loved Nicoletta and wouldn't want to be too far from her. They might consider hiring a manager for the store and just going in later if he could arrange that for them. That way, they could still be close to Nicoletta.

"We could always have a baby right away. They'd give up the shop for a baby," he suggested, straight faced.

She gasped and swung her head around to glare at him. "I did not just hear you say that. No one has a baby so their foster parents will close down a store and move next door."

"We could be the first ones."

Nicoletta stared at him a moment and then burst out laughing. "You're so awful. I'm going to have to get used to your terrible sense of humor."

He was going to have to make a list of the pros and cons of getting her pregnant. He hadn't thought about that. Cons were, no sex all over the house if they had kids right away, and he had to ease her into wild sex. That would take time. Babies meant she would find it harder to keep her running shoes on, and that was going to be a very hard pattern for her to break.

"Taviano, you have that look on your face."

"What look?" He tried for innocence.

"The one that says you're up to no good."

"I think my family is arriving." Just in the nick of time, too. No one was supposed to be able to read him. It was just his bad luck that his wife saw too much.

CHAPTER TEN

New York cousins are in town," Stefano reported. "Have you met them yet, Nicoletta? They came right away. Salvatore, Lucca and Geno are here with their bodyguards. The LA cousins are here as well."

Nicoletta knew Stefano was warning her so she wouldn't panic when they all showed up. Although she trained with them, she was still unable to overcome that uneasiness when the Ferraros were together in the same room. There were just too many of them and there was too much testosterone, too many alphas, although Stefano was always the acknowledged leader. Maybe it was that even with Mariko and Emmanuelle in the room, there weren't enough women to balance out the men.

Taviano shifted from his chair to hers, supposedly to make more room for the others, but she knew it was to give her more support and she appreciated it. He didn't make a big deal of it. Before he sat on the arm of her chair, he made certain everyone had something to drink and he gestured to

Ricco and Mariko to take his place, so it looked very natural that he would sit with her.

"I haven't met the cousins from New York yet," Nicoletta admitted, "although I did see some of the Los Angeles cousins when we were there." She hadn't really officially met them.

"And Elie Archambault? He's been working as a bodyguard with Emilio Gallo, another cousin. You've met him, of course," Stefano persisted.

Nicoletta nodded. "Yes, we've trained together a little here and there."

Elie smiled at her. "Stefano tells me that your father was an Archambault, a distant cousin of mine."

"So they say. I can't keep track of who is related to whom," she said. It was the truth. Every rider seemed related distantly to someone else. She resisted pressing a hand to her rapidly beating heart. Could they all hear it? They all seemed to have acute hearing, just like she did.

Mariko shifted in her chair, just a minute movement, barely perceptible, although Ricco noticed. His arm slid across his wife's shoulders, but he glanced at Nicoletta with one of his rare smiles. It was warm and genuine.

"I can barely keep track, either," he said. His lips, as he spoke, brushed Mariko's cheek. "And my wife doesn't ever try. She just smiles at everyone and assumes they're related in some way."

"Aren't they?" Mariko asked, looking surprised.

Nicoletta knew the couple was drawing attention away from her, and she was grateful to them. Mariko, almost from the first time they'd met, had been a gentle, exotic creature, so sweet it was impossible to think of her as a skilled and very experienced rider—but she was just as lethal as the men. She had, from the beginning, offered her friendship to Nicoletta.

Nicoletta glanced at Emmanuelle. She sat on the other side of Elie looking every bit a Ferraro. Even in the pin-striped suit she wore, she looked very feminine and beautiful. There wasn't a doubt that she was all woman. There was a sadness in her that hadn't been there a couple of years before. She had the same dark blue eyes that Taviano had. They used to light up when she smiled, but Nicoletta hadn't seen them do that, not in a couple of years.

She was always sweet and kind, she shouldered her responsibilities without a murmur and always took any extra rotation if any rider needed time off. If riders from other locations asked for help, it was Emmanuelle who volunteered to go. Nicoletta could tell that the entire family was worried about her, even the cousins. Even the bodyguards. Even Elie.

"Detroit Demons sent eighteen of their finest our way," Stefano announced. "They told Benito they'd soften us up and pick up Nicoletta for him. Benito did say they weren't to touch her. They could have whatever friend she cared about but not touch her. He would punish her his way, but no one else was to lay a hand on her."

"That's a big mistake," Nicoletta said. "Doesn't give his army a lot of room."

"I don't think they have a lot of control when it comes to women, so don't count on them listening," Taviano said. "I don't want any of them to ever lay eyes on you unless it's necessary for some reason we determine."

She nodded and leaned into him. "I'm good with that."

"Salvatore and the others have been monitoring the talk between Benito and the Detroit crew. They tried getting to him, but so far, they haven't been able to. He's moving all the time, and they can't pinpoint his location."

"Is he moving in this direction?" Taviano asked.

His hand settled around Nicoletta's neck. She was already acutely aware of him, but the moment he did that, surrounding her bare nape beneath her hair and stroking with the pads of his fingers, her entire focus jumped to those pinpoints of sensation. Each caress sent little streaks of lightning rushing through her bloodstream, creating heat. She knew she should stop him, because it was making it difficult to follow the conversation, but she didn't want him to stop.

Taviano made her feel connected to him, but more importantly, through that connection, she knew he needed to touch her. He hadn't had anyone to love him the way she did, so unconditionally. Giving herself to him when she didn't think she was going to get anything back mattered to him. She'd loved him for years. Even when she'd been pushing him away, he'd known she loved him. She *adored* him. He needed that from her. He needed to know that he was first in her life and that he always would be.

Nicoletta breathed through the lightning jolting her, the little strikes that seemed to carry such awareness to her breasts and then lower, between her legs, to her clit, to her core. She leaned into Taviano's hand and tried to concentrate on what was being discussed, telling herself it was good practice to learn to be aware no matter how pleasurable the circumstances.

"We have to assume that Benito is heading straight for us," Stefano said. He glanced at Nicoletta. "No matter what, *bella*, this man cannot have you. You are *famiglia*. None of this is your fault, and whatever they do, whoever they hurt, is on them. It is important to learn to disassociate. It's perhaps the most difficult of all the lessons."

Nicoletta felt the weight of their gazes on her. Her heart accelerated, and for a moment her breath was trapped in her lungs. Almost wildly, she looked around for the doors, or the windows, needing to know where the exits were. She'd already found them once—that was part of their training from day one—but she felt as if she needed to reassure herself that she could get to one of them quickly and no one was blocking any of them.

Taviano's fingers stilled their motion and then tightened on her skin, digging into her shoulders. There was a touch of possession there, but there was also the feeling of partnership.

"Breathe, *tesoro*. Everyone in this room is *famiglia*. No one will ever harm you."

She knew that. She hated that she still had panic attacks.

Stefano would never think she could go into the shadows with Taviano and be an asset to him, when she knew with a certainty that she could.

Mariko again came to her rescue. "It is true, Nicoletta. I have had a difficult time disassociating when the crime is too close to me."

Emmanuelle uncrossed her legs. "Unfortunately, I think all of us do. It's a human trait. We try, but when something is so close and we feel responsible, or someone hurts someone we love, we can't help wanting revenge."

Vittorio put his arm around his sister. "I chased a man, Grace's foster brother, a serial killer who had made her life a nightmare. He shot her, intending to shoot me, after selling her to the Saldis to pay a gambling debt. I wanted to hurt him before I delivered justice to him. It wasn't going to be justice, either. I wanted to kill him for the things he'd done to her. It took a great deal of self-control before I was able to fall back on my training and deliver justice for justice's sake. Disassociation is the hardest lesson and the most important there is, whether you are the victim or the one sent to deliver justice."

Nicoletta had gotten her breathing and racing heart under control, thanks to Mariko, Emmanuelle and Vittorio. She sent each of them a small smile of thanks.

"I understand what you're saying, Stefano, although, as everyone says, it is difficult, and I know if they get their hands on Lucia or Amo, I don't know how I would react." She could hear the raw honesty in her voice, but she couldn't help it. She loved her foster parents, and if Benito threatened them, she'd do anything at all to get them back. "I'd do whatever it took, including give myself up to him."

Taviano dropped his hand to her thigh and her heart nearly stopped. Her entire body reacted to his touch, in spite of the enormity of the conversation. Her core throbbed and burned. His declaration earlier, the promise of stripping her naked and devouring her, reverberated through her mind. She couldn't believe she could be distracted just by his hand on her thigh. His palm was burning a brand through her skirt to her thigh. His hand was high up, so close to where her heart beat right through her pulsing clit.

Taviano leaned down to press his lips close to her ear, but when he spoke even in that low tone, it was loud enough for everyone in the room to hear. "You wouldn't, *amore mio*. You would trust your *marito*, and your *famiglia*, to get them back. You will do what you are told and remain safe. We know how to handle these situations, and you have to have faith that we would get Lucia and Amo back unharmed."

She wanted to say she would do that. She really did, but she wasn't going to lie to Taviano. She'd promised herself— and him—that there would not be lies between them. "I swear I would try, Taviano, but they're . . . sacred." She couldn't come up with any other word. "I would try." That was all she could give him.

Stefano nodded his head. "I understand, *cara*. If someone took Francesca, I would feel the same. Trust us. Fight the inclination to give in, should that happen. The likelihood is slim, unless Lucia or Amo leave the safety of where we placed them. Valdez can't get to them where they are."

She was not going to go visit them, not until this was over, when she had intended to do just that. Now she knew Stefano had placed her foster parents somewhere very safe, and she wasn't about to jeopardize them by leaving a trail to them for selfish reasons. "What are you going to do? You said that some of the Demons were heading this way from Detroit."

Stefano nodded. "We intend to intercept this evening. The moment word gets to us that they stopped to eat, we'll visit them. We don't want them to get to our territory. I believe Valdez has several such branches of his army heading our way from various directions. We've got eyes on them. He's directing them. He'd like them to get here before his arrival."

She had heard that Benito used that tactic often, whenever he was going to take over a new territory. He would send out several branches of his army. They would pick off their rivals and then surround the territory before going in and wiping them out. It was always a bloody massacre. The idea that Benito Valdez was deploying his armies on Ferraro territory and the civilians who were just going about their lives was terrifying to her.

"He takes over that way," she informed them.

Taviano must have felt the quake in her mind, because it wasn't in her voice. She was proud of that. He used his thumb to stroke the inside of her thigh, once again distracting her beyond all reason. She was certain he meant to soothe her, but her body was already on fire. She felt torn apart, mind and body going in two different directions.

"He will end up with a bit of a shock when his army doesn't arrive," Stefano said. "Mariko and Ricco are going to intercept the ones coming from St. Louis. There's a contingency coming from Oklahoma City. Vittorio, Emme and Elie will take them. There's one coming in from Camden, New Jersey. Salvatore, Geno, Lucca, you're on them. Our cousins in Los Angeles are already tracking the very large group making their way from California to Chicago. Giovanni will head that way to help. They're going to take them when we give the go-ahead. We want them out of action permanently, but we don't want any witnesses or any way for Valdez to trace their deaths to us. Just like they found the Gomez brothers, these men will die with broken necks and no way to trace how or who. Watch for cameras. Always disrupt cameras. Be on guard for that."

"You didn't include us," Nicoletta objected.

"Valdez has people here in Chicago. He hasn't built his territory up here as large as he'd like, but he's called on them to step up," Stefano said. "We're going to visit them before they decide to show Valdez they don't have to wait for the others. Sasha has been keeping an eye on them, and there's already rumblings about a snatch and grab to incur Valdez's favor."

For some reason it surprised her that Stefano said Sasha

was keeping an eye on them, but she realized he meant ears. Sasha had learned to be very good with electronic equipment. She was working with Rigina and Rosina Greco, investigators for the Ferraro family. They were cousins, relatives, like everyone who worked for them. Sasha was learning from the best. Nicoletta was fascinated by all the different jobs and the way things worked. She hadn't realized what they were doing until Taviano had actually filled her in on what the investigations entailed. She thought they were private investigators and worked on divorces with slimy cheaters.

"We will be taking the fight to them," Stefano decreed. He glanced at his watch. "We'll meet around two in the morning. Streetlights give off plenty of shadows. I've scouted the streets where they live and hang out. We'll have easy access. They have one place they gather in, so if they're there, all in one place, it will be easier."

"Or more difficult," Giovanni said. "Someone is bound to notice when brothers start dropping dead on the floor."

Stefano shrugged. "Creating a little fear is good for their souls."

"You should hang back, Stefano, watch over our territory," Ricco said. "Taviano and Nicoletta can handle the Demons here. There's, like, what? Thirty total? Giovanni? What did you get? I doubt there's more than that."

Giovanni nodded. "Yeah. If that. Taviano can do that in his sleep. Or I can stay here and help him out. LA has seven riders including Velia, and she's every bit as lethal as her brothers. They don't need me."

Stefano looked around the room suspiciously. "What's going on here? Nicoletta can move in the shadows, but she can't help Taviano. She hasn't been given the necessary training yet. Giovanni, the LA chapter is enormous. The largest Valdez has moving our way. You know that. You said it yourself that it was going to take all the cousins to take them out, and then some. Why are all of you trying to keep me out of the shadows?"

His inquiry was met with silence. Nicoletta couldn't tell by the expressionless masks the others wore if there was a conspiracy to keep Stefano out of the fighting. It didn't make sense, when he was reputed to be so fast. She'd seen him a few times in action, and he'd worked with her several times. He was like greased lightning.

Ricco gave a small shrug. "You're the head of the family. We like to keep it that way. And someone needs to stay back just in case there's a fuckup and Valdez has an army that slips through. Who do we have on Francesca and Crispino, Sasha, Grace?"

"We have the best bodyguards in the world," Stefano said. "We're all going to be in the shadows. They'll be guarding the women. I think we're done here. Are there any questions?"

No one had any. When Stefano decreed something, it was rarely questioned. They had their assignments, and they were going to move on them fast. This time there would be no private jets and no parties. No alibis and paparazzi. They would ride the shadows to their destination from their homes, so it would appear as if they had gone inside and were in for the night. There would be no way to trace them to the "kill zone." Valdez wouldn't have a clue what had happened to his men, and neither would the cops, who would try to piece together the puzzle of who was killing off the Demons by breaking their necks one by one.

Nicoletta stayed in her chair in front of the fireplace while Taviano walked the others out. It was late afternoon, but the sun was still high in the sky and pouring beams down on the shrubbery. Through the panels of glass, she could see flowers lifting petals toward the rays. It was a beautiful sight. She looked around her. Everything in Taviano's house was beautiful. His home was peaceful. A work of art.

She could see why he had chosen the location, away from the city. There were no sounds of traffic. No noises other than the soothing symphony of nature. His home was hidden away from the world. Tucked up into the hillside, it was nearly impossible to spot until one was right up on it. The house felt cool, as if the hill and the woods protected it from the sun. The fireplace gave the illusion of heat even though there were no flames at the moment. The sunshine made her feel warm enough.

Taviano returned to her, a big man. Gorgeous. She would never tire of looking at him. She couldn't believe he was hers. That he really had fallen in love with her, but it was there in his eyes. She could get lost there.

"You told me you loved me."

"I do love you. The wonder is that you didn't know."

She thought the wonder was that he loved her. She wasn't yet that cool, confident woman that she was determined to become. "I'm not always going to be fragile."

Was that the reason? He was a Ferraro, and the men in that family were naturally dominant. They protected their women. She wasn't ever going to be a Francesca, or a Grace. She couldn't be sweet like Mariko, no matter how hard she tried. Sasha was the most like her, but even Sasha . . .

Nicoletta sighed. "I need to be strong, Taviano. So strong."

"You already are much stronger than you think, Nicoletta, but I understand what you mean. We have the training room, the gym and the meditation room. I'll do everything I can to give you whatever it is you need to build your confidence in your skills until you believe in yourself."

That hit her like an arrow straight to her heart, and she pressed her hand hard over her chest because she ached. He was wonderful. He had always given her everything. No matter what she did to push him away. Because she'd been so scared, because she'd thought she was so ugly and so covered in the layers of filth her step-uncles and Benito had visited on her, she hadn't wanted Taviano anywhere near her. Her golden man.

"Stefano is going with us to evaluate me, isn't he?"

"Yes."

His tone was mild. He didn't hesitate or attempt in any way to lie to her. She loved him all the more for that.

"I'm going to get sick the way I did before."

Taviano shrugged. "That doesn't matter. You handled it. He'll see that you handled being in the shadows and moving from one to the next. You'll be fine if you remember everything we've talked about, especially the breathing. You have to stay on top of that."

He was so matter of fact it was impossible to have a panic attack. It was impossible to think Stefano would decree she wasn't good enough to keep training. He hadn't sidelined her. He was allowing her to go along. In a way, she was grateful. The Demons chapter in Chicago had to be somewhat significant. She didn't want Taviano to face them alone and she didn't know how to make the Ferraro signature kill they all would be using. Having Stefano along ensured Taviano's safety. Above all else, she wanted that.

Heart pounding, she moistened her bottom lip. She wanted to be daring with him. She wanted to give him something huge. He deserved a brave, courageous partner. He deserved so much more than she was at that moment, but she was determined to grow and keep growing. She reached out to him, and he immediately wrapped his larger fingers around her hand. He made her feel delicate when she never had before.

He gently tugged until she was out of the chair and standing close to him, the tips of her breasts brushing his chest. Just that slight contact sent those little lightning strikes forking through her body in every direction. Where did women get confidence? Where did they learn to be sexy? She wanted that not just for herself but for Taviano. She wanted it with every breath she drew, but she couldn't quite gain the courage to lift her gaze to his.

He cupped her chin with exquisite gentleness, his thumb brushing along her lower lip. "I dream about biting this lip." He bent his head and brushed a kiss along her mouth. A brief, barely there contact, gone far too soon. "And then kissing away the sting."

She wanted to have the courage to challenge him to do it. More, she wanted to go up on her toes and bite his lower lip and kiss away the sting. She nearly did it. She actually rose on her toes, leaning into him so her breasts pushed against his chest, melting into him, her nipples two hard, aching buds. If the sensation hadn't been so acute, she might have succeeded, but she got stuck right there, her breath caught in her lungs, her pulse pounding between her legs.

Taviano took her mouth, somewhere between gentle and passionate. She wanted passionate and she went for it, kissing him back, her tongue shyly exploring, teasing his, dueling for a moment and then following his lead. She didn't know much about kissing—there were never kisses involved before, there was never anything to ensure she felt pleasure—so every sensation was new and shocking to her. She savored every single one.

Flames seemed to course through her blood, spreading through her body like a wildfire out of control. "I believe you promised me something." She whispered it, because she could barely say the words, but she wanted to experience everything he'd declared he'd do to her. She wanted it for both of them, but mostly to prove to herself that she could be a woman to her man. She could share passion with him. She could eventually make love with him. The horror of her past didn't have to destroy her future with the man she loved.

He kissed his way over her chin and down her throat. "I did? What did I promise you, *amore mio*? I always keep my promises."

Heart pounding, her fists clenched in his shirt, she closed her eyes, her head tilted back so he could kiss wherever he wanted. Little electrical sparks seemed to be dancing over her skin. She wanted more. She didn't know anything could make her feel so alive and so feminine. His mouth on her throat, moving down to the curve of her breasts, made her feel as if she were a goddess and he was worshiping her.

"What did I promise?" he prompted again.

His chin nudged her top down, the bristles on his jaw

scraping sensually over her sensitive skin, sending urgent demands thrumming through her body, straight to her sex. She felt the clench of need, a wave of desire dampening her panties and pounding through her clit.

"You said you would devour me." She managed the whisper on a gasp as he suckled right through her bra. She couldn't help cradling his head to her, his dark hair falling over her arm as she held him to her breast. She wanted more. She needed more. Her entire body was one living flame. "Taviano." She heard the raw ache in her voice.

That scared her. She was all but seducing him. She *was* seducing him, begging him to take things further, and yet she didn't know if she could really do anything with him. What if she couldn't? What if she panicked?

Before she could pull back, Taviano was already kissing his way up her throat to her chin, and then he took her mouth. When he was kissing her, there was no way to think. It was impossible to do anything but wrap her arms around his neck and give herself to him. She was lost there, kissing him back, giving him everything she was. Every kiss seemed better, hotter than the one before, so perfect.

Taviano shifted her enough to slide one arm under her bottom and he lifted her, his mouth still commanding hers. He carried her so easily through the house, kissing her as they went, making her feel as light as air. She felt as if she floated through the house, his arms around her, his kisses transporting her to a world of pure sensuality—one she wanted to know intimately. One she wanted to live in with Taviano.

He had to hold her up when he put her feet on the floor. She clung to him, her legs feeling as if they were shaky. When she looked up at his face, the light coming through the windows shone on him and he looked like a fallen angel. His dark hair spilled across his forehead in sharp contrast to the deep blue of his eyes.

The dark intensity of his focused look when it settled on her upturned face shook her. He looked like sensuality personified. Every line in his face was carved deep with a sensual lust that bonded with the dark blue of his eyes, sending her heart racing. Her body went into some kind of weird meltdown. A thousand butterflies took wing in her stomach as it did a crazy slow roll. He could make her nipples peak with that dark intensity every time.

"I don't know what to do, Taviano." She only knew that she had to do something. He had to do something. Her body was so hot and uncomfortable, every cell inflamed—for him. "What if I can't do this? What if I ruin everything?"

Taviano pointed to the bed. "Just kneel up on the bed, *piccola*. I love the way the light hits you. You look so beautiful. Face the window and look out. The wind is picking up. It always does this time of day." He gestured toward the bed. "You can't ruin anything, Nicoletta, because there is no wrong or right in our bedroom. There is only the two of us and what we decide to do together."

Dio, this man. *Her* man. She loved him more than life itself. She could do anything for him. She let him distract her. Let him help her over the first of the hurdles, because she was determined to give them both this time together.

Light streaked through the glass, hitting the bed from all the rows of windows and sliders, lighting up the duvet so that it shone like a watery image, almost as if it were a lily pad floating. Nicoletta hadn't noticed that the night before or in the morning when she'd awakened. She slid her palm over it in wonder. The texture of the duvet was soft like velvet, yet cooler. The swirling greens and blues with the sun playing over them really did appear to move like water. Everything in the house, even the linens, was art. She knelt up onto the bed, hiking up the skirt so her bare legs would feel the soft coolness of the fiber.

"Let me see your skin in the sun, *tesoro*."

His voice had dropped an octave, sounding like seduction itself. Now his voice brushed over her skin like velvet. She didn't need to feel the texture of the duvet when his tone could give her that sensual feeling.

"Do you feel the sun on you right through the glass? Just slip off your top and bra. Your skin is so beautiful. I'm not going to do anything but look at you. If you want, I'll go sit over there in the chair so you can feel safe."

He didn't wait for her to have to make the decision, he simply did so, removing his jacket and hanging it on the back of a chair before slipping into one of the two deep-backed comfortable chairs placed close together for morning coffee just inside, close to the slider leading to the terrace.

Nicoletta felt his eyes on her. She liked him watching her. She had always liked the way he focused so completely on her. He made her feel beautiful even when she'd never believed in herself. Now, she felt her nipples peak. Her breasts ached. Between her legs she grew damp and needy. It was okay because she was safe with him. She loved him all the more for making her feel it was all right to explore being sensual and not worry that she was going too far or teasing him and then refusing to go any further. Taviano didn't seem to put any limits on her—or expectations.

He didn't hurry her or insist. She knew if she crawled off the bed and got into his lap it would be okay and they'd try another day. Instead, she boldly unbuttoned her blouse, one little pearl button at a time. At first she was breathless. Scared. Then she slowed down and felt daring. Then she met his eyes and felt sexy. She let the material slide from her shoulders down to the duvet.

Before she could lose her nerve, she reached to the front of her bra where the little hooks were and quickly lifted them to spill her generous breasts free. She didn't look at him but at the woods where the wind was playing through the leaves, stirring them up, lifting them, the way her breathing was lifting her breasts.

"You have such a beautiful, feminine form. Truly beautiful, *tesoro*. Look down and see my mark on you. I love seeing it on you. If you were ever to be painted in the nude, I would want my mark on your breast, just like that."

She couldn't help it. She had already looked in the mirror a dozen times at it. She looked down at the dark reddish slash that declared she was his. Her hand crept under her breast to lift the soft weight higher, while her fingers traced the mark lovingly. A fresh flood of liquid heat formed between her legs and she wanted to rub her thighs together at the pulsing there.

With one hand, Taviano loosened his tie and then removed it. She liked that. She liked that just looking at her made him shift in his chair. She could see the bulge in the front of his trousers, and she liked that she had put that there. So far, panic hadn't crept in, but he was across the room from her and he'd given his word that she was safe. Taviano always kept his word.

"You ready for the next step or do you want to stop here?"

She ached inside. She ached for both of them. Her heart raced, but that was to be expected. All the while they'd sat through the meeting, Taviano's hand had been in her hair or at the back of her neck. Sometimes he had touched her thigh. Or her arm. She'd been so acutely aware of him. Mostly, she'd kept thinking about his declaration, that he was going to devour her. Eat her like candy. She wanted that. She wanted to experience what other women had. And she wanted to experience it with him. Just the thought had her aching so much between her thighs that she shook her head without thinking.

She took a deep breath and leapt off the cliff. "Tell me what you want me to do."

"Lie back and take off your skirt and then your panties. Just lie in the sun for a few minutes and feel it on your skin. Let me look at you."

Her heart nearly beat out of her chest. Could she do that? Could she do that for both of them? Was she that brave? She didn't have to take off her skirt. Taviano wasn't forcing her. He wasn't commanding her. There was no demand in his voice. She asked. He answered. She could pretend she was sunbathing in the nude. She'd done it before. More than once she'd done it. She'd been completely alone in Lucia's fenced backyard and she'd taken her clothes off in order to prove to herself she was that brave and to check if the pull of the shadows was greater without her clothes on, although she'd been so scared she'd only managed to make herself put her foot into the shadows.

Tentatively, while still on her knees, she shimmied the skirt down her hips, taking her underwear with it. When she brought them over her thighs, she turned sideways so she could slip them over her knees and down her legs to remove them. She was totally nude but not lying down. If she did, she would have to choose whether to lie down so her body faced him or not.

It was terrifying. Yet thrilling. Sexy as all hell because it was Taviano. He didn't say a single word. It was her choice. She hated and loved that it was her choice—that he gave her that. If he didn't, she couldn't possibly have gone through with it, but because he sat very still, a distance away from her, utterly silent with the exception of his steady breathing, she was able to match her breathing to his and slowly stretch her body across that amazing duvet.

The moment her skin slid over the soft fibers, they stroked her like fingers, adding to the already sensual sensation every cell in her body was on fire with. She tried not to squirm or rub herself all over the duvet. It was difficult not to move, and she found herself, as she bathed in the light, feeling as though a spotlight shone directly on her. She couldn't help moving subtly, letting the duvet send little sparks of electricity dancing through her bloodstream.

"Can you tell me what you're feeling right now?"

His voice floated to her on those beams of sunshine. She could see her breasts rising and falling, and she found the sight sexy, when she'd never thought of herself that way. She was connected with Taviano, and maybe some of his thoughts had crept into her mind, but for whatever reason, that added to the need rising in her like a tidal wave.

"So sexy. I want you to see me as someone beautiful and sexy. Someone desirable."

The chair creaked as he rose and walked slowly toward her. Ordinarily, it was impossible to hear a Ferraro walking, but he came across the floor deliberately making sounds. She turned her head to look at him, to watch him come to her.

Taviano was barefoot, his shirt off, wearing only his trousers. His upper body was all muscle and he looked powerful. So much more so than any man she'd ever been around. When he moved, muscles rippled, from his thick chest all the way to the vee disappearing into the pinstriped material of his slacks.

He didn't stop, he just kept walking until he was at the bottom of the bed and then he put a knee on it and was right there, his mouth on hers, kissing her until she couldn't think, couldn't be afraid of anything, because he transported her back into that wonder world of pure sensuality.

He lifted his head and smiled at her, his blue eyes staring directly into hers. "I love you beyond all reason, Nicoletta Ferraro. You are my sanity."

He brushed kisses over her chin and then his palm fit around her throat like a collar. So gentle. Loose. Her heart beat into his hand. She knew they both felt it. The hand slid down the valley between her breasts to her belly, where it stopped, fingers splayed wide.

"Someday, *tesoro*, our baby will be right here. I've thought of that so many times."

He slid lower on the bed while he framed her flat stomach with both hands, brushing kisses over her skin until she thought she might burst into flames. She hadn't known she was sensitive there. His strong white teeth suddenly nipped her, stinging, and her hips bucked as her sex clenched hard, a wild spasm of need, and her clit throbbed and pulsed, so inflamed she thought she would spontaneously combust.

"Taviano." She hissed his name.

His arm locked over her thighs, holding her to the bed while he licked at the sting. "I like to put my mark on you.

It pleases me to look at it. Or just to know it's there beneath your clothing."

"I'm on fire." It came out a wail. She hadn't intended to sound so . . . desperate, but she was. *Desperate* was the only adjective she could think of. He was making her desperate for him. For something. For anything. But he had to do it soon or she might not survive.

"Are you? For me? Are you on fire for me, Nicoletta?" His palm slid over her belly as he moved lower on the bed, then right off of it. She felt his movements more than saw them because she'd slung her arm over her eyes. Her hips were uncontrollable now, sliding shamelessly over the duvet, bucking, desperate for relief only Taviano could give her.

"Yes." Her breath hissed out in a long, painful admission.

His long, very strong fingers slid through her dark curls and found the betraying dampness she couldn't hide. He stroked caresses there and then his hands were on her thighs, pulling them apart. She felt the air, now cool on her hot entrance. She wanted to protest the way her thighs were spread so far apart, the way she was so open to him, but then his tongue ran up the inside of her right thigh and a dark moan slipped out instead of a protest.

The sensation of that velvet tongue lapping at her thigh, coupled with the rasp of the bristles on his jaw, built that terrible coiling pressure to an almost brutal need. She couldn't have protested if she wanted to. She needed more. She needed Taviano to do exactly as he'd promised, no matter the cost. She wanted to be devoured and eaten like candy. She wanted him to send her tumbling over the edge into a freefall. She could only hope that he would catch her.

CHAPTER ELEVEN

Taviano listened to the singsong sob hitching in Nicoletta's ragged breathing. It was difficult to keep himself under control enough to pay attention to minute details, but he reminded himself it was necessary. She tasted like heaven. He knew she would. His woman. *Dio*, but she was perfect for him in every way.

He took his time, savoring the liquid honey on her thighs, easing closer and closer to the heat emanating from her entrance. He put his mark there, several of them, on either side, both left and right. Strawberries with his teeth marks. Her gasps and groans, the addicting cream he captured in his mouth when he gave her those little reminders of who she was married to, made him feel a bit like a caveman.

Nicoletta was his woman. *His.* He had felt alone for so long. No one knew him. No one had ever accepted the real him. He knew that wasn't fair to his siblings, because chances were they would have unconditional love for him, but he also knew the knowledge of what had happened to him as a young boy would change their relationship subtly. Nicoletta just loved him.

Almost from the moment she'd opened her eyes on that plane ride back to Chicago from New York, he had seen the growing adoration in her eyes. She'd tried to hide it. She'd tried to escape him. He'd done everything in his power to encourage it. He'd found he needed her.

A year into her being with the family, he had gotten to the point that the nights he shared with other women after being in the shadows weren't nearly as satisfying as they had once been. He didn't like to be touched. Usually, he fucked a woman hard, was generous with jewelry or his photographs with the media so she could further her career, and then hc got away quickly. Now he craved Nicoletta's touch. He wanted her hands—and her mouth—on him. He wanted his cock buried in her body. And this—he wanted his mouth on her, tasting what belonged to him.

He was careful at first, lapping at her, suckling, watching her reaction before using his teeth to scrape along her clit and then suckle more. He used his tongue ruthlessly like a cock, stroking and caressing, fucking her, and then loving her. She writhed wildly, so he locked her down with his arm, his mouth doing exactly what he'd promised: devouring her.

Her hands found his hair, fisting there. At times she pulled on his scalp, the pain adding to the sensations whipping through his body like lightning strikes straight to his cock. She wasn't quiet, and he loved hearing her moans and her cries. The little sob in her voice as he took her up further and further and then backed off. She was so ready, but he hated to stop. He didn't want to lose this moment of intimacy with her. He might never get it back.

Her body shuddered and he put one hand on her belly, fingers wide to feel the tension coiling so tightly there. She was fighting the sensations, afraid now, near panicked at that pleasure spilling through her, fear creeping in at the unknown.

He added his fingers, curling one deep, stroking the little bundle of nerves while he worked her clit with his teeth and tongue. "Now, *amore mio*, let go. Just let go. I'm right here with you. You have to trust someone. Let that someone be me." He kept his voice gentle when he wanted to growl like a wild animal. His own body was making demands, so hard, full and painful, he feared he might make a fool of himself like some hapless teenager. He used his tongue, fluttering, probing, lapping, all the while keeping up that persistent stroking.

He knew the exact moment she chose to surrender to him. To give herself to him fully. To trust her body to him. One moment her entire body was shuddering, fighting the need to come, the tension in her making her almost rigid, and then she just gave in, relaxing, breathing, letting her body take over.

The orgasm swept through her like a tidal wave. Strong. Powerful. Sending shock waves through her. He felt ripples through her belly and down her thighs. He lapped at the hot liquid and then suckled, drawing that sweet honey out with his tongue so he could have more. He knew he should stop— her gift of trust to him was a tremendous one—but he couldn't quite relinquish his place between her thighs. Not yet. Not when her taste was so addictive.

He sent another orgasm crashing through her and then a third. She screamed through the third one, and when he licked at her, she nearly sobbed his name, jerking at his hair. He lifted his head. "Are you too sensitive for more, because I love this. I could do this all night."

He watched her face. She wanted this as much as he did. He could see the beauty there, the pleasure, the triumph. When he ducked his head and lapped at her again, he got the same reaction. The fist in his hair jerked hard, and this time her hips did the same. Yeah. She was too sensitive to continue.

Nicoletta flung her arm over her eyes, struggling for breath. "*Dio*, Taviano. If you kept that up, I think I would have died."

He laughed softly and rubbed his face on her thighs before kissing his marks on her. He loved looking at them. His cock hurt like a bear and he needed relief desperately. Any movement made it known that he was going to have to hit the shower soon. He tugged down his zipper and managed to get his trousers off. They didn't wear underwear in the shadows. It was one less thing to worry about. He took a deep breath the moment he was free of the confining material. He would have liked to climb on the bed with her, but not like this, not naked with his cock standing stiff and demanding. His fist circled the base. He gripped hard. Even that felt good.

"Taviano."

He closed his eyes. Her voice. There was too much temptation, too much seduction, and he was too far gone. He shook his head, but he didn't step away when she slid off the bed and went to her knees in front of him.

"*Piccola*, you did exactly what we'd hoped. We don't want to ruin it."

His fist slid up and down his cock. *Dio*, it felt good. He gripped harder, looking down at her mouth. Those lips. There was a faint mark on her lower lip where he'd bitten her. The thought of his cock in her hot mouth, his hand on her throat while she swallowed his come, all the while looking into his eyes—that would be sexy.

He dropped his gaze to her breasts. His mark was there as well. He could pump his cock and empty himself all over those beautiful breasts. Rub his essence into her like lotion. Feed her some with his fingers. Watch it drip from her nipples. The thought made him harder than ever, and drops leaked from the head of his cock.

He wished her thighs were open so he could see the strawberries he'd put there. Without thinking, he touched her knee with his foot, nudging just a little, his gaze still on her face. Her lashes fluttered, but her gaze remained on his fist sliding, pumping his cock. That fact that she watched him made him hotter than hell. She opened her knees wide and there was the evidence of his claiming, the bright chains of strawberries. She was slick; that addicting cream was all his.

Her hand brushed his heavy sac and desire shot through him like an arrow. She stroked and squeezed gently and then her mouth was there, licking and tracing every tight seam with her tongue. His breath caught in his throat. He knew he should stop her, but her hand was back, fingers splayed wide, and she was jiggling his sac. It felt as if the massaging waves rose in slow motion from his balls to the base of his cock, and then spread in a pounding ecstasy through his cock. He'd never felt anything quite like it.

"*Dio*, Nicoletta, you're killing me, *tesoro*."

A heartbeat went by. Two. Suddenly the gentle massage was gone, and she was doing something completely different, her fingers deftly rotating his large balls in her palm, at least it felt like that was what she was doing. That sent streaks of fire racing up his cock. Fast. The flames licked along the base, rushed along the shaft, burned under and then over the crown until he wanted to throw back his head and roar.

She moved then, her mouth sipping and then suckling at his balls, working her way up to the base of his cock. Her tongue flicked over his fist, teased between his fingers and then curled along his shaft. His heart nearly stopped as her eyes met his. His breath was instantly trapped in his lungs. He didn't know what he expected to see in her eyes, but it wasn't dark desire. It wasn't stark lust. It wasn't raw love. All three of those emotions were there, mingled together. Her gaze, her expression, was hot.

She licked her lips so that they gleamed at him. The little bite mark on her lower lip glistened. He couldn't help himself. He rubbed the head of his cock over the mark, deliberately leaving drops behind. Her tongue came out, licked slowly, sensuously, along her lower lip until she'd lapped up every bit. Never once did her gaze leave his.

"I want more."

"I think you're getting greedy." He loved teasing her.

"You took so much." She pouted, the lower lip coming out even more.

Dio, he was going to come just looking at her. More hot seed bubbled up like lava. Her tongue glided up his shaft. Featherlight. Just the tip. She flicked the vee beneath his crown over and over and then licked at the leaking drops as if they were her favorite ice cream. He didn't reprimand her. She was already back at his shaft, using the blade of her tongue, pressing into him, varying the pressure from one side to the other, until he was struggling to find his breath again. Her tongue was a wicked weapon and she wielded it with complete confidence.

Taviano pulled back. He needed some control. This was dangerous for both of them whether she knew it or not. She was enjoying herself and he was in paradise, but it could turn ugly in moments. He wasn't going to let that happen for her.

"Baby." It was a protest. "You had dessert. I get mine." She had a beautiful pout.

"How do I taste?" He couldn't resist asking.

"So good, the best. And all mine."

That was the right answer. He was all hers. He rubbed his brutally aching cock along her lower lip and then pressed down in a silent command. She opened her mouth immediately for him, stretching wide to accommodate his size. He pushed inside slowly. A single sound escaped his throat. A low moan of pleasure.

Paradise. Hot. Wet. Exquisite. He narrowed his eyes, closing until they were mere slits. He needed to see her, but he wanted to savor the incredible feeling of her mouth turning into a vacuum. A tight suction. One moment, her tongue was lashing him, flicking hard, stabbing at him, then lapping and curling as she bobbed up and down his shaft; the next, she was hollowing her cheeks and sucking as if she meant to pull every bit of his boiling semen from his tight balls.

His hand dropped to her hair. He had been careful not to touch her, but he couldn't stop himself. It was difficult not to feel dominant when she knelt at his feet, even though she was in that position voluntarily. He liked the way her gaze never left his face. He liked the expression of adoration in her eyes. She enjoyed what she was doing to him. She knew she was damned good at it.

Still, he needed to make it easier to stay in control. He felt for the bed. It was a good height. Slowly, he sank down, legs spread wide so she was between his thighs and he could push deeper. Just a little, watching her. Testing the waters to see if it scared her. She wrapped her hand around the base of his cock, freeing both his hands.

The tight erect buds standing up on her breasts called to him, and he reached down and caught her left one, first using his thumb to strum it, and then he flicked it before catching it between his finger and thumb and clamping down for just a moment. He watched her face the entire time. Watched the way she took the small sting and the blood rushing back when he let her loose. Color swept up her body and between her legs, fresh liquid glistened.

"You're so perfect, Nicoletta. Can you take more of me?" He pulled back to let her breathe. She gave him a wicked smile and lifted her right breast as she leaned into him, widening her mouth as he pushed his cock toward her lips.

His thumb strummed and flicked and then he pinched her nipple, this time pushing deeper as her breath hitched. More of his cock slid into her mouth and he felt the narrowing. The roof of her mouth. The velvet of her tongue. The suction. The cage of teeth. His heavy vein pulsed with his heartbeat as his cock bore its way into that exquisite tunnel. Another inch.

"I'm not going to be able to stop in another minute, *tesoro*," he admitted, his voice hoarse. He was barely able to control his hips. Already he was thrusting into her mouth.

Small little pushes, but he had promised himself he wouldn't take any control. His fingers had already fisted in her hair, holding her head tipped back and still. His other hand was wrapped around her throat so he could feel her heartbeat, that rapid rhythm that beat for him. It was possible, if she could do it, that he would feel the invasion of the thick bulge of his cock. The thought was exciting. His cock in her throat. Would she swallow him down? Swallow his semen? Take him that deep into her? Be that intimate with him?

He hoped he was man enough to stop when she said no. He needed her to tell him now. This minute, while he still had his sanity. Those dark chocolate eyes never stopped looking at him. Never once looked away. She didn't hesitate. She actually swallowed, the sensation like a wet massage, constricting him like a vise, and then she relaxed and did it again and again. All the while she breathed through her nose. As she did so, he watched more of his cock slip into her mouth, and under his palm he felt that monster like an invader, working its way into her. Deep. His woman.

His balls drew up in a frenzy. The volcano was a fiery mass of hot magma and then he couldn't think, only feel, as his body took over. He'd never experienced anything like she gave him, the release explosive, rocketing through his entire body, a wild ride that flung him somewhere into outer space. The orgasm encompassed every cell in his body, a violent, brutal eruption as jet after jet of semen was wrung from him.

Taviano was barely aware of anything but mind-numbing pleasure, that hot, wet cavern, the constriction, the ease and the lap of her tongue, so gentle, an exquisite torture. He collapsed across the bed, desperate to find his air, his lungs refusing to work, his mind nearly frozen. He was aware of Nicoletta moving, but he couldn't even turn his head to see what she was doing, he was that far gone, something that had never happened in his life. He felt thoroughly drained, thoroughly sated—and he hadn't even been inside her yet.

On that thought came another, his mind beginning to

slowly function again. Too slow. He groaned, rolled over and buried his face in the duvet. This was supposed to be for Nicoletta. All for her. An introduction to lovemaking, not just sex, but real love between a man and a woman. He wanted to show her something selfless. Unconditional. Give her something, her first real orgasm, a beautiful, loving gift between a husband and a wife. She had admitted she had perfected her oral sex techniques—just as he had—in order to avoid anything else.

He groaned into the duvet and then hit it with his bunched fist. Thumped the mattress twice. Had he played right into her hands? He hadn't planned to make love to her. He wanted her to choose when the time was right, but had she decided to ensure that he didn't touch her by falling back on a tried-and-true method? He *detested* that. He didn't want to be in the same category as her step-uncles, or Benito Valdez, a man she thought she had to control with her mouth.

The mattress dipped and he felt her crawling up onto the bed beside him. Her hand slid up his bare back. It was an intimate gesture and surprised him. Nicoletta rarely touched him of her own accord.

"What's wrong, Taviano?" She sounded hesitant but determined. "Did I do something wrong? You need to just tell me if I did."

He forced himself to turn his head toward her, his eyes on her face. If she could be courageous, so could he. She looked beautiful. Flushed. She had obviously washed her face and rinsed out her mouth and brushed her teeth. She'd thrown on his shirt but hadn't buttoned it up, and he could see the curves of her breasts peeking out at him. Her hair had slipped partially from the topknot and tumbled around her shoulders and down her back, a wild mass of unruly waves framing her face and breasts. The sight moved him.

"No, *amore mio*, this was all on me. I should have stopped you. I wanted this to be for you. A gift. I didn't want you to be afraid that I would expect something in return."

Her hand crept up the back of his neck and then her fingers were in his hair. Her touch sent little sparks of electricity down his spine. She began a slow massage, the pads of her fingers pressing into his scalp, relieving some of the tension that had begun to build just thinking about the mistakes he was making being selfish with her.

"I wasn't afraid you expected anything from me, Taviano."

Her voice was soft with love. The emotion was stark and raw and very genuine. She didn't try to hide it from him. She just laid it out for him to feel. She wrapped him in love and it felt damned good. He'd wanted to give her a gift, and she'd ended up giving him something priceless, something he'd felt he'd never have. He had to turn his head away from her. The lump in his throat was becoming too large to swallow and the burn behind his eyes too enormous to hide.

"I wanted to make you feel the way you made me feel, so we could share such an amazing moment together. It was beautiful and I'll remember it for the rest of my life. I hope you will as well. I wasn't putting you off. And I wasn't afraid you'd demand more than I was willing to give."

He had to say something, but it took a moment to get his emotions under control. "I won't ever forget this, either, Nicoletta. I'm still shocked that you're really mine."

She laughed softly and flung herself down beside him. "Well, I am. It seems you're stuck with me now. If for no other reason than I love the house. And your mouth. I could be addicted to that. And then there's your taste."

He wrapped his arm around her waist, pulled her to him so he could nuzzle her belly with the bristles along his jaw and then press kisses there before laying his head on her. "I want you to be addicted to me, Nicoletta, but you never have to get on your knees or put my cock in your mouth if that's not what you really want to do."

"I'm well aware of that," she whispered.

Her hand dropped back to the top of his head and then

her fingers were once again moving in his hair. He could stay there the rest of his life with her, just like this, and be happy.

"Dogs or cats?"

He frowned. "Not sure what you're going on about, *piccola*. You're going to have to spell it out for me."

"Which do you prefer? Dogs or cats?"

"I never really thought about it. We never had pets growing up. Can you imagine Eloisa with pets? She'd probably sacrifice them every full moon."

She tapped his head, but he heard her muffled laughter. "That's not nice. She's your mother."

"I'm not altogether certain of that," Taviano said. "I've often fantasized that one of my aunts got in trouble at a very young age and had to give all of us up. Eloisa took us in."

Nicoletta pretended to mull that over. "That doesn't sound very reasonable, Taviano. I doubt that Eloisa would have taken in any children."

"True, and I remember her being pregnant with Ettore. She complained all the time." He gave an exaggerated sigh. "My last childhood fantasy destroyed."

"I have the feeling if we had dogs, Eloisa wouldn't come around very often, and she definitely wouldn't walk in unannounced if they were big guard dogs," Nicoletta said.

Taviano tipped his head up at the speculation in her voice. She had a dreamy expression on her face, one he loved. He wanted to etch that image deep into his mind for eternity. She seemed to be concentrating on his hair, her fingers moving on his scalp, sending delicious sensations through him just with those small touches. It was her voice that convinced him she wasn't just idly making conversation.

"Do you want a dog, Nicoletta?"

Her gaze moved from his hair to his face. Her eyes met his and he felt that familiar jolt. An arrow piercing his heart. Hell. He loved her. There was no getting around that fact. It went deep, and he was so far gone there was never going to be any turning back.

"Maybe two. Big ones. Especially when we have children. If you want to have kids, Taviano, then we're going to have dogs trained to protect them."

"You know we have personal bodyguards."

She shrugged. "I want dogs. They'll alert us if someone comes near the house."

"You felt the energy in the house when Eloisa entered. If you hone that ability, you'll always feel an enemy—or even a friend—approaching."

Her expression turned stubborn and she lifted her chin. He had the crazy desire to kiss the look right off her face. Someday he was going to take a little bite of that chin when she did that to him. Right now, he contented himself with nuzzling her belly again and kissing his way up to the underside of her left breast. He nipped her there, and when she yelped, he used his tongue to ease the sting.

She tugged at his hair in retaliation, but not very hard. "I still want dogs."

Nicoletta sounded just as stubborn as her expression had been, and that made him smile. He kissed his way back down to her belly.

"If you come to rely on dogs to warn you, you won't rely on your abilities. You need to know your gifts won't fail you. You have to teach those same things to our children. I know you want dogs, *tesoro*, and I want to give you everything you want, but it is necessary to be able to feel a presence before an animal alerts us. Once you're capable of doing that, we can rethink the idea of guard dogs."

She studied his face for a long time. "I can't tell if you mean that."

"I don't lie to you. If you want guard dogs and they make you feel safer, then we'll get them. We have to compromise, because it is really necessary for you to feel the energy of danger entering our home. Of anyone entering, but the differences in the energy. You need to be able to teach our children. We both have to do that. Once we know we can, the dogs will add an additional layer of protection."

She was silent for so long; he lifted his head to look at her directly. "Nicoletta?"

"What if I can't have children? What if any of the wives can't have children? Francesca lost so many. She barely carried Crispino. Stefano doesn't want her to try for another. Mariko hasn't gotten pregnant and they aren't using anything to prevent pregnancy."

He hadn't known that. Women talked, but Ricco hadn't confided in the others. Neither had Stefano. "Sasha? Grace? What do you know about them?"

"Sasha and Giovanni are going to try. They haven't been. They liked being together and wanted to spend some time alone. Vittorio and Grace are the same. He wants her to himself for a while, and since her shoulder is still very fragile from that terrible infection she got, he definitely doesn't want her lifting babies and trying to take care of them. So they're waiting. I know Vittorio wouldn't care if Grace couldn't have children, but what about you? It's so important to the riders, so much so that they have to agree to an arranged marriage. If their wife doesn't produce, is there a set amount of time and then she's booted to the curb?"

"Booted to the curb?" He tightened his arm around her waist, holding her to him. "I can see why you'd think that. I wonder if Sasha and Francesca think that way, or Grace. I should warn my brothers. Mariko should know better, but it's possible, with her horrendous background, that she wouldn't know, either, so I'll just mention casually to Ricco to tell her, but we don't kick our women to the curb, Nicoletta. I married you."

"Yes, with the idea that I can produce riders. But if I can't, is another woman found that can produce riders? Do you take a mistress? Do you sever the shadows between us and get another woman pregnant so the rider lineage can continue?"

He caught the underlying anxiety in her voice. No matter what he said, the voices in Nicoletta's head were strong, and they told her she wasn't good enough for him. His mother had added to those voices. If she found she couldn't have children, she would be anxious that he would want to rid himself of her to find another woman who could give him what he wanted.

Taviano sat up and pulled Nicoletta into a sitting position as well. He framed her face with his hands. "I need you to hear me, *tesoro*. I call you treasure because, for me, you have always been that. My treasure. My love. The Ferraro family are riders, yes. We might want children to carry on that legacy, we might even need them, but in the end, Stefano, not Eloisa, raised us. And maybe that was Eloisa's gift to us. Stefano didn't drill it into us, as Eloisa's parents did to her, that we had to produce children no matter the cost to us."

"I don't understand. You said a marriage would be arranged."

He nodded. "Given time for us to find the one we wanted. If that failed, then a marriage would be arranged. Sometimes those marriages turned into love matches, and that hope was always there. I married you because I love you. I want you more than I want children. I choose you. If we can't have children, you will be my choice. If you want children and we can't have our own, we will explore other options. But our marriage stands, and there will be no going outside of it for any reason by either of us." He made that a decree as well as a promise.

He kissed her gently. She tasted like fresh mint. She tasted like what he was coming to associate with love. "Thank you for bringing up those fears, Nicoletta. If you have them, it's possible my sisters-in-law do as well. I'm going to make certain my brothers have talks with them so they know they would never be put aside because they can't produce a child."

"I know Francesca doesn't think Stefano would really get rid of her, but she does feel that he is disappointed. She's determined that she'll have more children. She's taking vitamins and working out, trying to make herself very healthy so she won't have problems. I overheard both Emmanuelle and Mariko telling her that being healthy was never her problem, but she won't listen to them. She said it doesn't make sense that when every other woman in the world can have children, she can't."

"Not every woman can," Taviano said. "That's just ridiculous and she knows better. She's too intelligent for that." He slid off the bed and made his way to the master bath, leaving the door open. "It's a wonder Stefano hasn't done something crazy like put her over his knee or something. That's just nuts."

She followed him slowly. "It's an emotional issue for a woman, Taviano, it isn't nuts. You should have a little more compassion. And when the pressure of marrying into a family like yours is added, it makes it all the worse."

He couldn't argue with that. "Are you going to shower with me?"

She had her hip against the doorjamb, draped artistically whether she knew it or not, his shirt looking like a dress on her, the open edges framing her midsection beautifully. She didn't avert her gaze from his body as he turned on the water from the various sprayers. He liked the water coming at him from all angles. He arched an eyebrow at her.

"I don't know if I can do that yet."

"What's the determining factor?" He couldn't keep amusement from his voice. She made his life fun. "Maybe I can help with your decision."

"Are you going to keep your hands to yourself?"

He cocked his head to one side and then stepped under the hot water. It fell on him from above and came at him from three sides. "I have to be honest, *amore mio*, I don't know. You're tempting. The idea of washing you is hard to resist. I thought we might exchange tasks, but I'm willing to do all the work."

She moved all the way into the room, slipping the shirt

from her shoulders. "How very sweet of you, Taviano. I think I can manage on my own, and I'll let you handle your own washing."

He refused to be disappointed. She had come a long way as far as he was concerned. He hadn't expected they would get as far as they had. And she was already pulling out the topknot and stepping into the double shower with him. That was a huge victory. He had hoped she would feel safe and comfortable enough to join him, but he honestly hadn't thought she would.

He tried to appear as casual as possible, flashing her a little grin before using the gel to soap his body thoroughly. He wanted to be exceptionally clean just in case she decided she wanted to repeat their exploration of each other's bodies later. He tried not to react in any way to the sight of her washing and conditioning her hair or gliding her hands over her breasts and lower to her belly and then those little ringlets that called to him, guarding the treasure just below.

No matter how disciplined he was, no matter how sated his body had been, the way her hands moved with the gel and then used the handheld water wand, his cock turned treacherous on him. He had to turn his back on her before his vicious erection had him in trouble.

"You're killing me, woman." He gave a little groan to prove it.

"I am?"

He glanced over his shoulder at her with open suspicion. She sounded just a little too innocent. There was definitely a little too much laughter in her eyes.

"Keep it up." It was an empty threat. He couldn't throw her over his shoulder—yet. There could be no tackling her. No play that involved holding her down. But verbal playing, he could introduce her to that.

"I intend to."

Now her laughter was open, and the sound teased at his

senses, creating an intimacy between them that surprised him. It was more emotional than physical, allowing his body a reprieve. He hadn't thought that just playing could achieve as great an intimacy as having sex with a woman, but he found everything he did with Nicoletta contributed to their closeness.

He brought tea to her on the back patio. She combed out her hair, taming the wild waves into a thick braid while he watched.

"You have a recording studio," she said.

She made it a statement, leaving it up to him whether or not he wanted to tell her about it. He debated. "I have an office, too." He did. He helped design racing engines. The Ferraro engines were mainly his designs.

"Yes, I was very nosy this morning when you were making breakfast, and I walked around. Mostly, I was lost, so I peeked into all the rooms. I saw all the engine diagrams on the walls. Or CAD drawings, whatever you call them. Emmanuelle mentioned that you're quite brilliant when it comes to that sort of thing. I think she was trying to tell me you weren't a bored playboy."

He laughed. Of course Emme would try to convince Nicoletta that Taviano was worth something. His sister knew he was in love with her.

"Francesca told me you are an amazing chef. That you'd learned in Europe and would be welcome in any of the best restaurants in the world."

"They were laying it on thick, weren't they?" But he was pleased his family would go to bat for him.

"That's not all," Nicoletta assured. She picked up the teacup and took a sip. "I love this. There's nothing quite like a great cup of tea, is there?" Her eyes were on the setting sun.

"What else did they tell you?" His voice darkened with suspicion. What else could they tell her? Everything went downhill from there.

"Sasha said you are so good with knives it's unbelievable. Throwing knives, but you don't even need the weighted real thing. She claims you can use a kitchen knife with deadly accuracy. I did see your targets and all the knife holes in them. It looked as if she might have been telling the truth."

"A by-product of being good in the kitchen."

She took her gaze from the sunset to glance at him for just a moment, amusement shining at him. "Is that what you're going with?"

He nodded. She turned her head to look back at nature's display of color and power.

"Mariko said you have the soul of a poet, the heart of a warrior and your hands were gentle enough to hold Crispino lovingly and yet strong enough to keep him safe."

His sisters-in-law spoke highly of him. He shouldn't have been surprised, but he was. And he was touched. They were good people. He admired, respected, and loved all four of them.

"Did they sway you at all toward me?"

"I'm here with you, aren't I?"

"I think I trapped you into marriage," he said, without remorse.

"That was my shadow trapping yours," she argued. "I saw the recording studio," she added.

They were back to that. She was his wife and she was living in the house with him. Sooner or later she would know. It was silly not to just tell her. She had her eyes on the sky, not on him, and that made it easier to act like it didn't mean a thing when it was intensely personal.

"I record music. Lyrics. I play a little guitar and sometimes I write songs. Nothing monumental, just mostly garbage, but I get them out of my head." Even to his own ears he sounded casual and he was proud of that.

She reached out to him and he immediately took her hand and brought her palm to his thigh, pressing it tightly to him. She knew he wasn't as casual as he sounded. That's what he loved about Nicoletta. She knew him. They knew each other.

"I've never seen you play an instrument."

"I'm not the best, *tesoro*. In my family, if you aren't the best at something, you keep practicing until you are. I play, but I don't play for others. Only for myself. I practice and I have friends give me lessons, but I don't let others hear me make my mistakes."

He knew that was a leftover childhood thing. Ferraros were expected to be perfect at everything they did. They had perfect accents when they spoke other languages. They got perfect grades and learned every subject fast. They were skilled in every form of self-defense and in the use of weapons. Any sign of weakness wasn't tolerated. No excuse was accepted. That had been drilled into them from the time they were toddlers.

Eloisa thought they had been coddled by Stefano. Taviano wasn't certain what his mother meant by being coddled. Stefano was a taskmaster, but he made his siblings aware that he loved them. If that was coddling, Taviano was all for it.

"I hope you get to a point that you feel you can share your music with me someday, Taviano," Nicoletta said. "I'd really love to hear it."

His heart clenched hard and his stomach did a weird pitching roll. He wasn't certain whether it was in joy at the thought or in protest. He wanted to share with her, because there were songs he was proud of. He wanted someone to hear them. He'd written them from his heart—maybe even his soul. He'd heard music outside in the woods, with the wind howling the way his mind did some nights when it wouldn't quiet. When the rain beat at the windows of his home, the way his tears did in his mind. She would understand. If anyone could, Nicoletta could.

He had listened to Kain Diakos's music because Nicoletta loved it so much. She played it all the time. He'd listened closely to the lyrics and he understood why she identified with his songs. There was always hope there after the initial terrible tragedy.

Taviano hoped that Nicoletta would identify with his lyrics even more. That his songs would give her that same lift, the same faith that there was more than just ugliness in the world. That there were choices and family was the best choice of all, whether blood or of the heart. Those were his beliefs. His hopes. His gifts. And they were for her.

CHAPTER TWELVE

Halfway between St. Louis and Chicago sat Blooming-ton, Illinois. Mariko and Ricco used the fastest tubes to take them to Bloomington. They stayed in the shadows of the little café where the Demons were reputed to hang out and eat while they refueled their cars when traveling. The owner of the café was friendly with them and the cops stayed away from that part of the city for the most part. Unwary travelers were parted from their wallets. A few bodies turned up but most of them simply disappeared.

Ricco and Mariko had endless patience. Both had grown up in a hard school. They had honed their skills and were excellent at their craft. Their craft just happened to be assassination. It didn't matter how long they had to wait; they could easily pass the time together anywhere. They took a shadow up the side of the building to the roof.

Ricco liked the fact that the café was a large rectangle. On the two shorter sides, two gaudy neon signs spelled **CAFÉ** in large red capital letters. On the front of the building, a sprawling, obnoxiously large sign on the bottom took up most of the long front, proclaiming in red neon letters on a gold background that it was "great eating." Stacked above that sign was another, forever claiming the café as belonging to Harold Peterbuilt and Son. The "son" had been x'd out with black paint. Ricco sarcastically thought that was very classy.

The roof itself was fairly flat. He took Mariko's hand and helped her across what looked like a tar rooftop. There were two outcroppings that were square, along with several giant fans. They made their way to the squares, where Mariko sat while Ricco scouted the area for cover and the best shadow tubes leading to the alleyway below as well as the parking lot to one side of the building and the landscaped front.

The front was mainly overgrown weeds and white rock that had long since been tossed around the parking spaces for the handicapped. Graffiti decorated the spaces in colorful language and art. The drawings added to the décor, along with sidewalks that were cracked and broken in places. The cement was more like waves than a straight line. Someone had written "fuck you, Harold" in bold black letters over and over right up to the door of the café. Ricco presumed it was the son who had been crossed off the neon sign.

His gaze swept the parking lots on all sides, seeking the cars they had been told the Demons were traveling in. Two SUVs, both with tinted windows, both dark navy blue with silver rims, traveling with a Ram truck with a cab. Fourteen members of the Demons coming in from St. Louis to Chicago, all to help Benito Valdez retrieve Nicoletta Gomez for whatever nefarious purposes he had in mind for her. That wasn't going to happen. Nicoletta was a Ferraro, and no one was going to take her from their family.

There were several cars in the parking lots, but not the vehicles they were looking for. He wasn't surprised. They had taken the fastest shadows possible in the hopes of arriving well ahead in order to scout out the premises and prepare a strategy.

Ricco walked back to his wife. She never failed to move him when he came up on her, no matter where she was or what she was doing. She was always very still. Peaceful. She was small. Half Japanese, half American. Surprisingly, she was a blonde. She had curves and pale skin. Her eyes always captured him, almond shaped, hazel, exotic like a cat's. She looked fragile, like a delicate flower. The fact that a warrior ran deep beneath her flawless skin and delicate image always amazed him.

Her gaze jumped immediately to his face. Focused completely on him. His body reacted immediately. He walked right up to her, towering over her as she sat so demurely, her pinstriped suit emphasizing her curves rather than detracting from them. Every breath she took made him aware of her breasts rising and falling beneath her jacket. He made out the tops of those sweet curves, just a hint beneath the lapels.

Ricco practiced the art of Shibari and was very thankful that Mariko enjoyed and allowed him to use her body as his canvas. The practice between them required a great deal of trust. He was very careful when he laid the ropes on her body and tied the knots, not wanting to hurt her in any way. What had started for him as purely art had taken a very erotic turn when Mariko had become his partner and then his wife.

"This is a perfect place to practice, Mariko." He gestured to the neon signs. They were huge, standing so tall and grotesque behind them, flashing their message for miles to anyone who cared to look. "I would have you naked and bound between the letters on this side of them. Wrapped in silks of gold and red so you would blend in. Only I would see you. Only the camera would capture you."

She didn't take her gaze from his, maintaining eye contact. "We don't know when they'll be here, Ricco."

He sighed. "No, we don't."

"Did you bring rope?"

"I always carry rope. You know that." He did. Silk. Silk

could go through the shadows. He didn't go anywhere without rope. In the past, sometimes rope had been his only sanity. Now, he always enjoyed the thought of binding her and taking her whenever he wanted. Coming off a job, coming out of the shadows, always brought on a savage need for release. Combining that with Shibari and his beautiful, erotic woman, the sex was always crazy, but he'd never considered actually staying close and using the actual location.

The rooftop was so perfect. The insanity of the grotesque neon signs hiding them from the world. The coolness of the night air. The shadows they could escape into should they need to. He could bind her close to the mouth of one and release her with one yank of the knots, catch her up and dive for the shadow if need be. Once the idea took hold, he began to consider how he wanted to bind her.

"You're really thinking of using *this* rooftop? Not after?"

"After. And then after again when we get home. Once won't be enough." He could tell that already. He was going to be wild with need for her. Just the thought of sex with her on the rooftop, surrounded by the neon flashing signs and his own artwork in stark contrast, was making him hard already. He had never bound her completely off the floor, she'd always been a little intimidated by the idea, but tonight, when they got home, he thought perhaps he could talk her into it.

"It could be dangerous, Ricco. If someone discovers the bodies and calls the cops too soon, we could be in trouble. I don't think we should take chances."

He could see the color sliding under her skin. Her breathing had changed, and her eyes had taken on a glow. He leaned down and took her mouth. Claiming her. Forcing her head back. Telling her he was in charge right then. Knowing she was already on board with his ideas.

"I hear cars, *farfallina mia*, I'll be right back." He always called her his little butterfly. She was so much more. She was everything to him. He kissed her again and then moved soundlessly across the flat rooftop toward the side parking lot where he could easily hear the noisy group of men getting out of their vehicles.

Two SUVs had parked under the tall lamps, the only two that weren't shattered. Clearly, they didn't want anyone messing with their cars. Five men descended from each of them. They wore their colors, shoving one another, laughing, each talking louder than the others. All ten bragging about what they were going to do to Valdez's enemies. The truck pulled up next to the SUVs and four more of the Demons leapt out. They swaggered after the others.

Ricco watched them go into the café before returning to Mariko. "The information is correct. We have fourteen opponents. Three vehicles. We'll take care of those first, just to ensure that no one escapes us and we have to give chase. It's easier to contain them here." And he had plans after.

Mariko stood up and stretched, easing her muscles into working order before she followed Ricco to the shadow that would take them both over the side of the building to the lot where the Demons had parked their vehicles, thinking them safe from any tampering. Ricco had chosen one of the slower tubes. It was wider and went over the side of the building and almost all the way across the parking lot. Thrown by the lamppost, the shadow touched the tube that reached out from the building itself.

The riders moved from one shadow to the next without hesitation. Ricco went under the hood of the first SUV and disconnected the ignition relay and then followed up with removing several of the other wires. He did the same in the other SUV and truck. Satisfied that it would take quite some time for the gang members to figure out what had gone wrong with their rides, Ricco and Mariko rode the shadows right up to the café.

The fourteen Demon members were swaggering around the café, taunting the waitress, who looked a little intimidated. She was older, her face drawn and tired. The cook could be seen throwing annoyed glances at the men, who were tossing napkins into the air and throwing spoons and forks at one another.

Two customers walked out. When they tried to pay, one of the men who had ridden in the truck grabbed the invoice from the waitress and tore it up, indicating for the couple to leave. He even opened the door for them. The couple hurried out, obviously afraid to stay and fight it out to pay the bill.

The same man who had let the couple go without paying sauntered over to sit on the table of another group of customers. Four men who looked like construction workers, big burly men with obvious muscles and tattoos that looked as if they might have gotten them in prison. The Demon member reached over and flipped a plate of food into the nearest construction worker's lap. Immediately, the other Demons howled with glee and gathered around the booth.

The moment he'd sat down, there had been a mass exodus from the café. Everyone else who had been eating there jumped up and, without paying, rushed for the door, ignoring the taunting laughter of the gang members as they ran to their cars. Ricco watched them drive out fast. Not a single one was on their cell phone reporting a disturbance at the Harold and x'd-out Son Café. And no one would. The café was known to be a safe haven for the various gangs.

The construction worker trapped in the booth tried to jump up as hot gravy and mashed potatoes burned through his jeans. The table and close booth seating inhibited his movements, causing him to teeter there, while the Demon member tipped more plates at the others sitting. One made the mistake of trying to punch the Demon while they all leapt up to protect themselves.

Instantly the construction workers were dragged from the booth. The waitress tried to pull out her cell phone but another Demon caught her in a vicious hold, forcing her to drop the phone. He stomped on it repeatedly.

"This café has the mark on it. You don't ever violate that

mark, or we kill every one of you, bitch, your families, and then burn your houses down. You got that?" As he threatened her, he kept putting more pressure on her arm until he nearly snapped the bone.

She nodded over and over. The cook refused to watch, not even when sprays of blood went up and construction workers were piled up in the corner. One was dead, two well on their way and the fourth struggling for every breath but trying to crawl for the door. No one stopped him, but they watched as he made his way, using elbows and toes down the center of the café, leaving a bloody trail behind him.

The plate-flipping member of the Demons smirked and then paced along beside him, kicking at him with his boots. "That was just a little warm-up, baby. Don't you want to play some more? I'm in the mood to play. You all are nothin' but pussies in here."

The gang member holding on to the waitress walked her over to the others. "Take their orders, bitch, and then get back here. Seems like you're going to be the only entertainment we've got." He leered at her and deliberately caught her breast and squeezed hard enough to bring on tears.

Ricco glanced at Mariko. She didn't change expression, but she was very focused on the gang member. He wore a blue plaid shirt. She didn't look away from him, not even when the one who seemed to be in charge leaned down and slit the construction worker's throat just as he reached the door.

The Demons laughed, as if seeing the blood running under the door was great fun. The one in charge wiped the blade of his knife on the man's shirt and turned back. "That's thirsty work. We've got to eat fast and get the hell on the road."

The one in the plaid shirt grinned evilly at the waitress. "You've got five minutes to take these orders, and then you meet me and some of the boys in the alley." He raised his voice. "I'm going out for a smoke. I want a Philly sandwich.

Hot." He gave her breast another twist and then sauntered out, stepping over the dead man.

Three others gave their orders and hastily followed him out. The man in charge shook his head and laughed. "He's always after pussy. Can't help himself. You'd better hurry, honey. He can get mean if he has to wait too long."

Ricco and Mariko took the shadow leading them to the narrow alley behind the café. It wasn't large enough to fit most vehicles. The garbage cans were in the back, but other than that, the asphalt was strewn with condoms, needles and cigarette butts. A few empty beer cans lay on the ground as well, and weeds pushed up along the broken seams, but for the most part, it was simply a narrow strip between a long fence and the building.

The four gang members smoked, one a cigarette, the other three passing around a joint, all laughing. The shortest member walked a distance away, unzipped and relieved himself on the fence.

Ricco slipped up behind him. A shadow in the dim light thrown by the hulk of the café. He caught the Demon member's head between his hands and twisted, delivering the signature kill. "Justice is served," he whispered as he lowered the body to the ground and disappeared back into the one shadow thrown by the bizarre flashing neon light from the massive overhead café sign.

Laughter continued. One member turned his head toward their fallen companion. He sobered and walked a couple of steps toward him. "Alejo?" He hurried his steps. The others hadn't turned around, still laughing as the side door opened and the waitress appeared framed there.

Ricco waited until the man concerned about Alejo knelt beside him. Once again, he slipped behind him and repeated the exact same thing, catching his head and delivering the signature kill as he murmured the satisfying reality, "Justice is served."

"Come here, bitch," the Demon member in the plaid shirt ordered, pointing to his feet. "Get on your hands and knees. We don't have a lot of time. Don't want my Philly to get cold." He laughed and glanced around. He could barely make out his two friends lying on the ground.

"What the fuck, Blas? What are they doing?"

"Don't know, Cleto, but Alejo's got his dick out." Blas giggled as he pointed. "I don't know what Don's doing, but he's looking interested." Don had fallen with his head very close to Alejo's exposed groin. Alejo looked as if he had his fist around his penis and was offering it to Don.

"What are you two doing? I bring you a present and you're sucking each other's dicks." Cleto grinned and turned back to the waitress. "Guess you only have the two of us, but we'll make it worth your while. I get your ass and Blas can have your mouth or pussy. It's his choice."

Blas giggled again, the sound high pitched. "Give me a second, Cleto, be right there." He rushed toward a bush, ripping down his jeans, eager to relieve himself, digging in his pocket for a condom at the same time. He heard Cleto slapping the waitress, heard her cry out and he winced. Cleto had slapped him a time or two, and he hadn't liked it. He was always low man and he didn't often get the opportunity to choose how he wanted a woman. Most of the time she was gangbanged and he got leftovers.

He never heard a sound as Mariko slipped up behind him. He didn't feel it as her hands caught his head in both hands and she delivered the sudden signature move of all riders, wrenching the neck for a quick kill. He didn't hear the softly whispered, "Justice is served."

Mariko lowered Blas's body to the ground. Cleto faced away from her. He had already forced the waitress to the ground, dragging her plain black skirt up to her waist and ripping her white panties off her.

"Shut the fuck up, bitch," he snapped. "I haven't given you anything to cry about yet. Put your fucking head on the ground. I'm going to give your face road rash."

Mariko walked right up behind him. She didn't use the shadows. She didn't need to. He was fully concentrating on the waitress. He liked hurting people. He'd all but forgotten his fellow gang members in his eagerness to degrade and hurt the waitress.

Mariko had to reach up to position her hands on his head, but she was used to height differences, and she'd trained endlessly for that. She waited a heartbeat to make certain she had them just right before she gripped and wrenched hard, using the signature move she'd practiced hundreds of times daily since she was a toddler. The neck snapped with an audible crack. She lowered the body to the ground as she murmured, "Justice is served." She then simply stepped into the nearest shadow and rode it to the café's doorway.

"Sooner or later, someone will come looking," she whispered to Ricco, nuzzling his neck.

He stroked his fingers lovingly down her throat. "Said the spider to the fly." He bent his head to brush a kiss into the shine of her blond hair. She had given him life back. She brought him to life. She made herself vulnerable to him and, in doing so, allowed him to do the same with her. She'd taught him how to love.

He kept his arm around her waist, breathing her in. That scent that was all Mariko. She had a taste that was unique to her. He would be able to find her in the dark, know her no matter how many other women were there with her. There was always an innocence about Mariko, and when he watched her perform her duties as a rider, he found her breathtaking. She was a double-edged sword, a beautiful, dangerous woman, and he wouldn't have her any other way.

The door to the café was thrown open and a man stomped down the two cement stairs, but still held on to the door to keep it open. "Cleto, Emidio says to get your ass inside if you want to eat. He wants to be on the road in five minutes."

Silence met his demand. He peered into the alley. The light was waning, and in the poorly lit alley, it was much darker. Light streamed from the café, but it only lit the fence. The waitress was still on her hands and knees, head down on the asphalt, wailing. Cleto lay on the ground behind her.

The Demon member scowled and let go of the door to walk closer.

"Cleto, what the fuck are you doing? Emidio is pissed. You know how he gets." He took two more steps.

Ricco glided up behind him and dropped him fast, not giving him a chance to turn around. There were five down and nine more to go. Now it was going to get tricky. If they were lucky, they might manage to get two more, maybe three, before someone realized there were dead bodies lying around and the Demons were under attack. It was extremely important that the two civilians not see Ricco or Mariko.

The waitress suddenly turned her head, no doubt shocked that Cleto hadn't raped her. She realized he was lying on the ground behind her and even then, she stayed where she was, afraid to move, frozen with terror for a few more minutes. Very cautiously she turned around, still on her hands and knees, and shuffled forward until she could look closely at Cleto. She gasped and drew back, realizing he was dead.

"Oh my God," she whispered and stood up abruptly. She flipped her skirt down and felt in her pockets for her keys. She looked wildly around and spotted the other bodies. She let out a high-pitched scream and ran for the tiny employee parking lot way in the back, where the alley opened up to four spaces.

Ricco and Mariko could hear her screaming the entire way to her car, which was a good distance away. They knew those inside the café and any of the neighboring businesses would put the screams down to whatever crimes were committed daily at the café. Women were often assaulted there, and no one cared.

The café door was flung open. At the same time, there was activity in the front of the café and more around the side lot. Emidio, the leader of the group headed to Chicago, had given the orders to leave, apparently with or without those in the alley. He must have sent others one last time to retrieve them.

"Cleto, Emidio is leaving now. He wants you in the fucking truck with him now."

Two men stepped out together, providing a menacing appearance. Both wore weapons in plain sight, apparently to convince Cleto to come with them. They slammed the café door behind them, as if that might give them more authority, and stalked right up to the two men lying on the ground.

Ricco and Mariko followed, two wraiths, stepping in the exact footprints of those they stalked. As they did so, three more members of the Demons came around the front of the alley, sent by Emidio to aid the enforcers in retrieving the five men still in the alley. Cleto must have had a reputation as a troublemaker, but Emidio wouldn't want to lose five men. He'd count on them to prove to Benito Valdez that the St. Louis chapter was worth more than any other.

Ricco and Mariko were in full sync when they performed their task, serving justice on the two enforcers, and then lowering them to the ground almost right on top of Cleto and the one who had been sent to find him.

"Seven down, *farfallina mia*. The odds are getting better," Ricco whispered as they stepped into the closest shadow and rode it to the nearest tube that would take them toward the three members striding toward the fallen Demons.

The tube was fast, one of the small ones that felt like greased lightning. It shook one's insides apart and ripped at the cells of the body until you didn't feel as if you were human. It was disorienting, and a rider got to the end of the tube and was in danger of being spit out before feeling as if he or she was back together. Ricco had stepped protectively in front of Mariko so he would arrive at the end first, blocking it for her.

Ricco could see that these men would be more difficult for Mariko to take just due to their size, although she always got the job done. He glanced at her. She tipped her head back and met his eyes. As always, she looked serene, and inside him, where before there had been rage burning, she brought a sense of peace. Of calm. His center. He was always amazed at the depth of his emotions for her. Even now, in the middle of a difficult mission, when there were so many of the enemy, she generated a sense of well-being.

Mariko was his partner in every sense of the word. They normally each took a rotation alone. There were so few riders that when requests came in from anywhere in the world, a rider was sent. It was rare to work in pairs. Ricco was grateful for the chance to be able to shape more memories of his woman being a warrior.

He inhaled and took her scent into his lungs, taking her with him as he stepped out of the shadows directly behind the man who had fallen one step behind the other two. Mariko kept pace behind him, her feet shadowing his. He didn't hear her, but he felt her energy, barely there, that vibration of feminine softness and steel. He matched the steps of the gang member exactly, his hands coming up in the classic kill. "Justice is served," he murmured as he wrenched the neck and took him down to the ground.

Without missing a step, Mariko was in the shadow of the footsteps of one of the two men coming up on Don and Alejo. The two Demons stopped abruptly. She stopped with them, turning as they turned. Her much smaller figure clad in the pinstriped suit blended easily with the shadows. Night had fallen and the streaks of neon red and gold threw out strange, macabre shadows that blazed and crept across the asphalt. The stripes of the suit allowed her to simply disappear when the gray hit her.

Ricco admired the way his woman went so still. Movement drew the eye and she never so much as flickered an eyelash. The two men crouched low to examine the two bodies. One rose slowly. The other took his time but stood as well, both turning to face toward the café where the other bodies lay. They weren't as visible, but neither man made a move to go search them out.

One pulled out his cell phone. "Emidio. Two are dead.

Necks broken. No, I don't know if Cleto did it. Alejo and Don. I don't see the others."

He looked at his partner and indicated to move forward. "He wants us to find Cleto."

He shoved the phone into his pocket and the two men reluctantly started forward, this time at a snail's pace. They both took out guns and pointed them straight ahead. Neither even considered that the danger might be coming from behind them. Ricco glanced at Mariko to ensure she was ready. She nodded without even looking at him. She always knew what he wanted from her; she was so tuned to him she felt his gaze on her. That was a by-product of Shibari. Or as he preferred to call it, Kinbaku—meaning "light binding." No matter what it was called, it was erotic and beautiful when he practiced the art with his wife.

They moved up on the two men as one. It felt powerful and connective to be in step like that. He reached and she moved, leaping, her hands flying to the man's head, positioning exactly while her legs wrapped him up. She wrenched, using her body weight, just as Ricco did the same with his hands. Audible cracks accompanied the whispers of "Justice is served." Mariko was just as graceful dismounting the body before it hit the ground as she was when she went flying through the air in her perfect attack.

Ricco locked his arm around her neck and dragged her to him, taking her mouth, because the combination of riding the shadows and seeing his woman in action was causing a powerful, intense reaction in his body. Every rider coming out of the shadows was desperate for sex. The drive was so brutal, they took care not to drink alcohol or go out in public until they could get themselves under control. He could feel the need, that terrible drive already on him, and they still had several shadows to maneuver and more tasks to complete before he could pay attention to the urgent demands of his body or those of his woman's.

She tasted like she always did. To the rest of the world

she was pure warrior, reserved, aloof, always in control. For Ricco, she was his woman, showing vulnerability, ceding control to him, allowing an exchange of power. Gifting him with her trust. She'd saved him when no one else could have. He loved her with every breath he took, and watching her in action strengthened his desire to make her life everything it should have been from the day she was born.

She'd never had a decent family life, and he wanted to give her that. Eloisa wasn't the best, she certainly wasn't ever going to be a great mother to her, but there were Stefano and Francesca—the true heads of the family—and they loved her. Giovanni and Sasha had become immediate friends. Now there was Vittorio and Grace. Nicoletta had always been a favorite of Mariko's. She'd treated her as a younger sister. And Mariko loved Taviano as much as he would let her. Taviano wasn't a man who let others really know him. Ricco had been the same way for so long, he hadn't really seen that in anyone else. It had been Mariko who had pointed that out. Then there was Emmanuelle. Everyone loved Emmanuelle.

He had definitely surrounded Mariko with a large family, and they all loved her. They weren't the only ones. He had an extended family that went on forever. Cousins. So many of them. They practically smothered the riders in protection. Mariko wasn't used to so many people and so much attention, especially bodyguards following them everywhere when they went out to eat or to a club. He could tell they made her uncomfortable, even though she liked them.

Mariko rubbed her hand along his jaw. "What is it, Ricco?"

"I was just thinking how much I love you."

"You were frowning. The thought of loving me makes you frown?" There was amusement in her voice.

Something about that soft laughter made his heart do a slow roll. "I was thinking how much you don't like the bodyguards that always surround us. It will get worse if we have children. There's very little I can do about it, and I promised you I'd do whatever it took to make you happy."

"I am happy, Ricco." She tugged on his hand. "Let's finish this. I'd like to get the job done and go back to being us."

He leaned down and nuzzled the suit jacket out of the way of her neck so he could kiss her pulse there. "You want to see what artwork I come up with on the rooftop, don't you?"

"That, and I have to confess, one more shadow and I might jump you before we get to the artwork. This is crazy."

He flashed a grin, took her hand and ducked back into the tube that would take them closest to the side parking lot, where the three vehicles had been left unattended. By now, Emidio had to have been told that none of them would start. There were four Demons left out of the fourteen that had come from St. Louis. Emidio had no idea what had happened to his men, and he would want to know.

The shadow was a long one, but fairly easy to ride. They paused just in the mouth of it, watching the Demons as they consulted together. Whispering. All of them were on their phones attempting to raise those not present. Emidio was furious. He punched the side of the truck, denting it, giving away the fact that he wore brass knuckles on his hand. He was prepared for a battle. He gestured toward the alley and indicated they all go armed together.

Ricco kissed Mariko and then indicated he would take the taller of the two men. Unfortunately, Emidio was very short. Mariko would have to serve justice on him, and he would be guarded by the other three. He would also be the wariest. Mariko simply nodded and waited for the four men to stalk past them.

Ricco caught the names of the two tall men. The one wearing a dark green shirt was called Juan, and the other Marcos. The shorter man pacing alongside Emidio was Carlos. Carlos was slim and wiry-looking. Ricco didn't like the look of him and hoped that Mariko noticed that of all of Emidio's soldiers, Carlos was the one most dangerous. That, Ricco decided, was the drawback to partnering with his wife. His attention was divided, even knowing she was excellent at her job. She'd trained from the time she was a toddler and excelled at her work, yet he still worried about her.

What of Nicoletta? She might be an anomaly. She had a fast learning curve, and he'd watched her. All of them had. They'd discussed the fact that she never had to be told something twice, that every week she was faster and deadlier on the training mats. That didn't take away from the fact that Mariko had years of training on her and Ricco still worried. He couldn't imagine what it would be like for Taviano if Stefano really gave the couple the go-ahead to work together as a pair.

Mariko fell into step behind Carlos, using the shadowing technique. Ricco couldn't move on the taller men until they were out of sight of the two others. He stayed in the shadows, watching them, keeping close to them by moving from one shadow to the next, using the darkness when he had to come out in the open. Part of his attention was on Mariko as she stalked Emidio's bodyguard.

"Stay close," Carlos hissed at Emidio when he quickened his pace. Juan and Marcos had a fairly good lead on them, their longer strides putting distance between the men.

"I don't want to get separated," Emidio snapped, but he slowed, taking a firmer grip on his weapon. "Shit, Carlos. Bodies."

Marcos and Juan had gotten to Alejo and Don. They went back-to-back and then Juan cautiously crouched down to examine the bodies.

Emidio halted a distance away when Carlos put a cautionary hand on his arm. "Who is it?" Emidio called out.

"Alejo and Don," Marcos answered.

"Necks are broken," Juan added, straightening. "They never saw it coming. Alejo was taking a piss."

Emidio swore savagely. "You see Cleto anywhere? Did he do this?"

"A pro did this," Juan said. "Someone who knew what they were doing."

Ricco was surprised that Juan would recognize that.

The man kept his cool when the three remaining Demons had to be a little panicked. He could understand why Emidio had kept these men close to him. Cleto was a wild card, probably useful in a fight but constantly a troublemaker. These three men were different, all business, and their business was to protect Emidio.

Mariko waited, her breath barely moving through her lungs, her energy so low nothing could possibly give her away. There was no warning to Carlos that danger stalked him. He might be the most lethal of the four men in the alley, but a beautiful woman wearing a pinstriped suit signifying she was a Ferraro, a bearer of justice, matched him footstep for footstep. He had one hand on Emidio's arm, while the other fisted his gun, and he looked around carefully to ensure no one was close that could harm the man he protected.

Ricco watched, his heart pounding, his mouth dry, as Mariko made her move, uncaring that Carlos stood so close to Emidio. She caught his head from behind, wrenched his neck and whispered, "Justice is served." Immediately she stepped into a shadow. She had chosen her moment based on the light coming and going from the gaudy neon signs overhead.

Ricco let his breath out in a long rush. She was beautiful. Magnificent. His body reacted, a rush of heat pumping through his veins, filling his groin with hot blood. She stepped out of the shadow directly behind Emidio as he turned to look at Carlos. Carlos's hand had slipped from his arm and the body was falling backward toward the rocky asphalt.

Emidio took a step forward, frowning, unable to believe his own eyes. He hadn't heard a sound and had no idea why his bodyguard would be falling. As he stepped forward, Mariko timed her moment and caught his head, wrenching hard. The man dropped almost on top of his guard. Mariko uttered the classic words in her soft voice and once more disappeared into the shadows.

Ricco had only to wait for Marcos and Juan to notice that both men were down. When no orders were given, the two tall men stepped into the light to try to catch a better look at the man they took orders from. When they saw the two bodies lying on the ground, they ran right past Ricco to them. Again, it was Juan who examined them.

"Same kill method," Juan said. "We've got to get out of here now."

"I didn't hear a sound," Marcos said.

"Yeah. Like I said, we've got to get out of here." Juan looked around carefully and then slowly straightened up. He indicated for Marcos to lead the way.

Marcos didn't protest, simply taking the lead, using longer strides to make his way toward the other end of the alley. Juan came behind him, watching all sides and occasionally throwing a glance over his shoulder. Ricco used the one shadow that would take him ahead and to the right of the rapidly walking men. Marcos passed him.

Ricco fell into step behind Juan and without hesitation, caught his head between his hands and wrenched. The crack was loud in the silence of the night. Marcos spun around, his gun coming up, looking for a target, finger on the trigger. Mariko was on him before he could squeeze and get off a shot. She had wrapped him up with her legs and her hands were already in the perfect position. She gave the same wrench, and both of them simultaneously uttered the required line. "Justice is served."

The bodies dropped to the ground.

Ricco stood looking for a long time at his wife. He couldn't see anything else. Only the perfection that was Mariko. Heat coursed through his body. Flames licked at his skin. Lust and love mixed together until he didn't know where one started and the other ended, the two emotions so intense and so intertwined. Her eyes shone at him, dark with her own need, watching him the way she did, that focused look that always told him she was all his.

He caught her hand and tugged her into the shadow

leading back up to the roof. The heat was so intense, burning through him as he stepped out of the shadow tube. He didn't try to control it as he normally would have.

"Take your clothes off, Mariko." Even in his heightened state, even commanding her, he used a velvet-soft voice. He watched her through half-closed eyes as he pulled the red silk rope from beneath his jacket and shook it out, beginning to run it through his hands to check for any splinters.

Dio, but she was beautiful. She wore nothing under her pristine pinstriped suit, and it was off in seconds, carefully folded and set aside near the shadow entrance. He slipped a rope around her wrist and bound her hand to the neon sign with the giant café letters. Stretching her arm out, he paced over to the end of the sign, as close as he could get, stretching her other arm, the rope a shackle around that slender wrist. He could easily slip the knots in seconds and break her free, or she could, if necessary, but she looked a prisoner, the huge letters standing tall behind her, going off and on while her naked body appeared small and vulnerable.

He could barely contain his raging cock as he began to frame her breasts in a harness of red. He worked fast, laying his ropes carefully, checking with her to ensure that no line was uncomfortable, his hands sliding over her soft skin, flicking her nipples, his mouth on the pulse at her neck. He spread her legs while he framed her sex, his thumb circling her clit and flicking it and rubbing. Several times he couldn't resist pushing his finger deep to coat it and then licking it clean. She tasted so good. Once he dropped to his knees to inspect his knots and he couldn't resist lapping at her. Once he started, he couldn't stop until her soft little moans and familiar music drove him insane.

He was on his feet again, lifting her. "Wrap your legs around me, *farfallina mia*, I'm not going to be gentle." He couldn't be. He was too far gone.

"I don't want you to be."

She was helpless in the ropes, but she looked so gorgeous, the red silk framing her breasts, emphasizing her feminine form, the ugliness of the sign a counterpoint to the beauty of a woman. Her sex, framed in the red harness, with intricate knots that dripped down her mound, over her hips and down her thighs but pulled tight around her lips and between her cheeks, gleamed with each pulse of the neon sign.

Ricco drove his cock into her snug, wet heat, wanting to fling back his head and howl as the fire raced up his spine. She was paradise. Sheer paradise. Everything to him. Wild sex on a rooftop and then home, where he could make love to her all night, knowing they had done what they could to keep Nicoletta safe. Yeah. He called that a win.

CHAPTER THIRTEEN

Nicoletta dressed carefully in the pinstriped suit Taviano handed her. His instructions were very clear. If she wore underwear, it had to be silk. There were a lot of new clothes in the drawers. She hadn't wanted to touch things that hadn't belonged to her, but she was Taviano's wife, and she would be expected to accompany him wherever he went. That meant wearing clothes that cost the Earth.

She ran her hand down the material of the suit. It felt very different from anything she'd ever worn before. Textures sometimes bothered her, but this felt right on her body. She had opted to wear silk panties beneath it. She hadn't quite gotten to the point where she was comfortable walking around knowing she didn't at least have little scraps of underwear protecting her.

She leaned her chin onto her palm as she paused by the hall mirror. That was the strangest thing of all. She probably was safer being nude. She could disappear into the shadows if she wasn't wearing clothes. All that time she'd been with her step-uncles, suffering their attacks, had she known she could have escaped by using the shadows, she would have done so. Her means to leave had been right there all along.

Taviano's attackers had been men who knew how to use the shadows. They were older and more experienced. She hadn't known, and he hadn't been able to leave.

Taviano came up behind her, close, so close she felt his body heat. He wrapped his arm around her, one hand sliding into the loose lapel of her jacket to cup her breast over the thin lace of the silk bra. His thumb and finger rolled her nipple. Her sex clenched and instantly she went damp and her stomach did that slow hot roll.

"What are you doing?"

"I like touching you." He didn't remove his hand. He tugged on her nipple through the silk. "Does it bother you?"

She pushed back into him. She wanted more from him. She wanted to be able to have a normal relationship, not be afraid every time he touched her that if he took it too far, she'd mess everything up by falling apart. Her first reaction was always fear. Her second reaction was an incredibly intense heat flooding her veins and pooling low and sinfully wicked. She laid her head back against his chest.

"Nicoletta? Does it bother you that I like touching you?"

"No." Her voice came out a husky whisper. She barely recognized it. There was no way to suppress the longing, and she didn't try. "I like that you do. I hope you always want to touch me like this, Taviano."

"Next time, *tesoro*, when Stefano isn't coming with us, you don't need to wear a bra or panties. I know you think you need them, but you don't. I want you to feel freedom. Not necessarily because you're going without them but from the idea of having to have clothes to protect you. First, you've gotten to a point where you can protect yourself. And second, I love your body and I love knowing no one else has a clue but me what's under that prim and proper little suit. Which, by the way, looks very different on you than it does on me."

She had to agree. He looked very handsome. All the Ferraros did. She looked . . . curvy. The jacket tucked in at her waist and flared over her hips. Emmanuelle had worn the men's cut for a long time and then she'd demanded a female version. The tailor had created a beautiful line, with the lapels fitting tight over her breasts and even tighter through the ribs before flaring out over the hips. The back was longer, a series of draping ruffles that framed her bottom deliciously. It was very feminine, but the material had a lot of stretch in it, allowing the women to move when they needed to work.

Nicoletta couldn't look away from the two of them in the mirror. She found the sight of his hand disappearing beneath her jacket lapel very hot. His fingers caressed her breast gently and then became rougher, more possessive, before going back to those hauntingly sweet strokes that drove her out of her mind.

He buried his face in that little spot between her shoulder and neck that he knew made her particularly squirm when he kissed and bit her there. Her entire body shivered. She wanted to ask him what he was doing. She worried that Stefano could be there any minute. Weren't they supposed to be heading out to go after the Demons who were going to come into Ferraro territory so no one could get hurt? The Ferraros were so casual about time. They acted like they had all the time in the world. She had no idea if they had to hurry or if they had most of the night to just be on call.

They'd spent time practicing traveling short distances in the shadows to acclimate her body and give her a chance to learn to ride them on her own, mainly from one part of the house to the other. It was much scarier than she'd thought it would be, even going that distance without holding on to him. He was right behind her, but she couldn't feel him there. The cold of the shadows and the absolute aloneness terrified her, compounded by the sensation of her skin coming off her bones, but she didn't get sick. The distance was short enough that she was able to maintain. Once she'd managed a few times to find her way around the house using the shadows, she had far more confidence.

Nicoletta opened her mouth, thinking she might protest Taviano's assault on her senses, but once his teeth scraped across her sensitive skin, she lost all ability to think clearly.

Taviano managed to open the first two buttons of her jacket while his mouth was busy at her neck, so the jacket framed her breasts. The silk bra was barely there, just a network of lace stretching around her generous curves. In the mirror, the marks from his roving fingers showed through the lace, and her nipples stood up temptingly. The bra was a pretty mauve, the color nice against her skin.

Her face was flushed that soft, delicate rose he loved to see over her entire body. His hands wandered down to the waistband of the trousers. It was easy enough to open them and slide his hand down inside. "I love your skin, *piccola*. Always so soft. When I held you at night, it was difficult not to rub my body all over yours just to feel how soft you are."

He massaged her feminine mound and those soft curls there. Waited a heartbeat. Two. She didn't protest. She didn't stop him. He tugged on the curls, watching her face in the mirror. Her breathing turned ragged. He let his fingers slide farther down, found her lips and rubbed and tugged. Her gaze jumped to his.

"Do you like that?" He whispered the question into her ear, his breath warm, his seduction blatant. "Does it feel good?"

She had to know he found her a desirable woman. He wanted her to know he loved her and loving her meant wanting her body as well as her heart. He stroked a finger over her clit and then her entrance. Tugged again on her lips. Gently. So gently but firmly, letting her know he could use every part of her to make her feel pleasure. The more she trusted him, the more pleasure he could give her.

Her gaze clung to his in the mirror. "Yes."

His finger slid into her. He felt the bite of her channel. She was tight. Achingly so. He bit down again on that sweet spot that had her squirming. "Keep looking at me, Nicoletta. I want you to pull your bra off your breasts, so it pushes them up."

He began to fuck her slowly with his finger, his eyes on hers in the mirror, his mouth on her shoulder. She looked so sexy with his hand in her trousers, working her body. Her hips began to subtly move, gliding with him. That was even sexier. Her hands came up to her bra and she dragged it down beneath the two rounded globes, pushing them up. Her nipples were even tighter. They looked so damned tempting he could barely contain himself.

"Can you roll and pinch your nipples for me?" He used one hand to show her and then pulled his hand free so he could lick off the coating of honey. He showed her his gleaming finger. "You taste so good, *tesoro*."

He held his finger to her mouth and waited for her to open. Pushing inside he watched in the mirror while she sucked. The sight made him so hard he found he was growing painful. "You're so sexy. I love that you do whatever I ask of you." His hand was back, sliding inside her trousers. He flicked her clit, strummed it and then flicked it again and again. "Keep rolling and tugging, Nicoletta. I love to watch."

Her breathing had grown ragged. She didn't take her gaze from his in the mirror, and he knew by the way her body was flushed and her hips bucking that she was finding the sight of what he was doing to her as sexy as he found it. He slid his finger into her again and began to fuck her harder and deeper, watching her closely as he added a second finger. Every now and then, he brushed along the seam of her cheeks with his thumb. She tugged harder at her nipples and her hips found his rhythm and matched him.

She was beautiful. So close. He couldn't take his eyes from her. This time he wasn't going to be selfish. This was for her. Although, he had to admit, it was for him, too. He loved seeing her like this. He loved knowing he could give this to her. He loved that she trusted him with her body enough to allow him to follow the things he asked of her and let him put his hands on her.

He felt the tightening of her body. The tension coiling in her. Her gaze turned frantic, fearful. "I've got you, *amore mio*, I'll always have you. Just let go. Give yourself to me." He bit down on her neck again, gently, his teeth scraping lightly, and then he kissed her there, his tongue lapping at the small sting.

She cried out, a soft little sound that sent an arrow piercing his heart, and he felt her channel clamping down, spilling hot honey around his fingers. The flush was on her breasts, her neck, her face. Her eyes had gone dazed, a rich haze of heat and pleasure mixed. She looked so gorgeous and abandoned, lying against him, her breasts thrust out, reddened, nipples inflamed, her trousers pushed down and the tops of her thighs glistening with evidence of her orgasm.

"I'm not sure I can stand up."

She still had her eyes open. Still watched him in the mirror.

"I've got you."

"I'm a mess."

"You're sexy as hell. You know you are."

"No, I mean a mess. Look at me. I need a washcloth."

She indicated the dark curls now damp and gleaming, along with the tops of her thighs. He grinned at her in the mirror.

"No problem, *piccola*, I've got this."

She looked at him suspiciously, but he was already on his knees, pulling her legs wide, wrapping his hands around her lower thighs to lock her in place, and he used his tongue to lick up the inside of her thighs, catching any honey that escaped. He took his time, devouring every drop, listening to her soft entreaties, her threats, her laughter. Her fists settled in his hair but she didn't pull him away as he used his tongue and teeth, getting creative, teasing her, inflaming her again, showing her that spontaneous sex between a husband and a wife in the light of day could be fun and playful.

He stroked her cheeks, bringing her closer to him, and

then, when he suckled and pressed deep, he stroked the sweet little star between her cheeks. Petting her. Soothing her. Giving that a rhythm, too. Letting her get used to the feel of him touching her everywhere but not demanding anything of her. Then she was crying out again and he was cleaning her up for real. For some reason, that soft little sound she made when she came for him went straight to his heart every time. The fact that she would trust him the way she did humbled him beyond reasoning.

He went up onto his knees and pushed his face into her belly, wrapping his arms around her. "I'm so in love with you, Nicoletta."

Her hands trembled as she stroked caresses through his hair. "I don't know how I got so lucky, Taviano. I was thinking about the two of us earlier. How, if I had known I could just be naked, gone into the shadows and disappeared, where my step-uncles and Benito wouldn't have been able to get to me, I would have done so. That you would have never been so lucky. But if I'd done that, I wouldn't have met you."

He stood up slowly. "Don't, *tesoro*. I wouldn't have ever wanted you to have to be with those monsters or have them put their hands on you."

"I know you wouldn't want that for me. But what I'm saying is, I wouldn't change what happened if it meant I couldn't be with you now."

He knew she meant it. She was killing him because she did mean it. She did love him that much. She had married him thinking he didn't love her and would never fall in love with her, but she'd married him anyway so that he could continue to be a rider. Nicoletta felt he was worth saving. Just being with her, he could admit to himself that had Stefano known what had happened to him, he would be like Nicoletta. He would have given Taviano that same fierce love, but he also would have treated him differently. He would have been more careful with him. He would have guarded his words. Been more protective. Taviano would never have been treated the way Stefano treated his other siblings.

Very gently he pulled her bra up over her breasts, hating to hide anything that beautiful from his sight. He buttoned the jacket. "I'll be right back with a washcloth."

"Are you certain your brother isn't going to come sauntering in?"

"I'm certain, Nicoletta. I wouldn't have started anything if there was that possibility. I can guarantee you that right now, Stefano has other things on his mind than the Demons."

We aren't going to have an exact location where the Oklahoma City chapter of the Demons might choose to stop," Vittorio said. He sat with Elie and Emmanuelle at a picnic table in an empty campground. They'd ridden the shadows for hours, trying to get ahead of the Demons before they made it anywhere near Chicago.

Rigina and Rosina Greco had eyes on the cars driving from Oklahoma to Chicago, using satellite surveillance. Having more money than most countries came in handy when you wanted—or needed—toys. They knew the Demons would have to stop soon for fuel and most likely would choose to eat something as well.

The Grecos, excellent investigators and cousins of the Ferraros, were monitoring the cell phones as well in the hopes of pinpointing Benito Valdez's exact location. So far, no one had called him to report in. The chapters had called one another but not their leader. Still, one could hope.

Emmanuelle sighed and rubbed the back of her neck. Immediately Elie reached up and began a slow massage without even looking at her.

"We're in the best position possible. The Northwye is the halfway point almost exactly, and it's the Y intersection in the road where the highway branches off north of town. We can follow them in any direction they take from here," Elie pointed out.

"All we can do is wait," Vittorio agreed. "Rigina indicated fifteen were sent out from the city. They have two

Ram trucks and a 4Runner. She thinks the one running the operation is in the 4Runner."

"How's Grace's shoulder doing?" Emmanuelle asked. "I couldn't believe she got an infection after injuring it again."

Vittorio flashed her a small smile. "She's better. Doing therapy. She's always trying to rush recovery and I have to slow her down. She gets herself into a lot of trouble that way."

"You're way too cautious." Emmanuelle mock scowled at him. "You wouldn't be with one of us."

"I'd be with you," Vittorio corrected. "And if she hadn't rushed her recovery in the first place, she wouldn't have needed a second operation."

"I know, Vittorio, I'm sorry," Emmanuelle said immediately. "I shouldn't tease you. Although Grace said she stumbled and hit her shoulder into a rock wall when she was checking out a place to hold an event." She turned to Elie, nudging him. "Grace took a bullet meant for Vittorio, and it shattered her shoulder, right about the time you came on board with us."

"I remember," Elie said. "I was training under Emilio. The call came in that someone tried to kill you, Vittorio. Emilio thought you were all tucked in for the night and he wasn't the least bit happy that you'd gone out without his knowledge."

Emmanuelle sent her brother a quick smile. "You got into trouble with Emilio, didn't you? I despise his lectures. Elie has the best of both worlds. Not only does he get to bodyguard, but he's a rider. So, you get to boss everyone around no matter what, just like Stefano."

"No one really bosses Stefano," Elie said. "Not even Emilio. Stefano is a law unto himself. Even my family walks carefully around him."

"I think of you more as a Ferraro than an Archambault," Emmanuelle confessed. "You've become such a part of our family."

Vittorio nodded. "Stefano treats him that way, doesn't he, Elie? He gives him the same hell he does the rest of us."

"And the same amount of work," Emmanuelle agreed. "Thanks for always being so good about it, Elie. There's so much now. It just seems like no matter how much we take on, there's always more."

Elie slung his arm around her shoulders and pulled her in close. "Because you're letting him send you all over the country, Emmanuelle. You're going to burn out if you don't slow down."

Emmanuelle stiffened and pulled away, glaring at him. "I work the same as everyone else does."

Elie glanced at Vittorio for confirmation.

Vittorio nodded. "You know it's true, Emme. I've already had the discussion with Stefano."

"Behind my back?" She looked outraged.

"Of course, behind your back," Vittorio said, sounding amused. "If you'd been there, you would have kicked our asses. No one was going to risk that."

Elie covered his mouth with one hand, but there was no hiding the sudden flare of laughter in his intense dark eyes.

A small smile flirted with the curve of Emmanuelle's lower lip. "You're not going to charm me, Vittorio. Or you, either, Elie. You're both in the doghouse." Suspicion crossed the perfection of her soft features. "Who else was there? Were all of my brothers there? Was *Mariko*?"

"Betrayal of the sisterhood? You know better. Even if Mariko thought it, she wouldn't voice it, not without talking to you about it first," Vittorio said. "While your brothers have always conspired to boss you around and protect you from your stubborn and willful behavior from the day you were born, your sisters-in-law wouldn't think of joining the many conspiracies we have. Fortunately, you have all of us, and now Elie as well, to look out for you. I know you are especially grateful." He sounded complacent.

"I love Grace," Emmanuelle told Elie. "I love her so very much. She's sweet and gentle and so deserving. Her one failing is that she's madly in love with Vittorio. If she wasn't, I'd be tempted to break something important on him and send him limping home. She'd be upset though, and I don't ever want her upset."

Vittorio smiled. "I don't like Grace upset, either. Have you talked with her about planning Nicoletta and Taviano's wedding? I thought maybe she could spend some time with Lucia and Amo. She might be able to keep them from worrying about Nicoletta until this is over."

"Do you think it will ever really be over for them?" Elie asked. "Benito has four brothers. In order to stop Benito from pursuing her, we've got to kill him. When he's dead, aren't the others going to come after her?"

"The hope is they will have no idea she has anything to do with his death, or the death of any member of the Demons," Vittorio said. "Although the manner in which they were all killed goes back to the same way her step-uncles were killed."

"That's true," Emmanuelle agreed, "but if they lose so many, and no one ever caught a glimpse of the assassins and lived to tell about it, I'd want to stay away."

"Taviano and Nicoletta will always have to be careful, but then we all do," Vittorio said. "In any case, we can hunt them if we have to. Elie, your family, in particular, has to be watchful at all times. It is rare to worry that shadow riders might come after us, but with the job your family has, that's a very real possibility."

The Archambaults were the only family sanctioned to kill other riders for breaking the laws of shadow riders.

Vittorio suddenly swung his head toward the highway. "I believe the Demons are close. Let's see where they plan on heading."

All three were immediately on their feet, stepping into the shadow that would hurtle them straight toward the Y in the highway that would determine which road the Demons would travel to fuel up on their journey, or if they would even stop.

Vittorio had taken the lead and Elie stepped in front of Emmanuelle. She hissed her ire at him as she emerged from the mouth of the tube, but he didn't so much as turn around or acknowledge that he noticed. The two Ram trucks and Toyota 4Runner were the only vehicles approaching the Y. Traffic wasn't busy.

The sun had already dropped, providing a purple and blue sky streaked with darker clouds. The vehicles pulled to the side of the road for a brief consultation, although no one got out.

"They're so lazy, they're using their cell phones instead of getting out and talking with one another," Emmanuelle observed.

The truck in the last position sat in the remaining light, engine rumbling, with the shadow of the trees cast right over it. Emmanuelle stepped into it and instantly felt the pull. The tube took her body, flinging her straight down and across the distance at breakneck speed, sliding her right under the door and throwing her into the very back, just missing one of the men in the back seat as the driver put the vehicle into gear and set the truck in motion.

She breathed deeply, crouching low, making herself as small as possible as she tried to rid herself of the disorienting effects riding the shadows always caused in her body. There was no shadow to immediately dive into if one of the five men in the cab of the truck should suddenly turn their head and spot her. As they drove down the highway, shadows occasionally striped the cab but streaked past and couldn't be counted on to hide in. She remained silent, slowing her heartbeat, breathing slowly and evenly, using calming meditation breathing to let her muscles relax and be ready to spring into action.

There was silence in the truck for the first few minutes and then one of them spoke. "Can't you put a little lead into it, Brio? Either that or pull the hell over."

Brio had to be the driver. Emmanuelle locked that into her memory.

"You had your chance, Cruz," Brio snapped. "You can hold it until we get to the diner. What are you, two?"

Cruz was sitting in the back seat directly to her left.

Cruz squirmed, and the man sitting directly in front of her shoved him. "Stop it. It's fucking close quarters in here. I told you to quit drinking, but you just kept it up anyway." He sounded annoyed. Frazzled even.

They'd come a long way, and riding together in the back seat probably hadn't been very comfortable. They weren't small men. She risked a look, just tipping her head up enough that she could see the backs of their heads.

Cruz swore in Spanish and elbowed the man. "Shut the fuck up, Eber, I'm tired of you."

Eber retaliated, slamming his elbow viciously into Cruz's jaw. It was hard enough to snap Cruz's head to one side. Eber didn't stop. He hit him two more times and then turned in the seat, facing slightly away from him.

The man to Emmanuelle's right snickered. "Hell, Eber, you just tore him up."

"What the fuck is going on back there?" Brio demanded. "Lon, what did Eber do?"

"Nothing, they're just going at it like always," Lon lied.

"Well, stop," Brio demanded.

Emmanuelle could see him peering into the rearview mirror, searching suspiciously to see what was going on. The front passenger turned to look as well.

Air moved through her lungs, in and out, no change as she waited for him to turn around.

The driver suddenly cranked up the radio so loud it blasted throughout the cab, making a statement, telling them all he didn't want any further problems. The moment they all settled, she put her hands on either side of Cruz's head and wrenched, using the signature kill of all the shadow riders.

"Justice is served," she murmured under her breath and settled his head in the exact position it had been in.

She waited a heartbeat. A second one. No one noticed. No one cared to check on Cruz to see if he was okay after Eber's vicious treatment. If someone did notice, they would hopefully attribute his death to Eber's elbow.

She watched Lon as he shoved his folded jacket under his head against the window and then removed it. He positioned it on the back of the seat under his neck twice and then moved it again. Clearly, he was uncomfortable, but he was careful not to bump into Eber, who was taking up more than his share of space on the seat.

Eber knew it, too. He inched his elbows out, shoving into both Cruz and Lon. Then when Cruz didn't give him a reaction, he turned his back toward Lon, shoving into him, forcing him closer to the window. There was a malicious little grin on his face.

Emmanuelle didn't hesitate. She gripped Lon's head and wrenched. The crack couldn't be heard over the blasting music, but his jacket started to slip out from under his neck. She had to catch it, and for a moment, the passenger in the front seat started to turn toward the back, and she froze. Brio said something to him and he turned back, leaning closer to the driver to hear. She positioned the jacket under Lon's head, whispered the required proclamation and sank back down, this time directly behind Eber. He would be the toughest one. Once she had him, she could crawl over the bodies and kill the passenger in the front of the cab and then the driver. That could be accomplished in seconds. Then she would drive the truck to wherever the destination was. Brio had programmed the address into the GPS. She just had to follow directions.

Watching in the rearview mirror, Emmanuelle took her time. One needed to be patient. Even if they reached their destination, she would still have time to kill Eber and possibly the others. It might be difficult depending on where they parked, but it wasn't out of the realm of possibility. She was fast, she knew that.

Eber played on his phone, eventually hunching to gain even more room, still uncomfortable. He straightened, spreading his knees wide as well as his elbows, head down, looking at his screen. The occupants in the front seat watched the road and discussed something she couldn't catch above the pounding beat of the music, so Emmanuelle ignored them.

She rose up, caught Eber's head between her palms and wrenched. The crack was satisfying. "Justice is served," she whispered.

Shoving him to one side, she was over the seat and on the passenger before either he or the driver even knew she was there. She took out the man in the passenger seat without a problem. The driver fumbled for a gun, shouting profanities at her as he tried to bring it up from where he had placed it in the console between the seats.

Emmanuelle had one foot on the console, preventing him from pulling the gun out while she gripped his head in her hands. He fought by throwing himself around, but he had one hand on the box between the seats, still trying for his weapon, and one on the steering wheel. He could do little more than throw his head around. She simply used the leverage of her body and the technique she'd learned from the time she was a toddler and broke his neck. The moment she did, she pushed his body away from the wheel.

It took strength to drag him up and off the gas pedal and shove him against the driver's side door, but she slid smoothly into the driver's seat, so the exchange barely took seconds. She was grateful for all the upper body work she did every day. She could never have pushed that deadweight off the seat had she not worked out so hard for so long. It sucked that he was squished up against her as she drove, but it couldn't be helped.

Fortunately, it was a fairly short distance before the lead vehicle was signaling to turn off the highway. At their destination, a small diner just on the edge of the city, she slowed as the other two vehicles pulled right up to the front. The 4Runner parked in the handicapped space. She didn't pull into the lot. Instead, she deliberately positioned the truck so a shadow, thrown by the only overhead light, fell across the driver's side door just to the right of the parking lot. Leaving the truck running, she opened the door, allowing the dead body of the driver to fall onto the ground into the brush. She hopped out, sliding straight into the shadow. It took her fast, shooting her up and over landscaping into a small patch of grass where an old dilapidated gazebo with the roof caving in sat on a cracked concrete slab, surrounded by rock and overgrown weeds.

"What the fuck, Brio!" a big man yelled as he stepped out of the 4Runner. "What are you doing?" He started toward the truck, and immediately, the others leaping out of the 4Runner surrounded him as he came purposefully across the parking lot.

Five more men wearing Demon colors joined them as they hurried toward the truck. The first man, obviously in charge, yanked open the door to Brio's truck. The passenger spilled out, hanging obscenely upside down.

The men jumped back as if bitten, surrounding the truck, weapons drawn, as if somehow they were going to find the killer in the bed waiting for them. The leader pointed toward two men and sent them toward the gazebo. Two others were sent toward a dark row of shrubs. Two others went in the direction of the small grove of royal empress trees that decorated what had once been an outdoor eating area but now was overgrown with weeds. The leader kept the last two men with him to inspect the truck itself and the other three bodies in the back seat.

Vittorio signaled to Elie to take the two men headed toward the shrubs. Thick green leaves grew so close to one another it was nearly impossible to tell where one plant started and another ended. There had been an attempt to start a garden there at one time. Elie could see the faint stone path every now and then twisting through the thick shrubbery, partially broken in places by overgrown roots.

If the two men were trying to be quiet, they weren't succeeding. He could hear their boots as they kicked up rocks and dirt and stumbled on the uneven, broken path. It was very dark, with the trees weeping overhead and the ominous clouds covering any light the moon might have provided. They were thorough in their search, splitting up, using their boots to kick under the shrubs when they couldn't see beneath the thick branches. It was easy enough to find them, come up behind them and administer justice when they made so much noise.

Vittorio followed the two men into the grove of royal empresses. The men stayed close to each other, spoke little and when they had to sweep low, they went back-to-back. They were smart about their search. He was patient. There was always one moment, one second that gave an opportunity. He just had to be ready. He paced along with them, stalking them from only three feet away, sometimes less. One of them was uneasy, looking around, peering into the darkness, sometimes right at him, but he went still and never moved a muscle, and the man always looked away. The uneasy Demon stopped abruptly and retraced his footsteps, whispering to his partner to wait for one moment. He only went back five steps, but his partner had gone ahead an additional five. That was far too big of a gap for either of them to survive.

Vittorio had shadowed the nervous one, knowing the Demon was more likely to know something was wrong and not wait to discover if his partner was dead before making a run for safety. He delivered justice fast, and, as his partner turned back, alarmed that he didn't answer, he killed him as well. Like Elie, he left the bodies where they fell.

Emmanuelle saw the two men headed her way. She didn't have much cover from the overgrown weeds, but the shadow remained, thrown by the light in the parking lot. She stayed in the mouth of it and let the two men come to her. Cloud cover blocking out the moon cast darkness around the gazebo, so the strange shadow seemed bizarre, thrown like a grayish fog in a stripe over the ramshackle building.

One of the men peered inside before stepping in, beads

of sweat gleaming on his face. His partner walked around the outside of the ruins. Emmanuelle waited until the man inside was close to her, his back to the shadow, his eyes on his partner. She delivered the signature kill, eased his body down and was back in the shadow all within two seconds, before his partner had time to turn his head.

"Ed?" His partner rushed inside, looking carefully around before dropping to one knee to feel for a pulse. "This is bullshit." He turned his head to look around again.

Emmanuelle took him from behind, dropping his body on top of his friend's. She stepped back into the shadow to ride it back to the parking lot, this time all the way to the pole where the lamp was, right in the middle of the lot. From the mouth of the shadow she could see Brio's truck with three men just climbing out of it. They consulted briefly, one of them gesturing toward the 4Runner. The large man, clearly the leader, shook his head.

Emmanuelle could see that he was angry. She couldn't blame him. He raised his voice, calling for his men to come back. He wanted whoever had killed those in the truck, but he also wanted his men to check in, and none of them had. She spotted Vittorio just to the right of the truck, stalking the three men. To the left was Elie.

The leader scowled and stepped around the hood of the truck almost directly into Vittorio's path. Vittorio didn't move a muscle. He just seemed to fade into the landscape. She'd seen him do it a million times, but it never failed to move her. She found her brothers extraordinary. They weren't small men, but they could disappear when they needed to, simply become invisible.

How many times had Stefano drilled it into them that movement drew the eye and they needed to know how to be still? She had the worst time with that. She had developed a nervous habit of twisting her fingers together when she was upset. She'd worked hard at overcoming it, but sometimes it still got the better of her. It was a flaw, and she had so many. Her worst trait was being a poor judge of character when it came to men.

She watched as the brush behind one of the men came alive and Elie wrenched the neck of one of the Demons smoothly and efficiently, lowered him to the ground and disappeared. It was over in less than a second. She hadn't even blinked. So fast. She admired him. Respected him. He was that good. That handsome. So sweet to her. She constantly looked to find what was wrong with him—because if she liked him, something had to be wrong with him.

The leader spun around, hands on his hips, shouting for his men. There was an ominous silence in answer. He snapped an order to the man who had stayed close to him. That one nodded and jogged around the hood, calling out for the one Elie had taken out. Instantly, Vittorio was on the leader, his hands expertly positioned for the signature kill.

Elie stalked the last one. As the leader fell to the ground, Elie was on the remaining man. It was going to take a few minutes to find decent shadows to start the long ride home, but as long as they were not seen on the way back, they were golden.

CHAPTER FOURTEEN

"S omething's on your mind, *piccola*," Taviano said. They
stood together just inside his music studio. He wanted to
share it with her, although he had to admit, he found the
thought of doing so a little nerve-wracking.

Nicoletta shot him a glance from under her long lashes,
something he found sexy and fascinating, but it also set off
his warning radar. Whatever it was she was wrestling with
was something big, not small. Her small teeth bit down on
her lower lip. She shrugged and walked away from him to
look out the window of the recording booth.

He didn't push her. Nicoletta would tell him in her own
time. If he pushed her, she'd close down. Right now, she
was struggling, and that surprised him. He thought they'd
gotten everything out between them. He picked up his guitar, sat on the stool he liked and ran his fingers over the
familiar strings.

Once he had the instrument in his hands, he immediately felt different. He imagined Ricco felt the same when
he moved rope through his fingers. His guitar felt a part of

him. The music inside of him he heard all the time struggled to come out. The moment the guitar was in his hands, his mind quieted. His fingers moved. He tuned it automatically. He could hear the slightest error, anything off pitch. He was certain that was one of the reasons he'd been so drawn to Nicoletta from the very beginning. Her voice was so tuned, so perfectly pitched. He would always remember the way it felt when he'd first heard her. Like a key turning in his chest to unlock something deep, something that allowed him to feel emotion, to let the lyrics he needed pour out of him with the right notes.

He played, watching her through half-closed eyes. Whatever it was she had held back hurt like hell. He wasn't going to like it, but he knew he had to hear it. He switched to a melody he'd written after he'd met her, when he'd first seen her, that warrior woman-child. Those men had torn her down until she had been forced to choose death over what life they chose for her. He saw her, so brave, so courageous, standing up to those brutes, refusing to let them make her choices. And then trusting in total strangers, determined to live, and trusting in herself to figure it out if that went bad. She'd been . . . magnificent. Nothing had changed his mind about her since.

He played the melody and then sang it softly, the lyrics about the warrior, the woman-child, courageous, standing up to vicious monsters. Overcoming all odds. She was strong. She was everything a woman should be. She would grow into that woman and learn that no one would ever defeat her. She was beautiful. Brave. She was his world.

She drifted across the room to stand beside him. She touched him, her hand skimming his neck to settle on his shoulder. "Is that how you see me, Taviano?"

"Yes." He kept his head down, his fingers moving lovingly over the strings.

"Even then, when I was so lost? You saw me like that?"

"You were still you, Nicoletta. I saw you. I always saw you. What happened to you threw you, just as what happened to me threw me. It didn't define either one of us, nor did it defeat us."

She ducked her head. "Benito Valdez raped me twice. It wasn't just my step-uncles. When he got out of prison, he saw me on the street. He wanted me and I ran from him." It came out in a rush. "I was so afraid. You've seen him. He's a great brute of a man and he's really mean. Especially to women. He really hurt me. And he told me he'd make my step-uncles give me to him. He decided I would provide him with children."

Taviano continued to play without missing a beat. He detested the pain in her voice. He knew what it was like reliving experiences. Of course he knew. He'd read the reports. She didn't have to tell him, but he knew she felt like she did. "*Tesoro*, this man is never going to get his hands on you again. Never again."

He looked at her then, holding her gaze so she could see he was a Ferraro. He had been raised to be an assassin, a shadow rider. He didn't like men such as Benito Valdez, and knowing how he treated women and children, he really despised him. Knowing what he'd done to Nicoletta made the man his number-one target. He wanted Nicoletta to see the killer in him. He was a predator. Benito Valdez was his prey—not just his but his entire family's.

"Do you understand, Nicoletta? Can you see what I'm saying to you?" He didn't stop playing, and never looked away from her.

She nodded her head. "I'm sorry I didn't tell you before. I should have. I don't know why it feels so much worse that he touched me, but it does. I didn't want anyone to know, but then it felt like I wasn't telling you the truth."

"Thank you, *amore mio*. Everything you tell me feels like a gift."

She rubbed her forehead against his shoulder. "I know there was a very detailed report and you probably already knew it, but it didn't come from me. I wanted it to come from me, not someone else. When I tell you things, Taviano, I feel like I'm letting them go."

He didn't deny that he already knew that Valdez had raped her. He'd read the reports the social worker had sent, her pleading letters, the recorded visit to the Ferraros in New York as well as the reports of the investigators in New York. The fact that he had found out three years earlier was the only reason he could find a way to distance himself from the crime enough to function at all. He wanted to wrap Nicoletta in a cocoon and protect her, but she wasn't that kind of woman and she never would be. She wanted to be actively participating against Valdez, but she knew she wasn't ready. This was more of a training exercise than anything else. She would stay in the shadows and Stefano would evaluate her ability to function.

He had utilized as much of their free time as possible in the meditation room, working with her on breathing techniques. That was more important than her self-defense skills at the moment, and she was already so good at that. She had to learn to handle the way the shadows ripped her body apart. The better she got at breathing her way through the pain and the way the ride screwed with imagination and feelings, the quicker she would learn to handle the pressure. Some riders never did. They had worked over and over at maneuvering through the house in the wider, easier shadows so her body had a chance to acclimate to the terrible toll riding took.

Taviano's own father had been trained as a rider, but he was never able to be one. He used the shadows occasionally to go from one place to another, but never for work. That required too long of a time actually being in the tubes. He'd used them only for his affairs.

"I like your music, Taviano. You said you weren't that good at playing, but that's not the truth. You play better than many professionals."

"I like your voice. You can sing, can't you?" he countered.

She actually stepped back away from him, those long lashes fluttering. He found himself flashing a grin, his fingers finally stopping their movement on the strings.

"You can sing. You were just about to try to tell me a giant whopper."

"I can't. My mother could sing. She had a beautiful voice. She sang all the time. When she was alive, the house was always filled with music. She would break into song whenever anyone was grumpy."

"Were you grumpy?" He set his guitar in its stand.

"Sometimes," she admitted reluctantly. "In the morning. I'm not really a morning person."

He found himself laughing. "I've seen you grumpy. I can tell I'm going to have to drag you out of bed in the mornings."

She glared, trying to look tough. He thought she only looked adorable. "I wouldn't do that if I were you. I'm not above retaliation."

He really laughed then and slung his arm around her neck, pulling her into him. "You're a sweet only child, Nicoletta. I'm one of the youngest of seven. You learn fast to think of evil things to do to those who prank you." He walked her out of his music studio.

She balked at the door, stopping him with a hand on his chest. "Your music is really good, Taviano. I suspect you already know that. Someone has to have told you, one of your friends. You know people in the industry. Don't you even own companies that produce music and videos? I thought the Ferraros had their own label."

"We're silent partners, although not so silent anymore," he admitted.

Some of the top musicians had jammed with him. They'd listened to his singles and wanted him to record the songs or allow the artists to record them. He'd refused. They were private, lyrics born of his private pain. Nicoletta's private pain. Their struggles to overcome their feelings of inadequacy. Their growing strength, finding it first in themselves and then in each other. Each song was a record of something very personal, although no one would ever know that. Just Nicoletta.

"My songs are for you."

She looked around the studio. It was as professional as it got. Then she looked up at him. He knew immediately, by the way her dark eyes glistened at him, that she got it. "You're such a beautiful man, Taviano." She put one hand over her heart. "I'll learn to sing the songs if you really want me to, if they're just for us. You gave me such an enormous, amazing gift. I want to hear every single thing you've ever written."

"I want to hear you bring them to life." Her voice would. She had that perfect pitch and the ability to make the lyrics weep with emotion or soar with hope.

"You really have never shared your music with your family? Not Stefano or Vittorio? Or Emme?" She knew he was particularly close to them.

"The lyrics were too close to the truth of my life. I would never sing in front of them anyway, but if they asked me to read the lyrics to them, Stefano would know just by listening to my voice or looking at my face. He's very in tune with all of us." Taviano walked her out of the studio and then locked the doors.

"Why lock them? Your family can just get in anyway."

"We use an invention of Ricco's to keep anyone from sliding under a door using shadows. I've installed them so no one can get into my studio. They would have to break in the conventional way. I would know, and I wouldn't be too happy. On top of that, all of us have a great deal of respect for one another and our privacy. When I'm not home, security is activated and it's very tight. If you're here by yourself, I would want you to have the security system on."

Taviano was careful not to make that an order. Nicoletta didn't need anyone ordering her around. She was intelligent and capable of making up her own mind about security. The Ferraros were always going to be at risk. She'd been around the family long enough to know there were always threats made against them. They were highly visible. They made enemies. They carefully cultivated a certain image that made others think they were useless with far too much money, or businessmen buying and selling companies others had worked to build up.

"I want to be able to go outside and utilize the patio and woods," she said. "Is there a way to do that and still have the security system intact?"

"Yes." Taviano hesitated. He didn't want to sound as if he was bragging. All of the Ferraros were born with various gifts. He had a knack with electronics and liked to tinker, to come up with new gadgets. He could disrupt security systems easily because he was always building new ones.

"You invented something new, didn't you?" she asked.

He shrugged. "Yes." His admission was low.

"There's so much to learn. All of you are light-years ahead of me." Nicoletta sighed. "I was studying night and day before we got married. You're a bit of a distraction."

He laughed again when she frowned. He couldn't help himself, he bent to brush her lips with his. The moment he felt that soft bow, his stomach did a slow roll and he locked his arm across her back, dragging her closer to him, tilting her head back so he could kiss her. That mouth. All flames. Alive with heat. With some special addictive aphrodisiac that roared through his body straight to his groin. A powerful, potent fire that invaded every cell and turned him inside out.

She made him feel things he'd thought impossible. She brought him roaring to life in so many ways. He tightened his arms around her when he lifted his head, just holding her close to him, letting the intense emotions wash through him.

"Am I doing the right thing taking you with us, Nicoletta? Should I keep you safe the way Stefano does Francesca? You're the most important person in my world. I don't want you ever to think I love you any less than he loves her, or Vittorio loves Grace, or Giovanni loves Sasha. I know every time you go into the shadows it's a risk."

"Why would you ask me that, Taviano?" Nicoletta tilted her head to look up at him, a small frown on her face.

She reached up and rubbed at his jaw, her palm cupping the side of his face. There was something so gentle and loving about the way she touched him that his heart turned over. She could just turn him inside out with such a small thing as framing his face or rubbing the pad of her finger along his jaw. He knew it was the way she touched him. He felt her love in the way she touched him. He saw it on her face.

"I *have* to be in the shadows with you. I can't explain it to you, but the compulsion is very strong. It's a drive. A need. I've had it since I was very young. I used to play like a bunny, hopping in and out of the shadows. My mom would watch me and tell me I was just like her when she was little. We'd laugh together all the time." She smiled up at him. "I'd forgotten that until just now. I'd forgotten so many things about my mother that I'm just letting myself remember. It wasn't like I disappeared or anything. I had clothes on, but I liked to play with shadows."

Taviano nuzzled the top of her head with his chin. "I know you want to be in the shadows, Nicoletta, but it is risky. We train for years to do the kind of work we do. You're not ready."

"I know I'm not. I'm not about to get in your way. But I have to start somewhere. I was careful when I was with you before. I wouldn't have insisted on going with you once we knew Pia and Bianca were safe at the hotel, but Clariss might have needed me. I couldn't let her be alone if those men had raped her. That was a very real possibility. I wasn't just insisting to be a pain."

"I'm well aware of that, *tesoro*."

Nicoletta wasn't the type of woman to throw a temper tantrum to get her way. She didn't insist she was as good as others who had trained for years at their job. She was highly intelligent and weighed each situation carefully before making decisions about the best thing to do. She tried to keep her emotions from ruling her. She was young, and that wasn't always possible. He was hotheaded, and at times it wasn't easy for him to push aside his own emotions and stay in control, making judgments impersonally.

"I want to learn. The more I'm exposed to this, the faster my body and my mind learn it. I don't know why I work that way, but I do. Each time I was in the shadows, I was sick, yes, but I could feel the difference in the way every tube worked both on my body and in the way the shadow pulled at us. Fast or slow, the way it moved us along. The corners, sharp or a steady curve. Eventually, I could anticipate them, and I couldn't see at all."

He knew everything she said was true. She had been sick, but she had also been more relaxed, riding with him, her body tuned to his, moving with his in a rhythm. She had been anticipating the curves and corners. "That doesn't mean there aren't very real dangers always present. The shadows won't protect you from one of our enemies spraying bullets through the room if you're sitting in the mouth of a tube. You can't navigate on your own yet. No one has taught you that. You'd be lost in the shadows, Nicoletta. Even if you didn't get hit by a bullet and you managed to dive into the tube and the shadows took you, you'd never find your way out again."

He closed his eyes with a groan of regret. "I never should have taken you with me in the first place. Not until you knew how to get from one place to another."

"You mean all the maps of Chicago Mariko and Emme insisted I memorize? They drilled it into me that I had to know my way around every single city that I went to. I needed to be studying all the time. Fortunately, I have a pretty remarkable memory. I can look at something and file it away. Mariko said that wasn't good enough and said she wanted me to study the map of Chicago, so I did. Now I know why she insisted."

"You think you could figure out how to maneuver through the shadows riding that fast, scared and in the dark, disoriented and possibly sick, alone, and know where you were in order to figure out where you have to go to get out?"

She put both hands on his chest and pushed to give herself room to step back so she could look up at him, her dark eyes meeting his. "The one thing I know above anything else, Taviano, is that you do whatever it is you have to do in order to survive. I would do it. And then I'd go back, and I'd find you. If you were in trouble, I'd get to you." There was calm conviction in her voice.

Taviano knew she meant every word. More, he was absolutely certain she would do just what she said. She might suffer a few agonies while she figured it out, but she'd get it done and she'd go back for him. He threaded his fingers through the weave of her braid at the nape of her neck, where it was thick and soft.

"I did pretty well here in the house, with you following me, not helping me, Taviano," she pointed out. "I didn't get sick going back to the plane, and I didn't, not once, here. I managed to find my way into each room. Granted, I was going slow, but it was me, controlling how fast I went." There was satisfaction in her voice. Pride, even.

"It's no wonder I'm in love with you. The wonder is, no one else knows what a treasure you are. I wish I could have met your mother, Nicoletta. She must have been something special."

"She was."

Taviano took her hand and they walked through the house back toward the kitchen. He'd glanced at his watch to see if Stefano had texted him, but the last message had merely said that no word had come in from the New York cousins. Rigina and Rosina had their eyes on Los Angeles and Chicago, and so far, there was no real movement. Stefano suggested they relax until he gave the word to move.

"Your parents never had any other children." Taviano made it a statement.

"Mom couldn't have any more after me. She always said

I was enough for her, and my father—adoptive father, but for me the only father I ever knew, and I loved him very much—said he was happy with me. He certainly made me feel that he was."

He waved her to a barstool so she could sit while he washed fresh berries he'd had brought in earlier for her. He mixed them up in a bowl and put them in front of her. She loved fruit. He'd also gotten dragon fruit and passion fruit, fresh mango and papaya, and cherimoyas, the last, one of his personal favorites. She loved cherries, and he had those brought in for her as well. He cut up a few mixes of the exotic fruits and laid them out for her, along with several different cheeses, honey, jam, crackers and spiced nuts.

"You're totally spoiling me."

"That's my intention," he admitted. He sat opposite her and nabbed one of the small plates he'd set beside the cheese plate. "Eat, woman. You always want to be well hydrated and have something in your stomach."

"So I can throw up all over your brother?"

"That won't happen this time." He poured confidence into his voice and hoped it wouldn't happen.

Stefano might use her being sick as an excuse to ban Nicoletta from the shadows until he saw fit to proclaim she was fully ready. Taviano knew she wouldn't be able to stop herself from practicing on her own. She had been telling the truth when she said it was a compulsion now, a need. It was for all shadow riders when they reached a certain point in their training. That was when they were usually sent out of the country to be trained with other families. That was the point when it was known to their parents and trainers that they were true riders.

He knew Nicoletta was a true shadow rider. He just hoped Stefano saw it as well. She had no experience and little training, but she had the instincts, and her body was strangely adapting faster than he had ever seen or heard of a rider adapting. He knew the Archambault family was different. No one ever spoke of why they were different, but they were the ones policing the riders for a reason. Elie was crazy fast in the shadows. He had amazing reflexes. Sometimes he was so fast, his hands or feet appeared a blur when he fought. All of the Ferraros preferred training with him. Working with anyone that good improved their speed as well. Nicoletta had Archambault blood running in her veins.

"I hope you're right," Nicoletta said. "I don't want Stefano to ban me from practicing. I don't intend to be a liability to you in any way, Taviano. I know I can learn. Mariko and Emmanuelle are assets to you. You said yourself that there are way too few riders."

He nodded. "Unfortunately, that's true. We're stretched pretty thin. So few children. That's part of the reason Eloisa and the older riders are so upset with our generation of riders. They want us to be old-school in our thinking and accept arranged marriages, produce children and train them immediately. I can understand that way of thinking, but it's difficult to agree with them."

"You're thinking of Emmanuelle."

He nodded and added honey and jam to his cheese. "She's in love with Valentino Saldi. The problem with a Ferraro falling in love is they only do it once if it's the real thing. Emme has indicated to Stefano she's willing to accept an arranged marriage. I don't want that for her. Neither does Stefano. As head of our family, he has to make that happen."

Nicoletta took several pieces of the fruit. Taviano noted which were her favorites. She was definitely fond of the dragon fruit. She did eat some of the cheese and honey, but far more of the fruit.

"Is Val really that bad? Could you talk to him?"

"I'd like to beat him to a bloody pulp," Taviano said, meaning it. Just the thought of the hell the man had put his sister through stirred the rage in him. "When she was just sixteen, he seduced her. It wasn't right. It was deliberate. His father ordered him to seduce her so that he could get information on our family from her. All along he was seeing other women. She caught him, and even heard him telling another woman who had confronted him about his relationship with Emmanuelle that he had no feelings for her whatsoever. It broke her heart."

Nicoletta looked up from where she'd been choosing a spiced nut, her dark eyes suddenly blazing. "Are you kidding me? And none of you have beaten the crap out of him?"

"Vittorio did," Taviano said. "Although not nearly as badly as he deserved. It's saying something that Emmanuelle didn't try to stop him, either. Normally, she would have been the first to defend Val. She hasn't spoken to him in two years. She's refused, and I know Val's tried to contact her several times. She's left the country a few times, and I think it was because he was pushing pretty hard to see her. I think she's afraid to hear whatever he has to say, even if it's an apology."

Nicoletta nodded. "I can understand that. Women forgive men they love way too easily. It's a failing most of us share."

He sent her a quick grin. "It's a trait you all need to have because men tend to screw up a lot. I'll need you to have that particular characteristic running deep, *tesoro*."

"I think it will have to be the other way around, Taviano." She sampled the passion fruit and then more of the dragon fruit. "This is so good."

"I had it brought in this morning for you."

She went very still. "You didn't."

"Of course, I did. I know you love fruit." He studied her face. She was just that little bit too still. "What's wrong, *piccola*?"

"You. You're so thoughtful. You really do love me. I don't know what to do with that. With you. All this time . . ." She trailed off. Nicoletta pressed her lips together and then her lashes swept up so her gaze met his. "You're the most amazing man. I realize I'm very lucky."

He couldn't help smiling. "You just remember that when

I screw up big-time, or Eloisa makes you crazy. Or Stefano does. And we all will."

Her smile was slow in coming, but when it did, it lit up her face and reached her eyes. His gut settled. She had him tied up in knots, and he hadn't even realized it. He didn't like her upset.

"Tell me about your cousins in New York. Emmanuelle and Francesca were talking about them a few weeks back when I was over playing with Crispino. I met Salvatore briefly, or I should say, I saw him. He was just leaving Stefano's when I arrived. He looked very intimidating. And sad. I don't know why I thought he was sad, but I did."

"Salvatore, like Emmanuelle, has resigned himself to an arranged marriage. So many women throw themsclves at men like us and they resort to all kinds of underhanded schemes to try to trick us into marriage. He wanted to find a woman to love him for who he is, not because he's wealthy, or a rider. That just doesn't happen so easily when you're a Ferraro and your picture is splashed across the world in every magazine there is."

"Your family doesn't exactly keep a low profile."

"That's true, but we do that for a good reason," he pointed out.

Nicoletta nodded. "Well, I felt bad for him. What's he like?"

"He's a really good man. Tough. Responsible. He's always the one who volunteers to take extra shifts even if that means going overseas. I like Salvatore. I always have."

"He has two brothers?"

"Lucca and Geno. Geno is the oldest. He's quite a bit like Stefano. Maybe a little rougher around the edges. He isn't a man you'd want to cross. He's loyal to the family and watches over his brothers. I know he's been worried about Salvatore for some time. I guess all of us have been. Salvatore is extremely good-looking, and the women go after him. He's gotten the most tricks played on him and I think that's taken a big toll. Geno is too tough for women to try to play him. They're smart enough to be afraid of him. Lucca appears to be the definitive playboy. He's a player and the women go after him, but they don't expect to win, and they don't."

"I find that so sad," Nicoletta said. "I'm glad I don't have money. It just seems to make everything a mess."

Taviano burst out laughing. "Honey, sometimes you're priceless. You do realize you're a Ferraro. You're married to Taviano Ferraro."

She nodded and took another bite of cheese with olallieberry jam on it. "Yes, of course, I know who I married. It's your money and your family's money, not mine."

He leaned across the short distance between them and brushed his mouth over hers, his tongue licking along her bottom lip, where a trace of jam lingered. "I love you so much, woman. It's *our* money and *our* family, so that money is yours as well."

She actually went pale. "We're not going to discuss this. I can't talk about it with you. Stefano will make more sense than you, and if he doesn't, I'll talk to the family lawyer. He'll have sense enough to protect you. We're going to draw up some kind of paper."

"*Amore mio*, on this one thing, you're not going to win, so don't bother fighting me on it. You know how stubborn I can be. Finish your fruit."

She shook her head. "Taviano, you just don't make any sense. And when you say the family's money, are you including the cousins as well?"

"Each part of the family makes their own money and builds their own financial empire, so to speak, but we contribute to the overall family wealth as well. That is overseen by a board consisting of a representative from each branch of the family."

"That's so crazy. How do you all get along?"

"We have a branch of the family that polices everyone. They make certain everyone does their jobs. The penalty for cheating or lying or doing the kinds of things that happened in Mariko's family, once found out, is extreme."

"I see."

Taviano was certain she didn't, but he didn't want to explain to her how things worked in their family when riders—or anyone else—went wrong. That would be for another time. Right now, he wanted their time together to be as smooth as possible.

Salvatore Ferraro stood in the shadow surveying the men wearing the colors of the Demons. Already drinking heavily, they didn't look like men on a mission to back up their president. They looked more like men determined to get drunk and push the locals around. The locals had, for the most part, already gotten wise and left for the night. The bartenders, three of them, were old hands in the business, and clearly knew they were in for a long night of broken glass and little pay.

Salvatore noted Lucca on the other side of the bar, just to the right of the flashing neon sign that proclaimed the best beer in town. Since the bartenders were pulling the beer out of a small refrigerator in the back rather than having it on tap, Salvatore doubted the sign was true. The leader of this crew of Demons was a man named Ed, and he was flanked by two others, Carl and Thomas. The three seemed more interested in where the women were. Several times they demanded the bartenders get on the phone and call some whores down to the bar so they could have some action.

"Get it done," Ed snarled, pounding his fist on the bar. "Otherwise, you'll be the one on your knees."

The other Demons erupted into laughter, one pointing to a bottle of tequila, and when the bartender tried to pour it into a shot glass, he snatched it out of his hands and just drank from the bottle.

"Pass it over, Adan," Ed demanded. He snagged it, drank and passed the bottle to Carl.

The Ferraros didn't want the bartender to call prostitutes. They didn't need more witnesses to work around. Two of the Demons headed toward the men's room. Lucca stepped into a shadow that took him directly ahead of the men sauntering toward the restrooms. He entered first and waited for them just inside the door.

One came in first, looked around, opened the doors to the stalls to make certain they were alone and then the two men immediately laid out lines of cocaine on the bathroom sink. The sink was unwashed. The bathroom smelled of urine and mold. It looked to Lucca as if it hadn't been cleaned in the last century, but then his standards were much higher. He told himself he might be considered a snob.

One of the two men leaned down to sniff the line up his nose. As he did, Lucca appeared behind the other one and very gently took his head in his hands, snapped his neck and murmured the appropriate phrase as he lowered him to the floor. He was gone before the other Demon straightened. The Demon giggled and then looked around, looked surprised, giggled again and then toed his friend.

"Get up, Moe. Stop fooling around." As he bent down, Lucca came up behind him and delivered the signature kill of the Ferraros. He left the cocaine on the sink untouched and once more slid outside the door to wait until someone noticed they hadn't returned.

Three of the Demons snagged beers and stepped outside to ensure no cops were around. They each took a separate direction to walk around the building. Geno slipped out behind them. He shadowed one man with long stringy hair. It smelled as if the Demon hadn't bathed in several days. Stringy hair walked briskly around the corner, not once looking behind him. If he was their best sentry, Geno thought they were in real trouble. He simply matched steps, caught his head, snapped his neck and lowered him to the ground with the appropriate phrase.

Geno took a shadow tube, a fast one, that shot him around the building to the other side, nearly dumping him out to the right of his next victim. This Demon was a little more aware of his surroundings, taking his duties seriously. The fence was on this side, and he had actually climbed up to peer over it. Geno stepped behind him and as he came down, simply broke his neck and left him where he lay.

The third man was just rounding the corner toward where the first victim lay on the ground. He halted, staring, as if he couldn't believe his eyes. It was dark on the side of the building, but the bar had neon signs on top of it, giving off light that cast shadows across the ground. The Demon could see his friend lying there, his beer spilled on the ground.

"Deke, you hurt?" he called out and then sprinted toward his friend.

Geno broke his neck and let his body fall over Deke's just as the man was pulling out his phone to call his boss and inform him of the loss. He rode a shadow back inside and waited for Ed and the others to notice that no one had come back in from sentry duty.

Ed paced back and forth, drinking more tequila and demanding "bitches and whores" be called. He wanted food. The bartenders put out peanuts and chips.

Two Demons, ones Salvatore overheard referred to as Berto and David, snagged several bags of the chips and moved to the back of the room to eat. Ed threw the empty bottle of tequila after them. Glass shattered and sprayed across the floor, but neither Demon seemed to care, which told Salvatore that they were used to Ed's tantrums. He found it interesting that these were the men sent to back up Benito Valdez. They seemed to be screwups. No matter. In the darkness and privacy of the booth where Berto and David had retreated to eat, they died quietly.

Four men headed toward the back room to play pool, although Salvatore was more inclined to think they were escaping from Ed's continual rants against the bartenders. He was drinking from his second bottle of tequila and passing it to Carl and Thomas, still demanding women and more food.

Salvatore and Geno followed the pool players into the back room. One of the men racked the balls on one table while another did so on a second table. The other two men hefted pool cues and then chalked the tips.

While those bent over the tables were concentrating their attention away from the men with the pool sticks, Geno took one of them and Salvatore the other. Both were eased to the floor with broken necks. They were on the two other men in seconds, so there was no possible way either would have time to call out a warning to those in the other room. They left all four men dead on the floor.

Ed glanced around and frowned. "Hugo, tell Moe and Boz to quit snortin' and get their asses back in here." He waved his hand toward the men's room.

Hugo sighed, put down his beer and stomped purposefully toward the restroom. He didn't like being an errand boy and he made that clear. He shoved open the door and took three steps in. The door closed behind him just as he spotted the two men lying on the floor. His first thought was a bad batch of cocaine finally got them. Then there was a wrenching pain.

Lucca dropped the third body over the other two. There was no point in blocking the door. If he was lucky, maybe Ed would check on his men himself. He had to have drunk so much by now, he was going to have to visit the men's room soon anyway.

Ed paced back and forth, glaring toward the booth in the back and then at the poolroom. He snapped his fingers for the bottle of tequila, took a long pull at it and then jerked his chin toward the front door.

"Thomas, Adan, go see what's taking them so long. What's got into everyone?" Ed demanded. "Is it just me? Carl? Is it just me?"

"Hasn't been that long," Adan muttered under his breath as he stomped out the door, Thomas behind him.

Geno rode the shadows and stalked them every step of the way. Thomas lagged behind, not wanting to bother going too far from the lights. He snapped his fingers at Adan and sent him toward the darker side of the building. The moment Adan disappeared, Thomas pulled out a joint and went to light it up. Geno was already on him, snapping his neck and lowering him to the ground before rounding the building and following Adan into the darkness.

Ed paced to the front door, took another healthy swig of tequila and handed the bottle to Carl. "Fuck it. Let's play pool. Come on. Benja, you can watch these fools."

Lucca and Salvatore were already waiting in the room. It was easy enough as Ed and Carl entered to get behind them as they stood staring, shocked, their alcohol-fueled brains unable to process what had actually happened to their friends. The two Demons dropped to the floor with broken necks as Benja stood with his back to them.

Salvatore gripped Benja's head and wrenched. "Justice is served," he murmured softly. Very carefully, knowing the three bartenders were most likely looking toward the poolroom, he pulled Benja inside and to the right of the doorway before laying him down on the floor.

He and Lucca caught a shadow to outside, where they joined Geno. The three shadow riders began the journey back to New York.

The bartenders washed glasses, waiting for the Demons to emerge from the poolroom. It was suspiciously silent. The music blared, but there was no more laughter or threats. No more loud conversation. They couldn't hear the sound of pool balls striking together. They looked at one another, but it took another few minutes before they ventured out from behind the bar to go look. What they found was more terrifying than the Demons coming into their establishment had ever been.

CHAPTER FIFTEEN

"S tefano is on his way here with two of our cousins from Los Angeles, Nicoletta," Taviano announced. "Are you ready for this?"

"Why would the cousins from LA be coming here? Did something happen to my friends?" Nicoletta spun away from the plants she was inspecting.

Taviano had overgrown greenery everywhere. The windows allowed light to come in from so many directions that the houseplants grew easily. They climbed toward the ceiling, thick and heavy, leaves green and silvery. That was another passion they both shared. He had discovered very early on that Nicoletta really loved plants. She had gravitated toward working in Signora Vitale's flower shop, much to his dismay.

Theresa Vitale's grandson Bruno had taken over the shop for his grandmother. He'd always been a bit of a hell-raiser, and he'd begun to run drugs out of the store once he'd taken over as manager and was without supervision. Nicoletta had even been accosted by one of his friends when she'd worked there. Later, Bruno's body had been found in a Dumpster, murdered, a victim of the ongoing feud between the Ferraro and the Saldi families.

An uneasy truce had continued over the last couple of years, but beneath the surface smoldered something deep and ugly only waiting for the lid to blow off. Both sides knew it, and both sides were preparing for war.

"Your friends are safe, *amore mio*," he assured. "I don't know why the cousins are here from LA. I'm sure they'll tell us. I'll put out some refreshments. We never serve alcohol before we work. We still have our run to make when Rigina or Rosina gives us the word."

She followed him to the bar and watched as he put ice into a bucket and then put out soda water and various organic syrups to make refreshers.

"Pay attention to the energy in the house, Nicoletta. This time, I want you to warn me when someone gets close or comes in."

She nodded and padded barefoot over to the window. She placed her palm on the glass, fingers spread wide. "Mom would give me a very bad time for getting my handprints on the glass."

"I doubt my mother would have noticed if we put our hands on the glass. Stefano taught us to read energy by touching shadows, the floor, glass, the wall, whatever worked for us. Do you have your gloves close and your shoes, just in case we have to leave fast?"

"Everything is right over by the entrance you told me we were going to use to leave. I can put them on in seconds." She didn't turn around or move her hand.

Taviano was pleased to see she was concentrating on the house more than she was on their conversation. She would learn to read the energy around her all the time. It would become second nature, so that she could carry on conversations and still feel when something wasn't right or know when someone was coming up on her.

"That's my woman. Always be ready. Always have your gear ready. That's the first lesson drilled into us."

"No, it really isn't, Taviano," she said, still not turning her head to look at him. "Stefano is already playing games with Crispino. Francesca isn't recognizing the movements, because she doesn't ever see the signature kill, but he's teaching him how to grip and snap a neck. He's just not using a head yet. He's just positioning his hands over and over on various objects. He's having me do it. All of you are doing it. Emme is. Mariko is. He's not even two and he's already learning."

"He isn't learning to kill anyone, *tesoro*," he said as gently as he possibly could. There was an ache in her voice, and he couldn't blame her. None of them liked the idea of a child learning those techniques, but on the other hand, it was the way to keep them safe. The younger they learned, the better they would be at it and the safer they were.

"I understand, I really do. I wish I'd had the training that young, but our children . . ." She trailed off. "I don't know, Taviano. It's such a terrible legacy to give them. To decide for them before they're born that they have no choice. They learn to kill, and if they can't find a man or woman to love them, they live without love but marry anyway and produce children. What anchors them? What could keep a person sane when they have to live a life with no one to love them and bring them peace and happiness when they return home?"

She turned her head then and met his eyes. His heart stuttered at what he saw there. So much love he could drown in it. He was never going to have to live that way because he had her.

"I don't want that for our children," she whispered.

"Neither do I. Neither does Stefano, or any of our family. That's what Eloisa fears the most. That's what the older generation is so afraid of, that we'll allow the riders to slowly dwindle out because we're not tough enough on our children." Taviano rubbed his jaw. "I don't know the right answer, Nicoletta. I do know that I felt hopeless until you came along. You were so young, and I felt a little like a monster for making certain our shadows tangled together.

I didn't want you getting away from me. I knew the connection between us would grow stronger each time we were together, and truthfully, I couldn't stay away."

"I was very mean to you."

"No, you weren't," he denied. "You were striking out against yourself, not at me. We both know that. You never sent me away." He gave her a small smile. "You do realize that, don't you? When you were so afraid, coming out of one of your terrible nightmares, fighting me, punching and kicking, you never sent me away."

"They're here, Taviano. I can feel them. Just now coming inside the door of the kitchen. Five people, four men and a woman. Stefano is one of them. And I could never send you away no matter how much I wanted to. You were always my anchor in the middle of the worst of everything. I was afraid if you left me, there wouldn't be anything of the real me left to find."

He understood what she meant. Nicoletta had been lost for a while. That strong woman her mother and adopted father had raised. That woman with a strong bloodline from both sides of her family. She was there, she just needed to fight her way to the surface again and remember who she was. He had to do the same thing. He had to remember he was a Ferraro. It didn't matter that his mother and father had rejected him. He knew, deep down, that Stefano, the one person in his life at the time that truly counted, would never turn his back on that boy.

"We're in the living room, Stefano." His voice carried, although he used a low tone.

There wasn't so much as a whisper of sound, but Stefano entered, leading the way. Behind him, one man, tall with broad shoulders and a wealth of dark hair, the same piercing blue eyes that marked him as a Ferraro, followed. Severino, the oldest of his cousins from Los Angeles, was very reminiscent of Stefano in that he had taken over his family early. His parents were deceased, a terrible blow to riders everywhere, leaving Severino to care for his siblings at a young age. He had refused to allow other families to break them up. Like Stefano, he'd taken full responsibility.

Behind Severino came a beautiful woman, his youngest sibling, Velia. She was tall and elegant, looking every inch a supermodel. Her hair was braided in a thick long rope, but Taviano had seen it many times falling in dark waves to her waist. She had the inevitable curves of the women in their family, and the pinstriped suit emphasized her narrow waist and long legs. She flashed a smile at him in greeting and turned that radiant smile on his woman.

Behind her were two more of her brothers. Marzio, one of the toughest of the Ferraros, had a reputation among the riders for being someone ready to defend his family immediately. He was quiet, much like Vittorio, but he stepped in front of any of his brothers or his sister if there was trouble.

Beside Marzio was Tore. Taviano had known him all his life, yet he was the cousin he knew the least about. Tore stayed in the background, and he was no different now. He greeted them with a nod, acknowledging the introduction to Nicoletta, accepting the refresher and then stepping back into the corner, as if standing guard over all of them.

"Thank you for providing Nicoletta with clothes, Velia," Taviano said. "We both really appreciated it."

Nicoletta nodded, coming around to seat herself beside him. Taviano immediately took her hand and pressed her palm to his thigh.

"Yes, I was wearing only Taviano's shirt, so I really needed them."

Taviano was proud of the fact that she didn't sound nervous. She seemed confident, a hostess in her own home. He liked that.

Velia smiled, looking somewhat amused. "I'll bet you had to roll the pants up in order to walk in them."

Nicoletta laughed. "That's true. You are a bit taller. Otherwise, everything fit nicely."

"I love the house, Taviano," Velia said. "It's different, but beautiful."

"I'm not someone who wants to live in a city," he admitted. "Fortunately, Nicoletta doesn't mind escaping from all the noise and lights with me."

"Let's get down to business," Severino said abruptly.

Velia heaved a sigh. "Seriously, Sev, you have to develop some kind of skills with people or you'll never find a woman to put up with you. This is called being civil. We're exchanging niceties."

Marzio might have snickered. Stefano hid a smirk behind his hand.

"Well, exchange them another time," Severino snapped, glaring at his sister.

She wasn't in the least bit fazed. "Nicoletta will think you're scary when you're really a teddy bear." She blew her brother a kiss.

He sent her a smoldering look, but Taviano could see that his dark eyes had softened when they rested on his sister.

"There appears to be a rift happening in the Demons with the leadership of the Valdez brothers," Marzio explained when Severino nodded to him. "We have their main meeting house in LA wired, and we've picked up some interesting conversations. Tonio Valdez is president in LA, but he answers to Benito, just as all the brothers do. The brothers all have their own territories that they've worked hard at building up. It seems that every time they get ahead, making money for their own locals, Benito takes it. He says it is his due as the president of the Demons."

Nicoletta inadvertently dug her fingers into Taviano's leg every time Valdez was mentioned. He felt the tremor run through her body. He knew she was afraid of the brutish leader of the Demons. There was no way to prevent her from feeling that same terror she had felt when she was a teen and the president of the Demons was determined to have her as his "wife."

"Nicoletta disappeared from the apartment, and the Demons had it completely surrounded," Stefano said. "Benito had been watching to make certain she didn't try to run from her step-uncles and him, so no one ever saw anyone going into the building or leaving it. No cameras or cells picked up anyone coming or going, yet all three of the Gomez brothers were dead from broken necks, and Nicoletta vanished. That left an impression."

"Yes, it did," Marzio agreed. "So, you can imagine what kind of craziness erupted when the same thing happened in LA, with Jorge running back to the warehouse and reporting that Armando Lupez, the man Benito sent out from New York and Tonio so graciously got tickets to the Kain Diakos concert for, was dead of a broken neck along with a member from LA."

Taviano felt the little shiver that went through Nicoletta's body. He didn't want to call attention to her, but he shifted just a little to put his body between her and his cousins.

"Then the news came in about the warehouse," Marzio continued. "Everyone dead, no Clariss and no explanation of what happened. No Nicoletta to hand over to Benito. The police never found a single body in the hotel where Jorge had claimed the others were killed. Now Jorge was dead in the warehouse as well. Tonio was going to have to tell his brother, and he knew Benito was going to be royally pissed and out for blood."

Stefano met Taviano's eyes. They had feared all along that Benito's brothers would be a problem.

"Tonio seems to be the driving force behind a revolt he and his brothers have planned against Benito," Marzio went on. "Benito's leadership has suffered, in their opinion, ever since he got out of prison and then lost Nicoletta. He became obsessed with her, with finding out what happened to her and with getting her back."

"What exactly is the revolt against Benito?" Nicoletta asked. "He's a very vindictive man and wouldn't hesitate for a minute killing his brothers and their families if they have them."

"They don't appear to have families at this time," Severino said. "We checked. None of the brothers have indicated in any way that they are in opposition to Benito. In fact, they all sent men to support him getting you back. It's just that the men they sent were their fuckups. The ones they have the most trouble with. It was discussed ahead of time which ones they didn't mind losing. Those they thought would be loyal to Benito no matter what. Those were the ones sent to aid him."

"What are the brothers planning?" There was apprehension in Nicoletta's voice.

Taviano wrapped his arm around her and pulled her beneath his shoulder.

"They don't want anything to do with Nicoletta," Severino said. His voice was grim. "It seems that Tonio has much grander ideas. He believes that Benito was stupidly wasting his time on a whore with no money. What could she bring to them? Nothing but trouble. Benito was making money the hard way. Tonio, it seems, likes to look at magazines. He sends them to his brothers and circles all the photographs of what he calls the 'useless' celebrities. The ones with far too much money and nothing to spend it on but toys."

Stefano and Taviano exchanged a long, puzzled look. Taviano shook his head. "What does that mean?"

"They watch reality television and the high life of the 'useless' celebrities," Marzio said. "Tonio has convinced his other brothers that they can make a far better living that way rather than running after someone like Nicoletta. You may not know this, Velia, but women with too much money like men from gangs. It's thrilling to bang men like them. Tonio thinks he's in the right place to get a deal for a reality show. They can make all kinds of money that way and put him in the path of the right kinds of bitches so they can have the kinds of toys where they can really have power. Not the kind of penny-ante shit Benito is into."

"He wants a reality show?" Taviano echoed, shocked. Disbelieving.

Severino nodded slowly.

Stefano laughed. "He'd probably get one, too."

"We could make it happen," Severino said. "Or at least begin negotiations with him and distract him from what's happening with his brother."

"All of his brothers want Benito gone," Marzio added. "His brother Thiago, president of the New Jersey Demons, is so sick of him insisting they take the fall for him and go to prison so he doesn't have to when he screws up, which he does more and more because he's drinking all the time now. Joaquin in Oklahoma City feels the same way. He told Tonio that he's just about had it with Benito's drinking, and he's not taking the fall for him."

"And there's Leonardo from St. Louis," Severino continued. "I think he despises big brother more than any of them. Benito took a couple of the women Leonardo's crew had, and Leonardo couldn't stop him without getting into it with his brother, and he wasn't strong enough at the time to oppose him. That made him look weak in his crew's eyes. They lost their women, and he lost their respect. He's since got it back, but that really tainted his view of his brother."

"Not a lot of love for Benito," Stefano said.

"There's a good reason," Nicoletta agreed. "He's a horrible man. Those women he took from St. Louis, where they were probably treated halfway decent, he most likely used in his trafficking ring. He didn't want them for anything but to prove to his brother and everyone else that he *could* take them. He pours favors on those who help him and utterly wipes out those who resist him. He rules with fear."

"Tonio lost some of the men he considers screwups," Marzio continued his report. "He didn't much care about them. And he was very happy that Benito's men were killed and couldn't tattle to big brother. He's handpicked the contingency he's sending to aid Benito. They're all men he doesn't trust. He figures they're all in Benito's pocket and have been paid to spy on him."

"Is he paranoid?" Stefano asked.

"I think he's a smart man in a lot of ways," Severino said. "And seriously, he may be onto something with this nonsense about a reality show. I can have our people reach out to him, Stefano, if you think it will distract him at the right time. He's running drugs and guns so he has a lot to lose if he doesn't juggle everything just right, because he could incriminate himself with cameras running all the time. I don't think he knows what reality television is."

"I hate to put him in a position of furthering his goals of meeting silly women who might do exactly what he wants them to do. That could turn out badly."

"I agree," Severino said, "but if we keep an eye on them, we could stop them before they get too far."

Stefano drummed his fingers on the arm of his chair. "Something this big, Severino, we usually talk about and put to a vote. What do your brothers and Velia think?"

"We just gathered the information and came to you."

"How soon can we expect the Demons in LA to make their move?"

"You don't have to worry about that. Giovanni is there with Maximino, Remigio, and Vico. They'll handle them, no problem," Severino said with confidence.

Taviano knew his other three cousins fairly well. Maximino was lightning fast when it came to handling any kind of weapon or working with his hands or feet. Taviano had trained with him often, both benefiting and improving their speeds.

Remigio was direct and to the point, all business when it came to work. He was quiet, had a soft touch and was in and out before anyone knew he was close by. He had trained in France with the Archambault family, just as Stefano and Severino had, and it showed in his direct, lethal style of fighting. He was very proficient with weapons but excelled with any kind of stick or cane.

Vico, like Ricco, had trained in Japan, and he was a mixture of both Ricco and Remigio. He had a grace and smoothness about him when he moved or worked. Taviano liked all of his cousins, but more, he respected them.

Severino's voice held absolute confidence when he said they would be able to handle those coming toward Chicago, and Taviano had that same confidence in his cousins and Giovanni. It didn't matter how many men Tonio had chosen to send after Nicoletta, they would be disposed of in the same manner as the other Ferraros had taken care of the Demons coming to their territory to aid Benito in taking her from Taviano.

"How's Francesca doing?" Velia asked. "Giovanni told me she wants to have another baby. That would be wonderful, Stefano."

Taviano kept his face expressionless but couldn't help the glance he threw at his brother. No way in hell had Giovanni disclosed that information. Velia had to have inquired in such a way that his brother had no choice but to answer her. Francesca did want another child, but she'd had trouble before, during and after she'd had Crispino.

Stefano's expression was pure stone. "Francesca had three miscarriages prior to carrying Crispino. During her pregnancy she was quite ill, and when she had him, she lost a great deal of blood."

"Does the doctor think she can successfully carry again?" Velia persisted.

Taviano had been there the night Francesca had gone into labor. They all had. Stefano had been with her right up until the time she'd begun to hemorrhage, and she'd had a seizure. He'd been ordered from the room while they did emergency surgery. Taviano would never forget the look on his brother's face. So lost. Completely and utterly lost.

There was a small silence. Taviano glanced warily at his brother. Nicoletta tightened her fingers in his. They both knew this was an ongoing argument between Stefano and Francesca. She wanted to try again. Stefano wasn't certain he wanted to try. The losses had been hard on both of them. The ordeal of Crispino's birth had been very traumatic on

Stefano. He had faced losing Francesca and didn't want to go there again no matter what the doctors told them.

"He does, yes. She carried Crispino, so yes," Stefano admitted finally after another small silence. "But she did have complications giving birth."

Velia pulled back, genuinely upset. "I'm so sorry, Stefano. I didn't know. Francesca never said a word. I thought all was fine."

"It is. She's very healthy and fit these days," Stefano assured.

"That's good," Severino said briskly.

Velia scowled at her brother, but he didn't pay any attention.

"I suppose you have to wait a decent amount of time between children. How long is the recommended period?"

Velia heaved a sigh. "You don't have to answer that, Stefano. Severino has no delicacy when it comes to actual relationships. If he ever meets the right woman, she'll run screaming for the hills when he opens his mouth."

Severino glared at her. "Why do you always say that? Having children is a real concern, Velia. There are too few."

"Perhaps that's so, Sev, but Francesca is more than a broodmare to Stefano. She's his wife. He actually loves her, in case that hadn't occurred to you. She's gone through a difficult time, as has he. Losing babies isn't easy."

Severino instantly turned to his cousin. "I'm sorry, Stefano. I didn't think before I spoke. Naturally you wouldn't want Francesca to get pregnant too fast. I really don't know how long one waits between children."

"I don't think there is a set length of time," Stefano said, taking pity on his cousin.

Taviano knew Stefano could and probably did relate to Severino. They both thought a great deal alike. And both had put the shadow rider program first for many years. It was only after Stefano had found Francesca that he had begun to think differently.

"You are going to have another child." Severino made it

a statement, proving that he was exactly like Stefano in that he could so easily read others.

Stefano sighed. "It isn't always so easy or as black and white as we think it is, Sev. The thought of losing another child, or watching Francesca suffer, isn't something I want to go through. Nor am I prepared to lose my wife in exchange for another child. I'm not having children for the sole purpose of producing them as riders. I am their father, and that means something. I didn't know what that was until I saw Crispino born and then I held him in my arms. It changes something in you."

Severino glanced at Velia and then across the room, where Tore had disappeared into the corner so silently. "There's a small part of me that understands. I had to take over when my parents died. I knew I wanted the others to be safe. We were spread out in age, and several of them were quite a bit younger. Velia was just an infant. Tore, a toddler. I made it my business to make certain they were safe. I'm certain you remember. You went with me. You, Geno and me."

Velia leaned forward and peeked around Marzio to look at her oldest brother. "What does that mean? I've heard vague references to something of that nature before. Keeping all of us safe, but no one talks about it. What does that mean, Sev?"

"It's of no consequence, *bella*," Severino said. "It's in the past and it can stay there."

"But no one ever says how Mom and Dad died," she pointed out. "Am I the only one who doesn't know? That's not right. Do you know, Taviano?"

He didn't. He only knew that Severino had come in the dead of night asking that Stefano come with him immediately. Vittorio had told Taviano later than none of them had ever seen Severino upset that way. He was always cool, calm, a boy, a teen and later a man who refused to be shaken by anything. Stefano had heard him out and then was gone. He hadn't consulted Eloisa or Phillip, but by then, as a boy in his teens, he didn't anymore. He simply left, and his parents never knew that he was gone or that he returned hours later. Taviano had been told by his brothers that there had been blood in the shower and sink, but they hadn't seen any signs of damage to Stefano.

"Leave it," Severino said softly, but his voice was a whip.

Taviano realized they all had history. He wasn't the only one. He brought Nicoletta's fingertips to his mouth and bit down gently to distract her from the byplay. They all deserved to have their own privacy if they wished it. He didn't want his siblings to know his story, and Nicoletta didn't want the cousins to know every detail of her story. The cousins had the right to their privacy.

"I would like a daughter," Stefano ventured.

Taviano knew he was deliberately changing the subject to distract Velia.

"Although I'm not certain I want Francesca to know that. A little girl who looks just like her. Unfortunately for me, if that happened, there would be two females in my house ruling me instead of one."

Nicoletta laughed. "Francesca would say you rule her. She says you're very bossy."

"I have to be. She sits on all those committees and visits every single household in our territory, just to make certain everyone is fine. Half the time the bodyguards can't keep up with her. She wanted to work two days after she had the baby. It was crazy. I had to put my foot down. Thank God for Mariko and Emmanuelle. They helped me sit on her for a few weeks after Crispino was born so she could heal. And you, Nicoletta, helping with the baby so we could keep her resting the way the doctors ordered."

"Sasha took over a lot of the visits," Taviano pointed out. "Emmanuelle showed her the ropes, although she didn't have the amount of time she needed because she was very involved with her brother's care. His brain injury is very severe, and she's determined to spend as much time with him as possible while she can. She knows she's going to lose him soon."

"Isn't there any hope at all?" Nicoletta asked. "Sasha loves him so much. She's lost everyone in her family."

Taviano hated to tell her otherwise, but he wasn't about to lie to her. "I'm sorry, *amore mio*, we had the best doctors available, and all of them came to the same conclusion. There is no recovery for Sandlin, and he's slowly deteriorating. Sasha is aware of it. Giovanni and Sasha spend most of their free time at the care facility with him, or they bring him to their home. He's used to both places now. A nurse accompanies him if they bring him home. They are amazed he has lasted this long. We believe it is his bloodline that has managed to keep him going, but even that will not save him forever. We all see the signs."

"I hate that for her."

"We all do," Stefano said. He turned his attention to his cousins. "You've met Giovanni's wife, Sasha, of course."

Severino nodded. "Yes, a beautiful woman. I actually have met Sandlin on two occasions as well. I needed to speak with Eloisa on an urgent matter and she was visiting him at the medical facility where he lives. He's quite interesting. He had the capability to be a very powerful rider. I imagine Sasha did as well."

"Eloisa visits Sandlin?" Nicoletta asked.

Her voice was so filled with disbelief that everyone turned to look at her. She didn't seem to notice, but Stefano's eyebrows went up and his eyes met Taviano's in a question. Why was it that Nicoletta was so adamant that Eloisa wouldn't ever go visit Sandlin? Especially when Nicoletta was aware Eloisa often visited the elderly and sick in the Ferraro territory. She looked incensed. She vibrated with outrage.

"*Piccola.*" He tried his gentlest tone to calm her, to remind her that one didn't ever give Stefano any kind of a puzzle. He always solved it.

"Is Eloisa still a terrible trial to everyone?" Velia did her best to turn the attention onto herself. "My aunt is a holy terror when she gets going."

Taviano shot her a grateful look. "She's made it very clear to both of us that she doesn't like Nicoletta."

"That's not unusual," Stefano said, leaning back in his seat, one arm stretched casually along the back of the chair, his piercing eyes on Nicoletta. "So far she hasn't approved of any of the women we've chosen. You've been around a long while now, *bella*, and she's been bad-mouthing you every chance she gets. How is it any different now that you're married to Taviano and a part of the family? There really isn't much she can do about it but make herself miserable. She can't tear your shadows apart."

"She would if she could," Taviano said, to keep Nicoletta from answering. He wasn't certain what she would say. She was still too angry with Eloisa for her choices when he was just a little boy.

"She was here," Nicoletta said, making an effort to smooth out her tone. She sent a smile to Velia, silently thanking her for the diversion while she got herself under control. "I lost my temper with her. It's just that this is our home and I feel that if she wants to be rude to me, that's all right, just not here. Not in my home and not in Lucia and Amo's home. It distresses them and I told her that. She doesn't have to speak to me, and I won't speak to her. But if she comes here, that's different. This is where Taviano and I live. This is where we should be able to have peace."

Taviano leaned into her, tilted her face up to his and brushed her lips with his. "I'm so in love with you, woman." It had taken one small reminder, and she'd gotten herself under control in seconds and immediately given Stefano a very good reason for her to be angry with Eloisa.

"I applaud the fact that you refuse to back down from Eloisa," Stefano said. "If you show her weakness, she will eat you alive."

"I made that mistake," Velia said, with a mock shiver, her fingers stroking her throat. "I thought she was going to rip my heart out."

Severino froze. A muscle ticked in his jaw. "When was this, *angioletto*?"

There was a sudden stillness in the room. Velia uncrossed her legs and pressed her lips together. "It was nothing, Sev."

When her brother continued to stare at her, her fingers stroked her throat again. Taviano recognized that gesture as a nervous habit. It surprised him that his cousin, so sophisticated, could have developed such a tic.

She shrugged, a delicate little motion. "I was visiting with Emmanuelle. Clubbing actually, and Eloisa dropped in. She was her usual charming self to her daughter, and I couldn't help myself. I don't like it when she's so ugly to Emme. Emme never stops her. Never. She's always so nice to Eloisa and yet Eloisa is venomous to her, stripping her raw, especially about Val Saldi. She knows it hurts her, but she just keeps lashing at her. I knew better, but I still told her to stop. She's my aunt and it was rude, but honest to God, Sev, she was tearing strips off Emme, and I was already worried that Emmanuelle might . . . I mean, what is she trying to get her daughter to do?"

"What did she say to you?" Severino bit out between his teeth.

Taviano had seen him like that a few times. Nothing good had ever come of it. He almost wished his mother was in the room. He knew exactly what Velia meant. Eloisa couldn't seem to help herself. The moment she was around Emmanuelle, she seemed to tear into her, hissing out the ugliest venom, throwing out recriminations, practically accusing her of selling out the Ferraro family for sex. Sometimes he'd like to remind his mother that she'd chosen Phillip over her son's welfare and see how that went over, especially when they all knew Emmanuelle had never once given Val a single piece of information on the Ferraro family.

"Sev, seriously, it was a while ago."

"You were here to go clubbing with Emme no more than three weeks ago, Velia. Answer me now."

Even Marzio moved closer, and in the corner, Tore actually stirred, making his presence known. Taviano was grateful to know that his LA cousins protected their sister with the same fierceness that he and his brothers did their sister and now, the other women in their family.

Velia sighed, the expression on her face telling all of them that none of them, including Stefano and Taviano, were going to like it.

"She said I was nothing but a beautiful whore like my mother. Everyone knew what she was like, and my father had to marry her because his father made him. She said naturally I'd side with Emmanuelle because look who I came from. She would expect nothing less of someone like me."

Her hand went to her throat again, and Sev caught it and pulled it down to her lap. "You had gotten over this habit, *cara*, but suddenly, in just this last couple of weeks, you're back to it. Now I understand why. I think I'll have a word with Eloisa if you don't mind, Stefano."

"Not at all, Severino. I will be going with you." Stefano stood up.

"Now?" Velia looked shocked. "Sev, you can't. Stefano and Taviano have work tonight. Don't say anything to her. She's vicious. She might say more ugly things about our mother. I don't want you to hear them."

She had her head down, and to Taviano's consternation, he saw tears glistening on her lashes. He'd never seen Velia cry, not since she was a little girl. She was a shadow rider, a very good one, seasoned and, like Mariko, a force to be reckoned with.

"*Angioletto*, look at me." Severino's voice was unexpectedly gentle, but it was nevertheless commanding, more than ever reminiscent of Stefano. It was very evident who the head of the family was and who the head of the LA riders was.

Velia lifted her head and Severino wiped at her tears with his thumb. "You are mine to protect. No one abuses you. They don't say vile things about our deceased mother, especially to you or to hurt you. I don't tolerate this from anyone, let alone a family member. This will never happen again."

"She'll think I'm weak. A tattletale."

"She said these things about my mother. About Marzio's mother. Tore's mother. She said these vile things to you, Velia. She is your aunt, and she should protect you. She should be protecting Emmanuelle. She said them about another shadow rider. I don't know why she's lost her way, but dragging everyone else down with her cannot be tolerated."

Without another word, Severino and Stefano turned, stepped into a shadow and were gone, leaving behind silence.

Velia closed her eyes and pressed her fingers to her temples. "I can't believe I just did that. Taviano, Eloisa is going to go after Emmanuelle. Whenever anyone confronts her, she turns around and gets ugly with her daughter."

Nicoletta had gotten up to refill Velia's refresher. She stopped and turned. "She does that? Taviano? Why didn't you say so earlier? I made her so angry. If she could have, she would have ripped my face off. She tried to slap me."

Velia gasped. "*Hit* you? Strike you? Physically? Eloisa actually tried to hit you?" She looked to Taviano for confirmation.

"Does Stefano know?" Shockingly, it was Tore who asked. He came out of the corner and handed Nicoletta his glass, but his gaze was on his cousin, demanding an answer.

Taviano shook his head. "No, I told her to leave. She wasn't welcome. I thought it better not to let Stefano know. Already, there is too much between Stefano and Eloisa. Much more, and there would be no going back. Eloisa needs to find her way, although it might not be our way."

Out of the corner of his eye, he caught a glimpse of Nicoletta half turning toward him, shaking her head, indicating that Eloisa's way was never going to be their way. She poured the refresher for Tore and handed it to him.

"She didn't manage to claw me, and I did provoke her. I

can get quite nasty when I want to, and I wanted to. She had been very ugly to Taviano. I didn't like it and I let her know."

A ghost of a smile played around Tore's mouth, making him look younger. "I'll bet you did. Your woman is quite the find, Taviano. I envy you."

Taviano smiled and put his arm around Nicoletta. "Believe me, I know how lucky I am. The moment I laid eyes on her, I knew. The first time I saw her with Lucia, she had my heart for sure. The way she loves Lucia and Amo gets me every time. I wanted a part of that."

He had. It had shocked him that Nicoletta had the capacity to love so deeply and so readily after what had happened to her. He hadn't thought she'd be open to Lucia and Amo. The Ferraros had watched her closely, fearing for the older couple, but from the moment she'd met them, Nicoletta had been more about taking care of them and protecting them than looking after herself. That had shown him her heart.

"Anyone want food? Who knows how long those two will be," he added.

"If you're cooking," Marzio said.

Velia and Tore nodded their assent and Velia hooked her arm through Nicoletta's. "We can get to know each other since we're now cousins."

Taviano gave his woman up to Velia as they followed him into the kitchen, happy to see she was in good hands.

CHAPTER SIXTEEN

Giovanni Ferraro peered down at the small group of men wearing the Demon colors of the LA chapter. These men were definitely loyal to Benito Valdez and spent more time reporting to Benito than to their president, his brother Tonio.

The leader of the group was a thin man with crooked teeth and a scar that ran the length of his face, from temple to jaw. He had multiple prison tattoos, creating sleeves on both arms and around his neck and up onto his face. Most were skulls, giving his face a strange, dead-like facade. His name was Victor and he appeared very driven. Giovanni pegged him for a plant.

If he could so easily see that Victor and most of those with him were really men Benito paid to spy on his brother, he was certain Tonio could as well. Tonio was an intelligent man. Giovanni was certain all the brothers were. Benito had succumbed to alcohol and drugs. He'd been on a power trip too long, and eventually the chemicals had eaten away his brain cells to the point that he had forgotten all about finesse and ruled his world with brute force. That worked sometimes, but not all the time. Real loyalty counted, and he'd forgotten that.

Tonio had sent the right army to support Benito's cause. Victor was happy that he was on his way, more than halfway to Chicago with his men. Benito had requested at least fifteen men from each city, and Tonio had been generous and sent eighteen of those he considered his "best." He'd had the conversation with his brother in front of Victor, and Victor had soaked that praise right up. He confirmed to Benito that the men Tonio sent were all very loyal to the president of the Demons and none of them were slackers.

They were fueling their vehicles and grabbing food and they'd be on their way. They weren't calling attention to themselves. They didn't want the cops to identify them or watch their progress to Chicago. They'd get the girl for Benito and make certain to identify anyone who had helped keep her from him. He could come in and kill them himself and then take her back to New York with him. Victor, on the phone, nodded several times and told Benito that they'd be there at the same time.

Giovanni exchanged a long look with his cousin Maximino. Benito was definitely on his way to Chicago. They had confirmation. If Rigina or Rosina could get a lock on Victor's cell they might be able to trace where Benito actually was, and they could send riders to intercept him. The family didn't want him getting anywhere close to Nicoletta.

Not one of the Demons was drinking. None of them appeared to be doing drugs. There were four vehicles. The drivers and two others stayed with each SUV. While they were putting gas in the cars, the others walked across the street to the diner. Six men walking into a diner didn't raise alarms. They went in quietly and sat down in two separate booths.

Giovanni immediately signaled to his cousins to choose a shadow that would take them to the parking lot where the drivers would bring the SUVs. The lot was on the small side but well kept, with trees shading many of the spaces from any afternoon sun. Two overhead lamps illuminated the lot, presumably making it safer at night. The lamps, coupled with the trees and their twisting boughs, threw interesting shadows in all directions across the lot, giving the riders quite a bit of tubes to choose from.

The first SUV pulled into the lot and the driver parked right in the front in a space to the right of the handicap parking. It was just out of sight of the plate glass window where the booths faced the lot. Vico, the youngest of Giovanni's cousins there, moved immediately, catching a shadow and riding it straight to the SUV and inside. He was on the man in the back seat, delivering the wrenching signature kill and out of the vehicle before the driver had turned it off.

The passenger opened his door and turned slightly in his seat to pick something up. Vico immediately caught his head between his hands and wrenched, murmuring that justice was served as he pushed the body back into the SUV and quietly closed the door. The driver had jumped out and slammed his door just as Vico closed the passenger door.

"What are you doing?" the driver asked, turning back toward the window.

Vico came up behind him, catching his head in his hands and wrenching. He heard two more of the SUVs in the parking lot, but those weren't his problem. He lowered the body of the driver beneath the vehicle and stepped into the shadow, allowing it to take him away from the parking lot and back to the vantage point overlooking the little diner. Giovanni signaled to Vico to watch the six men in the diner. They had a good view of the lighted parking lot. No one had emerged. No one had seen. It had taken him only seconds to kill the three Demons, and the bodies couldn't be seen in the dark where they lay.

Remigio and Maximino both stepped into two different tubes, each one small, the narrow ones that moved fast, tearing one's body into what felt like a million pieces, scattering them everywhere and hurtling one out as viciously as possible. The shadow riders couldn't be seen when they slipped out of the shadows and delivered the signature killing moves to those in the vehicles. They couldn't take chances that anyone in the diner would call the cops; Victor might alert Benito that someone was killing his army.

They wanted Benito to show himself, not go into hiding. As long as he thought he had a huge backing of his men behind him, he would swagger into Ferraro territory demanding everyone in his path to tell him where to find Nicoletta and anyone who might be hiding her from him. They needed Benito Valdez to show himself so they could dispose of the threat to Nicoletta.

Giovanni took the last SUV as the three Demons turned into the parking lot. He rode the shadow right to it, timing it perfectly to enter the back of the vehicle just as it entered. There was a dark strip to the left, and the driver chose that direction so he could park next to the other cars. He was driving very slowly, using care as he entered the lot.

Behind the Demon in the back seat, Giovanni gripped his head, wrenched and laid him gently to one side, and then was on the front seat passenger before either he or the driver knew anyone else was in the car. He killed the passenger just as the driver parked the SUV and turned off the ignition. As he turned his head slightly, just as if he might have sensed something might be wrong, Giovanni was already on him. It had taken only seconds to kill all three men.

It was necessary to exit the vehicle via a door, as there were no shadows to catch inside, but he was wearing gloves. He used the driver's side door and immediately stepped into a shadow, deliberately leaving the door to the SUV open behind him. No one could see the bodies unless they came up to the vehicle and looked inside.

He waited there, just in the mouth of the shadow. Vico came closer, as did Remigio and Maximino. It was only a matter of time before Victor and the others came out to see what was keeping the rest of their crew.

Shadow riders learned patience very early. As young

children they were taught to be still, no matter how long they had to lie in grass or rock or whatever the circumstances and wait. They couldn't fidget. They couldn't be seen. They had to remain absolutely still, and if they were spotted, the exercise was often repeated over and over until they could do it before they were allowed to stop for that day. Then it was done the next day and the next. Learning not to move was drilled into them, and yet being ready to move at a moment's notice was just as important as the next lesson to be learned.

Giovanni couldn't remember when he wasn't learning lessons. Granted, most of the earlier ones were couched in playing, just as what Stefano and all of the Ferraros were doing with Crispino, but they were still necessary life lessons to keep them all alive. He waited, knowing one wrong move could bring awareness to those inside the diner and not only end his life, or those of his cousins, but perhaps Nicoletta's as well.

Victor and the other Demons at his table continued to talk animatedly for some time. It was actually one of the Demons in a plaid flannel shirt that suddenly frowned, slid out of the booth and stood to look out the window at the SUV with the door open. He indicated it to Victor and the others. Those in the second booth swiveled around so they could look as well.

Victor nodded his head and the three in the other booth immediately rose and came toward the door. Giovanni remained still, his breathing easy, his heart rate steady and normal. The three men had to come up to the SUV in order to see the dead men inside, and to do that, they would have to pass through the dark section, which would make it difficult for those inside to see them. Waiting for them was death.

His cousins emerged from the shadows on that side of the SUV, moving into the shrubbery closer to the building, waiting for the three men to come along the sidewalk.

"Danny!" one called out, hesitating as the others walked

straight toward the SUV. The one doing the shouting hurried to catch up. "What the hell? Where'd they go?"

The three men stopped together, looking toward the other three vehicles. Vico, Remigio and Maximino came up behind them and simultaneously delivered the signature Ferraro kill. Rather than leave them where anyone could find them, the three were taken to the vehicle farthest from the windows and set inside with the other dead Demons.

Giovanni continued to watch Victor and the other two men. Victor had already signaled the waitress for both checks, paid them, and then was up and walking toward the door, flanked by his two guards, after the three he'd sent out to find his crew. He clearly didn't suspect anything was wrong.

Victor shoved open the door, came out onto the walkway and looked around. For the first time he looked confused. He turned back to his closest guard. "Where the fuck is everyone, Zeus?"

Zeus shrugged. "Hell if I know." He walked toward the corner of the building. "Try to get Danny on his cell. I'll take a look out back."

Victor pulled out his cell, but he paced along beside Zeus, as did the third man. He seemed more nervous, looking around him, standing on his toes to try to look into the darkened SUV.

"Victor. Wait. I think there's someone inside." The third man stammered when he delivered the bad news. "Laying down on the seat." He was standing by the last vehicle, the one farthest from the diner's doors, where Vico had put the last three men.

Victor and Zeus turned back toward him. As they did, Giovanni came up behind Victor while Remigio shadowed Zeus. The man facing them opened his mouth to shout a warning, but Maximino was on him, gripping his head while his two fellow Demons looked on in horror. Their heads were wrenched simultaneously. Three voices murmured at the same time, "Justice is served." Vico opened the door of the SUV, and all three bodies were put inside. Vico closed the door and then went to the SUV with the driver's side door open and closed that one as well. The four men immediately stepped into shadows to begin the journey home, three to Los Angeles and one back to Chicago.

I didn't exactly invite you into my home, Stefano," Eloisa said, staring coolly at her eldest son. "Nor do I remember giving you an invitation, either, Severino."

"I believe you use the shadows to enter any of our homes at will, Aunt Eloisa," Severino said. "As riders, it's a fairly common practice." He nodded his head at Henry, who sat looking extremely comfortable and at home in the overstuffed and very expensive French chair in front of the burning fireplace.

"It's nice to see you both," Henry greeted. "Stefano, is everything all right with the family? With the baby and Francesca?"

Eloisa's mask of indifference slipped, and she looked distressed. Her fingers gripped the stem on her glass of wine. She pressed her lips together as if refusing to inquire further, but she waited for Stefano to answer.

"Thank you for asking, Henry. They're both doing fine. Crispino is very healthy. He's a good boy and learning fast. Francesca is doing very well."

At his reference to Francesca's health, Eloisa did frown.

"And Grace? Is she doing any better?" Henry asked.

Eloisa's frown turned to a scowl. "Is there something to be concerned about with my daughters-in-law that you knew and didn't tell me, Henry?"

"I wasn't aware that you would want to know, Eloisa," he returned gently. "You've never asked a single question about either of them, and you know I visit them regularly."

Eloisa hissed her displeasure but simply turned her face

away from him, as if dismissing him. Henry didn't seem perturbed in the least by her actions.

"What can we do for you boys?" Henry asked.

"I've come to speak to Aunt Eloisa about an incident that happened a few weeks ago that I just learned of tonight," Severino said. "It came out by accident, and I could barely believe that such a thing would happen, but I was assured it did. Aunt Eloisa, I was told that you not only referred to my mother as a whore in front of Velia, but you informed her that my father was forced to take her in marriage and that Velia was like her."

Henry turned completely in his chair to face Eloisa. Stefano's dark blue eyes never left her face. Color stained her cheeks and her chin went up defiantly, but she avoided looking at Severino.

"Yes, that did happen," Eloisa admitted. "It was unfortunate. She was with Emmanuelle, and I was very angry with my daughter for her ridiculous attachment to Val Saldi. She just can't seem to get over that horrid man. It's treacherous on her part. She's a traitor—"

"Stop deflecting, Eloisa," Stefano snapped. "This has nothing to do with Emmanuelle. Your behavior is escalating out of control and you know it. What the hell is going on with you that you would say such a thing about Velia's mother? Her mother was a rider. A shadow rider who served our community with distinction and honor. We don't ever talk disparagingly about another rider, let alone one that is a Ferraro. *Your* behavior is a disgrace to our family, not Emmanuelle's, as much as you'd like it to be."

Eloisa rubbed her forehead as if it was throbbing. "I know, Stefano," she admitted in a small voice. "I'm very sorry, Severino, and I will apologize to Velia. I'll make it a point to go to your sister as soon as I can and tell her in person that I'm sorry for the things I said to her. I can't seem to stop myself, Stefano. I keep getting these headaches. I have for years, and they're so much worse now.

That's not an excuse, but I can't think clearly, and then I'm saying horrid things and I can't stop. I'm so afraid now, afraid for all of you . . ." She trailed off and looked at Henry as if she might crumble under a great weight.

There was a long, shocked silence while Stefano regarded his mother with a frown, his fingers steepled under his chin. The last thing he had expected was her frank confession of a physical ailment. In all the years he'd known her, that had never happened, and it alarmed him. "How long has this been happening to you?"

She shrugged and took a deep breath, waving it away. Stefano glanced at Henry. He wasn't in the least surprised that the man knew all about their lives; he'd been with the family too long not to.

"No, Eloisa, you just admitted something that may end up affecting all shadow riders. We don't know what long-term effects being in the tubes can have on our bodies or brains. Before, there were lots of riders, and so they didn't have to go in as often. We're riding all the time, long distances, staying in the shadows longer. Taking shift after shift. You took far more rotations than your share because Phillip didn't take any and most of your brothers and sisters weren't able to be riders. You should have told me immediately that you were having repercussions."

Eloisa was silent for so long Stefano sighed and started to speak, but Henry signaled him to wait. The older man reached across his armchair and took Eloisa's hand. At first, she resisted, looking stiff, but he didn't relinquish his hold.

"Tell him, sweetheart. He needs to know for the others. You've always kept them safe. They don't know the things you do for them. They don't know about the night patrols. You need to at least let Stefano know." His voice was very gentle but extremely firm.

Severino raised an eyebrow at Stefano. Stefano kept his gaze fixed on his mother's face. She was always such an enigma to him. A complete mystery. She seemed an utter contradiction, as if she were two people at constant war with herself. She hated her children and yet loved them.

"The headaches started years ago. I don't remember how far back they go," Eloisa said.

"The first time I found her in the garage, she was in tears, rocking back and forth, holding her head. I thought she had a migraine," Henry said. "It was just after Emmanuelle was born. Days after."

"My parents had quit riding after you were born, Stefano. My mother didn't want to ride, so my father retired and insisted I take over for both of them because Phillip wouldn't take a shift. He said riding made him sick and he never trained properly. His family hadn't provided that information to my parents when they looked for a husband for me," Eloisa said. "In any case, I was expected to resume taking my rotations immediately after giving birth. My mother told my father I really didn't need any time off."

Stefano leaned forward in his chair. "You're telling me after giving birth to your children, you were immediately sent out to work?"

"Yes. There was no one else. There weren't many riders, Stefano. That's why they were always pushing for children."

"And when you had Ettore?"

"I was sent all over the country. Even to Europe." She looked down at her hands. "I didn't ever go against my parents the way you did against Phillip and me." She rubbed her head again as if it really hurt. "It wasn't done. I think I'm going to be sick. If you'll excuse me." She got up and hurried out of the room.

Stefano turned his attention to Henry. "How much of this did you know?"

"I've worked for this family for years, Stefano. I've been in love with Eloisa since she was a teenager. Your grandparents were madly in love, but they had no time for her or any of their children. Life was very different when she was growing up. I didn't have a clue about shadow riding then, but as I worked over the years, I began to get a sense of things and guessed more and more of what was happening. Especially after Eloisa married Phillip and he had affairs. He wasn't exactly discreet with his comings and goings. I watched him, more than once, disappear into a shadow."

"Good old Phillip," Stefano said.

"He made it worse for your mother. Her headaches seemed like they were all the time. She would have to lie down, and I would see she would get nosebleeds, and sometimes she would bleed from her ears. Phillip knew, but he didn't care. I wanted her to tell you. I threatened to tell you, but she said if I did, she would never forgive me, and she'd never speak to me again. You know Eloisa. Even if it was for her own good, she would carry out that threat. I couldn't risk for her to be completely alone, without anyone to look after her."

"Has she been to a neurologist?"

Henry shook his head. "After seeing Sandlin, I think it scared her."

"It isn't the same thing."

"Head trauma is head trauma. Even at a facility where your family contributes millions of dollars, someone still leaked Sandlin's personal information, and the media was a circus there for a while. Can you imagine if Eloisa's information was leaked? Because she can."

"We can get ahead of that, Henry," Stefano said. "Every second she waits, more damage can be done. And she's still using the shadows. If every time she goes in, just to visit, just to speed up going from one place to another, she's damaging her brain more, then we have to know. We have to know how much is too much. We have to know if we all should be getting scans and comparing them year to year. Henry, this is huge."

"It also explains a lot," Severino said. "People with brain trauma can have unexpected outbursts of rage. If she goes into the shadows and it triggers that reaction in her, it's possible Aunt Eloisa has been having brain damage occurring for a while and no one has suspected."

Stefano steepled his fingers again. "All of us have bad tempers, Severino, including you. It's an unfortunate Ferraro trait."

"Great, we're going to have to have scans every other week."

"That's about the truth of it." The smile faded from Stefano's face. "I think we'll have to be stricter on the rotations and send out a caution to the board. Let them know that there might be a problem and the families should be careful about how much time is spent in the shadows overall. The only time I've ever had headaches or bleeds was at first, when my body was getting used to it. I'm trying to adapt Crispino slowly by letting him play in and out of the shadows without him getting sucked in. I never let a shadow touch him without his clothes on, and I've cautioned Francesca."

Eloisa returned to the room, her face pale. She slipped into the chair again. It was obvious she had tried to compose herself and put her mask back in place. She looked both haughty and regal. Stefano wasn't having any of it.

"Eloisa, I need you to go to the trauma facility with Henry and ask Dr. Elliot to do a scan on you immediately. I'll have all the boys and Emmanuelle do the same. We need baselines for all of us. You may have saved all the riders, and for that I have to thank you. The world of riders will owe you a huge thank-you. No one has ever considered the toll what we do might take on our bodies."

She had been shaking her head, but she stopped when he kept talking, as if he didn't see her resistance.

"It always amazes me that the Ferraro family seems to pioneer the leaps in our businesses and the way we do things," Severino said, "and thanks to you, Aunt Eloisa, we're still going to be the family in the forefront. I'll have my riders go in for scans. We'll use your facility as well, Aunt Eloisa. You'll have to tell us who the best doctor is, and how best to avoid any unwanted publicity. We'll need someone to handle that end of things, Stefano."

Eloisa made a little face. "That's easy enough. Dr. Elliot is a pioneer in the field of head trauma. And Grace is our answer on how best to handle this. She puts on all kinds of charity events for the Ferraro family, Severino. We can make it a huge event and invite the New York branch as well to participate. We'll do something with brain trauma, or PTSD awareness. Wearing helmets when riding motorcycles, maybe all of it."

Her face lit up. "We can put a large event together and then show scans of brains before injuries and after. We can say we volunteered to be scanned as well, showing brains that haven't been injured as opposed to those that have been, along with the various types of injuries. Naturally they won't label whose brain is whose."

She looked at Henry and then Stefano and Severino. "This is good. We could raise a lot of money for brain trauma centers all over. I like this idea. Trauma centers really need money."

"That's your forte, Eloisa," Stefano said. "Please, I'm asking you, stay out of the shadows until we get this cleared up. I need you for this. Let's keep all riders safe, Eloisa. It isn't just our family we have to consider. It's all of them. We're going to have to figure out if it is a problem and then how best to counteract it. I'll need your input for that. You can't take chances by slipping up and going in anymore. First thing tomorrow, call Dr. Elliot and tell him you need to get in, that it's an emergency. I want to know as soon as you do so he can call me in for the results." He poured authority into his voice.

Eloisa nodded. "I will."

"We've got to go. Taviano and I still have a job tonight. Benito Valdez is on his way to Chicago. I want the job done before he manages to get here. The hope is, we find his location before he makes his way here. We've stopped his army, so he'll be alone with whoever he brings with him. Nicoletta has Archambault bloodlines, and it's definitely showing when she's in the shadows. She's faster than anyone I've ever trained. He can't have her. Her children are going to be amazing riders."

Eloisa started to say something and then closed her mouth, pressing her lips together tightly. She just nodded.

The night air was cool on Taviano's skin. He threaded his fingers through Nicoletta's and stepped behind the dilapidated warehouse where the small band of Demons had tried to establish themselves. Stefano was on the other side of her, making certain she was always close to a shadow she could just slip into the mouth of and they would know she was safe while they positioned themselves where they could hear what was being said inside.

Nicoletta hadn't been in the least sick as they rode the shadows fast through Chicago to get to the part of town where the investigators had indicated the Demons appeared to have a small group ready to support Benito when he came to Ferraro territory. She moved easily with Taviano, as if she'd been doing it for years. She breathed easily; the few extra practices they'd gotten in helped, as if they'd practiced together from the time she was very young. Those trips in the shadows moving through the house had clearly helped her as well.

Stefano indicated for Nicoletta to remain silent while they moved into position, and she did so, staying still. Taviano knew that was one of the most difficult things for her. It was for all of the riders. Still, she was quiet, none of her usual fidgeting, and he was proud of her. It was all he could do not to send his older brother a grin of pure pride.

It wasn't difficult to see or hear what was going on inside the warehouse. Half a wall had crumbled away on one side, leaving steel rebar hanging and the two-by-four framework exposed, along with drywall and brick. There was no glass in any of the windows. Mold and weeds grew on the remaining walls. Water dripped steadily from somewhere inside and a greenish-brown sludge oozed from inside the torn wall to form an ugly puddle, mixing with the dirt just outside the crumbled walls.

The Demons didn't have much of a foothold yet in Chicago. The territory they tried to claim was already taken by a much larger, well-established street gang, which didn't want to give up a single block. That left the few men Benito had sent out, demanding they fight for a piece of Chicago, in a very bad position.

They'd started out with thirty men, and in two weeks had gone down to twenty-two. Three weeks later, they had retreated to the warehouse with nothing left, not even the vehicles they'd arrived in, and they had fourteen men left. Three of the fourteen were wounded. One of those was dying. Bario, the head of the Demons, had stopped checking on the wounded man because he smelled so bad it made him want to puke every time he got near him.

Bario paced back and forth, feeling like a rat in a cage. He swore they were being watched every second. He would have gotten out of there if he could, but stepping one foot out of the warehouse meant certain death. If they didn't leave, they were going to starve or die of thirst or Benito fucking Valdez was going to kill them all for not obeying orders. His cell phone rang continually, and when it wasn't ringing, it buzzed with persistent text messages from Benito, threatening to cut off his balls if he didn't respond. If he was dead, he couldn't very well respond, now, could he?

"Who do we have on the roof, Alan?"

"Hector and Angel. They're watching in case those bastards try to come back. We're going to have to find a ride out of here."

"I know," Bario snapped. He made an effort to calm his voice, glanced toward the three wounded lying in the corner along the wall. "I know. We can call for a van, shoot the driver and take it over. That's the best idea I've got. We might be able to take them with us, but not all of them. We won't have the room."

Alan looked at him and then pulled a gun out of his

waistband and stalked over to the wounded. He lifted the barrel, aimed and squeezed the trigger without hesitation three times. He stalked back. "Problem solved."

Bario laughed. "You're such a fuckin' bastard."

"Someone's got to be. Call for a van."

Taviano indicated for Nicoletta to slip into the mouth of the shadow, and he slid into one that would take him up to the rooftop. This was the most difficult part of having Nicoletta with him, and he knew he would have to get used to it if she was going to partner with him. He would have to reach a point where he knew she could take care of herself, the way Ricco knew Mariko could. His attention couldn't be divided. He had to be solely focused on his prey.

"Angel, did you hear shots?" the man who had to be Hector whispered, overly loud.

Angel was lying on the roof, facing the street. He was more difficult to spot than Hector, who faced toward the cross street, one much busier than the other side, which appeared more residential than business.

"Yeah, I heard them. They didn't come from the street, so just do your job." Angel didn't turn around.

Taviano was okay with that. He simply walked from the shadow right up behind Hector, bent down, caught his head in his hands and wrenched. "Justice is served," he murmured and stepped into the nearest shadow.

Angel turned slightly to glance back toward Hector. All he could see was Hector lying prone, staring out toward the street, just like he was supposed to do. He nodded his head, but it was clear he was uneasy. That was the way sometimes. Some people seemed to have a sixth sense about them. Taviano knew psychic gifts were real. His family certainly had them in abundance. That meant others could have various gifts as well.

He waited until Angel turned back toward the street and then he moved into place behind him. He used stealth, the freeze-frame stalk taught in childhood games, of large animals hunting prey. This was the leopard stalking the unsuspecting antelope. He was already playing the game with Crispino, who always wanted to make animal noises that had Taviano collapsing into laughter when his nephew leapt on him, baby hands curved into claws, dark blue eyes dancing with mirth, and growls emerging from his little throat.

The two would roll around on the thick carpet in Stefano's beautiful penthouse, laughing and making all sorts of animal noises until Stefano came in and stood over them with his hands on his hips, doing his best to frown at Taviano. Crispino and Taviano would sober for a moment and look at each other and then laugh again, Taviano hugging his nephew tight. Stefano always ended up smiling and shaking his head, declaring that the boy was never going to learn anything, but both knew that Crispino was already advanced in his games.

Taviano was just behind Angel when the man suddenly turned, rearing up, his gun swinging around with him, his radar clearly going off in full alarm. Taviano simply moved with him, like a dancer, staying behind him, his hands catching the man's head and wrenching. It was more difficult when Angel was in motion, but again, Taviano was ready for every type of reaction from his prey. He was gentle with Angel as he laid him on the roof. The man was a warrior, even if he didn't have any respect for women and children, working for a man like Benito Valdez.

Taviano rode the shadow back down to the small strip of overgrown weeds behind the warehouse where Nicoletta waited with Stefano. Her gaze quickly moved over him, inspecting him for damage, relief showing briefly before she managed to school her expression. He wanted to kiss her but just sent her a small smile before turning to his brother.

"Let's do this fast. The one called Bario has called a van. We want it done before the van gets here. They intend to kill the driver and take possession of the vehicle," Stefano informed him.

Taviano nodded. There were two men at the very ends

of either side of the warehouse, clearly lookouts. All of the Demons were nervous. The attacks on them had been instantaneous when they showed themselves. The local street gang knew where they had retreated and had eyes on them. The fear was that they would be attacked there in the warehouse. They had no food and no clean water and no real cover inside. They couldn't stay. For the first time, the predators had been turned into prey, and they didn't like the feeling.

"Anything, Felix? Ivan?" Bario demanded.

The two men watching the northern street turned toward him. "It's quiet," one reported.

"Elias? Luis?" Bario snapped out.

The two on the west end turned around and shook their heads. "Nothing. Not even headlights."

Taviano and Stefano slipped into the warehouse. There were fewer shadows inside because there was no electricity. The streetlights cast eerie streaks of gray through the empty holes where the windows had once been. Someone had attempted to board them up at some point, but the boards had long since been kicked out, and only a few broken, jagged pieces remained. Stefano immediately went toward the west and Elias and Luis, leaving Taviano to take the south end, the farthest from them, but one of the gray streaks was near and would allow him to get closer to the two men without the risk Stefano would have.

Taviano stepped into the shadow. It was wide and slow, an easy ride, ending just behind the two men. Neither so much as turned their heads at his approach. He was more concerned with Bario and Alan, who paced in opposite directions, casting looks around the warehouse and out the windows constantly. Because they kept looking into the lights of the streets and then into the warehouse, it was difficult for their eyes to adjust in the time given. Neither saw the four sentries go down or even noticed when they were no longer standing but were lying on the floor, tucked in close to the wall.

Taviano rode the shadow back toward the window where the gray streak originated. One man peered out the window there. Twice, the man called Alan had snapped orders at him, identifying him as Pablo. Taviano stayed in the mouth of the shadow, just waiting a few seconds. Pablo was nervous and he'd pop up, look out and then crouch low again. The moment the sentry crouched low, directly in front of Taviano, he stepped out of the shadow, crouching as he did so, gripped the Demon's head and delivered the signature kill. Immediately, as he laid the body down, he stepped back into the shadow.

Stefano stalked another of the remaining Demons, called Omar, into the dark, where he was relieving himself, one hand on the wall, muttering to himself, trying to give himself courage. Stefano dropped his body right there.

"Leo!" Bario bellowed. "Get up to the roof and tell Hector and Angel to get down here. Hurry. The van will be here any minute."

Leo nodded curtly and rushed toward the broken wall. It was the easiest way to climb to the roof. The moment he was on the outside of the building, Taviano was on him, breaking his neck and lowering him to the ground. He slipped back inside. Only Bario and Alan were left. Stefano was already close to the two leaders. Both were agitated, showing signs of breaking down under extreme pressure. The two were sweating profusely, unable to stop moving, muttering to themselves and then swearing loudly.

They occasionally passed inside and out of one of the gray streaks thrown by the yellow streetlights. Stefano signaled Taviano to use the shadow while he stalked the two men from the darker walls of the warehouse. Taviano detested that his brother always took the more dangerous route, but he'd been protecting the rest of his siblings all of their lives and he wasn't about to change now,

As Taviano reached the mouth of the shadow, close to ten feet from Bario and a good fifteen from Alan, both men suddenly turned toward Stefano. His brother was still in the darker part of the warehouse, but something had alerted the two men to his presence, or maybe they had become aware of the eerie silence. The pall of death hung in the air. Whatever it was, they lifted their guns, and Taviano's heart nearly stopped.

Something moved through the air so fast it whistled. A rock hit Bario in the middle of his back. On the heels of that missile came a second one. Alan was treated to the same fate. The rock was small, but the force was enough to send both men staggering. They whirled around to face the new threat, Alan stumbling.

Taviano covered the distance in seconds and had Bario's head in his hands, wrenching, muttering the prescribed "justice is served" and dropping him, and then whirling to try to get to Alan before the man turned back toward Stefano or caught sight of movement.

Alan started to turn, his gun swinging around, spraying bullets. Another missile announced its presence, whistling through the air with deadly accuracy, smashing directly into Alan's temple, driving his head sideways. His arms suddenly went limp, both dropping straight toward the floor, the gun falling from lifeless fingers.

Taviano was on him before he hit the floor. Alan's eyes turned toward him, filled with hatred. For a moment he looked as if he might struggle, but it was already too late. Taviano wrenched, and he was gone.

"Justice is served." Taviano laid him on the floor, where mold and sludge covered the cement. He turned and moved back into the shadow, following Stefano, going back outside to Nicoletta.

CHAPTER SEVENTEEN

Nicoletta lay very still, trying not to wake her husband. Husband. Taviano. That still didn't quite penetrate her brain. She'd been exhausted and she hadn't even waited for him to finish his conversation with Stefano when they'd arrived home. She just wanted to sleep. She had a whale of a headache, which she didn't want to mention to anyone. She also didn't want to hear Stefano's assessment of her abilities in the shadows. They'd both told her not to move under any circumstances—but she had, and she'd interfered by throwing rocks to keep Stefano from being shot. They probably could have gotten out of it by flying through the air with some double karate kick to the head, but she couldn't help herself. If he grounded her for that, so be it. Right now, she just wanted to sleep.

She'd made her way through the house to the bedroom, peeled off her clothes and tumbled into bed without a stitch on. That was how tired she was. She had awakened when Taviano came to bed. She smelled him, that masculine scent that seemed to surround her and always made her feel safe. He had slipped into bed beside her, under the covers, his body curling around hers.

Nicoletta was certain the reason she remained so relaxed was because she was so tired. She couldn't summon up the effort to stiffen and be afraid when he wrapped one arm around her rib cage right under her breasts and pressed his hips tight against her buttocks. She felt his heavy erection snuggled against her cheeks. His warmth took away the ever-present cold that lingered from the shadows. She'd felt his breath, warm on her shoulder as he leaned his head into her, his lips soft and firm as they kissed her before he settled on the pillow. Then she'd fallen back to sleep.

Taviano must have pulled the privacy screens because the bedroom was dark, and she knew it had to be daytime when she opened her eyes. She'd been asleep only a couple of hours, but her brain refused to stay quiet. She had so much to lose. Taviano. The love of her life. She knew he wasn't perfect; she wasn't foolishly blind or deceiving herself.

Taviano was a Ferraro, with a Ferraro's temper and arrogance. He'd been born into wealth and he had a sense of entitlement that he wasn't even aware of. With that, he was a generous, caring man, one who put her first before himself. He would do the same with their children.

She couldn't lose him. She just couldn't. More than anything else, finding a way to be a good partner to Taviano was the most important thing she could possibly do. She knew she had issues—big ones. Huge ones. He was so patient and so willing to wait until she was ready to be with him. She always felt like her body wanted his, and her brain certainly did, beyond anything else, but then panic would well up. Why? She knew she was safe with him. He would never hurt her. Why was she so afraid that she wouldn't try with him?

She also knew she was born to be a shadow rider. She *had* to be a rider. It was there in her blood, the need, the drive, a terrible compulsion that grew and grew until it consumed her, until it became who she was. A part of her soul.

She understood Taviano and his family. That compulsion wasn't to put their body into a shadow and move from one place to another, it was a burning need to give justice to those who had been denied it. People like her, those who couldn't receive it through normal means and never would.

She understood why they had to learn to separate themselves from the crimes that had been investigated so thoroughly. When emotions were involved, mistakes were made. They had to learn control and discipline. She had to learn those things. Could she do that with Benito Valdez? Separate what he had done to her and so many other young women so she could make his crime impersonal when it was so personal? She knew it would be impossible.

Stefano, as head of the family, with one word could take away her ability to live out that process of providing justice to others like her—and truthfully, she could see why he would do that. She was old to learn to be a rider. She could put them all in jeopardy. She could easily make one wrong move and put herself in a dangerous position.

Taviano's arm was heavy across her rib cage, and she needed to move. To breathe. She had to think. Very gently, because she couldn't lie there one more moment, she lifted his arm enough to slide to the side so she could sit up and scoot so her back was to the headboard and she could pull her knees up.

Taviano stirred immediately, his eyes opening. "What is it, *amore mio*?"

"Nothing, go back to sleep." She dropped her hand to the top of his head, fingers tunneling in his thick, dark hair. The moment she felt the silky strands, she couldn't help massaging caresses into his scalp. She wanted to spend a lifetime touching him like that. Soothing him back to sleep. Showing him without words, just by her touch, that she loved him.

"You certain, *tesoro*?"

She could see him making an effort to rouse himself from a deep sleep. The shadows had taken a toll, but it was more than that. When she had emerged from the shadows, there had been that terrible, deep craving for sex. She knew it would be far worse for him. He hadn't touched her. He hadn't demanded anything from her, not even oral sex—and as tired as she was, she would have provided him with that relief.

Nicoletta closed her eyes briefly, disappointed in herself. She had wanted him. The need was there, but it hadn't been a need rising from her love of him. It had been the adrenaline-laced aftermath of riding the shadows. She didn't want her first time with Taviano to be anything but making love with him.

"Go back to sleep, love," she whispered.

Taviano relaxed under her stroking fingers, taking her at her word. She was grateful he did that. She really needed to think things through. That was how she did things. She processed. And she had a lot to process.

She had used oral sex to keep from having a man touch her body. She didn't want to do that with Taviano. It had been so humiliating when she'd arrived at Lucia and Amo's home and the doctors had inspected her body, including her throat, explaining to her that more and more young women and men were developing sexually transmitted diseases in their mouths and throats due to oral sex, thinking it so much safer. It wasn't. Oral sex prevented pregnancy, but it didn't stop diseases. She had been treated and counseled on every disease under the sun. She had been placed on birth control to get her cycle back on track.

She had been put in counseling for her trauma. She had gone from a happy, loving home, with parents who rarely exchanged a cross word, to an environment she didn't understand or have any knowledge of. She had been a virgin. Of course she knew about sex, she'd discussed it with her mother and friends. It had been her decision to wait until the right man came along. She wanted him to be someone she was really into. Someone she cared about. Instead, three men had brutally raped her in every possible way they could.

Once Benito Valdez had spotted her, her life had become worse. Her step-uncles hadn't wanted to give her up, and he had become obsessed with acquiring her. In an effort to appease him, they had "shared" her on more than one occasion. He was every bit as brutal as they were, wanting to show her ownership and teach her lessons by beating other women in front of her and selling them into trafficking to show her what could happen to her if she didn't cooperate with him. All of that had contributed to making her feel very worthless and dirty. It had taken Taviano to shake her up and make her remember who she was and where she came from.

Nicoletta looked down at his sleeping face. Even with the privacy screens, she could see him well enough to appreciate the definition, the sheer power and raw masculinity in his bone structure. He was a beautiful man. Each time she looked at him, he moved her. Deep inside she always felt that shift, that wave of love that was so overwhelming it left her frozen, unable to move or speak at times. He didn't know how extraordinary he was.

Taviano Ferraro gave her everything. He might have gotten angry with her at times when she hurt herself, back when she was so out of control, but he was the one sitting on her bed when she woke from her nightmares. He was the one holding her when she cried. He came back night after night, even when she punched him and told him she didn't want him around because she was so ashamed. He never turned away from her. Never. His love for her seemed unconditional. She knew her love for him was.

She rested her chin on the top of her knees and kept her eyes on his face. That beautiful face she loved so much. She wanted to be normal for him, yet he'd never asked her to be normal. He'd never indicated in any way that it was important to him. He hadn't tried to hurry her or push her into having sex with him. No matter how many erections he got around her, he never asked her to take care of him. She had been the one to initiate the only time she'd done it, and even then, he had resisted at first, telling her she didn't have to.

A part of her had insisted at first because she did fear he would want to have sex, and she knew she wasn't ready. That hadn't been fair to him. She didn't want to be like that. He was so completely casual about communicating with her on all subjects, sex included. She needed to give him that same courtesy. She loved him so much. She didn't want to disappoint him—or, if she was honest, lose him. She was so afraid she would have a panic attack the moment they really had sex.

She pressed her lips together to keep from making a sound. She wanted him. Her body wanted his. So badly. So much. She couldn't sleep with wanting him. Waking next to him, inhaling that sandalwood scent that was uniquely his, sent her body into a slow burn that kept building until she felt like there were flames licking over her skin. In her veins ran thick lava, hot as hell, spreading through her entire body to pool low, a sinful heat. The temperature kept rising until little beads of sweat dotted her forehead and ran down the valley between her breasts. That was how much she wanted him.

He was right there. All she had to do was reach for him. It would be that simple. She was slick with need. Her breasts ached. Her clit pulsed with the blood pounding through it. She pressed her thighs together to try to calm the desperate craving for him. It would never go away. Every time she looked at him it was there. It had been almost since the moment she'd laid eyes on him, even back when her body had repressed every sexual reaction. For Taviano, there was still a reaction, a response, it was just buried deep, barely known, but it was there.

With the passing years, as she had been in closer proximity to him and she had grown to understand she was safe, her body had been free to respond. With that, the heat had matured, become a fire, then a firestorm, and now was just a conflagration burning out of control. She didn't have the first clue what to do about it.

"Nicoletta?" Taviano opened his eyes.

It was the last thing she wanted. He was instantly alert, frowning. Sitting up, concern on his face.

"*Tesoro*, tell me." His thumbs brushed at tears she hadn't known were even on her face.

She couldn't lie to him. She never wanted lies between them. She shook her head. "Go back to sleep, I'm just trying to think things through."

He looked her over, taking in too much. He framed her face with his hands. Her heart turned over. "Taviano." He always saw her. He always would. There was no hiding from him.

He leaned over her raised knees and brushed kisses over her eyes. So gentle. The touch of his cool, firm lips sent little shock waves rippling through every cell in her body. His tongue caught at her tears, taking them from her face. He kissed his way down one side of her face, following the path of her tears, and then the other, right to the corners of her mouth.

Her breath caught in her throat. The way he touched her was reverent. So different. Such contrast. So loving. Then his mouth was on hers, kissing her. Sweeping her away in the way he did, that slow gentle start, coaxing her to open her mouth for him. She parted her lips because it was Taviano and she wanted his fire. She wanted to feel the heat and possession. The safety and love that came with the flames that burned every time he kissed her.

Then she couldn't think, only feel, her body melting into his, legs sliding down the mattress, his arm behind her back locking her to him. Her arms went around his neck and she kissed him back, her tongue dueling and dancing with his. There were the familiar flames engulfing her, the burn that began in her throat and traveled through her body to pool into a steady pulsing need that refused to leave. Desire grew and grew until her hips bucked restlessly, seeking relief.

Taviano's hand cupped her left breast, his thumb stroking her nipple, and she arched her back, desperate for more. His mouth left hers and he kissed his way down her throat to the top of her right breast, all the while stroking and flicking the left nipple. His touch sent shock waves through her, each harder and more intense than the last. Her breath turned ragged. She'd never quite felt the sensations he was producing, and she wanted more.

His mouth closed over her breast and he sucked hard, using his tongue on her nipple while he tugged and rolled on her left nipple just a little harder. Now the waves rolled through her like a storm. She could barely catch her breath. She never wanted it to stop. The tension deep inside coiled tighter and tighter. She grew slicker and hotter. So hot.

He switched his attention to the other breast, his tongue swirling gently around her left nipple before his mouth closed over her breast. He began that tugging and rolling sensation on her other nipple, interspersing rough and gentle so she couldn't quite catch any rhythm. It was so perfect. So unbelievably perfect. But she needed more. She needed him.

His mouth left her breast and he began to kiss his way down her belly. She caught his head in both hands. He raised his gaze to her face. Her heart accelerated at the absolute love she saw there.

"I want you to make love to me."

"I am making love to you, Nicoletta," he said softly. "Don't you feel it?"

"Every time you touch me, I feel it. I want you inside me."

He went very still. "You have to be certain, *amore mio*. You have to be ready. Don't say that because you want to do it for me."

"For both of us. If it doesn't work this time, I know it will be all right." She poured confidence into her voice. Her fingers slipped into his thick hair and held there. She wished they weren't trembling, but there was no way to control the fear rising.

It wasn't fear of Taviano but of failing him. Of failing both of them. Of letting her step-uncles win. She was already afraid of being pinned down and looking for a way to escape.

Taviano pressed a kiss into her belly button and rolled over. "Come here, *piccola*. Be my beautiful little cowgirl."

She turned her head and looked at him, one eyebrow up, but she was used to doing what Taviano wanted, so she was already sitting up. "Your cowgirl?"

He caught her leg and tugged. "Ride me."

He looked enormous. One hand was casually fisting the base of his cock, the other tugging her leg over him so she would straddle his body.

"You might be a little intimidating, Taviano," she admitted, but she wanted him inside of her. She *needed* him there.

For the first time in her life, this was her choice. He made that very clear. No one was holding her down. He simply waited for her to decide, stroking himself, his eyes on her face, so much love shining at her it was close to worship.

She straddled him, sliding her body over his, her entrance slick and throbbing with desire so profound she shook. The moment he was pressed against her, that thick, velvet-steel crown, she hesitated, fear gripping her. He didn't move, just his fist, a lazy pump up and down, his gaze never leaving her face.

"You're so damn beautiful, Nicoletta. Sometimes, when I would come to your bedroom, I swear I could barely breathe when I looked at you. Now, without your clothes on . . ." He reached up and touched her nipple gently. "You're so gorgeous." His hand slid to her belly. "Someday, our child will be right here, and you'll ride me, just like this, and I'll get to see how beautiful my woman looks when she's carrying my baby and is about to come apart for me."

His voice was velvet soft. Compelling. So beautiful. He never pressured her. He never tried to get her to move, but she desperately wanted to. She pressed down and took the heat of the large thick crown into her body. She gasped as he invaded, pushing into her, spreading her open, touching so many nerve endings. It felt so good. It was exhilarating and yet terrifying at the same time.

Still, she was in control. He didn't so much as push deeper, even though she could see on his face the pleasure spreading through him. She was giving him that. She loved that she was. It gave her courage to continue. She wanted to see that expression deepen. Along with his pleasure, she could see approval, pride in his eyes. She loved that he felt that for her.

She flexed her hips and pushed down, swallowing more of him. He felt big. Thick. So hot. She forced air through her lungs as she moved her body in little circles, watching his face. His eyes darkened. The lines in his face deepened. She was doing that. She wanted more. She liked seeing the lust for her building in him. It was mixed with love. She could see that so plainly.

She pushed down, determined to take him deep. She hadn't considered that doing this would mean taking him so deep. She could feel his natural angle and immediately adjusted her body to angle hers with it, positioning herself so that her hips aligned with his. She began to move, sliding up and down, squeezing him, using her inner muscles, watching his face. Sometimes she rocked. Sometimes she ground down. Other times she did a little spiral. All the while she gained confidence because Taviano loved it all.

His hands went to her breasts, kneading and massaging, and then his fingers tugged and rolled her nipples so that little streaks of fire raced to her clit. He switched his attention from her breasts to her clit, flicking and teasing until it was inflamed, and she knew she was close. Before she could finish herself off, he caught her hips and stilled her.

"Try turning around and facing the other way."

Her breath caught in her throat. "Away from you?"

"That's right, *tesoro*, facing away from me. You're still in control."

She wasn't certain she could do that, although the idea

must have somehow appealed to her body because she went even slicker. She could feel the heat. She knew he was letting her know she could trust him in any position. She was in control, but she wouldn't be able to see what he was doing. If she was on her hands and knees, she wouldn't be able to see. If she was on her back, he would be pinning her down. For a moment, she couldn't breathe.

Nicoletta refused to give in to panic. She nodded and rose up on her knees, allowing him to help her, his hands on her waist as she slowly turned her back on him, turning, his thick crown swirling just in the mouth of her entrance. It felt so delicious, that slow, sweeping turn. Then she leaned forward in a slow, deliberate sprawl, sliding back down over that hot, steel shaft. The new angle drove her wild. It hit her bundles of nerves from different directions, and each streak as she rode him sent flames raging through her.

His hands went to her bottom, rubbing over her cheeks. For a moment her heart stopped and then began pounding, but she felt his heart pounding to the same rhythm right through his cock as he began to move with her. She wanted him to move, and she encouraged him. She liked his hands on her cheeks and then when he caught her hips and pressed into her for a few hard upward thrusts.

Fiery tongues licked over her skin. Flames raged between her legs, threatening to consume her. His finger slid from the nape of her neck and down her spine and stroked between her cheeks, gentle, possessive, all the while his hips thrusting into her. Her breasts bounced and jolted with each thrust.

"Your clit, *piccola*, flick your clit now."

She obeyed him because it was Taviano and she loved and trusted him with every cell in her body. The moment she did, fire erupted through her, a volcano of sensation. She ground down over him and then she was sobbing his name, her body clamping down on his like a silken vise, a thousand hot, hungry tongues milking him dry, greedy for every drop he could give her. She'd never felt anything like it, wave after wave of pure pleasure rolling through her, consuming her. Taking her. Taking him. It was perfection.

She lay over him, heart pounding, unable to move, limp and sated. Her lungs refused to work. She couldn't roll off of him to see if he was alive or if she'd killed him. That was entirely possible.

Beneath her, his body shook, and then his hand came down on her bottom. "I'm not dead. And I don't appreciate you thinking you killed me but you weren't going to check."

"Did I say that out loud?" she murmured, still not moving. She didn't even care that he'd smacked her on the butt. He'd been gentle and he'd rubbed her bottom right away, taking away any possible sting.

"Yes."

"Well, I can't move. I can't really breathe, so that's my excuse."

He laughed softly. "You're talking, Nicoletta. If you can talk . . ."

She waved her hand in the air dismissively, but she did manage to roll off of him to one side of the bed. She almost rolled right onto the floor, but he caught her by the hips and stopped her before she went over. She was that limp, feeling like a rag doll.

"I'm so in love with you, Taviano," she murmured. "Just in case I haven't told you today. You're the most extraordinary man. I'm lucky to have you and I won't ever take you for granted."

He sat up and kissed her spine, just above her bottom. "You slay me, woman. Every damn time. I'm going to run us a bath. Give me a minute and I'll come get you."

Nicoletta turned her head so she could watch him pad on bare feet to the master bath. He walked naked, with total confidence, the way he did everything else. Every muscle rippled deliciously beneath his skin, and if she wasn't so exhausted, she would have jumped him all over again. He was that beautiful. And she was that in love with him. What man turned control over to his woman so easily?

He had made it easy for her to trust him, always a choice. She didn't have to turn her back on him, but when she did, she'd been rewarded. She knew she would have more confidence if they tried a different position. She wanted to try now. She looked forward to it. She still wasn't so willing to have him pinning her down on the bed, but on her hands and knees, yeah, she could definitely try that. Just thinking about it had her blood pounding all over again.

She found herself smiling. She wanted to hug herself, but she still felt a little like a limp dishrag, so she let one arm dangle off the bed and kept her eyes on the master bath. She didn't want to miss one glimpse of Taviano's powerful body as he came back for her.

"You have a smug look on your face," she observed, as he prowled across the room toward her, making her heart beat faster. There was no other word for it. *Prowled* fit. He looked like a great jungle cat about to pounce on her.

He flashed a grin at her that looked suspiciously like he might just be a predator coming out of the trees. She watched him carefully, wondering if she might have to show him woman power—although it was going to have to be much later, when she got her strength back. How was it that he was up walking around, and she was just wanting to lie there?

He leaned down and nipped her bottom. She yelped and glared at him, batting ineffectively.

"Go away. You're annoying."

"I was a god a few minutes ago."

"My mind melted. It's back now. I forgot how really oral you can be. Keep your teeth to yourself. I'm drifting here. Dreaming a little bit. And before you get that goofy look on your face, *not* about you."

"Who else would you be dreaming about but me, woman?" He shifted her, and easily rolled her into his arms before she could protest. His mouth found her neck. "You know you love me, and you think I'm the hottest man in the world. You can't lie worth a damn, Nicoletta."

A little shiver went through her as his teeth scraped and

then he sucked on her skin. Every way he touched her seemed erotic. He kissed his way up her neck.

"I do find you hot, but that's because I'm a little insane."

He bit down on her earlobe. She let out a squeal and smacked him on the chest, glaring. "What did I say to you about your teeth?"

He just laughed and stepped into the giant bathtub. The water was a degree or two hotter than she liked it, and she let out another squeal and tried to climb out. He kept a firm grip on her.

"Don't be such a baby. The heat will take the soreness of the shadows out of your muscles—or if I was just a little too enthusiastic there at the end."

She caught the note of worry in his voice and immediately turned back to him, looping her arms around his neck. "Baby, you didn't hurt me, it was wonderful. Everything we did was perfect. I'm hoping the next time you'll be able to be the one to—" She broke off, unsure how to tell him what she wanted.

Taviano brushed kisses down the side of her cheek. "The one to what? Tell me what you want, Nicoletta. Next time what?"

She took a deep breath. They'd promised each other they'd talk things out, including about sex. Especially anything sexual. They were man and wife, and shouldn't that be every bit as important as any other subject? Maybe more so because it was the most intimate between them? The way they expressed physical love?

"I'm afraid to lie on the bed. I'm afraid I'll have a panic attack if you're on top of me, but I hope I'll get there one day soon. But I really want to try on my hands and knees, with you behind me. The idea is really hot every time I think about it. A little scary, but still, I think I could do it without panicking."

He nibbled on her shoulder. "I like that idea. It is hot. But you know what's even hotter?" His hands came up under her breasts and just stayed there, holding the weight casually, as if she belonged to him. As if he claimed her body. She loved the way he did that. He made her feel as if she were a part of him.

That voice. It got to her every single time. Excitement coursed through her. "What?" She could barely breathe all over again.

"I'll show you when we get out of here. We'll go down to the entrance hall, where the thick carpet is."

She licked her lips, trying to think why down there. Their bedroom had privacy screens, making the room at least a little darker. It would be very light in the wide foyer. The entrance was round and very wide, almost like a turret might be, the carpet very thick and rich, with a mirror curving from floor to ceiling along the entire foyer.

Her head jerked up and her eyes met his. The mirror. She would be able to see him if she looked up. She touched her tongue to her lips. His heavy cock stirred against her bottom.

He grinned wickedly. "Now you've got me hot all over again. Just the thought of watching me disappearing into you is too much to think about. Can't wait." He stood up, her in his arms, water pouring off of both of them. "And I can see your face."

It seemed so easy for him, his strength so casual as he caught up a large bath towel and pulled it around both of them.

"We're dripping everywhere, Taviano," she reprimanded, but she couldn't help laughing.

"It's our damn house," he pointed out, uncaring, hurrying down the hall, leaving behind a path of wet footprints.

She didn't care, either. Already the heat had started. He was nipping and kissing her shoulder. Her neck. She was doing the same. She licked at the drops of water on his chest. The moment he put her feet on the floor she went to her knees, surrounding his narrow hips with her arms and licking at his cock with her tongue, sweeping up his shaft and over his velvety crown.

Taviano's body was already hot. So hot. She loved that about him. The heat poured off his skin, and when she took him in her mouth, she felt as if he lit her on fire. The addicting taste of him nearly drove her out of her mind. She wanted more. Cupping his heavy sac, she stroked and caressed while she sucked and laved with her tongue.

"Want you on your hands and knees, Nicoletta. I need to be in you again."

There was a growl to his voice that had her gaze jumping to his. He looked the same, but different. Definitely hers, but most definitely Taviano Ferraro. He tugged on her hair, and she reluctantly let him slip from her mouth.

"Crawl over there, right in front of the mirror where it curves, so you can see anything coming at you from any direction."

The way he said it was almost an order, yet it was sexy as hell. That voice again. Low. His eyes blazing with heat. With carnal desire. With passion. At the same time, he was giving her a sense of safety. She could see anything coming at her in the mirrors.

"You'll be able to see my cock disappear deep. Your body rocking forward when I drive into you. Your breasts swinging with every thrust. It's so sexy, *amore mio*. So damn sexy. Your face. I want you to see your face, that beauty when I take you there. And the way we look together. There's nothing like it, Nicoletta."

Taviano could distract her so easily from fear. She put one hand and then one knee into the thick carpet, looking at herself in the mirror. Her breasts did sway. Her nipples peaked. Taviano's hand dropped to her left cheek, caressing and kneading the muscle as she moved into position.

"Look how sexy you are." He knelt behind her, his hand sliding between her thighs, spreading her legs apart farther. "I love how slick you get for me."

She watched in the mirror as his head lowered slowly. Her breath hissed out of her lungs and she couldn't breathe as his tongue ran up her inner thigh and then licked at her swollen lips. His teeth nipped, teased and then scraped at her clit. She moaned and tried to look away but was mesmerized by the sight of him as he moved to the other thigh and repeated the action. His dark hair spilled around her lighter skin. She not only felt it, soft and silky, brushing against her cheeks and thighs, but saw it, looking so erotic in the mirror.

The burning in her core seemed to increase beyond what she'd felt earlier, and that was a little scary. He licked at her, plunged his tongue into her, stabbing deep and then licking along the seam between her cheeks and thighs before straightening. She saw his fist clamp around his cock and he began to pump. He looked so sexy in the mirror. She pushed back into him.

"Taviano. What are you doing?"

"Waiting."

"For what?" She glared at him in the mirror. Or she tried to. Her gaze was on his cock. She couldn't help it. He looked huge and still growing and she was burning, her hips bucking, trying to push into him, trying to capture his slowly pumping cock.

"I'm a gentleman, *piccola*. I wouldn't want to just take advantage of your position without your consent."

She licked her lips again. "Taviano, I would very much like you to put your cock in me."

"How would you like that done? Hard? Gently?"

"Any damn way you like, just get it the hell moving."

He didn't wait. One moment he had his fist pumping his heavy erection, the next he had pressed the broad head to her slick entrance and thrust hard, burying himself deep. Lightning seemed to streak through her body as he drove her forward. She went to her elbows, her bottom up in the air, her head to one side, gaze fixed on the mirror, watching.

There was no way she could have looked away from the sight of his body moving in and out of hers. It was the sexiest thing she'd ever witnessed. He pulled nearly all the way out, and she could see his thick shaft glistening wet in the sunshine, gleaming in the mirror, and then disappearing again into her body.

She looked small and even delicate with Taviano's larger body looming over hers. His hands were at her hips, dragging her back into him, over and over. Each time he thrust into her, he buried himself harder and deeper, his fingers digging into her hips, jerking her into him. She couldn't take her gaze from the sight.

Every muscle in his body was defined. His face was carved with a kind of carnal lust mixed with passionate worship. He was a blend of sensuality and dominance that merged so perfectly, it only added to the fire sweeping through her. She could see her own body moving with his, thrusting back in rhythm, and he was right, it was sexy, the rippling of her muscles, the swaying of her breasts, the way he suddenly caught her hair and pulled her head back so her back arched and the line was extremely sensual.

Her breath sawed out of her lungs, turned ragged. Tension coiled. She didn't want it to end. She wanted him in her, filling her like this. It was beautiful. She felt triumphant. She felt exhilarated. She felt powerful. Most of all she felt loved and loving. This was a rougher sex, but no less loving, and she recognized that immediately. Every stroke, Taviano made certain, was for her pleasure. She pushed back, squeezing her muscles, making certain that everything she did was for his.

She felt him thickening, stretching her more, one hand stroking her clit, then her back, then her cheeks, soothing her, so that the flames banked just enough to keep her from flying apart. She found air and whispered his name.

"Taviano." Velvet soft. A whisper of love. So intense.

"You're my magic, *tesoro*," he said. "Look at you. Look at us. So damn beautiful, you make my heart ache."

He started all over again. A slow buildup, pulling almost all the way out until she could once more see the very edge of that thick, broad head. She wanted to hurry him, wanting the flames licking over her skin again. Desperate for him to send those fiery forks of lightning streaking through her body to every nerve ending. She wanted fast and hard. She got slow and easy. She got that smoldering burn that built and built until it was on her, and then it was crashing through her like a runaway train. Only then did Taviano go back to his furious pace, this one hard and deep, dragging her body into his all over again.

Nicoletta managed to match his rhythm only because she was so tuned to him, but it was a desperate tango, her mind telling her that she wasn't going to survive the wash of this next orgasm. It was too strong. Too big. Too everything. She was terrified to let go. She'd gone too high with him and didn't know how to come back from it.

"Look at me, Nicoletta."

His voice. Soft. Firm. Always there. Always her safety net. Her eyes met his in the mirror. Those dark blue Ferraro eyes. So turbulent, like a dark summer storm. He was right about the mirror. About how sexy, how sensual, they were together.

"Let yourself fall. I'm right here. I'll always catch you."

He had. Her nightmares. In the shadows. Here. Where there was pleasure. Her gaze safe in his, she gave herself up to the beauty and love between them. *Dio. Dio.* It truly was a firestorm of perfection, flinging them both outward, sending them soaring. She felt the jerk of his cock, sending jet after jet of his hot semen deep, triggering more massive quakes. They just seemed to roll through her entire body, one after another.

Nicoletta pressed her face into the carpet, grateful it was so thick and comfortable. Taviano wrapped his arms around her waist to keep her from totally collapsing forward. He rubbed his face on the small of her back.

"The mirror worked," he whispered.

"The mirror totally worked," she agreed and lay flat, closing her eyes. She intended to go back to sleep until they were absolutely forced to get up again and go out. Maybe, just maybe, they could someday make love in front of the mirror with Taviano on top of her, and she could stare at him the entire time, knowing she was safe. That would be heaven. Right now, she was happy, sated, and so in love she knew it would be all right if she never got there.

CHAPTER EIGHTEEN

Taviano made certain he appeared calm and relaxed when he was anything but. Stefano had called a family meeting. He knew that prior to having dinner with Francesca and the rest of the family, the riders would be gathering to discuss whether or not Stefano felt that Nicoletta could officially train as a shadow rider and actually take rotations with Taviano on the roster. They would have no choice but to abide by his brother's decision. Even if they tried to appeal his decision to the council, he knew the council would never go against Stefano's judgment.

Nicoletta sent him several speculative glances, letting him know she knew he hadn't told her everything, but she didn't push him. They were already there. The moment they walked into the penthouse, Taviano's stomach dropped; Eloisa was present. She was no longer a rider and she had no vote, no say in whether or not Nicoletta could be trained. *That* he could—and would—protest.

The room was full. Stefano had invited the cousins from New York, Geno, Lucca and Salvatore. That was unusual.

Taviano took Nicoletta's hand and pulled her close to him, wrapping his arm around her waist. He no longer had any idea what was going on. Whatever it was, this wasn't about Nicoletta, unless Benito Valdez had been spotted. If he had, surely Stefano would have said something.

His brothers were all there. Ricco with Mariko. Giovanni had returned, and both Vittorio and Emmanuelle were present. Of his seven LA cousins, the four that had come earlier—Severino, Tore, Marzio, and Velia—were still present. They sat as if they'd been waiting for everyone, although he could see by Velia's face that she wasn't nearly as comfortable as she'd like everyone to think with Eloisa in the room.

"Now that Taviano and Nicoletta have arrived, we can get down to business," Stefano said. "Before I go into the reason I've brought Eloisa here, I want to let all of you know that everyone did their job and the Demons heading this way were stopped. Unfortunately, Benito Valdez turned around before we could get a lock on his exact location, although our investigators have narrowed it down and I expect we'll have that very soon."

"He's aware his army coming this way is dead?" Giovanni asked.

"It appears so," Stefano said. "I doubt he would have turned around for any other reason. The cops were called to one of the locations. The bodies were discovered. It was bound to happen. We coordinated very well, but there were just too many of them."

Eloisa stirred and looked pointedly at Nicoletta, as if she shouldn't be there. "We are discussing rider business, aren't we, Stefano? Technically, we shouldn't be talking about anything that has to do with shadow riding if we aren't all riders." She sounded very stiff and annoyed.

Taviano tightened his arm around Nicoletta, drawing her beneath the protection of his shoulder. Damn his mother. He should have known she would continue her attack on Nicoletta, no matter how subtle or blatant. Given the opportunity, she was going to do it every time. His one consolation was that his older brother didn't make mistakes. He had deliberately included Nicoletta in the circle of riders. Francesca, Grace and Sasha were in another room with Crispino. If Stefano hadn't wanted Nicoletta there, she would have been asked to stay with the other family members in the sitting room or den, and she would have done so and probably been a hell of a lot more comfortable.

Nicoletta ran her hand up and down his thigh, and he realized she was attempting to comfort him. He was more upset by his mother's statement than she was.

Stefano regarded Eloisa steadily with his dark blue eyes. "If you would feel more comfortable waiting somewhere else while we have this discussion, Eloisa, you're welcome to wait in another room. I believe no one is using the den at the moment. I can check for you if this is too boring. I thought you would want to have this information, and I included you as a courtesy."

There was silence following his comments. Eloisa looked shocked and then color swept into her face. She glanced toward Nicoletta again, opened her mouth and then pressed her lips tightly together as her gaze swept around the room. She clenched both hands into fists as she shook her head.

"I presume that means you wish to stay," Stefano said, in the same low tone he used when discussing any business with the riders. It was a voice they were all very familiar with. He was in charge at all times, and he expected them to listen to what he was saying and remember it because it was important.

Eloisa nodded her head. This time she sent Nicoletta a poisonous glare.

Taviano threaded his fingers through his woman's and brought her hand up to his mouth, deliberately kissing her knuckles while meeting his mother's eyes. If she wanted a fight, he let her know it was with him or with both of them. If she came at Nicoletta, his woman wasn't going to be alone. Not ever.

"Benito Valdez has four brothers. They aren't as enamored with Benito as it first appeared. It seems as if he's been bleeding them dry for some time. They make money, and he takes it away from them, claiming they have to pay their dues to him. A few times he's gone in and taken some of their women, actual wives or partners to some of the men. That hasn't gone over very well, especially when those women were later sold into a trafficking ring."

Beside him, Nicoletta went very still. Taviano could feel her heartbeat hammering in her inner wrist. He rubbed very gently over that pulse, pounding so hard. Anything to do with Valdez was distressing. She'd witnessed firsthand how he'd treated the women.

Stefano noticed because nothing escaped his eyes. "Nicoletta, I'm sorry we have to talk about this man, but I feel it's important for you to hear this. If it becomes too much for you, Taviano can fill you in later."

She shook her head. "He's vile, Stefano. Everything he does to women is vile."

Taviano felt the shudder that ran through her, and he wanted to pick her up and carry her out of the room. He wished she didn't ever have to think about Benito Valdez again.

"He has to be stopped. No one seems to be able to do it. He's sold so many women and children into virtual slavery it's unbelievable. Girls as young as eight or nine." There were tears in Nicoletta's voice. Her eyes swam with them, but she didn't shed them. "If anything you say helps anyone in this room stop him, then I'll sit through listening a thousand times."

Emmanuelle looked up from where she was seated between Vittorio and Elie. She looked as if she might cry. "Well said, *sorellina*, we'll get him. There is no way he'll escape."

Stefano nodded. "He can't hide forever, Nicoletta. His brothers want him dead as well, he just is unaware of it. They sent the men they were certain were loyal to him and kept back the ones that are loyal to them. The brother that seems to be the appointed leader is in Los Angeles. His name is Tonio. His big dream is to have a reality television show and bring in all of his brothers from their locations. He thinks he can hobnob with the rich and famous and get a very wealthy celebrity to fall for him. He's got his eyes on Velia." He indicated his cousin.

Velia fanned herself. "I'm so flattered."

"You should be. He thinks a lot of himself," Marzio pointed out.

"The Ferraros have a network, and we can send someone to scout him out," Stefano said. "That would turn their attention from Benito and anything that happens to him onto themselves and their future. We can drag out the production and decide later if we think it's a good idea or not, but for now, it would deflect the rest of the Demons from continuing to come at Nicoletta."

"I like it," Vittorio said.

"Brilliant," Giovanni agreed. "Turn the tables on them and have cameras on them twenty-four hours a day. I doubt they know what they're going to be agreeing to."

Taviano was watching Eloisa's face. Even she was nodding as she considered what Stefano had said.

"Taviano?" Stefano asked. "Ricco?"

Both men added their assent. Emmanuelle and Mariko did as well.

"I don't have a vote anymore, but I agree with Giovanni, Stefano," Eloisa said. "You might make them famous, but on the other hand, if they are so stupid as to commit crimes on camera, they're incriminating themselves to the cops and providing evidence. Just make certain in the contract with them it states that the film will be permissible to be evidence."

Taviano was so shocked, he nearly fell off the couch. Looking at his brothers and Emmanuelle, he could see they were as astonished as he was. Their mother never praised them, least of all Stefano. No idea any of them had was a good one. Stefano, she seemed to want to crush every bit as much as Emmanuelle.

"Then I'll make a few phone calls," Stefano said, his expression exactly the same. There was no telling by his face or his inflection what he was thinking. "We all have to inform the families that we'll most likely be under scrutiny again after so many Demons were found with their necks broken. We're not tied to these deaths in any way, and there's no way to connect us, but there are rumors that continually surface about our family, and that means an undercover will be looking to infiltrate and try to find a way to prove we're somehow involved. Our greeters can't in any way make mistakes. That's more important than ever."

Eloisa leaned forward just a little more intently. She was the greeter for the Chicago Ferraros. Since Phillip was gone, the family relied on her. "I need to talk to you about that, Stefano. We do need help. I'd like to put out the word to the family to bring in greeters to give me some time off, if you don't mind. You'd have to interview them with me."

Again, there was a shocked silence, although Taviano was looking at his older brother's face and there was something in his eyes that told him maybe this revelation wasn't altogether unexpected.

"Of course, Eloisa," Stefano said smoothly. "I've wanted to get you help for some time. It's too big of a responsibility for one person. Now, with the threat of more scrutiny, I think we should take a break for a short while and regroup. All of us should, but that has to go before the council. The world is a much smaller place than it once was. We all deliver the same signature kill. That has become noticeable to some law enforcement officials worldwide."

"Even in our families, few know of the riders," Eloisa pointed out. "Not even close family members. Only those with direct responsibilities, or spouses. Sometimes not even spouses. Once in a while someone in the family wants to go into law enforcement, and we are supportive of that decision, but we are extra careful around them. Riders are protected at all times. They serve on the boards of the banks and hotels and are given jobs that take them all over the country and out of it, so no one thinks anything about them traveling."

"Or playing hard," Giovanni added. "Our cover is solid, that isn't what Stefano is saying. There isn't a need to panic. He's saying to be cautious, and he's right."

Elie nodded. "The council has to hear about what's happening and the fact that law enforcement will be investigating us thoroughly."

Eloisa sent him a sharp glance but refrained from saying anything. Technically, he wasn't a Ferraro, although he spent all of his time with them now. He rotated in with them and worked under Stefano's authority. When he wasn't working as a rider, he took jobs as a bodyguard, which Stefano objected to. Often, on his days off, he and Emmanuelle went to dinner or clubbing. Both liked to dance, and they were seen together out for pizza or they came to Stefano's on family night. Most importantly, he was a member of the famed Archambault family. Eloisa had a high respect for them as riders and held their bloodline in the highest esteem. More than anything, she wanted an alliance between the two families.

"Yes," Stefano agreed. "I've already spoken to Alfieri, and he was arranging a conference call for later this evening so that all members of the council would be able to be on."

"Alfieri is our uncle and a member of the international council," Taviano whispered to Nicoletta.

Stefano sank back in the chair. "That brings us to Nicoletta. She accompanied Taviano and me to the Chicago Demons who were coming to aid Valdez, or rather attempting to. I wanted to observe her. Already, just working with her, training her over the last couple of years, each of us had, including Elie, written reports on her. All of us had come to the same conclusions. No one had ever seen anyone like her. Reflexes were faster, learning curve, hand-eye coordination, the way her body reacted to the shadows, it was all very similar to Elie's." He indicated Elie.

Taviano smiled down at Nicoletta. He couldn't help the

surge of pride in her. Faint color swept up her neck to stain her cheeks. She didn't look at any of his brothers or cousins. He tightened his grip on her hand and glanced at his mother to see how she was taking the news. The look on her face was priceless. She'd gone very still. Almost frozen. She stared at Stefano as if she couldn't believe what she was hearing.

"We asked Elie to train with her because he's incredibly fast, and she actually kept up with him when they were kickboxing. We filmed her so we could send the live feeds to the head of the Archambault family. We know that her father was a member of the family, but not a rider. Nicoletta had never trained as a child, yet she not only didn't lose the ability to ride the shadows, but the compulsion, the need, grew in her to the point that she was doing it on her own." Stefano gestured to Taviano to take up the narrative.

Taviano pressed Nicoletta's palm into his thigh. "When she was attacked at the concert, she texted me immediately as she fought off her attacker and got her three friends to run. Her friends scattered, but she did exactly what I said and met me where I told her to. Unfortunately, I was shot."

He heard Eloisa gasp and realized she hadn't been told. Before, when they came off missions, they always reported injuries to her, but since her ugliness to Francesca, none of them did. He hadn't realized that until just that moment.

"I had Nicoletta strip and put my shirt on. She did so without hesitation, and she went with me, taking the shadows to the first aid station. She did get sick that first time, but she helped me with my wound, and she stayed alert and ready for action. From there, we took the shadow to the hotel. It was a long and very fast ride, with sharp turns and curves."

"Dangerous," Severino murmured. "So dangerous for anyone new to riding, let alone untrained. It was a terrible risk."

Taviano nodded. "We had to get there before the Demons did. She was very sick, and this time I could see there was bleeding. It alarmed me, but I consoled myself with the fact that all of us had some bleeding from the nose when we first rode the shadows as kids."

That was true enough, but he saw Stefano and Severino exchange a worried look, and there was no doubt in Taviano's mind that that exchange was one of concern. He found himself pressing Nicoletta's hand deeper into his thigh, more for his own reassurance than hers.

"The cousins took her two friends to a safe house, but Nicoletta was worried that Clariss, her friend still unaccounted for, had been taken by the Demons. When we discovered that was so, she didn't want to return to the plane. She knew what they did to women, and she wanted to be there for Clariss in case the men had raped her. She felt it was necessary to be there for her friend under those circumstances."

"That would be three jumps on an unskilled rider. Her body . . ." Severino trailed off. He looked at Nicoletta with respect. "That's unheard-of. We work up to that. We train from the time we're children. Shadows can tear apart a body."

"The third time was actually better in terms of her controlling the ride," Taviano explained. "She began to anticipate the curves and turns. She kept her head down, and her arms around me tight, but her body moved with mine, and she relaxed into the ride rather than fought it." Which was one of the hardest things to do. He knew that, as did every rider in the room.

"From the warehouse, we went to the plane, so all in all, Nicoletta rode the shadows four times in one day. She had the headache from hell and was exhausted, but there didn't seem to be any repercussions on her body, such as soreness with aches and pains, and she didn't get sick after riding to the plane. I watched her carefully. She didn't limp. She wasn't wincing. I had her meditating and doing breathing exercises, sitting with me on the floor, and we trained in my gym for a short period of time. She didn't so much as grimace. She never once has protested when asked to work out. All of us have had to stop her from pushing too hard."

"What does Marcellus Archambault say about her?" Severino asked.

"He says she's extraordinary and definitely indicative of their family, but one trained from childhood. Her body has to be made up of the muscle and cells theirs are made up of. He'd like to have their doctor examine her. He's extremely interested in her abilities, as no one has ever exhibited her talents before," Stefano said. "Not just coming in cold like this."

"Naturally, the Ferraros would manage to get her in their family," Elie said. "Her genetics are amazing even for my lineage."

Taviano felt Nicoletta stiffen.

"Well," Eloisa said, sitting back in her chair. "This is rather amazing. I didn't think this girl would be worth much to the family, and yet she's a prize beyond belief. Her children will be the riders we need to carry on the family name. It's just possible, Emmanuelle, that you won't need to have kids if she can produce several like she should, wouldn't you agree, Stefano? That really takes the pressure off everyone."

Nicoletta pulled her hand out from under Taviano's. When he reached for her, she stood up. "If you'll excuse me, I'm feeling a little sick to my stomach right now."

She didn't wait to see what anyone said. She walked away, not toward the inside of the house, where the other women were, or any one of the numerous bathrooms, but toward the elevator. She was leaving. Her back was ramrod stiff, her shoulders straight and her head high. She knew how to make an exit.

Stefano shook his head. "Why is it, Eloisa, that you always know exactly what to say to wreak havoc?"

"What did I say? I implied she was extraordinary. I wanted Emmanuelle to know she might be off the hook. It was a good thing. Nicoletta said she was ill. Maybe she's already pregnant." There was a hopeful note in Eloisa's voice.

Taviano ignored the exchange and, swearing under his

breath, hurried after Nicoletta. He stepped into the elevator just as the doors were closing. She didn't say anything to him, but her eyes all but dared him to talk to her. He didn't make that mistake. Instead, he remained silent and just stayed close to her.

Nicoletta stepped off the elevator and walked right into the middle of the Ferraro luxury hotel, oblivious to the sudden turning heads of those in the lobby. Taviano glanced around. Emilio and Enzo came hurrying in through the rotating door, no doubt called in by Stefano. They slowed down when they spotted Nicoletta striding toward the doorman, who had stepped up to courteously open it for her. She smiled at him without really seeing him and went right out onto the sidewalk without checking for danger first.

Taviano clenched his teeth. Nicoletta wasn't used to the danger she could be in just by being married to him. Fortunately, few people were aware of their marriage yet, but she needed to be more careful. He stepped close, ignoring the fact that she quickened her pace as if she wanted to get away from him. Enzo and Emilio fell into step behind them. They were smooth about it, as if they weren't really in any way shadowing them.

"I didn't say or even think what Eloisa said." He kept his voice low.

She sent him one smoldering look from under her long lashes. "Don't talk to me yet."

He counted to a hundred, his own temper mounting with each step rather than fading. He was trying to be understanding, but he wasn't the one who'd fucked up. That was Eloisa. That was his mother—trying to regulate Nicoletta into being a broodmare and their children into being nothing but shadow riders. He had never once said that was what he wanted. If anything, he had reassured Nicoletta over and over that he wanted *her*, not babies.

"Damn it, Nicoletta," he hissed under his breath. He caught her hand as they stalked down the street like two soldiers marching on Armageddon. At least she didn't pull away from him, and it was a damn good thing, too.

She glanced up at his set jaw. He knew his eyes were blazing fire. He felt like strangling his mother. And maybe Nicoletta, too. She could try believing in him. Her dark chocolate eyes went from a lethal smoldering to suddenly bright, brimming over with laughter. He didn't see anything the least bit funny at all about what had happened. His mother's behavior or hers.

Taviano set the pace now, and the direction, heading toward Petrov's Pizzeria. It was only the best pizza in Chicago as far as he was concerned, and if he was missing out on a home-cooked meal at Francesca's, even if he was helping to cook it, to hell with it, they were having pizza. He quickened his stride, texting Tito—the co-owner with his father and manager of the pizzeria—one-handed, to ensure he had the Ferraro private table available as well as a table close for Emilio and Enzo.

A small sound that sounded suspiciously like laughter escaped Nicoletta's throat. She had that sweet little musical laugh that was always on such perfect pitch there was no mistaking it. The sound always made him want to smile with her—but not this time. He glared at her.

"You don't get to storm out, mad as hell at me for no good reason, and then laugh."

"I'm thinking it isn't a good idea for both of us to get angry at the same time, Taviano," Nicoletta said. "You have a rip-roaring nasty temper, and mine isn't so hot, either. Can you imagine the kind of fights we're going to have?"

"We're going to have one right now, a big one," he said and kept walking straight down the sidewalk, nodding every now and again—rather curtly—to anyone who lifted a hand to him.

He half expected his woman to take offense and try to walk off in a huff, as she'd done at Stefano's, but she kept pace with him, even if she did have to nearly jog. He slowed down to give her shorter legs a break, but his temper wasn't in the least appeased.

"I should have been given the benefit of the doubt." He shoved open the door to the pizzeria.

Berta, the waitress and sometimes hostess, looked up and smiled at them as they came in. She gestured toward the back. The restaurant was large, and two tiered, with tables and booths accommodating all sizes of groups coming in. Petrov's was extremely popular. Aside from the locals, people came from all over to eat there. Take out orders were common as well. The pizzeria kept a few tables available for the locals to drop in when they got off work, which made them happy.

"Maybe you should have given me the benefit of the doubt," Nicoletta said cryptically, the smile fading from her face. Her dark eyes went right back to smoldering. "I think you're right. We might just get into a rip-roaring fight."

Alarms went off. He bit down on his retort, taking a deep breath and replaying the scenario in Stefano's penthouse. Taviano stepped back to allow Nicoletta to precede him. She followed Berta to the booth in the back, the one his family considered "theirs." It was mostly in the darker side of the restaurant, allowing the shadows to fall across it, making it difficult for other customers to see them as they had dinner, giving them a sense of privacy.

Nicoletta slipped into the booth first and Taviano slid in next to her. Close. Thighs touching. She shifted away from him. Just an inch or so. It annoyed him.

"What the fuck, Nicoletta?"

"Don't say *fuck* to me. I don't like it."

"I don't like being blamed for something I didn't do."

Berta smiled brightly at them. "I would be happy to bring you the antipasto plate and breadsticks. Do you already know what you'd like, or do you want a menu?"

"We know," Taviano said.

"A menu would be great, thank you," Nicoletta said perversely.

"She doesn't need a menu," Taviano snapped. "She's just being difficult. She likes pepperoni and black olive with extra olives and mushrooms. Thin crust, because she's not really Italian. She just looks like it."

Nicoletta kicked him under the table, but she didn't put much of an effort into it. "*She* would like an Italian soda to drink along with water. Peach, please."

Berta nodded. "What kind of pizza for you, Taviano?"

"I'm eating hers."

"I'm *not* sharing with you," Nicoletta declared. "Because you're all kinds of an ass."

"If you want ice cream, you're going to share with me."

"Fine, but only because I love the ice cream here."

"You love me."

"Sometimes I love you. I love ice cream *all* the time."

Berta nodded again, a small smile on her face. "Water for you, Taviano?"

"I'll have an Italian soda as well. Strawberry." He waited until she left before he turned fully in the booth to face his woman. "Look at me, Nicoletta."

She turned in the booth to face him. "I wanted to punch her. Right in the face. I know that's childish and absolutely wrong of me. She is your mother, and a rider, and I should find a way to be respectful, especially with everyone around, but I was so afraid of jumping up and attacking her or screaming insults at her right in front of everyone that I had to leave. I had to. I couldn't say anything because if one word escaped . . . I was so angry at her, I didn't know what might slip. She's just so above everyone else. She acts like she's so much better. That she can plan our children's lives and we're just going to let her do it. I'll burn in hell first, Taviano. She's not getting near our children."

Taviano couldn't take his eyes off Nicoletta's impassioned expressions as they moved across her face. The anger. The guilt. The ferociousness. The protectiveness. She was everything he could ever want. He'd wanted passion and he'd gotten it in abundance. Just seeing those expressions chasing across her face and blazing in her eyes had him wanting to sweep the basket of dried flowers off the table and lay her down on it. She was so beautiful.

"I'm not a mind reader, *tesore*. You could have indicated to me when we were alone in the elevator that it wasn't me you were upset with."

She frowned. "Why in the world would I be upset with you? And *upset* is a very insipid word for what I was feeling. Angry. Emotional. Wanting to commit murder. She was talking about our *children*. Weren't you just a little bit angry?"

He rubbed his jaw and the five-o'clock shadow already on full display there. "I really hate to tell you this, *piccola*, but Eloisa honestly thought she was giving you a compliment. Producing riders from a spectacular bloodline is the one thing she prizes in a woman. You have a spectacular bloodline."

"Yay me." Sarcasm dripped. "I'm so very glad your mother approves."

He hooked his palm around the nape of her neck, his thumb sliding along her cheek. "You are extraordinary, Nicoletta, in so many ways. Our children will be as well. No one will have a say in their lives but us. We'll decide what we want for them. And then they'll decide. That's a long way off. Right now, it's your life and you decide whether or not you're going to be a rider. Stefano would never have allowed you into that meeting if he wasn't going to say you were one of us. Obviously, you have to train more. You need to learn so much more before you can actually participate."

Nicoletta nodded. "I'm fine with that. I'm not ready to be whatever it is you call yourselves. I do want to go along though and learn. I want my body to get used to the feel and pull on it. I can tell each time I go, it's easier."

Taviano's phone buzzed. He glanced down. "Stefano says they're having dinner and to come back when we're finished here because there is quite a bit more to discuss."

"I guess I gave your mother a good opportunity to take another dig at me about not keeping my temper."

He tipped her chin up. "You can pretend with Stefano if you want, but you aren't feeling in the least bit guilty or remorseful. You wanted to punch my mother, woman. Own it. Don't give me that I-should-have-stuck-around mask."

"I was looking at my lap so I wouldn't have to try for the mask," she pointed out. "And don't say I wanted to punch your mother where someone might hear."

"Only Emilio and Enzo are close enough to hear us right now."

"My point exactly. They are related to you." She glanced over to the other table. "Please tell me that their mother or father isn't a sibling to your mother." She dropped her face into her palm.

Taviano glanced over to the bodyguards. Both men were valiantly looking at the menus. He knew they had the menu memorized, as many times as they came there. They'd already ordered. They were desperately trying not to laugh. He flashed them a small grin.

"Taviano." She hissed his name between her teeth.

He leaned over and kissed her. The moment he touched her lips, he knew he shouldn't have, not there in the privacy of that restaurant, not there in the dark. She ignited for him and burned, a fuse that detonated an explosive in him. She leaned into him as he put pressure on the nape of her neck, pulling her closer to him.

She slid her hands up his chest. His heart accelerated. She did that to him every time. Little flames licked at his skin while electricity snapped between them. Heat rushed through his veins and hot blood filled his cock. His heart beat there, throbbing and aching for her. He wished they were home and he could have her. He could be in her. He had to stop kissing her. That way was disaster, and it was also paradise.

Berta cleared her throat. Reluctantly, Taviano lifted his

head enough to press his forehead against Nicoletta's. "What is it, Berta?"

"Your drinks, Taviano."

"Put them on the table, Berta," he said without lifting his head. He kept his eyes closed, inhaling Nicoletta's scent. He was so in love with her. She mattered to him more than anyone or anything else.

"I have. And the antipasto as well. Um. Mr. Petrov doesn't like public displays of affection in his restaurant. He used to be cool about it, but ever since his wife died, he gets upset when couples start kissing and he throws them out. Just a heads-up warning. I'm sorry."

Taviano did look up then. He wasn't a teenage boy caught in the booth by the older Petrov sneaking kisses with a fifteen-year-old. He was grown, and Petrov had known him for years. He couldn't imagine the man kicking him out, let alone sending Berta to reprimand him.

Nicoletta's laughter escaped. "I'm *so* going to tell Francesca and the others. Especially Sasha. Taviano Ferraro, the playboy of the world, reprimanded in a pizzeria for kissing his wife. You weren't even getting all handsy. I'm dreadfully disappointed."

"I can get handsy if you want. They'll kick us out. It could be front-page news. I know most of the paparazzi by name now. Maybe a photograph as well."

"Think of the publicity it would generate. Do you have a race coming up? Something you need to market?" Nicoletta turned in the booth and put her feet back on the floor, reaching for her Italian soda. "I really am going to tell Francesca."

"If you do, it will get back to Stefano and the others," he warned. "We'll never hear the end of it."

"I know"—she sent him a wicked grin—"you mean *you'll* never hear the end of it. The boys are very careful of me. They treat me with kid gloves."

She was right. His brothers were very careful of her. They were all too aware of the terrible things that had happened to her. That had been one of the reasons, as he had gotten older, that he didn't want his family to know what had happened to him. The knowledge would change how he would be treated. It would be subtle, but they would be much more careful of him. There would be less teasing. Most likely, Stefano would yell at him less. The bottom line was, he didn't want his family to treat him any differently.

He understood what Nicoletta meant when she had told him long ago that it was humiliating that his family had read the reports. She hadn't known just how detailed those reports had been or she would have been even more humiliated. He would have had a very difficult time facing his brothers at the age of ten, given his parents' reaction. He didn't think they'd ever tease him, but he didn't know what children would do at that age. Now, he didn't want to find out even as a grown man.

He lifted the tall glass to his lips. There was condensation on the outside. Fresh strawberries and ice filled the glass, along with the light-colored liquid. It looked refreshing and tasted as good. Her glass was similar but filled with fresh peaches and ice. The color was more toward clear, just a slight peachy color, but when she tasted it, she smiled.

"Perfect. I have to learn to make these."

"The drinks and the pie are always the best here," he said.

"And the bread." She took a breadstick. She never used the marinara dip, but he did. She preferred the salty oil. She dipped the breadstick in the oil and took a bite. "This is so delicious. I was careful not to come in very often. I would end up weighing a ton."

He looked her over. "You'd look beautiful even weighing a ton."

She laughed. "You'd probably really think that. I don't want to get diabetes. No shots for me, thank you. I'll just keep Petrov's as a special treat." She looked up as Tito Petrov sauntered over with their very large pizza and placed it on the table.

"Made it myself, just the way you like it, Taviano. Nicoletta, you look beautiful tonight." He took her hand as if he might bend over it to kiss it, saw immediately she was wearing a wedding ring and straightened, looking shocked. His gaze jumped from Taviano to Nicoletta and back. "You two married?" He looked at Taviano's left hand. "Holy shit. You're married. To each other. You're fuckin' married. How come no one knows?"

"We're planning a big wedding soon, but I couldn't wait to get the ring on her finger. You know how she's always got one foot on the road leading out of here."

Nicoletta pretended to ignore them so she could get a jump on eating the pizza. She wasn't fooling him. He knew she loved pizza, and she was already calmly eating a slice and declaring it hot and good. Not to be outdone, Taviano took a slice and bit into it. She wasn't kidding when she said it was very hot. He nearly burned his mouth. She sent him a smug smile.

"Congratulations, you two. Should I keep it quiet? I mean, I'll tell my dad, but he won't say anything." Tito looked around the pizza parlor as if he wanted to make an announcement right then.

"We'd prefer that you didn't say anything yet," Taviano said. "We'd like to have a week to ourselves before the madness starts. You know what it's like. You've seen the circus enough times when one of us marries. Nicoletta wants things low key, and so do I."

Tito nodded. "I understand. I'll protect your privacy. Your family has always supported us, even through our darkest times. No matter what, you've come through."

"Don't be so nice to him, Tito. He was nearly kicked out for too much PDA."

Tito's eyebrows shot up. "What are you talking about?"

"Your dad's policy on public displays of affection. Taviano broke that rule so fast. He should have been thrown out but was shown mercy, which he didn't deserve." Nicoletta snagged another piece and smiled. "If you tossed him now, I could eat this entire pizza *and* have ice cream all to myself."

"She forgot her cash," Taviano pointed out with complete complacency. He grabbed the largest slice of pizza left, just in case the little monster he was married to managed to put away several slices to his one.

"Sorry, hon, no cash, he's gotta stay." Tito sounded regretful, but he winked at Taviano as he turned away.

CHAPTER NINETEEN

Once back at the penthouse, Nicoletta and Taviano took the same small couch they'd been sitting on before. Taviano liked how comfortable the sofa was, but mostly he preferred it because he could sit very close to his woman and shield her when he felt she needed it. Stefano had the fireplace going, the logs burning brightly, giving the room a soft glow that hadn't been there before. He rarely remembered to switch on the flames, not unless Francesca was around. Taviano knew his older brother had done that for Nicoletta, just to make the room seem more of a home to her.

Nicoletta had come to Stefano's penthouse often, especially in the last two years. She trained there in self-defense, and she was very disciplined about keeping her schedule. She didn't miss a single class. As she progressed, the family had scheduled more and more classes with her, and she had managed to make every one of them. After, she would often stay and play with Crispino and visit with Francesca, so she was very comfortable there.

Taviano thought those times, just relaxing with his siblings and especially his in-laws, helped bring Nicoletta closer to the family. She smiled more and even laughed at Crispino's antics. She had always liked the fireplace on, and when Stefano would light the flames, telling his son not to go near the grate to keep him from harm.

"We've come back to discuss some things that I think are extremely important for all riders," Stefano said. "I trust everyone has had dinner and is comfortable? Eloisa?" He looked to his mother.

She nodded. "Henry and I had a lovely dinner, thank you, Stefano." She took a deep breath. "I don't always say things the way I mean them. Clearly, when I spoke earlier, Nicoletta, I upset you. I am happy that you carry such strong Archambault genetics, but I didn't mean that all you're good for is to have baby after baby. I know it came out that way, and I'm sorry. Henry says I don't think before I speak, and he's right. I have no social skills."

Taviano nearly fell from his seat, so shocked by his mother's explanation he could barely comprehend what she'd said. Apparently, he wasn't the only one. Looking around the room, he saw his brothers, cousins and the other women were equally as stunned.

Nicoletta sent Eloisa a small smile. "Thank you for that. I certainly have no intention of being the family broodmare, although I want children."

"I've already spoken to Marcellus Archambault in France," Stefano said. "About a half hour ago, Nicoletta. He's reviewed all the videos of you. I told him, although I haven't had the chance to tell everyone here, about you stepping up when the two Demons turned their guns on me."

He paused, and Taviano knew he wanted Eloisa to realize he had really been in danger. Her head went up alertly.

"There was no shadow for me to hide in. Taviano was too far to reach one of them. At best, he might have gotten to the other. Nicoletta was outside, watching, where we told her to stay. She picked up a rock and threw it using a method one might for skipping it on a lake, but so fast it actually whistled through the air. The first struck one, and a second rock came right on the heels of the first, striking the other gunman. Both rocks were thrown with deadly accuracy. Not only did the sound distract them from shooting, but when they were struck, they both turned away from me."

Stefano glanced up at Taviano. "Had you ever seen that before?"

Taviano shook his head. "No. I was a little shocked that not only could she think that fast, but she could throw rocks that fast."

"My father, meaning my adoptive father, taught me to skip rocks from a very young age. He could make them whistle when he skipped them, and I loved it. I practiced until I had it down." Nicoletta gave a little shrug as if it was nothing.

"It was fast thinking," Stefano said. "Very fast. That was one of the things Marcellus was most impressed with. Not just Nicoletta's reflexes or the way her body reacts in the shadows, but her overall ability to adapt to every situation."

Taviano's heart suddenly dropped. "He wants her to go to France, doesn't he?"

"Stefano," Emmanuelle objected. "No. She's ours. He can't just demand she go to them because she has their blood. She's Taviano's wife. I hope you told him that. They're already married. We're planning a wedding, but they're already married." She was adamant.

"No one can force her to go," Stefano said, his voice calm. "But yes, he would like to train her himself."

Nicoletta's hand trembled in his. Taviano tightened his fingers around hers, giving her reassurance. She wasn't ready to go to other families, especially those predominantly male. She needed to establish herself where she was, gain confidence, build her own identity. He knew that as well as she did.

"What would you like to do, *tesoro*?" Taviano asked. "Whatever you decide, I'll be with you."

"This is my family," Nicoletta said. "The people here. I'm just starting to recover and find myself. I want to stay here and train. If, in the future, that advantage is still open for me, then I'll consider it when I feel I'm able, but right now, I know I'm not ready. Please thank him for me, Stefano, but I can't go to France at this time."

Taviano could hear the pleading in her voice for understanding, and he didn't like it. She didn't need to defend herself to anyone.

"I was hoping you would opt to stay with us," Stefano said.

Taviano could have kissed him. Over and over his brother proved why he was not only the leader of the Ferraro shadow riders but also of their family. He might have a ferocious temper, but he was also compassionate, and he seemed to know what each family member needed. Nicoletta had been treated as a member of their family almost from the moment they had brought her back from New York with them. Stefano had so easily just made her feel as if she was wanted there by all of them. A few simple words were all it took from the head of the family, voiced in that casual way he had that spoke volumes.

"Elie is here, and he's indicated he's willing to help with your training in and out of the shadows. He's been working with Vittorio, Ricco and Mariko as well as Emmanuelle and me. Giovanni and Taviano were scheduled next. Severino and Geno have both indicated, as heads of their families, that they would like additional training for their families as well. We all know that no matter how much we train, our bodies do dictate some of what we can do. That's why we train with those faster than us to try to always be better. What Marcellus was getting across, Nicoletta, is that your genetics will allow you to be faster and see more in the shadows than most others can." Stefano sent her a smile. "That's a good thing. But it also means that you might have a tendency to, once you're comfortable, not train as hard."

She shook her head slightly but didn't respond to Stefano's indictment.

Taviano's hand tightened around hers. He brought her knuckles up to his mouth to press a kiss there because she was still trembling, and he wanted to reassure her that no matter her choice, he was with her.

"I know that most riders work alone, Stefano," Nicoletta said. "Even if I get to the point where I'm good enough to go out by myself, I would prefer to work in partnership with Taviano. Is that ever done?"

Eloisa rolled her eyes. "Seriously? What's the point of teaching you, then? Or having the kind of genetics you have? Does Mariko need her husband to hold her hand when she goes out? She holds her own, the same as Velia or Emmanuelle. Female riders are every bit as good as male riders. It's ridiculous to think that you would need a man to be with you once you know what you're doing." There was a sneer to her voice.

Taviano opened his mouth to defend Nicoletta, but she got there before him.

"I'm sorry, Eloisa, but you must have misunderstood me. I didn't say I needed Taviano to hold my hand, although . . ." She turned her head to smile adoringly up at him, brought their joined hands up and kissed his fingers. "I do love holding his hand. I said I preferred to work in partnership with Taviano. I am not certain what part of that you don't understand. My preference for working with my husband? I believe I was asking a question about whether a team was ever sent out or whether it was always a lone rider."

She turned back to Stefano, all wide-eyed innocence, which Taviano knew was the epitome of total bullshit. It was all he could do to keep from smiling. His woman was giving no quarter. No matter what, she wasn't going to like his mother, not after what he had revealed to her about the way Eloisa had reacted to his childhood assault.

"Is there something wrong with asking questions, Stefano? I'm not yet familiar with protocol so you'll have to forgive me if I'm making blunders."

"No, of course not, Nicoletta. Often, in the past, riders went out in pairs. That ensured the safety of the riders, but we are too few at this point and we need the riders in the rotations to give one another breaks. Having said that, it doesn't mean we won't accommodate the preferences of riders. Taviano stated the same thing. If both of you feel strongly, I have to take that into consideration. All of us have instincts and it would be wrong of me to ignore your instincts, especially if both of you are feeling them."

Eloisa shook her head, pressed her lips together and clenched her fists, as if that were the only way she could keep her opinions to herself.

"This brings us to another matter that could very well affect every shadow rider, not just those of us in this room," Stefano went on. "When we were first learning to go into the shadows, all of us suffered headaches and nosebleeds. Some severe, and some less so. The symptoms lessened as we grew accustomed to being in the shadows, and we could stay in for longer periods of time. Eventually, even the longer, faster shadows rarely bothered us."

Taviano frowned, watching his older brother carefully. Stefano was definitely worried. He saw his older brother's gaze flick to Severino. His cousin knew whatever it was that Stefano did and he was equally worried.

"Eloisa has been having severe headaches and nosebleeds for several years. Unbeknownst to us, when we were children, she was sent out over and over even days after giving birth because, according to her parents—the heads of the family and riders at that time—she didn't need the rest and there were no other riders available to go. The headaches and bleeding became worse and more severe. She began experiencing blackouts. Or at least times when she couldn't stop herself from acting in ways that she might not normally behave."

There was sudden silence in the room. Taviano felt his heart thud hard in his chest. He didn't want to look at his mother, but he couldn't help it. Eloisa had her head down, not looking at anyone in the room. She was a proud woman, and he couldn't imagine how she felt with all of them staring at her, suddenly aware of very private medical information. He had no idea how Stefano had gotten her to agree to allow him to share that data with everyone.

"Over the last few years, the headaches and bleeds have grown worse. Even after she stopped officially riding in rotations, she was still using the shadows to move from one place to another. Those bleeds seemed to compound, and the headaches were so severe she would sometimes go blind. When she confessed this to me, I asked that she go to the Hendrick Center and have Dr. Elliot do an MRI on her brain to look for trauma. We have to know if going into the shadows can cause the rider brain damage."

Giovanni reached out to touch his mother's shoulder, a rare gesture for any of them. "Eloisa," he said softly. "You could have shared this with me."

She shook her head, but to Taviano's astonishment, she didn't pull away from Giovanni as she normally would have. She didn't like sympathy or a show of compassion from anyone ever, not even when her husband died. He thought perhaps it was because Sasha's brother had such severe brain injuries.

"Unfortunately, Eloisa's scan did show she is suffering from fairly severe brain injuries," Stefano announced in that same matter-of-fact voice that he used as if speaking about the weather.

Taviano closed his eyes and pushed his head back against the couch. He had allowed Nicoletta over and over into the shadows. She had headaches. She had nosebleeds. He had thought them a natural part of learning. *"Tesoro,"* he whispered. Aching inside.

"Don't, Taviano," Nicoletta said immediately.

"I know that sounds bad for all of us, but before we all

panic, we need more information. Eloisa came forward, and she has ideas that I think will help us to better figure this situation out and let us know what to do and where we can go from here. This is a good time for us to take a step back from our work, since law enforcement may suddenly be taking a hard look our way once again," Stefano continued. "Eloisa thought this might be a great time to organize a worldwide fund-raiser for traumatic brain injuries. The Ferraros could lead the fund-raiser by getting scans of our brains to use for comparison with those that have been injured in accidents. At least, that will be the excuse we use. Every member of the Ferraro family will participate. Our New York cousins as well as our Los Angeles cousins. I'll talk to the council and they'll have the members of the other families get scans as well."

Stefano got to his feet and poured himself a glass of sparkling water, looking around the room to see if anyone else wanted their glass filled. No one took him up on the offer. Taviano thought they were all too stunned to move or really think. He knew he was. The idea that doing what they'd been born to do was harming them seemed ludicrous.

"I don't think anyone should panic yet," Stefano said, leaning one hip against the bar. "I haven't had a headache in years, nor have I gotten a nosebleed. I think, if I were having a problem, I would have had signs. Nevertheless, I will be going in to get an MRI immediately. I think it's necessary for all of us to do so. In fact, for my family it will be considered mandatory, or there will be no putting you into the roster. Anyone wanting to be pulled from the roster, of course, just make that request and it's done. Having said that, if you do get a headache or a nosebleed, no matter how minor, I want to know about it."

Severino looked around the room at his siblings. "I want to know the same. We're all participating as well. Eloisa had a terrific idea not only to raise money for a worthy cause but as a great cover for all of us to use to get scans. The doctors aren't going to question why we're going in when we're volunteering to allow our scans—anonymously, of course—to be used in comparison to those who have had trauma."

"And if trauma is discovered? What is the explanation?" Ricco asked.

"For you and your idiot brothers," Stefano said, "driving race cars and the accidents you were in. I imagine Severino can say the same. Geno and every other family member are going to have reasons because you're all adrenaline junkies."

"I think the idea of a fund-raiser is brilliant, Eloisa," Emmanuelle said. "No one would ever think twice about it. The Ferraro family does them all the time."

Giovanni nodded. "And Sasha's brother has a brain injury. Thanks to the fuckin' paparazzi, always paying everyone for photographs and any private information they can get, the world knows about him. We've donated money to the hospital and to his care facility several times for equipment and buildings. This will just be on a much larger scale."

"Grace and Katie Branscomb are excellent at planning details, and they can handle something this large," Eloisa said. "I'm well aware they're working on wedding details for Taviano and Nicoletta, but they can do both. They work on several events at the same time as a rule. I think they can manage easily. I can check with Katie and see if she can find a location for an event of this size," Eloisa said.

Taviano was a little shocked to hear the excitement in his mother's voice. Few things seemed to ever bring her to life. He brushed the pad of his thumb back and forth over the back of Nicoletta's hand.

"We can forgo a formal wedding," Nicoletta said, a little too hopefully for Taviano's liking. "We did get married in Vegas."

"You're a Ferraro," Eloisa snapped, before Stefano could say anything. "To the people who live here, that means something, and you have a duty to them."

"Eloisa," Stefano cautioned. He smiled at Nicoletta, but his dark eyes were very serious. "The wedding is already being planned, Nicoletta, and as much as you'd like to get out of it, just like the rest of us, you're going to have to see it through."

The others laughed. Even Taviano. He wished he could get over the feeling that at any moment the room might explode from the tension between Nicoletta and Eloisa. He couldn't blame Nicoletta. She knew one of Eloisa's darkest secrets, and brain injury or not, there was no excuse for sending her son out four years before he was supposed to go, to a family he wasn't supposed to go to, because she didn't want to bother with him and all because Stefano was not available to parent. She'd used the excuse of sending him to the family in Italy because they were friends, but then, when he should have returned home, she didn't want him back and she'd sent him on to the only place available.

Taviano broke out into a sweat. He had to stop thinking about it. His mind seemed to be in chaos. Suddenly he couldn't understand what the voices in the room were saying. They were loud, and then receded. Back and forth. Ringing through his ears, reverberating through his head. His heart pounded. His chest hurt, the pressure building until he pressed his hand hard there, fearing he was having a heart attack. His lungs felt raw, desperate for air, but he couldn't draw a single breath.

He thought he heard Nicoletta's soft voice and Stefano's deeper one. Someone bent over him and he started to fight that shadowy figure, self-preservation taking control.

Nicoletta knew exactly what was happening to Taviano because it had happened to her a thousand times. She had no idea what had triggered a flashback, but he was suffering from post-traumatic stress, and clearly, none of his family had ever seen him have an event. He was violent, impossible to get near.

"Get everyone out of here, Stefano," Nicoletta ordered, taking charge. Taviano was her husband, and she had his back.

"Call a doctor," Eloisa snapped. "You don't know what

the hell you're talking about, Nicoletta. You don't have a clue what's wrong with him."

"I know *exactly* what's wrong, and so do you. Get out of here. Everyone needs to get out of here, *especially* you," Nicoletta snapped back. "I mean it, Stefano, get them out."

Eloisa went white. Stefano turned his dark, speculative gaze from his mother to Nicoletta and then to his brother, who was on the floor, sweat beading on his skin as he clutched his chest. He looked as if he was having a heart attack. Eloisa backed up as if afraid of Nicoletta.

"Everyone please leave," Stefano said calmly. He gestured toward Taviano. "Nicoletta, tell me what to do."

"Get me a cool washcloth and some water." She knelt beside her husband but didn't touch him. "Baby. Can you hear my voice? Listen to me. To the sound of my voice. I'm right here with you. Taviano, it's Nicoletta, and I'm right here." She took the cloth from Stefano. "I'm going to just put this cloth on your head."

She did so fearlessly, uncaring if he struck her. For a moment he caught at her wrist, fingers biting deep into her flesh, his gaze bouncing all over the place, but he didn't hit her.

"That's it, baby. Just take a breath. Breathe with me. Like we do when we're together. At night, all those nights when you came to my room and I was panicking just like this. You put a cloth on my head, and you helped me to breathe. You said I was safe. You're safe. No one can touch you. You're here with me. I won't ever let anyone touch you. You're always safe with me, just the way I know I'm safe with you."

Beside her, she felt Stefano freeze. Every muscle in his body. The room temperature seemed to go down several degrees. She didn't take her eyes from Taviano, afraid to look away from him. Afraid of losing him to a nightmare world. She'd been lost in that world so many times and he had been the one to help her find her way out. She had to do the same for him.

"Baby, look at me. Don't look inward. Just look at me. See me. Breathe with me. I'm real." She took a chance and placed her hand gently on his shoulder, waited a heartbeat to see if he recognized her touch enough to let her slide her hand down to his. "I love you, Taviano. I know you're somewhere else right now, but come back to me. That's not a good place for you to be. Breathe with me." She used the words he had sometimes used with her.

His long lashes fluttered. Those eyes of his, so intensely blue, so dark, looked at her, lost beyond imagining, haunted beyond description. Behind her, Stefano made a sound so agonized it tore at her heart. He saw what was in those eyes. The eyes of a lost child, a little boy so bewildered and tormented, so hopeless and hurt and completely alone.

Nicoletta didn't realize she was weeping until she saw tears falling on Taviano's shirt. She dashed at her face. "Come on, honey. Look at me. See me."

The lashes fluttered again. Taviano looked confused. His breathing changed. He drew in one long, shuddering breath. Nicoletta immediately moved the washcloth over his face. "That's right. You're good. I've got you."

He sat up and pulled her into him all in one motion, dragging her in so fast and hard he smashed her into his chest, driving all the air out of her lungs and just holding her. Her lungs burned, and for a few moments she thought she couldn't breathe, but she managed to turn her head enough to find a way to draw in air, and that was all that mattered. They clung to each other.

"*Dio, tesoro*, what the hell happened?"

"It's okay. You had a flashback. You're okay. No one got hurt. You're okay." She kept murmuring reassurances over and over to him, remembering how disoriented she'd been at times when she'd found herself in his arms in the middle of the night in Lucia and Amo's house, tight against his chest, sobbing.

"What the hell," he muttered against her neck. "That hasn't happened in years."

He rocked her. Or she rocked him. She didn't know which one of them needed more comfort at that point. Taviano had always been her rock, her anchor, and it had really thrown her that he had unexpectedly and without warning gone into a flashback. She knew that when he fully realized the event had happened in front of his siblings and cousins he was going to be very upset, but the worst was still waiting for them, sitting directly behind them on the floor.

She still hadn't looked at Stefano. Other than that one agonized sound, much like a wounded animal, the head of the Ferraro family hadn't so much as stirred.

It was some time before Taviano loosened his grip on Nicoletta and looked around him. "I don't even know what triggered that, it hasn't happened to me in years. One minute I was sitting there and the next, I couldn't breathe. I felt like I was having a heart attack."

"You scared everyone," Nicoletta said.

"Everyone?" he echoed. Then it hit him where they were and that they'd been in a meeting with his siblings and cousins.

He gripped her arms hard and looked around the room. She knew the exact moment when he saw Stefano sitting on the floor just a few feet from them. Taviano went very still. She turned to face the oldest Ferraro brother as well. Stefano looked as destroyed as she felt. He had his head down, his fingers pressed into the corners of his eyes. Before either of them could speak, Stefano came to his feet in a swift, graceful movement. He reached down and offered Nicoletta his hand without really looking at her face.

"I have to get out of here. Let's go for a walk."

Nicoletta took his hand without hesitation, her heart going out to him. She could feel Stefano's distress. It was overwhelming and very genuine. Anger. Sorrow. He reached for Taviano's hand and pulled him up as well and then turned away from both of them toward the elevator, already texting those in the other room to let them know they were leaving and that Taviano was all right.

Nicoletta and Taviano followed Stefano onto the elevator. She couldn't think of a word to say to break the uncomfortable silence, so she just stood as close to Taviano as possible to offer him comfort. She knew he had never wanted this—his brother to know what had happened to him. It was obvious that he knew—or at least guessed what it was that had triggered Taviano's flashback. They walked straight through the lobby of the Ferraro Hotel out into the coolness of the night and turned toward the businesses that made up a portion of the Ferraro territory.

"They sent you away while I was gone for training. I wasn't here to stop them." Stefano made it a statement.

Taviano didn't reply. He kept walking, but his fingers tangled with Nicoletta's. She glanced from his set face to Stefano's. They looked so much alike they could have been twins had they not had an age difference between them.

"I knew something was wrong, but you wouldn't tell me when I asked. I shouldn't have stopped asking, but the more I did, the more it felt like I was driving you away from me." Stefano shook his head. "Sometimes, Taviano, I despised them so much. I looked at all of you and saw these beautiful, intelligent children deserving of parents who loved them, and what did you get? They couldn't be bothered with even tucking you in at night, let alone looking after you. I never should have left. I'm so fucking sorry that I did."

Nicoletta's heart nearly stopped. If Stefano actually cried, she didn't know what she'd do. He sounded like he was either going to weep or kill someone. She'd rather he kill someone. He *was* the Ferraro family.

"Stefano," Taviano said gently. "You keep saying we deserved parents. *You* deserved them, too. You gave us the best of everything we ever had. You don't have anything to be sorry for. Anything good in my life, I have you to thank for it."

"Who was it?"

"They're dead. She killed them."

Stefano walked for nearly a block. "They? More than one. Fuck, Taviano." He spat the last two words out and then walked to the corner in silence. "At least she did that. Why wasn't I told?"

"Phillip wanted me gone. I was an embarrassment."

Stefano swore in Italian, a long litany of so many colorful phrases, Nicoletta couldn't possibly keep up with them all, nor did she think it was a good idea that she try. She just kept walking with the two men until Stefano had gotten his temper back under control. She knew it was be angry or cry. Stefano's love for Taviano was more than that of a sibling. He'd practically raised him, although he'd been a boy himself. He was crushed and trying to do what was best for his brother in spite of his own pain.

"He threatened to leave unless she sent me away. She wanted to continue to be a rider. She made a deal with him. They wouldn't tell you and I would stay, keeping out of his sight, and she would continue as a rider. Phillip could do his thing and no divorce."

Stefano's face looked like thunder. "*Dio*, Taviano, it's a good thing she isn't here at this moment. I would strangle her with my bare hands. Had they sent you away, I would have found you. I hope you know that. I never would have stopped looking for you. Fuck them. Damn them both to hell."

Nicoletta knew it wasn't helpful, but she couldn't stop herself. "No counseling, of course, because you might ask questions about why your little brother needed to go into counseling."

That brought more swearing, and she glanced up at Taviano to see if he was angry at her.

Stefano's phone buzzed. He dragged it out of his pocket and looked down so furiously that at first the text didn't seem to register, but then he passed his phone to Taviano.

"It's from Rigina," Stefano explained to Nicoletta. "They have the exact location of Benito Valdez and his crew. It's not that far from here. Apparently, they were close, did a slow circle and came back. If you don't mind, I would very much like to take this one. Actually, I very much need to take this one."

"How big is his crew?" Taviano asked, handing back the phone.

Nicoletta hadn't seen the location.

"He brought thirteen with him. His lucky thirteen. Geno's family did the investigation, and these thirteen men always surround Benito. They do his killing for him. They bring him the women he wants, and while he was in prison, they made certain all of his operations ran smoothly for him. They kept him informed through his lawyer of anyone that was out of line, and he sent back word what action he wanted them to take, and they carried it out."

"He trusts them more than he does his brothers?" Taviano asked, a little shocked. "Why in hell would you put more stock in strangers?"

"Others were willing to follow his brothers," Stefano said. "You're a Ferraro. You could have a huge following if you wanted, where someone in our employ wouldn't be able to muster an army against us."

That made sense. Nicoletta nodded her head. "Are you going to ask any of the others to come with us?" Silence met her inquiry. "What?" She raised an eyebrow.

"Didn't you hear what I said about brain trauma?" Stefano asked. His phone buzzed again, and he glanced down at it. "He's on the move again." He glanced down the street.

Nicoletta followed his gaze. The streetlights illuminated the various stores. About a block away was Masci's, the popular deli owned by Pietro Masci. The deli carried meats and goods from all parts of Italy. It was right next door to Lucia's Treasures. Nicoletta had worked at Lucia's Treasures almost continually from the first few weeks that she arrived in Chicago.

Lucia and Amo owned the boutique. The merchandise was handpicked by the couple, beautiful, unique and very expensive, because often, each item was one of a kind.

Clothing was often from designers not yet known from France, Spain, Italy, India or the United States, treasures that Lucia and Amo had uncovered and were willing to take a chance on because they found them beautiful.

"You're saying that because you're men, you can take the risk, but I can't?" she asked.

"No," Stefano answered, looking impatient with her. "I wouldn't expect that of you. I'm saying we both have been riders for years and have no known complications. You haven't. Until we get a baseline for you and know that the bleeding and headaches you suffered are just that initial starting adjustment, we aren't taking chances with you. In any case, I need the outlet of action right now. I just found out that my brother, one I love more than life itself, suffered a horrendous attack at a young age, one beyond my comprehension, and I need to put that all somewhere before I have to face my parent again. I don't want to strangle her and end up in prison when I have a son, wife and family I love. Give this to me, Nicoletta, because I swear to you, I need it."

She believed him. But she needed to make certain they were both safe. "He's heading to Lucia's Treasures," she guessed. "Or our home. One or the other. I can walk to the store or take a cab home. You do what you have to do, and I'll text the other riders to meet you where you think they're going to be."

Stefano gave her a faint smile and shook his head. "Benito is headed for your home." He stood there a moment looking at her. "What you did there in my home for your husband, taking control and getting Taviano out of a bad situation, was extraordinary. I am more than grateful that he has you, Nicoletta. So grateful."

The raw sincerity in his voice burned through her chest straight to her heart. She managed a watery smile.

"Former home," Taviano corrected. "Benito is headed for your former home." He leaned into Nicoletta, caught the front of her shirt and pulled her into him to kiss her. "If you have to step into a shadow, and you should always have one close, just step into the mouth of it. Stay safe. Let us do the work."

There was no use commanding her to stay away. This was Benito Valdez, and if Taviano was the one being asked to stand on the sidelines, he would still want to make certain Valdez couldn't harm another person she loved or come after her ever again.

"I will," she assured. "Did you already alert the others, or should I?"

"You go ahead," Stefano said. "Although most likely, Rigina sent a group text to them already." He handed her his cell phone, and Taviano did the same. The two men turned and walked around the corner to the alleyway.

Nicoletta trailed after them, already texting Mariko just to be certain. She'd trained the most with Mariko, and she immediately told her that Benito and thirteen of his men were on their way to Lucia and Amo's home. Stefano and Taviano had gone after them. She was going to follow in a car. She was about to call for a cab but then saw the number already programmed into Taviano's phone for the body-guards. She called for Emilio. It didn't take more than a few minutes for him to arrive.

Enzo, his brother, drove while Emilio sat in the back with her. "They all went. Every one of the riders," Emilio said. "Not the cousins or Elie," he corrected, "but all of Taviano's brothers, Emmanuelle and Mariko. They aren't supposed to do that."

He sounded so annoyed and so mournful she thought he could have rivaled Eeyore in the movies and books. She had to hide a smile behind her hand. "Why can't they all go? There're fourteen Demons if you count Benito, and he's armed to the teeth and every bit as lethal as any one of his men," she pointed out. "If they all went, that's still only seven of them."

"They don't ever go where they all could be killed, leaving no one behind to carry on the name," Emilio said. "I suppose there's Crispino, but he's years out from being a rider. It's bullshit for them to do this. Stefano has lost his mind. You should have seen Eloisa. I thought she was going to have some kind of a fit. She turned purple and started choking."

Nicoletta might have imagined that there was satisfaction in his voice. She had never considered it before, but Emilio and Enzo were also related to Eloisa, and they must have heard the way she was with her children over the years.

Whatever terrible things had happened to her as a child, however she'd been raised, didn't excuse her for the neglect and terrible decisions she'd made with her children, at least that was Nicoletta's opinion. She didn't mean to be harsh, but she would never get over what Taviano had told her, not in a million years.

She knew, someday soon, Stefano was going to ask his younger brother to talk to him about what had happened. She knew Taviano would, and it would be difficult for both men. Eloisa could have prevented the trauma now by dealing with it then. Or just never having it take place by sheltering her son a little better.

"Are you all right, Nicoletta?" Emilio asked.

She sat up straight, realizing she once again had tears swimming in her eyes. She loved her husband more than anything, and no matter the things that had happened to her, she found it almost harder to accept what had happened to him because he had a family that could have prevented it.

"I'm good," she lied as the car cruised up to a walkway a good block from her foster parents' home.

She stepped out of the car, Emilio pacing beside her. She knew the way home through the network of backyards. She'd taken that route numerous times. They were all connected, those massive parklike courtyards. They came across two bodies, both wearing Demon colors, by a wrought-iron bench that Lucia loved to sit on when she went to the koi pond. Both had their necks broken.

Emilio stepped in front of her and Enzo took up the rear,

sandwiching her in between them. The next two Demons were right at the edge of the pool, one practically lying in the tall blue grasses Amo had planted because Lucia loved them. The other lay across the stone path, neck broken, staring up at the sky.

Nicoletta recognized all four men. These were the men closest to Benito. He never went anywhere without them. There was satisfaction in knowing she was getting close to him.

Two more bodies were just outside the Japanese maple garden, the one meticulously planted and cultivated for Amo's beloved wife. Both Demons had their necks broken. One had been particularly brutal, and she remembered him laughing when Benito had beaten her.

There were two in the maple garden, and she really didn't like that. In fact, it upset her so much that she almost asked Emilio to pull the bodies out of the garden. Lucia loved to have her morning tea there. Often, Nicoletta would sit with her and they would talk of nothing important, but that was where she first learned to trust her beloved foster mother. She forced herself to stay quiet and keep moving.

The Ferraro family was proving themselves to be silent, deadly assassins. She knew they had all come on her behalf. She was *their* family, and this man had hurt her. He had done despicable things to others, and they would have gone after him for his crimes had someone pointed them at him, but he had come at her, and she was theirs. She was a Ferraro. Family. *Famiglia.* That meant something wonderful. Beautiful. She hugged the knowledge to herself.

There were two more dead just on the side of the house, leading to the front, as if someone had tried to creep around without being seen. She had to step over their bodies to get to the corner of the house. At once she could see her family surrounding Benito Valdez and his three closest men. They were silent shadows, moving out of the shrubbery and flowers and back into them, barely noticeable.

Taviano emerged directly behind Benito. Stefano was

behind Benito's first lieutenant. They were facing the other two men, whose faces she couldn't see. Clearly, neither Demon had any idea they were in danger, but the Demons looking toward Benito and his lieutenant tried to call out warnings. It was too late as Ricco and Giovanni wrenched their necks in the signature kill, delivering justice.

Simultaneously, Taviano and Stefano did the same. Nicoletta's legs nearly turned to jelly as she saw Benito go to the ground. He was gone. Really dead. Her worst nightmare. Emilio had his arm locked around her, and she turned into him and let him hold her for just a moment until she could get her strength back.

"These bodies can't stay here," she announced when Taviano came striding over to take her into his arms.

"No worries," Stefano said. "I've called Uncle Sal. He'll make certain no one ever hears from Benito Valdez or any of these men. Lucia and Amo will never have so much as one hair left behind on their property. You go on back to the penthouse with Emilio and Enzo. We'll meet you there, and then everyone will leave in their respective vehicles."

CHAPTER TWENTY

"You look so beautiful, *cara*," Lucia Fausti said, reaching up to touch the delicate Italian lace making up the barely there neckline adorning her foster daughter.

An ivory silk sheath clung to every curve, accenting Nicoletta's figure, giving her the look of a long-ago Hollywood screen star. She could barely recognize herself in the full-length mirror.

Hand-embroidered lace florets were scattered throughout a sheer duster of designer lace flowing to the floor and forming a train that fell with elegance around her, adding to the look of an ageless beauty. The delicate peekaboo cap sleeves were made of the same sheer Italian lace, with the hand-embroidered florets falling gracefully down her arms.

Her dark hair had been plaited into several intricate braids and then woven into a long chignon at the back of her head. She wore a tiara of chocolate diamonds, which matched the ones dropping in two chandeliers from her ears and those in the necklace that sparkled so close to the silk and lace of her gown.

Nicoletta turned away from the mirror to her foster mother. "I don't even have the right words to tell you how much I love you, Lucia. How much you and Amo mean to me. You saved my sanity, my life. You gave me a home when I was so messed up, I didn't think I even deserved to live."

She stepped close, inhaling the fragrance of orange, caramel and mandarin she associated with Lucia. That scent would always mean home. Reaching out, she framed the older woman's face with her hands and leaned in to brush both cheeks with a kiss.

"I love you so much, Lucia. So much. I want you always to be close to me. I told Taviano we have to live near you and Amo. Wherever you decide to retire—and I know you've spoken of going to Italy—we'll follow. He's promised me, and Taviano would never go back on his promise."

Lucia had tears in her eyes, but she shook her head. "We can't cry on your wedding day, *vita mia*. We aren't going anywhere. Taviano has already offered us a beautiful home on our retirement and a chance to help you when you have your babies. I don't want to miss out on the chance to spend time with my grandchildren."

Nicoletta looked over Lucia's shoulder to smile at Amo. Her heart actually ached she loved them so much. There was no way to repay them. They had been the ones to teach her what true unconditional love was. "Did you notice she said grand*children*? In the plural. I think there's a conspiracy."

Amo nodded solemnly. She could see the sheen of tears in his eyes as well, but he didn't shed them. "Of course there is a conspiracy, *vita mia*. You are our heart and soul. You always will be. We are so incredibly blessed to have you in our lives, an unexpected gift that came when we had given up all hope. You brought joy and laughter to us. You brought a brightness we hadn't known in years. Thank you for that. And thank you for allowing us to love you."

Nicoletta didn't care about the very carefully applied makeup Sasha had spent an hour on. She burst into tears and flung her arms around Lucia. Amo came close and hugged both of them tight. They clung to one another for a few minutes, the tears turning to laughter.

"What are you doing?" Emmanuelle demanded, coming into the room. "You can't cry on your wedding day. Isn't it bad luck or something? I'm certain it is. In any case, you're going to have to pull it together fast because Grace is right behind me and she runs a tight ship. You've only got a few more minutes with Lucia, and then she'll be sending her straight into the church."

"No, no, I can't leave yet," Lucia objected. "I have something very special for my girl. I believe you need something old." She turned to her husband.

Amo smiled gently at his wife, his eyes shining with his love for her. It had always been that way when Amo looked at Lucia, Nicoletta knew. It was one of the first things she'd noticed about the couple, the way they treated each other with such care. She saw that same light shining in Taviano's eyes when he looked at her.

Amo took an antique jeweler's case from behind him, where it was sitting on a table. The case was square, black, and worn in places, but rather tall. He opened the lid and handed it to Lucia. His wife looked down at it for a long moment and then up at Nicoletta.

"My mother gave this to me on my wedding day. Her mother gave it to her. You're my daughter, so I'm giving it to you, and I hope when your daughter gets married you give it to her, and she treasures it the way I know you will."

Lucia looked into the jewelry box for a long moment and then lifted the piece out slowly. Nicoletta's breath caught in her throat. She heard Emmanuelle gasp. The bracelet was a series of thin gold bangles held together by woven gold braided knots. The piece was to be worn from wrist to shoulder.

Nicoletta didn't know the first thing about jewelry, but just looking at it, she knew it was absolutely unique. Emmanuelle stepped closer to watch as Lucia slid the bangles up Nicoletta's arm and tightened the knots. They were actually slipknots made of the finest thin gold.

"That's so clever," Emmanuelle said. "That's a genuine Italian piece from the earliest craftsmen. Lucia, it's worth a fortune."

"It was my grandmother's. And then my mother's," Lucia reminded in her gentle way as she turned each bangle on Nicoletta's arm until she was satisfied the gold enhanced the perfection of her skin. "I wore this same bracelet, and now our girl is wearing it. To loosen each bangle, you simple pull the slipknot, see, Nicoletta?" She demonstrated with the last tiny braided knot.

Nicoletta should have protested wearing it, let alone accepting it. A piece of jewelry in such pristine condition from so long ago, crafted by Italian jewelers for wealthy patrons, was only seen in museums and then, rarely. But this was Lucia's, and it was given to her from the heart, handed down from mother to daughter. The gesture was huge, and the meaning behind it even greater. She never wanted to take the bracelet off.

"Thank you, Lucia. I'll treasure this incredible gift always, and when my daughter weds, she will wear it," she vowed.

Nicoletta wrapped her arms around Lucia again and gently hugged her. Lucia always seemed delicate to her, a fragile flower, yet she'd lost two children and she remained standing straight, loving her husband, supporting him through every difficult time. She had a backbone of steel, just as Nicoletta's birth mother had. Nicoletta was going to maintain that same backbone and make certain her children—boys or girls—did the same. She wanted Lucia and Amo close to be grandparents to her children, to be the amazing examples they were.

"I made certain to show Taviano the piece so he could match the gold with your earrings and necklace," Amo pointed out, to keep the women from bursting into tears again.

Nicoletta turned back to the mirror to look at herself. Immediately her gaze was drawn to the golden circles going up her arm, complementing her skin. The ivory silk sheath dress could have been planned around the piece. The sheer duster, with its peekaboo shoulders and wispy sheer lace, looked as if it had been made specifically to be worn with the bracelet.

Even the tiara she wore in her hair with the chocolate diamonds had the same Florentine gold woven around the glittering gems.

Emmanuelle beamed at her. "You truly are beautiful. I can't wait for my brother to see you coming down the aisle to him."

The door opened and Grace leaned in. She beckoned to Lucia and Emmanuelle. "Everyone is waiting. We don't want them to get restless, and if we're not on time, Taviano will panic and come looking for Nicoletta." She stopped to really look at her newest sister-in-law. "You look absolutely gorgeous."

Emmanuelle took Lucia's arm. "She does, doesn't she? We don't want to panic Taviano by being late."

Lucia blew Nicoletta kisses and walked with Emmanuelle out of the room. Grace glanced at her watch. "I'll come get you in a couple of minutes." She closed the door, leaving Nicoletta alone with Amo.

"I'm so nervous, Amo, and I don't even know why. Technically, I'm already married to him. He took my ring back." She rubbed her finger. It felt bare without her ring. "Even without his ring, I'm still married to him. I shouldn't be nervous, but look at this." She held out her hand to show him her trembling fingers.

Amo took her hand and kissed her fingers. "You've never liked to be the center of attention, *vita mia*. That is why you have these nerves, not because you are having second thoughts. You would marry Taviano a hundred times."

She would. She knew she would. More. He would always be her choice. She nodded. "You're so right. I love him more than life itself."

"I feel that way about Lucia. I always have, and nothing

has ever happened through the years to make me feel any differently." Amo guided her hand and put her fingers in the crook of his arm. "Always remember, this is your marriage. Your partnership. No one else knows what is between you. Keep that sacred and have each other's backs at all times. Put each other first, and I promise you, Nicoletta, if you both do that, you will have what Lucia and I have had, and it is good."

Throughout her time living under Amo's roof, when he imparted advice, it was always in the simplest of terms, and yet upon examination, she had continuously found his guidance to be profound. "Thank you. I'll remember. You look very handsome in your suit. I forgot to tell Lucia how elegant and beautiful she looks."

"The Ferraro boys didn't forget," Amo said, with mock annoyance. "They try to steal her out from under me."

Nicoletta laughed. "You always say that. I love that you do. You make her smile no matter what she's thinking about at the time."

"A sense of humor is always of the utmost importance in a marriage."

She knew that it was. She'd seen Amo turn the worst situations around with his wonderfully timed humor.

"Before we join the others, I just want to say one more thing, my beautiful girl. I couldn't have asked for a better daughter. I know you would have preferred a quiet little wedding, without the photographer underfoot and all the many guests, but this big affair was Lucia's dream for our daughter. You've become that for us—our daughter. She needed this dream to be fulfilled."

"I know she did," Nicoletta agreed quietly. She had known.

Lucia would have never voiced a single objection had Nicoletta held up her ring and stated she wasn't going through a huge church wedding just to satisfy the curious masses. Lucia, more than once, had talked to her about the wedding she had dreamt of for her daughter. Choosing the dress together, the cake and bouquet, jewelry, all the planning. It was extremely important to Lucia, and therefore, it became important to Nicoletta. She could take being in the glow of that hot spotlight for a few hours for her foster mother.

"Thank you," Amo said simply.

"I love you both very much," Nicoletta said.

Before Amo could reply, Grace pushed open the door, and at once they could hear the music signaling that the bridesmaids were to begin their walk down the aisle. She would have had Mariko stand up for her, and Taviano would have had Stefano, but since Lucia wanted a large wedding, there were several bridesmaids.

Emmanuelle, Sasha and Grace were escorted down the aisle by Elie, Giovanni, and Vittorio. They looked elegant as only the Ferraros could, dressed in their suits and the long silk dresses. Following them were Pia, Bianca and Clariss, escorted by Ricco, Enzo and Demetrio. Bianca, especially, looked ecstatic. Enzo looked pretty happy as well.

Nicoletta tightened her fingers on Amo's arm as Mariko turned her head to look at her, sent her a serene smile and then started down the aisle.

Her heart began to beat wildly. Amo patted her hand, and then they were walking through the double doors following Mariko. The entire church was filled with people, all on their feet. She didn't see anyone. She was looking down that long white strip leading to the man standing at the end of it.

Taviano was in a dark suit with the thinnest of stripes. He was so handsome he took her breath away, but then he always did. Mariko moved to one side, and Nicoletta had a clear vision of Stefano standing beside Taviano, but it was really only Taviano that she saw. His eyes were on her. There was that look on his face, and she knew she had a matching one on hers. Love. Adoration. Taviano was her everything, and she was his.

She felt the weight of the three generations of Italian gold bangles on her arm, proclaiming the love between the man and wife exchanging vows. She had that. She had that man, that family. It didn't matter how difficult some of her trials and issues were and would be for the rest of her life, or the scars both Taviano and she bore, they had this amazing love and family to see them through.

Amo kissed both of her cheeks and put her hand in Taviano's. He closed his fingers firmly around hers as he stepped up beside her. Their eyes met, and she let herself get lost in his gaze, safe there through the ceremony that joined them together in front of their family and friends.

Keep reading for an excerpt from the next novel
in the Torpedo Ink series by Christine Feehan

DESOLATION ROAD

Available July 2020 from Piatkus

Aleksei Absinthe Solokov loved books. He loved the smell of them. The sight of them. The information in them. He especially loved the places he could go in them. Books had saved his life on more than one occasion. He'd originally come to this place needing the quiet and peace, needing the scent and the words. And once again, books had led him to find something so unexpected, so spectacular, he still hadn't accepted the offering, the gift, not quite believing yet, but he couldn't walk away.

He sat in his favorite place right in front of the tallest stacks. The table was smaller and less inviting, due to the crowded space. He didn't like being disturbed. He came to the library to get respite from the continual bombardment of other people's thoughts and emotions. He could command with his voice, and sometimes the temptation to tell everyone to not think or speak for five minutes was brutally hard to resist. He needed to feel normal when he wasn't. He wanted to see if he could fit in somewhere but he knew he couldn't. He needed to stand on his own but it was impossible.

His small table, nearly hidden beside the taller stacks, not only protected him from unwanted company but gave him a direct view to the desk where the librarian checked out books, recommended reads and sometimes—make that often—helped teens with their homework. He had been coming for over a month. Six weeks to be exact. And he just watched her. Like a fucking stalker. The librarian. She was so damn sexy he was shocked that the place wasn't overrun with single men—because she was single. He'd made it his business to find out.

When he first came to the library, he hadn't worn his colors. It was more to be anonymous than for any other reason—at least he told himself that. Sometimes he just got a feeling. Whenever it happened, he acted on it—and he'd had that feeling, the one that often saved his life, so he'd removed his colors and gone into the library, feeling a little naked without them.

He didn't want to be noticed, although he was covered in tattoos and scars that couldn't be seen beneath the tee that stretched tight across his chest. Just his sleeves showed, those tattoos that meant something to him but wouldn't mean anything to anyone else. Memorials to his lost family and the children that hadn't survived that nightmare he'd lived through.

Now, he still didn't wear his colors for the same reason, although he felt like a fraud, because he was Torpedo Ink. His club colors were tattooed onto his back, but it was more than that. His identity went beyond skin and sank right into bone. He knew with absolute certainty that he couldn't live without his club, nor would he want to. Torpedo Ink was his identity. His life. His family—brothers and sisters—and their lives were bound together irrevocably.

They were woven together like an old tapestry, and nothing could take them apart, and yet he felt as if he had betrayed them. Skulking away. The members rarely went off alone, certainly not daily for six weeks. And they didn't go six weeks without wearing their colors. It wasn't done. He might as well have gone naked. He didn't know why he kept this place to himself . . .

He did though. It was the librarian. The little redhead. She moved like poetry. Flowing like words across the pages of a book. One moment she could be a lady in a historical novel, taking the hand of a gentleman and gracefully emerging from a carriage, the next, a modern-day woman striding down the busy street in a business suit with her briefcase. Or a sexy librarian dressed in a pencil-straight skirt that hugged her curves and gave him all kinds of very dirty and graphic thoughts, like bending her over that desk of hers when the rest of the world went away.

Still, that feeling of staying anonymous, of keeping his identity secret so that no one had a clue what or who he was, persisted while he unraveled the mystery of the woman who ran the library so efficiently.

He was back. Oh. My. God. The most gorgeous man in the entire world and he just walked in off the street like he owned the place. Like the library was his home and gorgeous men came in every single day. He was tall with broad shoulders and a thick chest and arms. Really great arms. Muscles. Really great muscles. Scarlet Foley spent a *lot* of time perving on his muscles. And all those delicious tattoos. Who knew she'd fall for tattoos when she'd never been all that fond of them?

He had thick blond hair, a lot of it, and it spilled across his forehead, making her fingers itch to smooth it back. His eyes were very different. Blue. But not. More crystal blue. But not. Like two really cool crystals. She couldn't decide. When she wasn't perving on his muscles or fixating on his fascinating mouth, she was definitely wondering how to describe his eyes, and she was really good with words as a rule.

She knew she shouldn't be around him. He left her breathless and tongue-tied. If she had girlfriends, she would be over at their houses every night after work so she could share the mythical pictures she would secretly sneak of him like a crazy stalker. They would have dropped by the library to see him and giggled like schoolgirls.

Instead, she acted the part of the librarian. Dignified. Hiding behind the glasses she didn't really need. She had that role down perfectly. No giggling. No snapping contraband pictures to stare at in the middle of the night and fantasize over and pretend she might actually have some sort of love life. Or worse, get out every single toy known to single women, which wouldn't even help because he was *too* gorgeous and nothing was *ever* going to match the real thing. But as long as he kept coming to her library, she was going to do some daydreaming. No one could take that away from her.

He liked science fiction. He read psychology books. Not self-help books but the real thing, industry books. He also read a lot of obscure reference books on the pyramids of Egypt. The building of them. She knew because she watched his every move, and sometimes she helped him find the books he wanted. Up close, he smelled like cedarwood, and at night, when she was alone, she couldn't get that scent out of her mind. She knew she would always associate it with him. Man. Muscles. And sex. Worse.

Yes. It did get worse because she'd looked down his body. It wasn't her fault. She hadn't meant to. She'd practiced keeping her eyes up on his chest. But she handed him the book and her gaze just dropped and there it was . . . in all its glory. Hard as a rock. The full ultra-impressive package. So now she had it all to take to bed with her. And quite frankly it sucked that the man wasn't in bed with her as well.

He would ask her for help in finding a particular book, and when he asked, his voice was mesmerizing. Velvet soft. She swore she felt the sound sliding over her skin. Stroking her. An actual physical sensation. A little shiver always slid down her spine and a very inappropriate flutter in her sex accompanied that shiver. Now that she knew what he had, her wayward gaze strayed often, and her panties went damp more than they should have. She had no respect for herself. None. But that didn't stop her.

She'd never had that kind of reaction to any man, not in college and not when she'd traveled to other countries. His voice was always pitched low, very soft, but it was commanding, and she heard a little twist of his words, as if he had an accent under the English pronunciation, but she couldn't place it. She'd never heard a voice like his before, and she'd traveled extensively. He was very much a gentleman, and yet he gave off an extremely dangerous vibe. She'd been around dangerous men, and she would have placed him right there with them, but she didn't know why. He seemed as if he'd be more at home in a suit and tie than casual clothes. And he wore his clothes like a model.

She had a lot of time—too much time—to think about him when she went home from the library and sat alone in her reading chair, surrounded by her books and little else. He was the fastest speed reader she'd ever seen in her life, and she knew he was for real. At first she thought he was faking his ability to read that fast, but then she realized after some time that he was clearly reading the books and must be comprehending what he was reading.

She was impressed. She'd taken several speed-reading courses and, in the end, had gone with the advice of the fastest reader in the world, learning from his books. She picked up things fast; she always had. The more time spent, the faster she learned. It was a gift she had, and she used it often, which made it all the more readily available to her.

She'd made certain to touch him. The first time had been a brief brush of their fingers as she handed him a book. Frankly, she hadn't been certain if he'd made that initial contact or if she had, but she would never forget it as long as she lived. The spark had gone up her finger to every nerve ending in her body, spreading like a wildfire, bringing her to life as if she'd been asleep—or dead—her entire life and it had taken him to wake her up.

She *had* been dead. She'd chosen to be dead. She'd shoved the woman in her aside out of necessity and become what she had to be. Now she was simply surviving. Until he walked in. She had no idea what to do with him—but she wanted him. She'd sworn she would never—not *ever*—go there again. Put herself in a situation where the dark things inside of her had a chance to escape. She'd seen the results of that, and yet she couldn't stop thinking about him . . . wanting him.

Touching him was dangerous, but she couldn't seem to resist no matter how hard she tried, and every touch brought something new. She couldn't get to him, couldn't uncover him or strip him in layers like she did others, but something connected them so strongly, melded them so tightly together, that there was no going back, and she knew it. Every time he was close to her, he melted away that shell of a hardened human being that wasn't real, and for a moment, she felt alive and genuine—and vulnerable.

Right now he sat in her library, disturbing her beyond all measure. She hadn't thought it possible. She thought she was stone cold when it came to the opposite sex, but she lit up around him. On fire. Hot as hades. She apparently had red hair for a reason, and it wasn't her temper. Okay, maybe it was that, too. She hadn't made up her mind how she felt about Mr. Aleksei Solokov. That was the name on his library card. She didn't know if her body coming to life was a good thing or a bad thing. If fantasies were wonderful or a curse. There was a lot to think about, but then she had a lot of time to think.

"Miss Foley?"

She jerked her head up, her breath exploding out of her lungs. No one had managed to sneak up on her in years, and yet just perving on Aleksei Solokov, she failed the first lesson in survival. She turned slowly, already knowing who was behind her, identifying him by his voice.

"Hi, Tom." He was sixteen and trying desperately to learn to read at his level. His English teacher was no help, giving him assignments far beyond his comprehension. It made Scarlet angry that the man couldn't take the time to help the boy. "I was hoping you'd come in today. I have plenty of time to help you." She flashed him a reassuring smile.

The boy's face flooded with relief. "Thanks, Miss Foley."

She waved him toward the table where they often worked together, and where she was most comfortable. She could see out the windows, but no one could see her or the boy she tutored. She was always careful just in case, so no one could ever harm any of the teens just because of her. She put aside the rest of the evening's work and settled down to help Tom do his homework. She would have plenty of time to finish her own work before the close of her shift.

The librarian moved, drawing Absinthe's attention. It was growing late, and she walked the boy she'd been helping with his English paper to the door, reassuring him he was getting better with every paper and she was proud of him. She moved like someone who could handle herself, always balanced, even when she was carrying stacks of books. He'd noticed that almost immediately about her. When one was as fucked up as he was, you always assessed the men and women around you to see who the fighters were. Under that sexy prim-and-proper librarian facade, she could handle herself.

She wore her hair up in an intricate, twisted bun, but twice after work he'd seen her let it down. It was bright red, shiny red. There was no other word for the color. Just red, and that color hadn't come out of a box. It was a waterfall of true, thick, silky red. Her hair, once let loose, refused to be tamed. It snaked down her back to her waist, drawing attention to just how small her waist and rib cage were and how curved her hips were. She had an ass, and tits that were high and firm, and very generous. Her curves were deceptive considering she was very fit.

Absinthe's entire body reacted to her in an entirely unprecedented way. He didn't have normal erections. Those had been beaten or raped out of him when he was a child. To achieve one, he had to command his body to cooperate, and why the hell bother? To sit in the library—that quiet and peaceful place—and feel his body respond to a beautiful woman was a form of magic. He enjoyed the feeling, knowing he would never take it for granted—and it happened every damn time he looked at her.

He had experimented after he'd had a reaction to her, going to various bars and even the market in the hope that his body would respond to someone else after it had come to life, but it seemed it was only the little librarian with her bright red hair that did it for him. That was just fine with him. He liked her. He liked the way she was so gentle and calm—so patient with the kids that came in, asking her homework questions. If she noticed there was a much higher percentage of boys than girls, she didn't make a big deal out of it. She spoke in soft, melodic tones, but hushed, in keeping with the library rules.

After seeing the boy out, she turned and looked straight at him. He could never quite interpret the expression on her face. He was always careful not to touch her for too long. He didn't want to read her thoughts. He was enjoying their dance around each other too much for that. She was fascinated but nervous—anxious, even, which he found interesting as well. She was always so calm with everyone else. She couldn't know he was in a club, so it wasn't that.

She came toward him, flowing across the room. She was breathtaking. Beautiful. All woman wrapped up in that sweet package. Her name was Scarlet, and he loved that name. It said Scarlet Foley on her nameplate, and she'd finally introduced herself formally to him three and a half weeks earlier. It had taken quite some time before she actually spoke to him. She'd smile, but she didn't come near him at first. Even now, she was extremely reserved with him.

"You've been here for hours. Are you doing research again? I might be able to help you," she offered. "Although we're closing soon."

He glanced around. The library was empty. It was definitely near closing time. He decided to take a chance. "I stayed late on the off chance you'd have time to have dinner with me. Nothing fancy, just across the street there." He indicated the more upscale restaurant facing the front of the library.

He liked the location of the library. It was on a block that was also quieter than most of the town's streets. Foliage was abundant; in fact, the front and sides of the library were covered in ivy so that it appeared to drip down the brick walls and fall like a waterfall over the second story to the first. Everything about the place proclaimed it was cool and inviting.

Scarlet stood very still, her large green gaze, behind her glasses, moving over his face slowly. For a moment she looked scared. Not scared exactly. That wasn't the right word. Leery, maybe. Assessing the risk? He wasn't certain, but she wasn't jumping at his invitation. She glanced over her shoulder toward the restaurant. Absinthe stayed silent, letting her make up her mind. He needed her to feel safe with him, and he wanted her to *want* to spend time with him, the way he wanted to spend it with her—just the two of them. Walking across the street with her vehicle close was a good start.

"I think that sounds fun," she said finally. Almost reluctantly.

He could hear lies. She wasn't lying, but there was something he couldn't quite put his finger on. For the millionth time, he glanced at her hand to see if she was wearing a wedding ring. She wasn't. There was no faint tan line that might indicate she'd worn one. She had very pale skin. A dusting of freckles was across her nose, spreading out just a bit, very faint, but he had the unexpected urge to kiss each one.

"I'll wait here for you while you close up, and we can walk over together," he said. He made it a statement. She more than likely would want him to go out the door first. She didn't walk outside with anyone, even if one of the teens stayed late. Not one time in the six weeks he'd been coming. She always stood at the door for a long period of time, scanning the entire block, the buildings and even the rooftops.

Her small white teeth caught at her lower lip for a moment, and his heart nearly stopped. Why he found that sexy, he had no idea, but he did. His body stirred, and heat rushed through his veins like a drug. Just being close to her was addicting. Her eyes did that reluctant drop, as if she couldn't help herself. He fucking loved that. For just one moment her gaze rested on the bulge at the front of his jeans, and he hardened even more. She turned red and averted her eyes. He resisted grinning.

"I have a few things to do. You could grab us a table and I'll meet you there."

Yeah. She didn't want to be seen with anyone. That was a red flag. He held up his cell phone. "I'll text them to hold us a table. I scoped it out earlier and they have a few tables for two. They're kind of in the shadows, but if you'd rather sit on the main floor . . ."

"No, I think a table for two sounds excellent."

She jumped at that. A little too fast. She didn't want to be seen with him. Fuck.

"I'll make us a reservation and you finish up."

She hesitated again, but then turned away with a little nod. He watched her go back to her desk. He'd already made the reservation. If she'd said no, he simply would have canceled it. He kept an eye on her while he made a show of writing down a few facts from the book he had pulled out to reference. Truthfully, he didn't need to write anything down. He could read and absorb over twenty thousand words per minute. He retained everything he saw or read. He could compel truth and make suggestions that others would follow. He had highly developed gifts. Some were a curse, no matter what others thought. Most were. Or maybe it was how he'd had to use them.

He was uneasy without his fellow Torpedo Ink members close by, and even more so now that he could see just how nervous she was. They had survived their childhood and then later, as teens and adults, by sticking together. The rule had always been that one or two stuck close to a third. Sometimes they were unseen, up on a rooftop with a rifle, and sometimes they were in the shadows, but there was always someone close to protect another.

Absinthe knew if the pull toward the librarian hadn't been so strong, he never would have continued to come without at least one of the others. He wanted them close. Eventually he would have to ask them to ride with him, but there would be so many questions, and he wanted this time with her to be real. He wanted to unravel the mystery of Scarlet Foley alone. If he enlisted the aid of his club, Code would be involved, and her life would instantly be an open book. No one escaped Code's ability to uncover their past with his genius computer skills. There was something to be said for the old-fashioned way of conversation and courtship.

He drummed his fingers on the table, reminiscent of Czar, their Torpedo Ink president. When Czar was thinking, he often kept time with his fingers. Absinthe found himself with the same habit, and he'd never bothered to try to break it. Twice, there in the library, his little redhead had sent him a small frown. Now he often drummed his fingers on the table just to see that frown because he found it provocative. Sensual. Hell. Everything she did was sensual.

He waited for her to turn the lights off before he got up and made his way down the aisle between the tall stacks to her. She knocked her purse off the desk and then when she picked it up, she dropped it again. Absinthe recovered it and handed it to her. That was absolutely, entirely unlike her, especially the fact that she hadn't caught it before it hit the floor. He'd seen her catch dozens of books and other objects over the last six weeks even when others had dropped them.

Scarlet took the purse with a rueful expression. "I'm a little nervous," she confessed, not looking at him. "I don't go out very often."

He'd already guessed that. He also was very sure she was afraid of someone. "Does your family live here?"

He held the door open for her. He wasn't used to making conversation with an ordinary citizen, and certainly not one who made his cock feel so diamond-hard he was afraid he might not be able to walk. Wasn't that a perfectly ordinary question? One any man might ask a woman on a first date? Date. Hell. He didn't date. He'd never been on a date in his life.

She had dropped back, not walking with him, and he just stood there, waiting for her to exit. Scarlet's gaze slid up and down the street before she reluctantly stepped outside and allowed him to close the door behind her, take the keys from her hand and lock it, and then hand them back to her.

"No, but my grandmother did. I used to visit her here. I had a lot of good memories, so I came back and was able to get the job at the library. What about you?"

He shook his head. "No, but now I live in Caspar, which isn't all that far from here." It was by some people's standards, but he found it peaceful riding his motorcycle, and the roads were perfect for cruising between the coast and inland, so distances didn't matter to him.

Her face lit up. "I've been to Caspar. It's on the coast, right? I love it there. The sea is always changing. One day it will be quiet and calm, and the next, it's wild and crazy. You're lucky to live there, although I imagine there aren't very many jobs available."

Was there a wistful note in her voice? He hoped so. He

needed the stars to align and let him have this miracle of a gift. He needed her in his life. He just had to find a way to make it happen and have it be real. He was most afraid of that—needing her too much and creating a false relationship.

He opened the door to the restaurant for her, scanning the room quickly for potential trouble before allowing her to do the same thing while he turned back toward the street and gave that another quick once-over. Certain no one was paying attention to either of them, he closed the door and followed his librarian's amazing ass. She was in a black skirt with small white polka-dots scattered over it. The material clung to her curves. He appreciated that particular skirt very much.

Absinthe held the back of her chair for her, ignoring the waiter, who looked as if he might conk him on the head and abscond with the girl. She looked regal as she took the seat, smiling up at Absinthe, nearly taking his breath away. Whatever it was, she had affected him like some kind of aphrodisiac. Her small teeth. That mouth, with her full, pouty lips that were made for a man's dirtiest fantasies. He hadn't had them until she'd come along. Not like this. Mostly he'd had nightmares. The erotic, very graphic dreams were a welcome change.

"Are you a wine drinker?" Absinthe didn't know the first thing about wine. He could make her any kind of drink she wanted, or talk beer, but wine eluded him. If she loved wine, he was going to be taking a crash course. It wouldn't take him long to catch up.

She shook her head. "I actually don't drink very much. Once in a while, if it's really hot out, I'll have an ice-cold beer. But other than that, it's a very occasional drink, and usually I go for something girly like a cosmopolitan."

"I don't drink wine," Absinthe admitted. "Like you, I'm not a big drinker, but mostly that stems from wanting to be alert all the time."

"You don't put your feet up, relax and have tons to drink?"

There was the merest hint of amusement in her voice. Mostly she was serious.

He loved the look on her face when she gave him her full attention. He focused completely on her once he was certain the few couples already eating or waiting to be served weren't in the least interested in them.

"No, that wouldn't work for me. I do like to put my feet up though," he admitted. "I'm going to be very up front with you." It was confession time. If he didn't say it straight up, she'd find out anyway. "I'm not good at this. I never know what to say, and I come off stilted and awkward, but I don't want to be that way with you."

Her green gaze was hard to stay still under. She seemed to see right through his skull into his mind, where chaos reigned—thanks to her.

"I'm not so great at this, either," she declared. "I guess we're going to have to learn. I'm very competitive, and I have a fast learning curve. Very fast. Wait." She frowned at him. "You weren't reading a self-help book on dating, were you?"

"Do they have those in the library?"

Her lashes swept down and then back up. A small smile teased the curve of her mouth, causing his heart to accelerate. He found himself staring. Shit. He was going to lose before he got started because he couldn't stop staring at her.

She laughed. "I'm not telling you. I'll read them and turn into a scintillating conversationalist in minutes, leaving you in the dust."

He instantly learned three things. There were multiple self-help books on dating, she read extremely fast and she really was competitive. He flashed a small grin, looking at her with hawklike eyes, giving her the predator look just for a moment. Just to see the shiver that crept down her spine.

"I'll have to be there first thing in the morning, before your shift."

"You know my shifts?" The smile faded, and she sounded uneasy.

He shrugged. "How was I going to ask you out? I went multiple times without seeing you, so clearly you had a shift and only came into the library during those times. I kept having to trade work with friends and drive here from the coast, so I found out when you worked. I came as often as I could and just waited until we'd established that a very tentative woman can charm the socks right off a shy man any day of the week."

"Is that what we established?"

Her laughter got him every time. He found himself actually relaxing. The waiter hovered, and both guiltily studied the menu. She ordered a pasta dish and he ordered a steak. Fresh-baked bread was put on the table and he suddenly realized he was very hungry.

"I watched you right back," she admitted as she buttered a small piece of bread. "You're quite fascinating."

"I am?"

"The way you read. Even the books you choose. They're reference books on just about every subject. Three were language books. All on Hindi. Are you planning on going to India?"

He shook his head. "I like languages. I study the various ones to see how alike they are, and how different. There are at least seven hundred twenty dialects spoken in India, but most speak one or more of the official twenty-two languages."

"Do you speak other languages?"

"Yes, I've studied them so much over the years, I've picked them up. Some more than others. You know how some people are good at mechanics? I've got a gift with languages. I can pick them up easily."

"How did you learn to read so fast?"

She really had been watching him. He liked that, although it could be dangerous.

"I started practicing when I was really young. I practiced every single day for hours. I have a gift there as well. I read and absorb very quickly now, and I never miss a day that I don't keep up the practice. I like books."

"That's so awesome that you started so young. I read this really cool article on the Internet about speed-reading and how to comprehend what you were reading at the same time," she explained. "It's funny that you speed-read, too. I started practicing about seven years ago. It comes in handy when you want to learn about various subjects."

"That and YouTube."

She nodded. "Right? I've found help from a tremendous number of videos. I rent this little house out in the middle of nowhere and it's always falling apart. Repairs are my responsibility, so I just read or YouTube whatever I need."

She was so fucking perfect for him. She made him ache inside. It was a good kind of ache after a lifetime of nothing but bad.

"Tell me about this boy you work so much with. Tom. He seems like a nice kid. What's his story? You work with a lot of the kids, but he seems very special to you."

She shrugged and buttered another piece of warm bread. He liked that she didn't stint on the sweet, salted butter and worry too much about her figure. She had curves and he wanted her to keep them.

"He's a nice kid. He has a great mom. Single. She works all the time. She came in once to thank me for helping him and even brought me some cupcakes she'd made. They were delicious."

She flashed him a grin that said he'd missed out. His cock jerked hard at that mischievous grin. He could fall hard for her. He thought maybe he already had. Six weeks staring at her and she'd cast her spell.

"He was deaf the first few years of his life and then they operated on him, but he's had trouble hearing sounds correctly and so has been slow reading and identifying words.

He fell behind and she can't help him because she works nights and isn't home with him."

Scarlet shrugged again but he had the feeling she wasn't as casual as she tried to sound. She was upset on the boy's behalf.

"He puts in the time, but he needs a tutor. I work with him after hours sometimes and he's catching up now. He's getting it."

He knew immediately she was tutoring him as well as working with him in the library. He didn't bother asking but knew she didn't get paid for it. She didn't want him to ask. He liked her all the more for it. He dipped his bread into oil and balsamic. "I'm glad the kid's picking it up and that he wants to learn. That's really what it takes, the desire."

"You know what I do—the library. What do you do?"

He made a point of sighing. "I was afraid you'd ask. It's very boring. I'm an attorney."

She stiffened. She tried not to, but she did. He could see she had a major aversion to anyone with his particular career choice. He had thought perhaps it would gain him some points, but he just lost any advantage he might have had.

"Hate it. Don't work much. Looking for another career. Kind of fell into it because I like to debate but feel like criminals always get off and no justice is ever served. So, I'm kind of a lousy attorney." He kept his voice low and pushed a little persuasion into it. Just the slightest to see the effect on her. She was different. He'd noticed that right away when he was with her in the library just observing her, and then later, when he would ask for various books.

She was susceptible to his voice, and yet he could see she could build up a resistance to things fairly quickly; she reacted so fast. He wasn't going to let her find a way to stop his subtle influence on her until he had already managed to get her to fall completely under his spell. He intended to put everything he had into this war and win. She already admitted she had a fast learning curve. She had gifts, the same as he did, and they were strong in her, already developed. He had to be cautious. This was one war he was determined to win.

Scarlet visibly relaxed a little, taking a breath, studying her bread before she took another bite and washed it down with a sip of water. "What kind of lawyer are you?"

He shrugged. Now that was a very good question. He was whatever he had to be. In the days of specialization, Code's paperwork was invaluable. Absinthe's ability to devour law books and keep up with the latest on whatever was needed for Torpedo Ink was equally as valuable. "I'm kind of a jack-of-all-trades, the fill-out-papers boring kind of work."

She relaxed even more. "Do you have your own practice?"

He nodded. "I get by. It's not my passion though."

"What is?"

He wanted to say he'd walked into the library and found it, but he knew that wasn't going to fly. "Books. Languages. The written word. Dead languages. History. Art. Martial arts from around the world. Legends. Weapons. Poetry." That was all true. He didn't bother to hide the enthusiasm because he actually felt it and that was who he was. If he wanted the real her, she had to want the real him.

A slow smile spread across her face. "You are an amazing man. I can't imagine you as a lawyer."

"Neither can I," he agreed. "I should have been a librarian, although I did volunteer in a library once. I read all the books and then had to quit." That was sort of true. He worked there, read as many of the books as possible, assassinated a member of the ministry and then returned to Sorbacov's hellhole. That had been in Russia. "Do you like the outdoors?"

She nodded and looked up as the waiter returned to place a salad in front of her and then one in front of Absinthe. The waiter stood a little too close to Scarlet, and she shifted in her chair slightly, edging away from him. She waited until he was gone before she spoke.

"I actually prefer to be outdoors if the weather's good.

Well," she hedged. "Sometimes I find the most amazing places and take a book when it's storming just to be outside when it's raining. I love storms."

She was perfection. Who knew that it was possible to have a woman be perfection for him? He hadn't thought it was. He hadn't thought one was made for him. He could look at her all day. He knew he could because he had. He'd sat in the library and studied every single inch of her body. She was clothed, but often her clothing was tight and moved with her body, and he had mapped every curve, every valley, every sweet inch of her that he could.

"I really love storms as well. I particularly love to sit above the ocean and watch the storms move in while the waves rise up to meet the lightning. There's something very freeing in the wildness of it."

She regarded him over a forkful of romaine lettuce. "That's poetic, Aleksei. I haven't experienced that, but now I want to."

"What about motorcycles? How do you feel about them?"

Scarlet took a sip of her water and then smiled up at the water boy who rushed to fill her glass. It was already mostly full. Absinthe thought the boy just wanted an excuse to be closer to her. He couldn't blame the kid. Even the waiter was trying to find excuses to visit their table. He didn't have to like it though—and he didn't. The boy he didn't mind. She didn't, either. The waiter was a different story. He actually seemed to brush his body up against Scarlet's when he got close to her. Absinthe had never been a jealous man, but then he'd never had a reason to be jealous. He wanted her attention centered on him, which was childish. He was a grown man and very confident. He didn't whisper "go away" to either of the two servers, but he thought it.

"I take it you like motorcycles."

"You could say I'm passionate about motorcycles. I love the freedom of riding on them. The way the road opens up and you become part of the world around you. You can't get that in a car or truck. Even a convertible doesn't give you

that same feeling of being part of the landscape and highway around you as you ride. You can see everything. The
road stretches out in front of you, and it's like the entire
world is yours to see."

"You make riding motorcycles sound very different than
I ever thought about them."

"What did you think about them?" He braced himself.
Most people were very judgmental about motorcycles and
the men and women who rode them. He was prepared for
her poor opinion and knew he'd just have to work to change
her mind.

She took off her glasses for a moment, blinking at him
with her vivid green eyes. She had very long lashes, reddish
gold tipped with more gold. For some reason just looking at
those lashes framing her large eyes made his cock come to
life all over again. She had no idea what that meant, as it was
unheard-of. The men of Torpedo Ink, his brothers, commanded their cocks. Women didn't do that. Nature didn't do
that. The reality was, the ability had been beaten out of
them so they could be trained to order their erections, to
always be in complete control of every sexual response.

Until now. Until Scarlet Foley. The redheaded librarian,
complete with her black or purple or red square glasses
framing her gorgeous eyes, seemed to have taken command
of his body. She was definitely his lady. His *literaturnaya
ledi*, literary lady. He loved that she was as much into books
as he was. That she loved the written word and she could
read and comprehend what she was reading fast.

"I don't know exactly, I haven't been around motorcycles. I think I thought of them as death traps. One accident
and bye-bye brain." She pushed her salad away. She'd eaten
most of it. "You don't like salad."

He looked down at his plate. "It's lettuce. Ruffled lettuce, but green all the same. Bugs thrive on this stuff."

She burst out laughing, and that dark place inside him,
which was so solid nothing could penetrate, cracked. It just

cracked like an iceberg. The sound of her laughter was incredible. Low. Soft. Intriguing. The tones played over his skin like the dance of fingers. He felt the brush of the notes on his chest and down his spine, the stroke of them on his cock and balls like caresses whispering over him. He wanted to close his eyes, all the better to savor the sensation. He had to file it away to take out later, but he knew he would never forget it. She had given that to him, just as she'd given him the first natural erection he could remember.

"So, you're afraid of lettuce but not of motorcycles. I suppose, since you put your argument for riding motorcycles so eloquently, I'll have to concede it sounds pretty awesome, as long as you ride with a helmet."

"Babe, there's a law in this state that makes that mandatory."

The waiter arrived with their food, stepping very close to Scarlet so that when he bent to place her plate in front of her, his face was almost nuzzling her neck. She pulled her head immediately to the side to get away from him with a look of distaste. The move was almost reflexive.

"Step away," Absinthe commanded, his voice low, but there was no mistaking the threat. He "pushed" blatantly, although no one would know. Only the waiter would feel it—and the threat that was all too real. "She doesn't like you so close."

The waiter immediately complied. There were very few people who didn't comply when Absinthe used his voice at that level. It was rare, and he was shocked that it came out so aggressively when the indiscretion had been a small one. There was silence as the man finished giving them their food. Once they were alone, Absinthe reached across the table to gently cover her hand.

"I'm sorry, are you all right?" He removed his hand immediately before she could be the one to withdraw it. He wanted her to feel his touch, to be comforted, not offended by it.

"He just startled me, that's all. I don't like anyone I don't know coming so close to me. It's just a thing I have."

"It's not a bad thing to have, Scarlet. It's called self-preservation. You're a beautiful woman and men are going to find you very attractive. Most will just look. Others take advantage when they shouldn't."

"What do you do?"

"I ask you out and see if you're interested." He flashed a little self-deprecating grin. "I confess my worse sins, including not liking lettuce, and let you decide." He was a fucking liar and he was going to burn in the fires of hell, but she was worth it.

She flashed him a smile and pointed to his steak. "Eat up before it gets cold. Do you actually own a motorcycle? Is that what you ride all the way from Caspar to here on? Because it gets cold, you know."

It was his turn to laugh. They spent the next hour and a half talking and laughing together. He enjoyed every minute with her far more than he had expected. He spent all of the time watching her every move, absorbing her as if he could just take her inside of him. It was interesting to be able to relax wholly in her company. He didn't know why he didn't worry about making mistakes with his voice, but he didn't. He just felt at peace, the chaos in his mind receding until it was gone completely.

After dinner, he walked her to her car and told her he'd had a great time and he'd see her in a couple of days. She didn't object or pull away when he brushed a light kiss across her forehead. Touching her skin was a mistake. Inhaling her scent was a mistake. Taking in her laughter and the poetry of her lyrics was even worse. It didn't matter. He'd done it and he'd do again. She was his addiction now and he would return again and again. He hoped she felt the same about him.

He walked the two blocks to the parking garage where he'd left his Harley. Parked on either side were two other motorcycles and, sitting on them, were two familiar men.

Both wore Torpedo Ink colors and they were grinning at him.

Maestro tossed his vest to him. "You've been holding out on us."

He had been. Absinthe caught his vest and shrugged into it, his colors fitting over his body like a second skin. "How long have the two of you been following me?"

Maestro and Keys exchanged a long, amused look between them. "About two weeks now," Keys admitted. "We hung back, stayed up on the roof across from the library, just to make certain you were safe." He shook his head. "Even if she's yours, Absinthe, you know to be careful."

"*Especially* if she's yours," Maestro corrected.

Absinthe nodded and slung his leg over his bike. The moment he did, most of the chaos that had been returning in him settled. His bike. His colors. His brothers. His little redheaded librarian. "Yeah. What blows the most is I wasn't aware you were following me."

"We only had to stay close the first time. After that, we knew where you were going. You like books. You like to hang out in libraries. We weren't aware for the first week that the librarian was the big draw."

There was a questioning note in Maestro's voice. Absinthe nodded. "Yeah. She's mine. I don't have her yet. She's somewhat of a mystery and I'm taking my time with that." And enjoying it. He liked watching her. Uncovering her little secrets. Watching her with the teens that came in and the infinite patience she had with them.

She was attracted to him and shocked that she was. Shocked and a little embarrassed, yet at the same time, she wanted to go for it. He was certain she would have tried for a purely sexual relationship had he suggested it, but because he had asked her to dinner and kept it light, talking about himself and asking questions about her, pushing more for a relationship, she was confused and didn't know exactly what to do.

"Code look into her yet?" Keys asked cautiously.

"No. Tonight was the first real contact I've had with her," Absinthe said. "When I said I was taking it slow, I meant really slow. I would have lost had I gone too fast."

Maestro's head went up alertly. "You didn't use any influence?"

Absinthe shook his head. "No, of course not. If she comes to me, I want it to be because she wants me as much as I want her. Something's not quite right though. I did lift the fork she used tonight and got her prints. I also got a very good picture of her on my cell. Code should be able to give me the information I need if she needs protection, or if I do."

He sent them a brief grin, but he wasn't kidding. She had abilities. He was certain of it. He just didn't want to give Code the opportunity to find out about her yet. He wanted to take his time and uncover her himself, one layer at a time. He knew he was giving them the impression he was turning over the fork and picture to Code immediately, but he didn't intend to do it, not yet. He really did want to take his time with Scarlet.

"I'm just taking my time right now and enjoying myself." That was the best he could do, give them the truth of it. They seemed to understand, both nodding.

"Let's ride, gentlemen. It's getting late and we've got a distance to go," Keys said.

"She know you're in a club?" Maestro asked.

Absinthe should have known he wasn't going to get off that easily. He'd expected the question. "No. Not yet. I went into the library without my colors and kept it up. Didn't tell her tonight. I had a feeling . . ." He trailed off. Why hadn't he told her? He was Torpedo Ink. The club logo was inked into the skin of his back, but more importantly, he was part of his brothers, and they were part of him. One didn't work without the other. It was that simple. It always would be.

"A feeling?" Maestro prompted.

Absinthe shrugged. "I just had a feeling I shouldn't. She's skittish, and I'm not losing her. I'm reeling her in slowly.

Once I have her hooked, then I'll tell her. I just need to set that hook in good."

Maestro shook his head. "I hope to hell you know what you're doing, man."

Absinthe hoped so, too.

CHRISTINE FEEHAN

"The queen of paranormal romance...
I love everything she does."

—J. R. Ward

piatkus